W9-CJF-466

Dear Reader:

Dreams should be magic. They should be intimate. Laura Templeton's were. In the first book of this trilogy, *Daring to Dream*, Laura's dream of a fairy-tale marriage shattered. She now struggles to build a new life focused on her two young daughters and the risk of a new business with her two closest friends, Margo and Kate, in a boutique called Pretenses.

Laura Templeton was the daughter of the house, and she continues to live in, and care for, the majestic Templeton House in Big Sur. She's raising her children there and is determined to provide them with the loving, secure home she'd always known.

In *Holding the Dream*, Laura watched Margo thrive in her new marriage, and Kate blossom as she fell in love. Laura learned to stand on her own, to become an independent woman, a single parent with a home and a business to run.

In *Finding the Dream*, Laura faces a new challenge. His name is Michael Fury. Rather than the golden fairy-tale prince she once dreamed of, he is a man of passion and action and heat. He disrupts the ordered life she believed she wanted, and disturbs the heart she was sure she had locked.

Laura, like Margo and Kate, will discover that if you dare, and hold fast, you'll find your most precious dreams. I hope you enjoy her story. And here's wishing all your dreams come true.

Nora Roberts

Finding the Dream

Finding the Dream

Titles by Nora Roberts

HOT ICE
SACRED SINS
BRAZEN VIRTUE
SWEET REVENGE
PUBLIC SECRETS
GENUINE LIES
CARNAL INNOCENCE
DIVINE EVIL
HONEST ILLUSIONS
PRIVATE SCANDALS
HIDDEN RICHES
BORN IN FIRE
BORN IN ICE
BORN IN SHAME
TRUE BETRAYALS
DARING TO DREAM
HOLDING THE DREAM
FINDING THE DREAM
FROM THE HEART (*anthology*)
MONTANA SKY

SANCTUARY
in hardcover from G. P. Putnam's Sons

Titles written as J. D. Robb
NAKED IN DEATH
GLORY IN DEATH
IMMORTAL IN DEATH
RAPTURE IN DEATH
CEREMONY IN DEATH

FINDING THE DREAM

Nora Roberts

JOVE BOOKS, NEW YORK

FINDING THE DREAM

The Berkley Publishing Group, 200 Madison Avenue,
New York, New York 10016.

ISBN: 1-56865-422-7

PRINTED IN THE UNITED STATES OF AMERICA

To dreamers

Finding the Dream

Prologue

California, 1888

It was a long way for a man to travel. Not only the miles from San Diego to the cliffs outside of Monterey, Felipe thought, but the years. So many years.

Once, he had been young enough to walk confidently along the rocks, to climb, even to race. Defying the fates, celebrating the rush of wind, the crash of waves, the dizzying heights. The rocks had bloomed for him in spring once. There had been flowers to pick for Seraphina then, and he could remember, with the clear vision of age looking back to youth, how she had laughed and clutched the tough little wildflowers to her breast as if they were precious roses plucked from a well-tended bush.

His eyes were weak now, and his limbs were frail. But not his memory. A strong, vital memory in an old body was his penance. Whatever joy he had found in his life had been tainted, always, with the sound of Seraphina's laughter, with the trust in her dark eyes. With her young, uncompromising love.

In the more than forty years since he had lost her, and the part of himself that was innocence, he had learned to accept his own failings. He had been a coward, running from battle rather than facing the horrors of war, hiding among the dead rather than lifting a sword.

But he had been young, and such things had to be forgiven in the young.

He had allowed his friends and family to believe him dead, slain like a warrior—even a hero. It had been shame, and pride, that caused him to do so. Small things, pride and shame. Life was made up of so many small blocks. But he could never forget that it was that shame and that pride that cost Seraphina her life.

Weary, he sat on a rock to listen. To listen to the roar of water battling rock far below, to listen to the piercing cry of gulls, the rush of wind through winter grass. And the air was chilled as he closed his eyes and opened his heart.

To listen for Seraphina.

She would always be young, a lovely dark-eyed girl who had never had the chance to grow old, as he was old now. She hadn't waited, but in despair and grief had thrown herself into the sea. For love of him, he thought now. For reckless youth that hadn't lived long enough to know that nothing lasts forever.

Believing him dead, she had died, hurling herself and her future onto the rocks.

He had mourned her, God knew he had mourned her. But he hadn't been able to follow her into the sea. Instead, he had traveled south, given up his name and his home, and made new ones.

He had found love again. Not the sweet first blush of love that he had had with Seraphina, but something solid and strong, built on those small blocks of trust and understanding and on needs both quiet and violent.

And he had done his best.

He had children, and grandchildren. He had a life with all the joys and sorrows that make a man. He had survived to love a woman, to raise a family, to plant gardens. He was content with what had grown from him.

But he had never forgotten the girl he had loved. And killed. He had never forgotten their dream of a future or the sweet, innocent way she had given herself to him. When they had loved in secret, both of them so young, so fresh, they dreamed of the life they would have together, the home they would build with her dowry, the children they would make.

But war came, and he left her to prove himself a man. And proved himself a coward instead.

She had hidden her bride gift, the symbol of hope that a young girl treasures, to keep it out of American hands. Felipe had no doubt where she had hidden it. He had understood his Seraphina—her logic, her sentiment, her strengths and weaknesses. Though it had meant that he was penniless when he left Monterey, he had not taken the gold and jewels Seraphina had secreted.

Now, with the dreams of age that had turned his hair to silver, that had dimmed his eyes and lived in his aching bones, he prayed that it would be found one day by lovers. Or dreamers. If God was just, He would allow Seraphina to choose. Whatever the Church preached, Felipe refused to believe God would condemn a grieving child for the sin of suicide.

No, she would be as he had left her more than forty years ago on these very cliffs. Forever young and beautiful and full of hope.

He knew he would not return to this place. His time of penance was almost at an end. He hoped when he saw his Seraphina again, she would smile at him and forgive a young man's foolish pride.

He rose, bending in the wind, leaning on his cane to keep his feet under him. And left the cliffs to Seraphina.

There was a storm brewing, marching across the sea. A summer storm, full of power and light and wild wind. In that eerie luminescent light, Laura Templeton sat content on the rock. Summer storms were the best.

They would have to go in soon, back to Templeton

House, but for now, she and her two closest friends would wait and watch. She was sixteen, a delicately built girl with quiet gray eyes and bright blond hair. And as full of energy as any storm.

"I wish we could get in the car and drive right into it," Margo Sullivan laughed. The wind was fitful and growing stronger. "Right into it."

"Not with you behind the wheel," Kate Powell sneered. "You've only had your license a week, and you already have a rep as a lunatic."

"You're just jealous because it'll be months before you can drive."

Because it was true, Kate shrugged. Her short black hair fluttered in the wind. She took a deep gulp of air, loving the way it thickened and churned. "At least I'm saving up for a car, instead of cutting out pictures of Ferraris and Jaguars."

"If you're going to dream," Margo said, frowning at a minute chip in the coral polish on her nails, "dream big. I'll have a Ferrari one day, or a Porsche, or whatever I want." Her summer-blue eyes narrowed with determination. "I won't settle for some secondhand junker like you would."

Laura let them argue. She could have defused the sniping, but she understood it was simply part of the friendship. And she didn't care about cars. Not that she didn't enjoy the spiffy little convertible her parents had given her for her sixteenth birthday. But one car was the same as another to her.

She realized it was easier, in her position. She was the daughter of Thomas and Susan Templeton, of the Templeton hotel empire. Her home loomed on the hill behind her, stunning under the churning gray sky. It was more than the stone and wood and glass that composed it. More than the turrets and balconies and lush gardens. More than the fleet of servants who kept it shining.

It was home.

But she had been raised to understand the responsibilities of privilege. Within her was a great love of beauty and symmetry, and a kindness. Aligned with that was a need to live up to Templeton standards, to deserve all she'd been given by birthright. Not only the wealth, which even at sixteen she understood, but also the love of her family, her friends.

She knew Margo always fretted at limitations. Though they had grown up together at Templeton House, as close as sisters, Margo was the daughter of the housekeeper.

Kate had come to Templeton House when her parents had been killed. An eight-year-old orphan. She was cherished, absorbed into the family, as much a part of the Templetons as Laura and her older brother, Josh.

Laura and Margo and Kate were as close as—perhaps closer than—sisters who shared blood. But Laura never forgot that the Templeton responsibility was hers.

And one day, she thought, she would fall in love, marry, and have children. She would carry on the Templeton tradition. The man who came for her, who swept her up in his arms, who made her belong to him, would be everything she'd ever wanted. Together they would build a life, create a home, carve out a future as polished and perfect as Templeton House.

As she pictured it, dreams budded in her heart. Delicate color bloomed on her cheeks while the wind tossed her blond curls around them.

"Laura's dreaming again," Margo commented. Her grin flashed, transforming her striking face to stunning.

"Got Seraphina on the brain again?" Kate asked.

"Hmm?" No, she hadn't been thinking of Seraphina, but she did now. "I wonder how often she came here, dreaming of the life she wanted with Felipe."

"She died in a storm like the one that's coming. I know she did." Margo lifted her face to the sky. "With lightning flashing, the wind howling."

"Suicide's drama enough by itself." Kate plucked a wildflower, twirled the stubby stem between her fingers. "If it had been a perfect day, with blue skies and sunshine, the results would have been the same."

"I wonder what it is to feel that lost," Laura murmured.

''If we ever find her dowry, we should build a shrine or something to remember her by.''

''I'm spending my share on clothes, jewelry, and travel.'' Margo stretched her arms up, tucked them behind her head.

''And it'll be gone in a year. Less,'' Kate predicted. ''I'm going to invest mine in blue chips.''

''Boring, predictable Kate.'' Margo turned her head, smiled at Laura. ''What about you? What will you do when we find it? And we will find it one day.''

''I don't know.'' What would her mother do? she wondered. Her father? ''I don't know,'' she repeated. ''I'll have to wait and see.'' She looked back toward the sea, where the curtain of rain was inching closer. ''That's what Seraphina didn't do. She didn't wait and see.''

And the sound of the rising wind was like a woman weeping.

Lightning jagged, a flashing pitchfork of brilliant white through the heavy sky. The blasting boom of answering thunder shook the air. Laura threw back her head and smiled. Here it comes, she thought. The power, the danger, the glory.

She wanted it. Deep inside her most secret heart, she wanted it all.

Then came the squeal of brakes, the angry pulse of gritty rock and roll. And an impatient shout.

''Jesus Christ, are you all nuts?'' Joshua Templeton leaned out of his car window, scowling at the trio. ''Get the hell in the car.''

''It's not raining yet.'' Laura stood. She eyed Josh first. He was her senior by four years, and at the moment he looked so much like their father at his crankiest that she wanted to laugh. But she'd seen who was in the car with him.

She wasn't certain how she knew that Michael Fury was as dangerous as any summer storm, but she was sure of it. It was more than Ann Sullivan's mutterings about hoods and troublemakers—though, to be sure, Margo's mother had definite opinions on this particular friend of Josh's.

Maybe it was because his dark hair was just a little too

long and too wild, or because of the little white scar just above his left eyebrow, which Josh said Michael had gotten in a fight. Maybe it was his looks, for they were dark and dangerous, and just a little mean. Like a greedy angel's, she thought as her heart fluttered uncomfortably. Grinning all the way to hell.

But she thought it was his eyes. So startlingly blue they were in that face. So intense and direct and intrusive when he looked at her.

No, she didn't like the way he looked at her.

"Get in the damn car." Impatience shimmered around Josh in waves. "Mom had a fit when she realized you were out here. One of you gets hit by lightning, it'll be my ass."

"And it's such a cute one," Margo added, always ready to flirt. Hoping to make Josh jealous, she opened the door on Michael's side. "It'll be a tight fit. Mind if I sit on your lap, Michael?"

His gaze shifted from Laura. He grinned at Margo, a quick flash of teeth in a tanned, hollow-cheeked face. "Make yourself at home, sugar." His voice was deep, a little rough, and he accepted the weight of a willing female with practiced ease.

"I didn't know you were back, Michael." Kate slipped into the backseat, where, she thought sourly, there was plenty of room for three.

"On leave." He flicked a glance at her, then looked back at Laura, who still hesitated at the car door. "I ship out again in a couple days."

"The merchant marine." Margo toyed with his hair. "It sounds so . . . dangerous. And exciting. Do you have a woman in every port?"

"I'm working on it." As the first fat drops of rain splatted the windshield, he raised a brow at Laura. "Want to sit on my lap, too, sugar?"

Dignity was something else she'd learned at an early age. Not sparing him a reply, Laura got into the backseat with Kate.

The minute the door was closed, Josh sent the car streaking across the road and up the hill toward home. When her eyes met Michael's in the rearview mirror, Laura deliberately looked away, then back. Back toward the cliffs, and her place of comfortable dreams.

Chapter One

On the day of her eighteenth birthday, Laura was in love. She knew she was lucky to be so certain of her feelings, and her future, and the man who would share them both with her.

His name was Peter Ridgeway, and he was everything she had ever dreamed of. He was tall and handsome, with golden good looks and a charming smile. He was a man who understood beauty and music, and the responsibilities of career.

Since he had been promoted in the Templeton organization and transferred to the California branch, he had courted her in a fashion designed to win her romantic heart.

There had been roses delivered in glossy white boxes, quiet dinners at restaurants with flickering candlelight. Endless conversations about art and literature—and silent looks that said so much more than words.

They had taken walks in the garden in the moonlight, long drives along the coast.

Her fall into love had not taken long, yet it had been a

gentle tumble with no scrapes or bruises. Very much, she thought, like sliding slowly down a silk-lined tunnel into waiting arms.

Perhaps, at twenty-seven, he was a bit older than her parents might have liked, and she a bit younger. But he was so flawless, so perfect, Laura couldn't see how the years could matter. No boy of her own age had Peter Ridgeway's polish, his knowledge, or his quiet patience.

And she was so much in love.

He had hinted at marriage, gently. She understood that this was to give her time to consider. If only she knew how to let him know she had already considered, already decided he was the man she would spend her life with.

But a man like Peter, Laura thought, needed to be the one to make the moves, the decisions.

There was time, she assured herself. All the time in the world. And tonight, at the party to celebrate her eighteenth birthday, he would be there. She would dance with him. And in the pale blue dress she'd chosen because it matched his eyes, she would feel like a princess. More, she would feel like a woman.

She dressed slowly, wanting to savor every moment of preparation. It was all going to be different now, she thought. Her room had been the same when she'd opened her eyes that morning. The walls were still papered with those tiny pink rosebuds that had grown there for so many years. The winter sunlight still tilted through her windows, filtering through lacy curtains as it had done on so many other January mornings.

But everything was different. Because she was different.

She studied her room with a woman's eyes now. She appreciated the elegant lines of the mahogany bureau, the glossy Chippendale that had been her grandmother's. She touched the pretty silver grooming set, a birthday gift from Margo, studied the colorful, frivolous perfume bottles she'd begun to collect in adolescence.

There was the bed she had slept in, dreamed in, since childhood—the high four-poster, again Chippendale, with its fanciful canopy of Breton lace. The terrace doors that led to her balcony were open, to invite the sounds and scents of evening inside. The window seat where she could curl up and dream about the cliffs was cozy with pillows.

A fire burned sedately in the hearth of rose-grained marble. Atop the mantel were silver-framed photos, the delicate silver candlesticks with the slim white tapers she loved to burn at night. And the Dresden bud vase that held the single white rose Peter had sent that morning.

There was the desk where she had studied all the way through high school, where she would continue to study through what was left of her senior year.

Odd, she mused, tracing a hand over it, she didn't feel like a high school student. She felt so much older than her contemporaries. So much wiser, so much more sure of where she was going.

This was the room of her childhood, she thought, of her youth and of her heart. As Templeton House was the home of her heart. Though she knew she would never love any place as much, she was prepared, even eager to build a new home with the man she loved.

At last, she turned and looked at herself in the cheval glass. And smiled. She'd been right about the dress, she decided. Simple, clean lines suited her small frame. The scoop neckline, the long, tapered sleeves, the straight column that skimmed down to flirt with her ankles—the effect was classic, dignified, and perfect for a woman who met Peter Ridgeway's standards.

She might have preferred that her hair be straight and flowing, but since it insisted on curling frivolously, she'd swept it up. It added maturity, she thought.

She would never be bold and sexy like Margo, or casually intriguing like Kate. So she would settle for mature and dignified. After all, those were qualities that Peter found appealing.

She so badly wanted to be perfect for him. Tonight—especially tonight.

Reverently she picked up the earrings that had been her parents' birthday gift. The diamonds and sapphires winked flirtatiously back at her. She was smiling at them when her door burst open.

"I am not putting that crap all over my face." Flushed and flustered, Kate continued her argument with Margo as both of them strode inside. "You have enough on yours for both of us."

"You said Laura would be the judge," Margo reminded her, then stopped. With an expert's eye she studied her friend. "You look fabulous. Dignified sex."

"Really? Are you sure?" The idea of being sexy was so thrilling, Laura turned back to the mirror. All she saw was herself, a small young woman with anxious gray eyes and hair that wouldn't quite stay in place.

"Absolutely. Every guy at the party is going to want you, and be afraid to ask."

Kate snorted and plopped onto Laura's bed. "They won't be afraid to ask you, pal. You're a prime example of truth in advertising."

Margo merely smirked and ran a hand over her hip. The lipstick-red dress dipped teasingly low at the bodice and clung to every generous curve. "If you've got it—which you don't—flaunt it. Which is why you need the blusher, the eye shadow, the mascara, the—"

"Oh, Christ."

"She looks lovely, Margo." Always the peacemaker, Laura stepped between them. She smiled at Kate, spread out on the bed, her angular frame intriguing in thin white wool that covered her from throat to ankle. "Like a wood nymph." She laughed when Kate groaned. "But you could use a little more color."

"See?" Triumphant, Margo whipped out her makeup bag. "Sit up and let a master do her work."

"I was counting on you." Complaining all the way, Kate suffered the indignity of Margo's brushes and tubes. "I'm only doing this because it's your birthday."

"And I appreciate it."

"It's going to be a clear night." Margo busily defined Kate's cheekbones. "The band's already setting up, and the kitchen's in chaos. Mum's rushing around fussing with the floral arrangements as though it's a royal reception."

"I should go help," Laura began.

"You're the guest of honor." Kate kept her eyes closed in self-defense as Margo dusted shadow on her lids. "Aunt Susie has everything under control—including Uncle Tommy. He's outside playing the sax."

Laughing, Laura sat on the bed beside Kate. "He always said his secret fantasy was to play tenor sax in some smoky club."

"He'd have played for a while," Margo said as she carefully smudged liner under Kate's big doe eyes. "Then the Templeton would have come out, and he'd have bought the club."

"Ladies." Josh loitered in the doorway, a small florist's box in his hands. "I don't mean to interrupt a female ritual, but as everyone's slightly insane, I'm playing delivery boy."

The way he looked in his tux shot heat straight through Margo's loins. She sent him a sultry look. "What's your usual tip?"

"Never draw to an inside straight." He struggled not to let his gaze dip to her cleavage and cursed every man who would be offered a glimpse of those milky white curves. "Looks like more flowers for the birthday girl."

"Thanks." Laura rose to take the box, and kissed him. "That's my tip."

"You look wonderful." He caught her hand. "Grown up. I'm starting to miss my annoying little sister."

"I'll do my best to annoy you, as often as possible." She opened the box, sighed, and forgot everything else. "From Peter," she murmured.

Josh set his teeth. It wouldn't be fair to say that she was already annoying him in her choice of men. "Some guys think single roses are classy."

"I'd rather have dozens," Margo stated. And her eyes met Josh's in perfect agreement and understanding.

"It's lovely," Laura murmured as she slipped it into the vase with its mate. "Just like the one he sent this morning."

* * *

By nine, Templeton House was overflowing with people and sound. Groups of guests spilled out of brightly lit rooms onto heated terraces. Others wandered the gardens, strolling down bricked paths to admire the blooms and the fountains, all lit by the white ball of a winter's moon and the charm of fairy lights.

Margo had been right. The night was clear, a black sky stabbed by countless diamond-bright stars. Under it Templeton House stood awash in lights.

The music pulsed, inviting couples to dance. Huge tables elegantly clad in white linen groaned under the weight of food prepared by a fleet of caterers. Waiters trained by Templeton Hotels standards wandered discreetly among the guests, carrying silver trays filled with flutes of champagne and tiny delicacies for sampling. Half a dozen open bars were set up to serve mixed or soft drinks.

Steam rose off the swimming pool in misty fingers, while dozens of white water lilies floated on the surface. On terraces, under silky awnings, over the lawns, dozens of tables were draped in white linen, centered with a trio of white tapers ringed by glossy gardenias.

Indoors, there were more waiters, more food, more music, more flowers for those who wanted the warmth and relative quiet. Two uniformed maids upstairs stood ready to assist any lady who might wish to freshen up or fix a hem.

No reception ever held at any Templeton hotel around the world was more carefully planned or executed than the celebration of Laura Templeton's eighteenth birthday.

She would never forget that night, the way the lights flashed and glowed, the way the music seemed to fill the air, mating with the scent of flowers. She knew her duties, and she chatted and danced with friends of her parents and with her contemporaries. Though she wanted only Peter, she mixed and mingled as was expected of her.

When she danced with her father, she pressed her cheek against his. "It's a wonderful party. Thank you."

He sighed, realizing she smelled like a woman—soft,

elegant. "Part of me wishes you were still three years old, bouncing on my knee."

Thomas drew her back to smile at her. He was a striking man, his bronzed hair lightly touched with silver, the eyes he had passed on to both of his children crinkled at the corners with life and laughter.

"You've grown up on me, Laura."

"I couldn't help it." She smiled back at him.

"No, I suppose you couldn't. Now I'm standing here aware that a dozen young men are aiming arrows at my back, hoping I'll keel over so they can dance with you."

"I'd rather dance with you than anyone."

But when Peter glided by with Susan Templeton, Thomas saw his daughter's eyes go soft and dreamy. How could he have predicted, he thought, when he brought the man out to California, that Ridgeway would take his little girl away?

When the music ended, Thomas had to admire the smooth skill with which Peter changed partners and circled away with Laura.

"You shouldn't look at the man as though you'd like to flog him, Tommy," Susan murmured.

"She's just a girl."

"She knows what she wants. She's always seemed to know." She sighed herself. "Apparently it's Peter Ridgeway."

Thomas looked into his wife's eyes. They were wise, always had been wise. She might be small and delicate-framed like her daughter, and perhaps she gave the illusion of fragility. But he knew just how strong she was.

"What do you think of him?"

"He's competent," she said slowly. "He's well bred, well mannered. God knows, he's attractive." Her soft mouth hardened. "And I wish he was a thousand miles away from her. That's a mother talking," she admitted. "One who's afraid she's losing her little girl."

"We could transfer him to Europe." He warmed to the idea. "No—Tokyo, or Sydney."

Laughing, she patted her husband's cheek. "The way

Laura looks at him, she'd follow him. Better to keep him close.'' Struggling to accept, she shrugged her shoulders. ''She could have fallen for one of Josh's wilder friends, or a gigolo, a fortune hunter, an ex-con.''

He laughed himself. ''Laura? Never.''

Susan merely raised an eyebrow. A man wouldn't understand, she knew. Romantic natures like Laura's most usually were drawn to the wild. ''Well, Tommy, we'll just have to see where it goes. And be there for her.''

''Aren't you going to dance with me?'' Margo slid into Josh's arms, fit there, before he had a chance to agree or evade. ''Or would you rather just stand there brooding?''

''I wasn't brooding. I was thinking.''

''You're worried about Laura.'' Even as her fingers skimmed flirtatiously up the nape of his neck, Margo shot a concerned glance toward Laura. ''She's mad for him. And bound and determined to marry him.''

''She's too young to be thinking of marriage.''

''She's been thinking of marriage since she was four,'' Margo muttered. ''Now she's found what she thinks is the man of her dreams. No one's going to stop her.''

''I could kill him,'' Josh considered. ''Then we could hide the body.''

She chuckled, smiled into his eyes. ''Kate and I would be happy to help you toss his lifeless corpse off the cliffs. But hell, Josh, maybe he's right for her. He's attentive, intelligent, apparently patient in certain hormonal areas.''

''Don't start that.'' Josh's eyes went dark. ''I don't want to think about it.''

''Rest assured your little sister will walk down the aisle, when the time comes, in blushing-bride white.'' She blew out a breath, wondering why any woman would consider marrying a man before she knew if he was her mate in bed. ''They have a lot in common, really. And who are two jaded cynics like us to judge?''

''We love her,'' Josh said simply.

''Yeah, we do. But things change, and before much longer we're all going to be moving in our own directions.

You've already started,'' she pointed out. ''Mister Harvard Law. And Kate's chafing at the bit for college, Laura for marriage.''

''What are you chafing for, duchess?''

''Everything, and then some.'' Her smile turned sultry. She might have pushed the flirtation a bit farther, but Kate swung up and pried them apart.

''Sexual rituals later,'' she muttered. ''Look, they're going off.'' She scowled in Laura's direction, watching her walk away hand in hand with Peter. ''Maybe we should go after them. Do something.''

''Such as?'' But understanding, Margo draped an arm over Kate's narrow shoulders. ''Whatever, it won't make any difference.''

''I'm not going to stand around and watch, then.'' Disgusted, Kate peered up at Josh. ''Let's go sit in the south garden for a while. Josh can steal us some champagne.''

''You're under age,'' he said primly.

''Right, like you've never done it before.'' She smiled winningly. ''Just a glass each. To toast Laura. Maybe it'll bring her luck, and what she wants.''

''One glass, then.''

Margo frowned, noting the way he scanned the crowd. ''Looking for cops?''

''No, I thought Michael might show after all.''

''Mick?'' Kate angled her head. ''I thought he was down in Central America or somewhere, playing soldier of fortune.''

''He is—was,'' Josh corrected. ''He's back, at least for a while. I was hoping he'd take me up on the invitation.'' Then he shrugged. ''He's not much for this kind of thing. One glass,'' he repeated, tapping a finger on Kate's nose. ''And you didn't get it from me.''

''Of course not.'' After tucking her arm through Margo's, Kate wandered toward the gaily lighted gardens. ''We might as well drink to her if we can't stop her.''

''We'll drink to her,'' Margo agreed. ''And we'll be there, whatever happens.''

* * *

"So many stars," Laura breathed in the night as she and Peter walked across the gently sloping lawn. "I can't imagine a more perfect evening."

"Much more perfect now that I have a moment alone with you."

Flushing, she smiled at him. "I'm sorry. I've been so busy, I've hardly had a moment to talk with you." Be alone with you.

"You have duties. I understand. A Templeton would never neglect her guests."

"Not ordinarily, no. But it is my birthday." Her hand felt so warm and sheltered in his. She wished they could walk forever, down to the cliffs, so she could share that most intimate place with him. "I should have some leeway."

"Then let's take advantage of that." He guided her toward the fanciful white shape of the gazebo.

From there the sounds of the party became muted background, and the moonlight filtered through the latticelike lace. Scents from the flowers perfumed the air. It was precisely the setting he'd wanted.

Old-fashioned and romantic, like the woman he intended to have.

Drawing her into his arms, he kissed her. She came so willingly, he thought. So innocently. That lovely mouth parting for his, those delicate arms winding around him. It stirred him, this youth combined with dignity, eagerness flushed with innocence.

He could have her, he knew. He had the skill and the experience. But he was a man who prided himself on control, and he drew her gently back. He wouldn't soil the perfection, or rush into the physical. He wanted his wife untouched, even by himself.

"I haven't told you enough how lovely you look tonight."

"Thank you." She treasured those warm, liquid pulls of anticipation. "I wanted to. For you."

He smiled and held her tenderly, letting her head rest against his heart. She was so perfect for him, he thought.

Young, lovely, well bred. Malleable. Through the slats he spotted Margo, flashy in her clinging red dress, laughing bawdily at some joke.

Even though his glands stirred, his sensibilities were offended. The housekeeper's daughter. Every man's wet dream.

His gaze shifted to Kate. The prickly ward, with more brains than style. It amazed him that Laura felt this childish attachment for those two. But he was sure it would fade in time. She was, after all, sensible, with a dignity admirable in one so young. Once she fully understood her place in society—and her place with him—she could be gently weaned from inappropriate attachments.

He had no doubt she was in love with him. She had so little experience in coyness or deception. Her parents might not completely approve, but he was confident that their devotion to their daughter would sway them in his favor.

They would find no fault with him personally or professionally, he was certain. He did his job, and did it well. He would make a suitable son-in-law. With Laura beside him, with the Templeton name, he would have everything he wanted. Everything he deserved. The proper wife, the unshakable position in society, sons. Wealth and success.

"We haven't known each other long," he began.

"It feels like forever."

Over her head, he smiled. She was so sweetly romantic. "Only a few months, Laura. And I'm nearly ten years older than you are."

She only pressed closer. "What does it matter?"

"I should give you more time. God, you're still in high school."

"Only for a few more months." Her heart beat wildly with anticipation as she lifted her head. "I'm not a child, Peter."

"No, you're not."

"I know what I want. I've always known."

He believed her. And he, also, knew what he wanted. Had always known. That, too, he mused, they had in common.

"Still, I told myself I would wait." He brought her hands to his lips, watched her eyes. "Another year, at least."

She knew this was what she had dreamed of, had waited for. "I don't want you to wait," she whispered. "I love you, Peter."

"I love you, Laura. Too much to wait even another hour, much less another year."

He eased her down onto the padded bench. Her hands trembled. With all her heart she absorbed every aspect of the moment. The sound of music in the distance that carried over the clear night air in quiet notes. The scent of night-blooming jasmine and hints of the sea. The way the shadows and lights played through the sheltering lattice.

He got down on one knee, as she'd known he would. His face was so beautiful in the delicate, dreamy light, it broke her heart. Her eyes were swimming with tears when he took a small black-velvet box from his pocket, opened it. The tears made the light that glinted off the diamond refract into rainbows.

"Will you marry me, Laura?"

She knew what every woman felt at this one shining moment of her life. And held out her hand. "Yes."

Chapter Two

Twelve years later

When a woman turned thirty, Laura supposed, it was a time for reflection, for taking stock, for not only shuddering because middle age was certainly creeping closer and closer around that blind corner, but for looking back over her accomplishments.

She was trying to.

But the fact was, when she awoke that morning in January on her thirtieth birthday to gray skies and unrelenting rain, the weather perfectly mirrored her mood.

She was thirty years old and divorced. She had lost the lion's share of her personal wealth through her own naïveté and was struggling mightily to fulfill her responsibilities to her family home, raise two daughters alone, hold down two part-time jobs—neither of which she had prepared herself for—and still be a Templeton.

Crowding the minus side was the failure to hold her marriage together, the personal and somewhat embarrassing fact that she had slept with only one man in her life, worry that her children were being penalized by her lack, and fear that the house of cards she was rebuilding so carefully would tumble at the first brisk wind.

Her life—the unrelenting reality of it—bore little resemblance to the one she had dreamed of. Was it any wonder she wanted to huddle in bed and pull the covers over her head?

Instead, she prepared to do what she always did. Get up, face the day, and try to somehow get through the complicated mess she'd made out of her life. There were people depending on her.

Before she could toss the covers aside, there was a soft knock at the door. Ann Sullivan poked her head in first, then smiled. "Happy birthday, Miss Laura."

The Templetons' longtime housekeeper stepped inside the room, carrying a fully loaded breakfast tray accented with a vase of Michaelmas daisies.

"Breakfast in bed!" Scrambling to reorganize her schedule, which had room for a quick cup of coffee at best, Laura sat back. "I feel like a queen."

"It isn't every day a woman turns thirty."

Laura's attempt at a smile wobbled. "Tell me about it."

"Now don't you start that nonsense."

Brisk and efficient, Ann settled the tray over Laura's lap. She'd seen thirty herself—and forty, and Lord help her, she'd just run smack into fifty. And because she understood just how those decades affected a woman, she brushed Laura's sigh aside.

She had been fretting after this girl, as well as her own and Miss Kate besides, for more than twenty years. She knew just how to handle them.

Ann went to rekindle the fire in the hearth not only to chase away the January chill but to add light and cheer. "You're a beautiful young woman with the best of her life ahead of her."

"And thirty years of it behind her."

Ann methodically pushed the right buttons. "And nothing to show for it but two beautiful children, a thriving business, a lovely home, and family and friends who adore you.''

Ouch, Laura thought. ''I'm feeling sorry for myself.'' She tried the smile again. ''Pathetic and typical. Thank you, Annie. This is lovely.''

''Drink some coffee.'' As the fire caught, crackling briskly, Ann poured the coffee herself, then patted Laura's hand. ''You know what you need? A day off. A full day just for yourself, to do exactly as you choose.''

It was a fine fantasy, and one that not so many years before she would have been able to indulge. But now, she had the girls to ready for school, a morning in her office at Templeton Monterey, and an afternoon at Pretenses, the shop she and Margo and Kate had started together.

Then it was a quick dash to take the girls to their dance class, time out to go over the bills and to pay them. Then there was homework to oversee, as well as dealing with any and all of the myriad problems her daughters might have encountered during the day.

And she needed to carve out time to check on old Joe, the gardener. She was worried about him but didn't want him to know it.

''You're not listening, Miss Laura.''

At the faintly censorious tone, Laura pulled herself back. ''I'm sorry. The girls need to get up for school.''

''They're up. As a matter of fact . . .'' Pleased with her surprise, Ann walked to the door. At the signal, the room filled with people and noise.

''Mama.'' The girls came first, rushing in to jump on the bed and rattle plates on the tray. At seven and ten they weren't babies any longer, but she cuddled them just the same. Kayla, the younger, was always ready for a hug, but Allison had been growing distant. Laura knew the extended embrace from her elder daughter was one of the best gifts she would receive that day.

''Annie said we could all come and start your birthday off right.'' Kayla bounced, her smoky gray eyes bright with excitement. ''And everybody's here.''

''So they are.'' With an arm around each girl, Laura

grinned at the crowd. Margo was already passing her three-month-old son to his grandmother so she could supervise as Josh opened a bottle of champagne. Kate slipped away from her husband to help herself to one of the croissants on Laura's tray.

"So how does it feel, champ?" Kate asked with her mouth full. "The big three-oh?"

"It was feeling lousy until a minute ago. Mimosas?" She raised a brow at Margo.

"You betcha. And, no," she said, anticipating Ali, "straight o.j. for you and your sister."

"It's a special occasion," Ali complained.

"So, you're going to drink your o.j. in a champagne flute." With a flourish, she passed juice to the girls. "For a toast," she added, then hooked an arm through her husband's. "Right, Josh?"

"To Laura Templeton," he began, "a woman of many talents—which includes looking pretty great for a kid sister on the morning of her thirtieth birthday."

"And if anyone brought a camera in here," Laura said, pushing back her tumbled hair, "I'll kill them."

"I knew I forgot something." Kate shook her head, then shrugged. "Well—let's get to the first gift. Byron?"

Byron De Witt, Kate's husband of six weeks and the executive director of Templeton California, stepped forward. He touched his glass lightly to Laura's and grinned. "Ms. Templeton, if I see you anywhere on hotel property before midnight tonight, I'll be forced to pull rank and fire you."

"But I have two accounts I have to—"

"Not today you don't. Consider your office closed. Somehow Conventions and Special Events will have to limp along without you for twenty-four hours."

"I appreciate the thought, Byron, but—"

"All right." He sighed. "If you insist on going over my head. Mr. Templeton?"

Enjoying himself, Josh joined ranks with Byron. "As executive vice president, Templeton, I'm ordering you to take the day off. And if you've got some idea about going over my head, I've already talked to Mom and Dad. They'll be calling you later.''

''Fine.'' When she discovered she was getting ready to pout, she shrugged instead. ''It'll give me a chance to—''

''Nope.'' Reading Laura well, Kate shook her head. ''You're not setting foot in the shop today.''

''Oh, come on. This is just silly. I can—''

''Lie in bed,'' Margo continued, ''walk the cliffs, read a book, get a facial.'' Over the sheets, she grabbed Laura's foot, waggled it. ''Pick up a sailor and . . .'' Remembering the girls, she backtracked. ''Go for a sail. Mrs. Williamson is planning an elaborate birthday feast for you tonight, to which we have all invited ourselves. At that time, if you've been a good girl, you'll get the rest of your presents.''

''I have something for you, Mama. I have something and so does Ali. Annie helped us pick them out. You have to be good so you can open them tonight.''

''Outnumbered.'' Laura took a contemplative sip of her mimosa. ''All right, I'll be lazy. And if I do something foolish, it'll be your fault. All of you.''

''Always willing to take the credit.'' Margo took J. T. back as he began to fuss. ''He's wet,'' she discovered and, laughing, handed him to his father. ''And it's your turn, Josh. We'll be back at seven sharp. Oh, and if you decide on that sailor, I'll want to hear every detail.''

''Gotta go,'' Kate announced. ''See you tonight.''

They went out as quickly and as noisily as they had come in, leaving Laura alone with a bottle of champagne and a cooling breakfast.

She was so lucky, she thought, as she settled back against the pillows. She had family and friends who loved her. She had two beautiful daughters, and a home she had always called her own.

Then why, she wondered as her eyes swam with sudden tears, did she feel so useless?

The trouble with having free time, Laura decided, was that it reminded her of the days when most of her free time had been eaten up by committees. Some she had joined because she enjoyed them—the people, the projects, the causes. Others, she knew, she'd involved herself with because of pressure from Peter.

She had, for too many years, found it easier to bend than to stand.

And when she had rediscovered her backbone, she had also discovered that the man she had married didn't love her, or the children. It had been the Templeton name he had married; he had never wanted the life she dreamed of.

Sometime between Ali's birth and Kayla's, he dropped even the pretense of loving her. Still, she stuck with it, maintained the illusion of marriage and family. And the pretense was all hers.

Until the day she walked in on that most pathetic of clichés: her husband in bed with another woman.

Thinking of it now, Laura crossed the beautifully tended lawn, strolled through the south gardens and into the grove beside the old stables. The rain had subsided to a mist that merged with the swirl of fog crawling along the ground. It was, she thought, like walking through a cool, thin river.

She rarely walked here, rarely had time. Yet she had always loved the play of sunlight or shadow through the trees, the scent of the forest, the rustling of small animals. There had been times during her youth when she imagined it was a fairy-tale woods and she was the enchanted princess, searching for the one true love who would rescue her from the spell cast upon her.

A harmless fantasy, she thought now, for a young girl. But perhaps she had wanted that fairy-tale ending too badly, believed in it too strongly. As she had believed in Peter.

He had crushed her. Quite literally he had crushed her heart with simple neglect, with casual disinterest. Then he had scattered the pieces that were left with betrayal. At last, he had eradicated even the dust when he had taken not only her money but the children's too.

For that, she would never forgive or forget.

And that, Laura thought as she wandered a path under an arch of lazily dripping branches, made her bitter.

She wanted to swallow the taste of that bitterness once and for all, to get beyond it, fully, and move ahead. Perhaps, she decided, her thirtieth birthday was the time to really begin.

It made sense, didn't it? Peter had proposed to her on her birthday twelve years before. On a starry night, she remembered, raising her face to the misting rain. She'd been so sure then, so positive that she knew what she wanted, what she needed. Now was the time to reevaluate.

Her marriage was over, but her life wasn't. In the past two years she'd taken quite a few steps to prove that.

Did she mind the work she'd taken on to rebuild her life and her personal finances? Not the work itself, she decided, stepping over a fallen log and going deeper into the forest. Her position with Templeton Hotels was a responsibility, a legacy, that she'd neglected too long. She would damn well earn her keep.

And the shop. She smiled to herself as her boots squished on the soggy path. She loved Pretenses, loved working with Margo and Kate. She enjoyed the customers, the stock, and the sense of accomplishment. The three of them had built something there, for themselves, for each other.

How could she resent the hours and the effort that she put into raising her girls, seeing that they had a happy, healthy life? They were her heart. Whatever it took to make up for the loss of the home she had somehow helped break, she would try to do.

Kayla, she thought, her little Kayla. So resilient, so easy to please. A loving, happy child was Kayla.

But Allison. Poor Ali had needed her father's love so desperately. The divorce was hardest on her, and nothing Laura did seemed to help her adjust. She was doing better now, Laura thought, better than she had been during those first months, even the first year. But she had pulled in, and back, and was only rarely spontaneous with her affections, as she had been.

And wary of her mother, Laura thought with a sigh. Still blaming her mother for a father who had no interest in his daughters.

Laura sat on a stump, closed her eyes, let the faint breeze that was the music of the forest surround her. She would handle it, she promised herself. She would handle all of it—the work, the rush, the worry, the children. No one was more surprised than she herself that she was handling it well.

But how, she wondered, how in God's name would she continue to handle the loneliness?

Later, she snipped deadheads out of the garden, did some pruning, hauled away the debris. Old Joe simply couldn't keep up any longer. And young Joe, his grandson, couldn't afford more than a few hours a week in between his college courses to add his help. Since it would cut too much into her budget, and old Joe's pride, to hire an assistant, Laura had convinced Joe that she wanted to take on some of the gardening tasks.

It was partially true. She had always loved the gardens of Templeton House—the flowers, the shrubs, the vines. As a child she had often dogged Joe, nagging him to teach her, to show her. And he would pull a pack of cherry Life Savers out of his pocket, thumb one out for her, and demonstrate the proper way to train a creeper, to deal with aphids, to prune a tea rose.

She had adored him—his weathered face, old even then, his slow, thoughtful voice, his big, patient hands. He had come to work in the gardens of Templeton House as a boy, in her grandparents' day. After sixty years of service, he had a right to his pension, to spend his days tending his own garden, to a life sitting in the sunshine.

And, Laura understood, it would break his heart if she offered it.

So she picked up the slack under the guise of wanting a hobby. When her schedule allowed, and often when it didn't, she would stand with Joe and discuss perennials and bonemeal and mulch.

Today, as afternoon faded to dusk, she took stock. The gardens of Templeton House looked as they should in winter: quiet, waiting, the hardiest blooms splashes of defiant color. Her parents had given the house into her hands for tending, and for cherishing. Laura did both.

She stepped out onto the skirt of the pool, nodded in approval. She maintained the pool herself. It was, after all, her indulgence. Whatever the weather, if she could squeeze in a few laps, she did so. She'd taught her children to swim in that pool, as her father had taught her. The water sparkled, a delicate blue, thanks to some of her recent dickering with the pump and filter.

The mermaid lived beneath, a mosaic fantasy of flowing red hair and glossy green tail. Her girls loved to dive down and touch that smiling, serene face, even as she had.

Out of habit, she checked the glass tables for smudges, the cushions of the chairs and lounges for dampness or dust. Ann would have already done so, but Laura didn't turn toward the house until she was certain everything was perfect.

Satisfied, she walked down the stone path and chose the kitchen door. Scents assaulted her, made her taste buds yearn. Mrs. Williamson, ample of hip and bosom, stood at the stove, as she had done for all of Laura's memory.

"Leg of lamb," Laura said and sighed. "Apple chutney. Curried potatoes."

Turning, Mrs. Williamson smiled smugly. She was well into her seventies. Her hair was the hard glossy black of a bowling ball and approximately the same shape. But her face was soft, full of folds and wrinkles and as sweet as her own cream centers.

"Your nose is as good as ever, Miss Laura—or your memory is. It's what you always want for your birthday."

"No one roasts a lamb like you, Mrs. Williamson." Because she knew the game, Laura wandered the spacious kitchen, making her poking about obvious. "I don't see a cake."

"Maybe I forgot to bake one."

Laura expressed the expected dismay. "Oh, Mrs. Williamson!"

"And maybe I didn't." She chuckled, gestured with her wooden spoon. "Now off you go. I can't have you around pestering me while I'm cooking. Get yourself cleaned up—you're carrying garden dirt.''

''Yes, ma'am.'' At the kitchen door, Laura turned back. ''It wouldn't be a Black Forest cake, would it? Double chocolate?''

''Just you wait and see. Scat!''

Laura waited until she was well down the hallway before she chuckled. It would be a Black Forest cake. Mrs. Williamson might be a tad forgetful these days, and her hearing wasn't what it had been. But vital matters such as Laura's traditional birthday meal would be remembered in every detail.

She hummed to herself as she climbed the stairs to bathe and change for dinner. Her mood had lifted, but it plummeted quickly when she heard the sounds of a sibling argument in full swing.

''Because you're stupid, that's why.'' Ali's voice was shrill and bitter. ''Because you don't understand anything, and I hate you.''

''I am not stupid.'' There were tears trembling on the surface of Kayla's retort. ''And I hate you more.''

''Well, this is pleasant.'' Determined to lose neither her temper nor her perspective, Laura paused in the doorway of Ali's room.

The tableau seemed innocent enough. In a girl's pretty mint-and-white room, dolls from around the world wearing their countries' traditional dress ringed the shelves that flanked the wide window. Books, ranging from *Sweet Valley High* to *Jane Eyre*, filled a case. A jewelry box with a twirling ballerina stood open on the dresser.

Her daughters faced each other from either side of the canopy bed like mortal enemies over embattled soil.

''I don't want her in my room.'' Her fists clenched, Ali whirled to face her mother. ''This is my room and I don't want her in it.''

''I just came in to show her the picture I drew.'' With trembling lips, Kayla held it out. It was a clever crayon sketch of a fire-breathing dragon and a young, silver-clad knight with a raised sword. The natural youthful talent in it reminded Laura that she needed to arrange for Kayla to have drawing lessons.

"It's wonderful, Kayla."

"She said it was ugly." Never ashamed of tears, Kayla let them fall. "She said it was ugly and stupid and that I had to knock before I came into her room."

"Ali?"

"Dragons aren't real, and they're ugly." Ali thrust her chin out, challenging. "And she can't just come into my room if I don't want her."

"You're entitled to your privacy," Laura said carefully, "but you're not entitled to be mean to your sister. Kayla—" Laura crouched down, brushed tears off her daughter's cheeks. "It's a wonderful picture. We can frame it if you like."

Tears dried up. "We can?"

"Absolutely, and we can hang it in your room. Unless you'd let me hang it in mine."

The smile bloomed, brilliantly. "You can have it."

"I'd like that very much. Why don't you go back to your room and sign it for me, just like a real artist. And Kayla . . ." Laura rose, kept a hand on Kayla's shoulder. "If Ali wants you to knock on her door, then that's what you'll do."

Mutiny flared briefly. "Then she has to knock on mine, too."

"That's fair. Go on now. I want to talk to Ali."

After sending her sister a smug look, Kayla sailed out.

"She wouldn't leave when I told her to," Ali began. "She's always running in here whenever she wants."

"And you're older," Laura said quietly, trying to understand. "There are privileges that go along with that, Ali, but there are also responsibilities. I don't expect the two of you never to fight. Josh and I fought, Margo and Kate and I fought. But you hurt her."

"I just wanted her to go away. I wanted to be alone. I don't care about her stupid picture of a stupid dragon."

There's more going on here, Laura thought, studying her daughter's miserable face, than sibling sniping. She sat on the edge of the bed so that her eyes were level with Ali's. ''Tell me what's wrong, honey.''

''You always take her side.''

Laura bit back a sigh. ''That's not true.'' Determined, she took Ali's hand, pulled her closer. ''And that's not what's bothering you.''

There was a war going on inside this little girl, Laura realized as she watched Ali's eyes swim. With all her heart, Laura wanted to find the right way to make peace.

''It doesn't matter. It won't make any difference.'' Tears came closer to the surface. ''You won't do anything about it.''

It hurt, but then, this recent distrust from Ali always hurt. ''Why don't you tell me, then we'll see. I can't do anything about it if I don't know what it is.''

''They're going to have a father-daughter dinner at school.'' The words burst out, full of anger and pain. ''They're all going to bring their dads.''

''Oh.'' No peace here, Laura admitted and touched her daughter's cheek. ''I'm sorry, Ali. That's hard. Uncle Josh will go with you.''

''It's not the same.''

''No, it's not the same.''

''I want it to be the same,'' Ali said in a furious whisper. ''Why can't you make it be the same?''

''I can't.'' There was relief when Ali went unresisting into her arms. And there was grief.

''Why don't you make him come back? Why don't you do something to make him come back?''

Now there was guilt to layer on top of grief. ''There's nothing I can do.''

''You don't want him to come back.'' With her eyes bright and hot, Ali jerked back. ''You told him to go away, and you don't want him to come back.''

This was a thin and shaky line to travel. ''Your father and I are divorced, Ali. That's not going to change. The fact that we can't, and don't want to, live together anymore doesn't have anything to do with you and Kayla.''

''Then why doesn't he ever come?'' Tears poured out

again, but they were hot now, and angry. "Other kids have parents that don't live together, but their dads come and they go places together."

The line got shakier. "Your father's very busy, and he's living in Palm Springs now." Lies, Laura thought. Pitiful lies. "I'm sure once he's more settled, he'll spend more time with you." When did he ever?

"He doesn't come because he doesn't want to see you." Ali turned away. "It's because of you."

Laura closed her eyes. What good would it be to deny it, to defend herself and leave her child vulnerable? "If it is, I'll do what I can to make it easier for him, and for you." On legs that weren't quite steady, Laura rose. "There are things I can't change, I can't fix. And I can't stop you from blaming me for it."

Fighting to control both grief and temper, Laura took a slow breath. "I don't want you to be unhappy, Ali. I love you. I love you and Kayla more than anything in the world."

Ali's shoulders slumped. "Will you ask him if he could come to the dinner? It's next month, on a Saturday."

"Yes, I'll ask."

Shame eked through the anger and misery. She didn't have to look at her mother's face to know she would see hurt. "I'm sorry, Mama."

"So am I."

"I'll tell Kayla I'm sorry, too. She draws really good. And I . . . I can't."

"You have other talents." Gently Laura turned Ali around, cupped her shoulders. "You dance so beautifully. And you play the piano so much better than I did at your age. Better than I do now."

"You never play anymore."

There were a lot of things she didn't do anymore. "How about a duet tonight? We'll play. Kayla can sing."

"She sounds like a bullfrog."

"I know."

And when Ali looked up, they grinned at each other.

* * *

Another crisis averted, Laura decided, as she settled down with her family after dinner. There was a cheery fire blazing in the hearth and rich, creamy cake to be devoured. The curtains in the parlor were opened to a starry night. And the lights inside glowed warm.

Birthday presents had been unwrapped, opened, and admired. The baby was sleeping upstairs. Josh and Byron were puffing on cigars, and her daughters, fences mended for the moment, were at the piano. Kayla's booming frog of a voice competed with Ali's skillful playing.

"Then she went for the Chanel bag," Margo was saying, comfortably curled on the sofa as she talked shop. "It took her more than an hour, and she just kept piling up stock. Three suits, an evening gown—your white Dior, Laura—four pairs of shoes. Count them, four. Six blouses, three sweaters, two silk slacks. And that was before she started on the jewelry."

"It was a red-letter day." Kate propped her bare feet on the Louis XIV coffee table. "I had a hunch when the woman pulled up in a white stretch limo. She'd come up from L.A. because a friend of hers had told her about Pretenses."

Kate sipped herbal tea, hardly missing the punch of coffee. "I'm telling you," she went on, "this woman was a pro. She said she's buying a country home and she's going to come back and choose some of the furnishings and whatnots from the shop. Turns out she's the wife of some hotshot producer. And she's going to tell all her friends about this clever little secondhand shop in Monterey."

"That's wonderful." So wonderful, Laura could almost accept not being in on the kill.

"It's making me wonder if we shouldn't think about expanding sooner. Maybe in L.A. rather than Carmel."

"Hold it, hotshot." Kate eyed Margo narrowly. "We're not talking seriously about another branch until we've been in business two full years. Then I run some figures, do some projections."

"Always the accountant," Margo muttered.

''You bet your ass. So, what did you do with your day off, Laura?''

''Oh, a little gardening.'' A little bill paying, closet cleaning, moping.

''Is that J. T.?'' With a mother's superhearing, Margo tuned in to the sounds whispering out of the baby monitor beside her. ''I'd better check on him.''

''No, let me.'' Laura rose quickly. ''Please. You get to have him all the time. I want to play.''

''Sure. But if he's . . .'' Margo trailed off, glancing toward the two young girls at the piano. ''I guess you know what to do.''

''I think I have a pretty good idea.'' Aware that Margo might change her mind, Laura hurried out.

It was amazing and gratifying to see the way her impulsive, glamorous friend had taken to motherhood. Even two short years before, no one would have believed Margo Sullivan, supermodel, the rage of Europe, would be settled down in her hometown, running a secondhand shop and raising a family. Margo certainly wouldn't have believed it herself, Laura mused.

But fate had dealt her a tough hand. Rather than fold and run, she'd stuck. And, with determination and flair, had turned fate on its ear.

Now she had Josh, and John Thomas, and a thriving business. She had a home she loved.

Laura hoped that somehow, someday, she could deal fate the same blow.

''There he is,'' Laura cooed as she approached the antique crib that she and Ann had hauled out of storage. ''There's the darling. Oh, what a handsome boy you are, John Thomas Templeton.''

Truer words were never spoken. He'd had a rich gene pool to choose from, and he'd chosen well. Golden hair grew thick around a glorious little face. Round with babyhood it was, with his mother's stunning blue eyes, his father's well-sculpted mouth.

His fretful whimpering stopped the moment she lifted him. And the feeling, one that perhaps only a woman understands, soared through her. Here was baby, beginnings, beauty.

"There, sweetheart, were you lonely?" She walked him, as much to pleasure herself as to soothe. She'd wanted more children. She knew it was selfish when she had two such beautiful daughters. But, oh, she'd wanted more children.

Now she had a nephew to spoil. And she intended to do so, lavishly. Kate and Byron would have children, Laura mused as she laid J. T. on the changing table. There would be more babies to cuddle.

She changed him, powdered him, tickled him to make him giggle and kick his legs. He grinned at her, wrapped a fist around a curl and tugged. Laura went with the pull to nuzzle his neck.

"Bring back memories?" Josh asked as he stepped inside the nursery.

"Does it ever! When Annie and I were putting this room together for his visits, we wallowed in memories." She lifted J. T. high over her head, where he could gurgle in delight. "Both my babies slept in that crib."

"So did you and I." He ran a hand over the curved rungs before moving to his son. Josh's fingers itched to hold him, but he held back, allowed Laura to cuddle the baby.

"Everyone who's been there says it, but I can't stop myself. The years go so fast, Josh. Treasure every second of it."

"You did." He touched her hair. "You are, and have been, the most incredible mother. I've admired you for that."

"You're going to make me sloppy," she murmured, and buried her face in the sweet curve of J. T.'s neck.

"I figure you and I had the best possible examples to follow. We've been lucky, Laura, to have people like Mom and Dad for parents."

"Don't I know it. I know they're in the middle of negotiating the construction of the new hotel on Bimini, but they called today just to wish me happy birthday."

"And Dad told the story of how he drove Mom through

the worst winter storm in the history of central California when she went into labor with you.''

''Of course.'' She lifted her head and grinned. ''He loves telling that story. Rain, floods, mud slides, lightning. All but an appearance of the Angel of Doom and the seven plagues of Egypt.''

'' 'But I got her there,' '' Josh quoted his father. '' 'With forty-five minutes to spare.' '' He stroked his son's hair. ''Not everybody's as lucky. Do you remember Michael Fury?''

Images of a dark, dangerous man with hot eyes. Who could forget Michael Fury? ''Yes, you used to hang around with him and look for girls and trouble. He went into the merchant marines or something.''

''He went into a lot of things. There were some problems at home—an unpleasant divorce. Well, two actually. His mother got married for the third time when he was about twenty-five. This one seems to have stuck. Anyway, he came back to the area a few weeks ago.''

''Oh, really? I didn't know.''

''You and Michael never ran in the same circles,'' Josh said dryly. ''The thing is, he took over the old place, where he grew up. His mother and stepfather relocated in Boca, and he bought the property from them. He's raising horses now.''

''Horses. Hmm.'' Not terribly interested, she began to walk the baby again. Josh would get to his point eventually, she knew. Sometimes he was such a lawyer, caging the meaning with words.

''Those storms we had a couple weeks ago?''

''Oh, bad ones,'' she remembered. ''Almost as bad as the fateful night of Laura Templeton's birth.''

''Yeah, more mud slides. One of them destroyed Michael's place.''

''Oh, I'm sorry.'' She stopped walking and tuned in. ''I'm really sorry. Was he hurt?''

''No. He managed to get himself and his stock out. But the house is a loss. It's going to take some time to rebuild, if that's what he wants to do. Meanwhile, he'll need temporary lodgings for himself and his horses. Something he could rent, you know, for the short term. And I was thinking, the stables and the groom's apartment above them aren't being used.''

Alarm came first. ''Josh.''

''Just hear me out. I know Mom and Dad were always a little, well, wary of him.''

''To say the least.''

''He's an old friend,'' Josh returned. ''And a good one. He's also handy. No one's done any maintenance or repairs on that building in years, not since—'' He broke off, cleared his throat.

''Not since I sold off the horses,'' Laura finished. ''Because Peter didn't care for them, or the amount of time I put in with them.''

''The point is, the building should be looked after. Right now it's just sitting there empty. You could use the rent, since you refuse to dip into Templeton capital to run this place.''

''I'm not going over that ground again.''

''Fine.'' He recognized that set to her mouth and didn't bother. ''The rent from a building you're not using would help you out. Right?''

''Yes, but—''

He held up a hand. He would cut through the logic and practicalities first. ''You could use someone around here, in the short term, to do some heavy work, to put the stables back in shape. That's something you simply can't do yourself.''

''That's true, but—''

Now, Josh thought, for the clincher. ''And I have an old friend whose home has been washed out from under him. I'd consider it a personal favor.''

''Low blow,'' she muttered.

''They're always the most effective.'' Knowing he'd scored, he gave her hair a quick, affectionate tug. ''Look, it should work out for everyone, but give it a couple of weeks. If it's not working, I'll find an alternative.''

''All right. But if he starts having drunken poker parties or orgies—''

''We'll try to keep them discreet,'' Josh finished and grinned. ''Thanks.'' He kissed her and took the baby. ''He's a good man, Laura. One you can count on in tight squeezes.''

Laura wrinkled her nose at his back as he carried J. T. out of the room. ''I don't intend to count on Michael Fury, particularly in a tight squeeze.''

Chapter Three

The last place Michael Fury had expected to take up residence, however temporarily, was on the great Templeton estate. Oh, he'd visited there often enough in the past, under the subtly watchful eyes of Thomas and Susan Templeton and the not so subtly watchful eye of Ann Sullivan.

He was well aware that the Templeton housekeeper had considered him a mongrel let loose among her purebreds. And he assumed that she'd been worried about his intentions toward her daughter.

She could have rested easy there. As lip smackingly gorgeous as Margo was, and always had been, she and Michael had never been more than casual friends.

Maybe he'd kissed her a couple of times. How was a red-blooded man supposed to resist that mouth? But that had been the beginning and end of it. She'd been for Josh. Even that long ago and despite the shortsightedness of youth, he'd realized that.

Michael Fury didn't poach on a pal.

Despite their different backgrounds, they had been

friends. Real friends. Michael didn't consider many people real friends. He would, and had, gone to the wall for Josh, and he knew he could depend on the same.

Still, he would never have asked for the favor and would likely have refused it but for his horses. He didn't want them boarded any longer than necessary in a public facility. He'd gotten sentimental over them, and he wasn't ashamed of it. In the last few years they'd been one of the few constants in his life.

He'd tried a number of things. He'd drifted. He liked to drift. Joining the merchant marine had been an escape, he'd reveled in it. He'd seen a lot of the world, and he liked some of it.

It had been cars for a time. He still had an affection for them, liked to drive full out. He'd had some success on the race circuit in Europe, but it hadn't satisfied him in the long term.

In between the sea and the cars, there had been a brief stint as a mercenary, during which he'd learned too much about killing and warring for profit. And maybe he'd been afraid he was too good at it, afraid it would satisfy him too well. It had fattened his wallet but scarred his heart.

He'd been married once also, only briefly, and could claim no success from that experience either.

It was during his stuntman stage that he fell for horses. He'd learned that craft, gained a reputation, broken several bones. He jumped out of buildings, rioted in staged bar fights, was shot off roofs, set on fire. And he tumbled off of countless horses.

Michael Fury knew how to take a fall. But he wasn't able to roll when he fell in love with horses.

So he bought them, and bred them, and trained them. He had put down a sick horse and labored through the birth of a foal.

Though he knew the odds were long, he thought he'd found what he'd been looking for.

It seemed like fate when his stepfather called, telling Michael that he and Michael's mother were going to sell the property in the hills. Though he had no sentiment for it, Michael heard himself offering to buy it.

It was good horse country.

So, he'd come back, and nature had delivered a hard backhanded slap in welcome. He didn't give a good damn about the house. But his horses—he would have died saving them, and he'd come dangerously close as those acres of mud tumbled down.

There he was, filthy, exhausted, alone, looking at what had been his next start. The oozing rubble of it.

There had been a time when he would have simply cut his losses and moved on. But this time he was sticking.

Now Josh had offered him a hand, and weighing his pride against his horses, Michael had accepted.

As he swung up the drive toward Templeton House, he hoped he wasn't gambling on the wrong roll of the dice. He'd always admired the place. You couldn't help it. So he stopped in the middle of the drive, got out, and took a long look.

He stood in the mild winter air, a rangy man with an athlete's disciplined body, a brawler's ready stance. He was dressed in black, his most usual attire, because it saved him from thinking when he reached for clothes. The snug black jeans and sweater under a scarred leather bomber jacket gave him the look of a desperado.

He would have said it wasn't far from the truth.

His black hair danced in the breeze. It was longer than practical, sleek and thick by nature. When he was working, he often pulled it back in a stubby ponytail. He hated the barber and would have suffered torments of hell going to what they called a stylist.

He'd forgotten to shave—he'd meant to, but he got involved with the horses. The stubble only added to the dangerous appeal of a rawboned face. His mouth was surprisingly soft. Many women could testify to its skill and generosity. But whatever softness was there was often overlooked when the observer was pinned by hard eyes the color of ball lightning.

Over them, his brows were arched, the left one marred by a faint white scar.

He had others on his body, from car wrecks, fights, his stunt work. He'd learned to live with them, just as he lived with the scars inside.

As he studied the glinting stone, the spearing towers, and glinting glass of Templeton House, he smiled. Christ, what a place, he thought. A castle for modern royalty.

Here comes Michael Fury, he thought. And what the hell are you going to do about it?

He chuckled to himself as he drove up the winding lane, cutting through rolling lawns accented by stately old trees, shrubs waiting to burst into bloom. He didn't imagine that the reigning princess was too happy about his impending stay. Josh must have done some fast talking to persuade his proper society sister to open even the stables for the likes of Michael Fury.

They'd both get used to it, he imagined. It wasn't for long, and he was sure they could manage to stay out of each other's way. Just as they had in the past.

For Laura, carving out this hour in the middle of the day was problematic but necessary. She had sent the maid Jenny to do what she could about cleaning the groom's apartment above the stables. God knew it was a mess of dust and debris and spiderwebs. Mice, Laura thought, shuddering as she hauled up a bucket of soapy water.

She couldn't expect the girl to perform miracles. And there just hadn't been enough time. It hadn't been possible to ask Ann's help. At the mere mention of Michael Fury's name, the housekeeper had sniffed and gone stone-faced.

So, Laura had decided the final work fell to her. She wasn't about to welcome anyone into her home, or a part thereof, and not have it spic and span.

An extended lunch hour away from her duties at Pretenses, a quick change of clothes, and now, she thought, a great deal of elbow grease. The state of the bathroom in the apartment had shocked young Jenny speechless.

Small wonder. With her hair pulled back, her sleeves

rolled up, Laura climbed into the tub and began to attack the worst of the grime. When her guest—tenant—whatever the hell he was—arrived the following day, at least he wouldn't find scum on the tiles.

As far as the stables themselves went, she'd decided after one look that they fell into Michael Fury's territory.

While she worked, she rattled through her head for the rest of her day's schedule. She could get back to Pretenses by three. Close out by six-thirty. A quick dash to pick up the girls from piano lessons.

Damn it, she'd forgotten to look into finding a good drawing instructor for Kayla.

Dinner at seven-thirty. A check to make certain both girls were prepared for whatever tests and assignments were coming up.

Was it spelling for Kayla tomorrow or math for Ali? Was it both? Good God, she hated going back to school. Fractions were killing her.

Puffing a bit as her muscles sang, she swiped soap and grit over her cheek.

She really did have to go over that report on the cosmeticians' convention next month. She could do that in bed, once the girls were down. And Ali needed new ballet shoes. They would see to that tomorrow.

"Well, that's quite a sight." Michael stepped into the narrow doorway and was treated to the appealing view of a pretty female butt straining against faded denim. A butt that he assumed belonged to some nubile Templeton maid. "If this is among the amenities, I should be paying a hell of a lot more rent."

Yelping, Laura sprang up, rapped her head on the shower nozzle, and slopped filthy water over her feet. It was a toss-up as to who was more surprised.

Michael hadn't realized until that moment that he'd carried an image of Laura in his head. Perfect. Perfectly lovely, gold and rose and white, like a glossy picture of a princess in a book of fairy tales.

But the woman facing him now, eyes huge and darkly gray, had wet dirt smeared on her cheeks, her hair was a mess, and her tea-serving hands held a scrub brush.

He recovered first. A man who'd lived on the edge had to have quick reflexes. And he grinned widely as he leaned on the doorjamb. "Laura Templeton. That is you in there, isn't it?"

"I wasn't—we weren't expecting you until tomorrow."

Ah, yes, he thought. The voice hadn't changed. Cool, cultured, quietly sexy. "I always like to get the lay of the land. The front door was wide open."

"I was airing the apartment."

"Well, then. It's nice to see you again, Laura. I don't know when I've had someone quite so attractive scrub out my john."

Humiliated, knowing her cheeks were hot, she nodded. "As Josh probably told you, we haven't been using the building. I wasn't able to spare the staff to put things to rights so quickly."

It surprised him that she knew which end of a scrub brush was which. "You don't have to bother for me. I can handle it myself."

Now that he took a close look, he could also see for himself that she was just as lovely underneath the grime as ever. Delicate features, soft mouth, the aristocratic hint of cheekbone, and those dreamy storm-colored eyes.

Had he forgotten how small she was? Five two, maybe three, and slim as a fairy, with hair the color of gold in dim sunlight. Subtle again, with the richness but not the flash.

She remembered he had often stared, just as he was doing now, saying nothing, just looking, looking until she wanted to squirm.

"I'm sorry about your home."

"Hmm?" He lifted a brow, the scarred one, drawing her eyes to his. "Oh, it was just a house. I can always build another. I appreciate you providing a place for me and my horses."

When he offered a hand, she took it automatically. His was hard, rough with calluses, and held on to hers even when she tried to slip away.

His lips curved again. ''You going to stay standing in the tub, sugar?''

''No.'' She cleared her throat, allowed him to help her out. ''I'll show you around,'' she began, then her eyes went cool when he remained where he was. ''I'll show you around,'' she repeated.

''Thanks.'' He shifted, enjoyed the waft of scent, again subtle, that she carried with her.

''Josh would have told you this was the groom's apartment.'' Her voice was clear again, the polite hostess. ''It's self-sufficient, I think. Full kitchen.'' She gestured toward an alcove off the main room, where Jenny had dutifully cleaned the white stove, the stainless steel sink, the simple white countertops.

''That's fine. I don't do a lot of cooking.''

''Josh mentioned that you'd lost your furniture, so we brought over a few things.''

She waited, hands folded at her waist as he wandered about the room. The sofa had been in the attic and could have used re-covering. But it was a good solid Duncan Phyfe. Some Templeton or guest in the past had scarred the Sheridan coffee table with a careless cigarette, but it was functional.

She'd added lamps, simple brass ones that she felt suited a masculine taste, an easy chair, other occasional tables, even a vase of winter windflowers. She was too much the innkeeper's daughter not to have put thought and effort into her temporary inn.

''You've gone to some trouble.'' Which surprised and humbled him. ''I figured on roughing it for a few months.''

''It's not exactly Templeton Paris.'' She unbent enough to smile. ''The bedroom's through there.'' She gestured toward a short corridor. ''It's not terribly large, but I went with instinct on the bed. I know Josh likes room to, ah . . .'' She trailed off when Michael grinned. ''Room,'' she finished. ''So we stuffed a queen size in there. We had the iron head- and footboards in storage. I've always liked them. There's not much of a closet, but—''

''I don't have much.''

"Well, then." At a loss, she wandered toward the front window. "The view," she said and left it at that.

"Yeah." He joined her, intrigued by the way her head fit neatly below his chin. He could see the cliffs, the azure sea beyond, the splits of rock islands, and the fuming water that charged them. "You used to spend a lot of time out there."

"I still do."

"Still looking for treasure?"

"Of course."

"What was the name of the girl who tossed herself off the cliff?"

"Seraphina."

"Right. Seraphina. A romantic little tale."

"A sad one."

"Same thing. Josh used to laugh about you and Margo and Kate haunting those cliffs and looking for Seraphina's lost dowry. But, I figured he secretly wanted to find it himself."

"We look every Sunday now. Margo and Kate and I, and my daughters."

That brought him up short. He'd forgotten for a moment that this small, delicate woman had given birth to two children. "You've got kids of your own. Girls."

"Yes." Chin lifted, she turned back. "Daughters. My daughters."

Something here, he mused, and wondered which button he'd pushed. "How old are they?"

She hadn't expected him to ask, even out of politeness. And she softened all over again. "Ali's ten. Kayla's seven."

"You got started early. Girls that age usually go for horses. They can come by and see mine whenever they like."

More of the unexpected. "That's kind of you, Michael. I don't want them to get in your way."

"I like kids."

He said it so simply that she believed him. "Then I'll warn you, they're both eager to see them. And I suppose you're eager to see the stables.'' Out of habit she glanced at her watch, and winced.

''Got an appointment?''

''Actually, yes, I do. If you don't mind taking the rest of the tour on your own, I really have to change.''

To get her hair done, he imagined, or her nails. Or to make her fifty-minute hour with some society shrink. ''Sure.''

''I left the keys in the kitchen,'' she continued, juggling details. ''There isn't a phone. I didn't know if you wanted one. There's a jack. Somewhere. If you need anything, you—''

''I'll be fine.'' He slipped a check out of his pocket and handed it to her. ''Rent.''

''Oh.'' She slipped it into her own pocket, sorry that she couldn't welcome one of her brother's old friends as a guest. But the rent would go a long way toward new ballet shoes and drawing lessons. ''Thank you. Welcome to Templeton House, Michael.''

She went to the door and down the steps. He walked to the side window and watched her cross the rolling lawn toward Templeton House.

''And there I was,'' Laura muttered, ''standing in the bathtub.'' She sighed, grateful for a lull in the customer flow in Pretenses so that she could vent to her friends. ''Wearing rags. Holding a scrub brush. Stop laughing.''

''In a minute,'' Kate promised, holding a hand to her aching stomach. ''I'm perfecting the image in my mind first. The elegant Laura Templeton caught fighting pesky bathtub ring.''

''Ring, hell. It's more like bathtub plague. And maybe I'll think it's funny in a year. Or two. But right now it's mortifying. He just stood there grinning at me.''

''Mmm.'' Margo touched her tongue to her top lip. ''And if memory serves, Michael Fury had one hell of a grin. Is he as wickedly, dangerously handsome as ever?''

''I didn't notice.'' Laura sniffed and gave her attention to rubbing a fingerprint off the glass display case.

''Liar.'' Margo leaned closer. ''Come on, Laura. Tell.''

''I suppose he looked a bit like a twentieth-century version of Heathcliff. Dark, brooding, potentially violent, and rough around the edges.'' Her shoulders shrugged again. ''If that sort of thing appeals to you.''

''It wouldn't make me look the other way,'' Margo decided. ''Josh said he was a mercenary for a while.''

''A mercenary?'' She'd forgotten that and remembering now, nodded. ''Figures.''

''And I ran into him once in France when he was racing. Cars.'' Margo tilted her head as she brought the memory back. ''We had an interesting evening together.''

Laura lifted a brow. ''Oh, really?''

''Interesting,'' Margo repeated and left it at that. ''Then it was stunt work in Hollywood. And now it's horses. I wonder if he'll stick around this time. I know Josh hopes he does.''

''At least the situation has pushed me into getting the stables in shape.'' Wanting busy work, Laura moved to the shelves and began to tidy glassware. ''I've neglected them too long. In fact, I may think about getting a horse myself once I can manage it. The girls might like that.''

''So what kind of horses does he raise? Breed. Own. Whatever,'' Kate wondered.

''I didn't ask. I just showed him around the apartment, gave him the keys. I suppose he's competent. Josh seems to think so. And if his rent check doesn't bounce, I'll assume he's reliable. I can't imagine I'd want any more out of a tenant. Horses take a lot of time and work.'' Which meant, Laura thought, she couldn't even consider having them again for at least a decade. ''He'll be busy. I doubt we'll see much of him.''

The door opened for a pair of customers. Recognizing them as regulars, Laura smiled, stepped forward. ''I'll take them,'' she murmured to her partners. ''Good to see you, Mrs. Myers, Mrs. Lomax. What can I show you today?''

As Laura led the customers into the wardrobe room, Margo considered. ''She's trying not to be interested.''

''Hmm?''

''Laura. She had the look of a woman who's been intrigued by a man and is trying not to be.'' After a moment's thought, Margo smiled broadly. ''Good.''

''And why would that be good?''

''It's time she had a little distraction in her life. A little male distraction.''

''And do you ever think of any other kind of distraction?''

''Kate—'' Amused, Margo patted her friend's hand. ''From a woman newly married to a certified hunk, that's a very stupid question. Laura's never let herself cut loose when it comes to men. I think Michael Fury might just be the perfect thirtieth birthday present.''

''He's a man, Margo, not a pair of earrings.''

''Oh, but darling, I think he might look wonderful on her. So to speak.''

''And I don't suppose it occurs to you that they might not be interested in each other, in a sexual way. Wait.'' Kate held up a hand. ''I forgot who I was talking to.''

''Don't be snide.'' Margo tapped her fingers on the counter. ''You've got a man and a woman, both unattached as far as we know, both attractive. Josh has put them in close proximity. Though I doubt it was his intention, he's created a very interesting situation.''

''When you put it like that.'' Concerned, Kate glanced toward the wardrobe room. ''Look, I always liked Mick, but he was a wild child. We could have a lamb and wolf situation here.''

''I certainly hope you're right. Every woman needs at least one close encounter with a wolf. But . . .'' They were talking about Laura, after all. ''I'll have to invite Michael over for dinner. Check him out myself.''

''And I suppose we'll have to bow to your greater judgment and experience.''

''Naturally.'' The door jangled open again. ''Back to work, partner.''

In the wardrobe room Laura was patiently showing their selection of cashmere sweaters. If she had been aware of the direction her friends were taking she would have been both amused and appalled.

Men in general simply weren't of interest to her. She didn't hate them. Her experience with Peter hadn't turned her into a shrew, made her frigid, or narrowed her vision so that she considered men the enemy. Too many good men had touched her life for that. She had her father as a prime example. Her brother was another. And over the past months, she had come to love Byron De Witt.

Family was one thing. Intimate, even casual, relationships were another. She didn't have the time, inclination, or energy for one. In the two years since she had ended her marriage, she had been struggling to rebuild her life on all levels. Her children, her home, her work for Templeton. And Pretenses.

While her customers debated their selections, she eased back to give them room, musing on the events that had led to starting the shop. It had been an impulse, a step she'd taken for Margo as much as for herself.

Margo's career and finances had been in ruins when she returned to Monterey from Europe. The idea of liquidating her possessions and creating an intriguing space in which to sell them had been a risk, but it had paid off from the first moment.

Not just in dollars, Laura thought, as she wandered back into the main showroom. In pride, in confidence. In friendship and fun.

When they bought the building, it was an empty space, dusty, scarred, smelly. Their vision, their effort had turned it into the remarkable. Now the glass of the wide display window sparkled in the sunlight and teased passersby with clever hints of what was offered inside.

A sassy cocktail dress in emerald, with the nostalgic touch of peacock feathers at the shoulder, was draped over the elegant chair of a woman's vanity. Colorful bottles stood on the glossy surface, along with a jeweled collar. One of the drawers was open so that glittery rhinestones and shimmering silks spilled out. There was a lamp shaped like a swan, a single crystal flute beside an empty bottle of champagne. A man's cuff links and carelessly tossed formal black tie mingled with the woman's trinkets. A pair of red spike heels was artfully positioned to give the impression that their owner had just stepped out of them.

The little vignettes in the display were usually Margo's domain, but Laura had designed this one. And was proud of it. As she was of the shop as a whole. Throughout the spacious showroom was scattered the unique, the fanciful. The warm rose walls complemented glass shelves filled with treasures. Porcelain boxes, silver services, gold-ringed stemware. A velvet settee—the third they'd had to stock—provided customers a chance to sit, enjoy a cup of tea, a glass of champagne.

Gilded tightwinder stairs spiraled up toward the open balcony that ringed the room and led to the boudoir where negligees, peignoirs, and other night apparel were displayed in a gorgeous rosewood armoire. Everything was for sale, from the rococo bed to the smallest silver trinket box. And nothing was duplicated.

The shop had quite literally saved all three of them. And though she wouldn't have thought it possible, it had brought them even closer together.

As she hovered outside the wardrobe room, she watched Margo show a customer a sapphire bracelet from the display. Kate discussed the origins of an Art Nouveau lamp with another. A new customer studied an opal snuff bottle while her companion perused the selection of evening bags.

Mozart was playing on the stereo, softly. Through the window, Laura caught glimpses of the busy traffic on Cannery Row. Cars chugged or streamed or jockeyed for position. People strolled by on the sidewalk. A man passed with a young boy giggling from his perch on Daddy's shoulders. A couple, arm in arm, stopped to admire the display—and moments later came inside.

''Ms. Templeton?''

Pulling herself back from her reverie, Laura turned to the wardrobe room. ''Yes, Mrs. Myers, did you find something you like?''

The woman smiled, held out her choice. "I never leave Pretenses disappointed."

The glow of pride was swift and satisfying. Laura accepted the cashmere. "We're here to see that you never do."

Chapter Four

"Pretty good digs, right, boy?" Michael groomed Max, his pride and joy while the enormous buff-colored Tennessee walker snorted in agreement.

The Templeton horse palace was a far cry from the simple working stables that Michael had built in the hills, then watched collapse under walls of mud. Not that it had looked much like a palace when he stepped inside that first afternoon, when he ran into Laura. Then it bore more than a slight resemblance to some fairy-tale cottage long under a wicked spell, deserted by all who had once inhabited it.

He had to grin at the thought, and at the fact that everything about the Templeton estate made him think of fairy tales with golden edges.

What he found in the stables was dust, disuse, and disrepair.

It had taken him the best part of a week to ready the building. No easy task for one man and a single pair of hands, but he wasn't willing to move his horses in until their temporary home had been cleaned and organized to his specifications.

On the other hand, for that week he'd had to endure the public stables, the painfully high fee for boarding, and the fact that his own lodgings were miles away from his stock. But the results were well worth the investment of a few sixteen-hour, muscle-aching days.

It was a good, solid building, with the stylish touches that the Templetons were known for. The loose boxes had plenty of space and light and air, a more important feature to Michael than the intricately laid brick flooring, the decorative tiles around the mangers, or the ornate ironwork above them, with its center stylized T in polished brass.

Though he did consider the fancy work a nice touch.

The layout was practical, with the tack room at one end of the block, the feed room at the other. Though he was baffled by the obvious neglect and disuse, he put his back into it and dug in to correct the situation. He hauled and hammered, swept and scrubbed until every stall met his stringent standards for his babies.

He thought of them as such, secretly.

He'd had fresh hay and straw delivered that morning and had been grateful that the boy who delivered it had been willing to make a few extra dollars by helping Michael store the bales.

Now each stall was deeply bedded with wheat straw—expensive and difficult to come by, but these were his babies, after all. Some tools and some ingenuity had put the automatic drinking bowls back in working order. He oiled hinges on stall doors, replaced hooks that had rusted away.

Since he'd lost all of his supplies in the mud, he had to restock grain, electrolytes, vitamins, medicines. He'd managed to salvage some tack, some tools. Every piece had been cleaned and polished, and what couldn't be saved had been, or would shortly be, replaced.

His fifteen horses were housed as royally as he could manage, but as yet, he hadn't done more than sleep in the upstairs apartment.

"You've come up in the world, Max. You might not

know it, but you are now a tenant of the Templeton estate. That is one big fucking deal, pal, take my word for it.''

He slapped the horse affectionately on the flank and pulled a carrot out of the pouch tied at his waist. ''I've already started designing your new place. Don't worry. Maybe we'll add a few of the fancier touches ourselves this time around. But in the meantime, you can't do much better than this.''

Max took the carrot politely, and the dark eye he turned to Michael was filled with patience, wisdom, and, Michael liked to think, affection as well.

He stepped out of the stall, latched the bottom half of the door with its foot bolt, then moved down the block. The floor might have been fancy enough for a garden party, but it sloped perfectly. His boot heels clicked. In anticipation, a chestnut head poked over the adjoining stall door.

''Looking for me, baby?'' This was his sweetheart, as kind and gentle a mare as he had ever worked with. He'd bought her as a foal, and now she was heavily pregnant and had been assigned to the foaling stall. He called her Darling.

''How's it going today? You're going to be happy here.'' He stepped inside and ran his hands over her enormous sides. Like an expectant father, he was filled with anticipation and concern. She was small, barely fourteen hands, and he worried about how she would fare when her time came.

Darling liked to have her belly rubbed, and she blew appreciatively when Michael obliged her. ''So beautiful.'' He cupped her face in his hands as a man might hold the face of a cherished woman. ''You're the most beautiful thing I've ever owned.''

Pleased with the attention, she blew again, then lowered her head to nibble at his pouch. Chuckling, he took out an apple—she preferred them to carrots. ''Here you go, Darling. You're eating for two.''

He heard the voices—young, excited, almost piping—and stepped out of the stall.

''Mama said we're not supposed to bother him.''

"We're not going to bother him. We'll just look. Come on, Kayla. Don't you want to see the horses?"

"Yeah, but . . . What if he's in there? What if he yells at us?"

"Then we'll just run away, but we'll get to see the horses first."

Amused, wondering if Laura had painted him as an ogre or a recluse, Michael stepped out of the shadows of the stables and into the sunlight. If he'd been a poetic man, he would have said he'd encountered two angels.

They thought they were looking into the face of the devil himself. He was all in black, with shadows behind him. The hard, handsome face was unsmiling and dark with stubble. His hair reached almost to his shoulders, and he had a black bandanna tied around his forehead, like a wild Indian, or a pirate.

He seemed big, huge, dangerous.

Her heart jittering, Ali put a hand on Kayla's shoulder, both to protect her sister and to steady herself. "We live here," she stammered. "We can be here."

He couldn't resist playing it out a little. "Is that so? Well, I live here. And I don't look kindly on trespassers. You wouldn't be horse thieves, would you? We have to hang horse thieves."

Shocked, appalled, terrified, Ali could only shake her head vigorously. But Kayla stepped forward, fascinated.

"You have pretty eyes," she said, dimpling into a smile. "Are you really a troublemaking hoodlum? Annie said so."

All Ali could do was whisper her sister's name in mortification and fear.

Ah, he thought, Ann Sullivan, sowing his youthful reputation ahead of him. "I used to be. I gave it up." Christ, the kid was a picture, he thought. A heart melter. "Your name's Kayla, and you have your mother's eyes."

"Uh-huh, and that's Ali. She's ten. I'm seven and a half, and I lost a tooth." She grinned widely to show him the accomplishment.

"Cool. Have you looked for it?"

She giggled. "No, the Tooth Fairy has it. She took it up

into the sky to make a star out of it. Do you have all your teeth?''

''Last time I checked.''

''You're Mr. Fury. Mama says we have to call you that. I like your name, it's like a storybook person.''

''A villain?''

''Maybe.'' She twinkled at him. ''Can we see your horses, Mr. Fury? We won't steal them or hurt them or anything.''

''I think they'd like to see you.'' He offered a hand, which Kayla took without hesitation. ''Come on, Ali,'' he said casually. ''I won't yell at you unless you deserve it.''

Biting her lip, Ali followed them into the stables. ''Oh!'' She jolted back, then giggled at herself when Max stuck his huge head over the stall door. ''He's so big. He's so pretty.'' She started to reach out, then stuck her hand behind her back.

''You can pet him,'' Michael told her. The older girl was a little shy, he decided, and pretty as a picture in a book. ''He doesn't bite. Unless you deserve it.'' To demonstrate, he hauled Kayla up on his hip. ''Go ahead, meet Max. He's a Southern gentleman.''

''Our uncle is a Southern gentleman,'' Kayla announced. ''But he doesn't look like Max.'' Delighted, she stroked the soft cheek. ''Smooth,'' she murmured. ''Hello, Max. Hello.''

Not one to be outmatched by her kid sister, Ali stepped forward again and touched Max's other cheek. ''Does he let you ride him and everything?''

''Yep. Max and I have fought wild Indians together, been wild Indians together, robbed stagecoaches, jumped ravines.'' Looking down into two pairs of wide eyes, he grinned. ''Max is a Hollywood star.''

''Really?'' Enchanted, Kayla touched one velvet ear, giggling when it flicked under her fingers.

''Really. I'll show you his press clippings later. Come meet Darling. She's going to have a baby soon.''

''Aunt Margo just had one.'' Kayla chattered gaily as they made the new acquaintance. ''His name is John Thomas, but we call him J. T. Do horses have babies the same way people have them?''

''Pretty much,'' Michael murmured and skirted the issue by distracting the girls with the mare.

They met Jack, the dignified gelding, and Lulu, a frisky mare. Then Zip, the fastest horse—so Michael claimed—in the West.

''Why do you have so many?'' Suspicion of the man couldn't hold out against delight with horses. With shyness outmatched by curiosity, Ali dogged Michael's every move and peppered him with questions.

''I train them. I buy them, sell them.''

''Sell them?'' The very idea had Kayla's lip poking out.

''All but Max and Darling. I won't sell them, ever. But the others will go to people who'll appreciate their talents and take good care of them. They all have a destiny. Now Jack here, he's going to make someone a good saddle horse. He'll ride forever if you ask him. And Flash, he'll be a hell of a stunt pony when I'm finished with him.''

''You mean he'll do tricks?''

''Yeah.'' Michael grinned at Kayla. ''He's already got a few up his sleeve. But Max—now Max knows them all. Want a show?''

''Really, can we?''

''It'll cost you.''

''How much?'' Kayla demanded. ''I have money in my bank.''

''Not money,'' Michael said as he led them back to Max. ''If you like the show, you have to come back and work it off.''

''What kind of work?'' Ali wanted to know.

''We'll talk about it. Come on, Max.'' Michael took a bridle and slipped it on. ''You've got a couple of ladies to impress here.''

At five, Max was a veteran performer. He high-stepped it outside, pleased to have an audience. Michael led him to the small paddock beside the building. ''You girls stay at the fence there. This could get hairy. Take your bows, Max.''

Max gracefully bent his front legs and lowered himself. When the girls erupted with applause, Michael could have sworn that Max grinned.

''Up,'' he ordered.

Using voice and hand signals, Michael took Max through his routine. The big horse reared, pawed the air, let out a high whinny. He pranced, sidestepped, danced, circled. Then when Michael swung up onto his bare back, he repeated the routine with variations.

''Now here's his 'we've been walking in the desert for three days without water routine.' '' At the signal, Max drooped, his head fell limply, and he plodded along as though each step would be his last. ''Now, look out, rattlesnake.'' Max leapt back, bunched up, cowered. ''God almighty, the posse shot my horse right out from under me. Dead horse, Max.''

For his finale Max wheeled, cantered to the left, and dropped to the ground. Michael tumbled off, rolled. As he got to his feet, he caught sight of Laura, racing in skinny little heels across the yard.

''Oh, God, are you all right? How did it happen? Oh, your horse!''

Though he started to speak, Michael found himself too involved in watching that nifty length of bare leg as she vaulted the fence in her neat little lady's suit.

Max lay dead, hardly flicking an eye when Laura knelt at his head. ''Poor thing, poor thing! Is it his leg? Who's your vet?''

At the sight of the horse lying with his big head nestled in the lap of Laura's pretty blue skirt, Michael tucked his tongue in his cheek. ''Looks like it's curtains for old Max.''

''Don't say that,'' Laura snapped back. ''He might have just bruised something.'' But what if he hadn't? She pushed back the hair that curled flirtatiously at her jaw. ''Girls, go back to the house now.''

''But, Mama—''

''Don't argue.'' She couldn't bear the idea of either of them witnessing what might have to be done.

''Laura,'' Michael began.

''Why are you just standing there?'' Worry and temper warred in her eyes. ''Why aren't you doing something? The poor thing is suffering, and you're just standing there. Don't you care about your own horse?''

''Yes, ma'am, I do. Max, cut.''

On cue, and to Laura's astonishment, the big horse rolled again, then got to his feet.

''It was a trick, Mama.'' Kayla laughed gaily at the shared joke while Michael pulled Laura up. ''Max does tricks. He was playing dead. Like a dog does. Isn't he wonderful? Isn't he smart?''

''Yes.'' Under a ragged cloak of dignity, Laura brushed off her skirt. ''He's certainly talented.''

''Sorry.'' A wise man knew when to smother a grin. Michael rarely chose to be wise. ''I'd have warned you if I'd seen you coming. Then you were off and running.'' He scratched his cheek. ''Seemed a lot more worried about my horse than about me. I could have broken my neck.''

''The horse was down,'' Laura said primly. ''You weren't.'' But everything faded into admiration as Max bent his head to her. ''Oh, he is beautiful. Aren't you gorgeous? Aren't you clever?''

''Max has been in lots of movies.'' Ali moved closer. ''So has Mr. Fury.''

''Oh?''

''Stunts,'' Michael explained. He took a carrot out of his pouch, handed it to Laura. ''Give him that, he's your slave for life.''

''Who could resist?'' As she offered the treat, she spoke slowly. ''Didn't I tell you girls not to pester Mr. Fury?''

''Yes, but he said we weren't.'' Kayla smiled hopefully up at Michael. Standing on the rail of the fence, she lifted her arms, confident.

''Because you weren't.'' He hauled her up, fit her so naturally on his hip that Laura frowned. ''I like the company,'' he said to Laura. ''So do the horses. They get tired of looking at me all day. The kids are welcome to come by anytime. If they're in my way, I'll tell them.''

To Kayla's delight, and Laura's momentary horror, he plunked Kayla onto Max's wide back.

"It's high. Look how high up I am."

"I'm trying not to," Laura said, her hand automatically going to the bridle. "He's a stunt horse, not a saddle pony."

"Gentle as a lamb," Michael assured her, then lifted Ali over the fence and put her behind her sister. "He'll carry the three of you if you want. He's also strong as a bull."

"No, thank you." Her heart settled as she looked into Max's eyes. They were indeed gentle. "I'm not exactly dressed for it."

"So I noticed. You look good, Ms. Templeton. And you looked damned good climbing over the fence."

She looked back, into Michael's eyes. Gentle? No, indeed, she thought. But just as compelling. "I imagine I made quite a picture."

"You don't know the half of it, sugar."

She stepped back. "Okay, girls, party's over. You need to wash up for dinner."

Ali started to complain, stopped herself. She didn't want to risk being told she couldn't come back. "Can Mr. Fury come to dinner?"

"Oh." Discomfort and manners. Manners always won. "Of course Michael, you're welcome to come."

And if he'd ever received a cooler and less enthusiastic invitation, he couldn't remember. "Thanks, but I have plans. I'm heading over to Josh's to meet his son."

"Well, then." She reached up, lifted Kayla, then Ali to the ground. "We'll get out of your way."

"There were a couple of things I wanted to run by you. If you've got a minute."

"Of course." Her feet were killing her. All she wanted was to take off those damn heels and sit down. "Girls, tell Annie I'll be in shortly."

"Thank you, Mr. Fury." Her mother's daughter to the core, Ali offered a hand.

"You're welcome."

"Thanks, Mr. Fury, for showing us the horses, and the

tricks and everything. I want to tell Annie.'' Kayla started to race off but stopped at the fence. ''Mr. Fury?''

''Yes, ma'am?''

She giggled at that, then sobered. ''Can you teach dogs, too? If you had a puppy, or somebody did, could you teach him tricks like Max?''

''I expect I could, if he was a good dog.''

She smiled again, wistfully, then hurried away behind her sister.

''She wants a dog,'' Laura murmured. ''I didn't know. She never said. She asked years ago, but Peter. . . . Damn it. I should have realized.''

Intrigued, Michael watched the varied emotions play over her face. And the weightiest was guilt. ''Do you always beat yourself up this way?''

''I should have known. She's my child. I should have known she wanted a puppy.'' Suddenly tired, she dragged her hands through her hair.

''So get her one.''

Her chin set. ''I will. I'm sorry.'' Shaking off the guilt, she looked back at Michael. ''What did you need?''

''Oh, I need a lot of things.'' Casually, he draped an arm around Max's neck. ''A hot meal, a fast car, the love of a good woman—but what we both need is a couple of mousers.''

''Excuse me?''

''You need some barn cats, Laura. You got rodents.''

''Oh, God.'' She shuddered once, blew out a breath. ''I should have realized that, too. We used to keep some when we had horses, but Peter—'' She broke off, shut her eyes. No, she was not traveling down that road again. ''I'll be making a trip to the pound, it seems. I'll get a couple of cats.''

''You're going to get your kid a dog from the pound?''

''And why not?''

''No reason.'' He led Max toward the fence. ''Figured you for the purebred type, that's all. That's the way some people are about horses. They want Arabians, Thoroughbreds. I've got me one of the prettiest fillies you could want in that stable. She's smart as a whip and quick as a snake. She's what you'd call a mongrel, though. Always liked mongrels myself."

"I prefer character above lineage."

"Good for you." In an absentminded movement, he bent down, plucked a struggling buttercup out of its patch of grass, and handed it to her. "I'd say you've got both in those girls of yours. They're beauties. Heartbreakers. The little one's already wrapped her fist around mine. And she knows it."

"You surprise me." She stared down at the sunny yellow flower in her hand, baffled. Despite fatigue and aching feet, she followed him into the stables. "You don't strike me as a man who'd take to children. Little girls."

"Mongrels are full of surprises."

"I didn't mean—"

"I know you didn't." He settled Max in his stall, latched the door. "The little one's got your eyes, smoke and storms. Ali's got your mouth, soft and wanting to be stubborn." He grinned then. "You breed good, Laura."

"I suppose I should thank you, though no one's ever put it quite that way before. And I appreciate your entertaining them, but I don't want you to feel obligated."

"I don't. I said I like them. I meant it. Besides, they owe me for the show. Me and Max don't work for free. I could use some help around here."

"Help?"

"Mucking out, hauling hay. Unless you've got a problem with your progeny shoveling manure."

She'd shoved plenty herself in her day. "No. It'll be good for them." Automatically, she lifted a hand to stroke Max's nose. "You've worked a minor miracle here," she noted, glancing down the spotless building.

"I've got a strong back and plenty of ambition."

"For?"

"Making something out of this. Saddle horses, trick ponies, jumpers. I've got a way with them."

"If Max is any example, I'd say you've got a major way with them. Were you really a mercenary?"

"Among other things, including the troublemaking hoodlum Mrs. Sullivan claims I am."

"Oh." She rolled her eyes at Max, cleared her throat. "I expect Annie's remembering the boy who gave Josh his first cigarette."

"One of my lesser crimes. I quit six months ago myself. Easier than worrying about setting fire to the hay."

"Or dying of lung cancer."

"You gotta die of something."

She turned just as he reached up to slip the bridle off Max. Their bodies bumped. As much out of curiosity as to steady her, he took her arms.

Soft. Fragile as he'd imagined. And as he shifted, just a little, the gentle swell of her breasts pressed against him. Her eyes had whipped to his at first contact. They stayed there as her heart hammered.

"I always wondered what kind of handful you'd be." He smiled, let his hands run up and down those pretty arms. "Never had the opportunity to find out before. Of course, you were too young for me back then. You've caught up close enough now."

"Excuse me." That was her voice, calm and cool. She was able to manage that, though everything inside her was hot and unsteady.

"You're not in my way." Easily, he lifted a hand to toy with a curl that flirted with her cheek.

"Then you're in mine." She didn't know how to handle men. Had never had to, really. But she was smart enough to know that now she needed a crash course. "I'm not interested in flirtations."

"Me either."

She borrowed a page from Margo's book, made her eyes bored. "Michael, I'm sure scores of women would be flattered. If I had the time, I might be flattered myself. But I don't have the time. My children are waiting to have their dinner."

"You've got that down," he acknowledged. "Lady of the manor. You were born for it." He stepped back. "If you find yourself with time on your hands, you know where to find me.''

''Give my best to Josh and Margo,'' she said as she set out on watery legs for the house.

''Sure. Hey, sugar?''

Bristling only a little at the term, she looked back. ''The mousers. Don't come bringing me some furry little kittens. I want big hungry toms.''

''I'll see what I can do.''

''I'm sure you will,'' he murmured as she walked away. ''Christ, what a package,'' he said to Max. Amused at himself, Michael rubbed the heel of his hand against his heart. It had yet to settle down for him. ''She's the type that makes a man feel like a big hungry tom. And clumsy with it.''

Shaking his head, Michael headed upstairs to wash off the stable dirt.

''So, Margo's a mommy.'' Michael grinned at his hostess, who failed to look the least bit maternal in a peach-toned jumpsuit that clung glamorously to every curve.

''I'm a great mommy.'' She kissed both his cheeks, European fashion. ''I love being a mommy.'' Drawing back, she took a long look and wasn't disappointed. ''What's it been, Michael? Six years, seven?''

''Longer. I was trying to tear up the European circuit, and you were taking the Continent by storm.''

''Those were the days,'' she said lightly and, tucking her arm through his, led him inside.

''Great place.'' He wasn't surprised by the elegance of the California Spanish, but he was by its coziness.

''Kate turned us on to it. You remember Kate Powell.''

''Sure.'' They strolled out of the tiled foyer into a spacious room with a blazing fire and twin sofas in deep maroon. ''How's she doing? I heard she's married now.''

''Still a newlywed. You'd like Byron, I think. We'll have to have a party when you're settled. Introduce you around.''

''I'm not much of a partier these days.''

''A small one, then. What can I get you to drink?'' She

glided behind a deeply carved bar. "Josh will be right down. He had a meeting run over."

"Got a beer?"

"I think we can manage that." From the small cold box under the bar she chose a bottle. "So it's horses now."

"It seems to be."

He watched her open the bottle, pour beer smoothly into a pilsner. On the third finger of her left hand diamonds and gold flashed. Her hair was more gold, soft, flowing waves of it. And there were more diamonds at her ears. Still, he saw that it was her eyes that shined the brightest.

"You look good, Margo. Happy. It's nice to see you happy."

A little surprised, she glanced up. "Really?"

"You never seemed to be really quite there."

"Apparently you were right." She set the glass on the bar and pried the silver wine saver off a bottle of champagne. "But I've gotten there."

"A wife, a mommy, and a shopkeeper." He lifted his glass in a toast. "Who'd have thought it?"

"And doing a marvelous job at all three." After pouring herself a flute of champagne, she toasted herself in turn. "You'll have to come by Pretenses, Michael. We're on Cannery Row."

"I'll come see your shop, you come see my horses."

"That's a deal. I'm sorry about your house."

He shrugged his shoulders. "No big deal. I didn't like it anyway. I was more pissed off about the stables. I'd barely gotten them finished when I lost them. Still, it's just wood and nails. I can buy more."

"It must have been horrible. I've seen film of mud slides and the aftermath of some. I can't imagine being in the middle of it."

"You don't want to."

He still had moments when the image of driving rain, thundering earth, and wicked winds flashed into his mind. And the panic that came with the flash that he wouldn't be quick enough, strong enough, smart enough to save what mattered to him.

''Anyway, I'm working on the plans for rebuilding, got a contractor lined up. It's mostly just time and money.''

''I'm sure you'll be comfortable at Templeton House until you've rebuilt.''

''It's hard not to be. I met Laura's kids today. Beautiful kids. The older one's reserving judgment on me, but Kayla—'' He chuckled. ''She just moves right in.''

''They're wonderful girls. Laura's done a terrific job there.''

''She hasn't changed much.''

''More than you might think. The divorce was hard on her. Terribly hard. But she's got that strong Templeton core. You never met Peter Ridgeway, did you?''

''Nope.''

''Trust me,'' Margo said and drank deeply. ''He's a bastard.''

''Sugar, you hate him, I'll hate him, too.''

Laughing, she took his hand. ''It's good to have you back, Michael.''

''Moving in on my wife already, Fury?'' Josh came in, an owl-eyed baby on his hip. ''My kid and I'll fight you for her.''

''I think he could take me.'' Curious, Michael set his beer aside and walked over to study J. T. The baby studied him right back, then reached out and grabbed a handful of Michael's hair. ''Come here, slugger.''

Even as Margo opened her mouth, dozens of maternal warnings on her tongue, Michael nipped J. T. neatly out of Josh's arms and settled him on his own hip. The natural move made Margo's eyes blink in surprise, then narrow with speculation.

Enjoying the stranger, J. T. gurgled.

''Great job, Harvard.'' Michael gave J. T. a quick nuzzle. ''Congratulations.''

''Thanks.'' Josh grinned at his wife. ''I had a little help.''

Chapter Five

Laura did bring home a fuzzy little kitten. In fact, she brought home two. And a pair of lean, sharp-eyed toms. And a big-footed puppy with a spotted coat and an eager tongue.

The small zoo in her car caused her a bit of trouble but gave her a great deal of pleasure. She drove home with cats meowing bitterly in their boxes, kittens sleeping on the car mat, and an adoring puppy sprawled in her lap.

"Wait until the girls get a load of you." Already in love, she stroked the puppy's head. "And I guess if they fight over you, I'll just have to go back and pick up a brother or sister for you."

Laughing, she turned into the drive at Templeton House. So foolish, she realized, not to have done this before. Old habits, she mused. Peter hadn't wanted pets, so there had been no pets. But Peter had been gone nearly two years. And that was two years too long not to have made some simple adjustments.

After parking the car, she glanced around at her menagerie and blew out a breath. "How the hell am I going to manage to get you all inside?"

She had a leash for the pup, which she attached to his brand-new collar. She held out no hope that he would understand the purpose. For a brief moment, she considered laying on the horn until someone came out to give her a hand. Which, she assumed, would send her new petting zoo into a frenzy.

So she'd deal with it herself. "You first," she decided, and opened the door. The puppy cowered, sniffed at the empty space on the other side of her lap. Then, gathering his courage, he jumped. If she hadn't been laughing so hard, she would have held on to the leash. But the pup landed in a sprawl and looked so surprised that she roared with laughter and the leather slid out of her hands.

He was off and running.

"Oh, damn it." Still laughing, she sprang out of the car. "Come back here, you idiot."

Instead, he raced in circles, then cut through old Joe's pampered bed of narcissus, yapping joyously all the way.

"Oh, that's going to be a problem," she realized. Wincing, she walked around the car to retrieve the sleepy kittens. In the back, the toms continued to complain at the top of their lungs. "All right, all right. Give me a minute here."

Inspired, she tucked a kitten in each of her jacket pockets, then hauled out the cat boxes. "You two are Michael's problem." Following the excited barks, she headed toward the stables.

The sight that greeted her when she stepped through the arbor of wisteria was worth every moment of annoyance. In the far yard, her daughters were kneeling on the ground embracing and being embraced by a wildly enthusiastic spotted mutt.

She took the picture in her mind, slipped it into her heart.

"Look, Mama!" Kayla was already shouting as Laura started toward them. "Come quick and look at the little puppy. He must be lost."

"He doesn't look lost to me."

"He has a leash." Ali giggled—a sound Laura could

never hear often enough—as he scrambled into her lap. ''Maybe he ran away from home.''

''I don't think so. He is home. He's ours.''

Ali simply stared. ''But we can't have pets.''

With a smile, Laura adjusted her boxes. ''He doesn't seem to agree with you.''

''Do you mean it?'' Kayla rose. The expression of stunned joy on her face carved itself into Laura's heart. ''Do you mean he can be our puppy and we can keep him? Forever?''

''That's exactly what I mean.''

''Mama!'' In one leap, Kayla had her arms wrapped around her mother's waist. She clung hard, fierce. ''Mama, thank you. I'll take such good care of him. You'll see.''

''I know you will, honey.'' She looked over at Ali, who remained still, staring. ''We all will. He needs a good home and lots of love. We'll give him that, won't we, Ali?''

Inner conflict held her back. Her father had said pets were a nuisance, messy. They shed hair all over the rug. But the puppy was sniffing at her leg, wagging his tail and trying to jump into her arms.

''We'll take good care of him,'' she said solemnly. She started to step forward, stopped. Her mouth went lax in shock. ''Mama, your pockets are moving.''

''Oh.'' With a laugh, Laura set her boxes down, reached in and plucked out two furry balls, one silken gray and the other sassy orange, from her pockets. ''What have we here?''

''Kittens?'' Kayla squealed, grabbed. ''Kittens. We have kittens, too! Look, Ali, we have everything.''

''They're so tiny.'' Gently, cautiously, Ali took the mewling gray. ''Mama, they're so tiny.''

''They're just babies. Just over six weeks old.'' Every bit as much in love as her daughters were, Laura stroked a fingertip down the sleepy gray. ''They needed a home too.''

''It's really all right?'' Half afraid to hope, Ali looked up into her mother's eyes. ''It's really all right for us to keep them all?''

''It's really all right.''

''More!'' Tuning in to the sounds coming from the cardboard boxes, Kayla pounced.

''No, those aren't ours. Those are barn cats, for Michael.''

''I'll take them to him.'' Desperate to share her fabulous news with anyone who would listen, Kayla handed her kitten to Ali and hefted both boxes by the straps. Grunting a little, she headed toward the stables. ''Come on, cats. Come on, I'll take you home.''

''Do they have names?''

''Hmm.'' Absently Laura stroked her daughter's hair, then made herself look away from the comical picture of Kayla, bobbling along with two boxes full of impatient felines and a puppy racing around her legs in clumsy, big-footed circles. ''They will have, when we pick them out.''

''Can I name one myself? Pick out the name all by myself? For the little gray kitten?'' Ali lifted it to her cheek.

''Of course you can. What name would you like?''

''Is it a boy or a girl?''

''It's—I don't know,'' Laura realized. ''I forgot to ask. It's probably on one of the papers I filled out.'' With one arm around Ali's shoulders, she walked after Kayla. ''The puppy's a boy, and both big cats are boys because that's what Michael wanted.''

''Because he likes boys better?''

Uh-oh. ''No, honey. I guess he figured tomcats would be meaner, and he wanted mousers.''

Her eyes went huge. ''He's going to let them eat mice?''

''Baby, I'm afraid that's what cats do.''

Ali pressed the little ball of fluff to her cheek. ''Mine won't.''

Kayla's voice was already echoing in high, excited chirps, accented by the yaps of the pup, who had raced inside the stables with her. When Laura stepped in and her eyes adjusted to the dim light, she saw Michael and Kayla crouched together on the brick floor, taking stock of Templeton House's new mutt.

''Looks like a good dog to me,'' Michael stated, giving the pup an energetic scratch between the ears.

''So you can teach him tricks, right, Mr. Fury? How to sit and play dead and shake?''

''I expect.''

The pup sniffed curiously at one of the cat boxes and was rewarded with a spitting hiss. Yelping, he streaked away and cringed behind Laura's legs.

''He's already learned something.'' With a grin, Michael opened the first box. ''Don't mess with a cornered tom. No, honey.'' Michael took Kayla's hand before she could reach in to pet the cat. ''I doubt he's in a friendly mood at the moment. Don't like being cooped up there, do you, big guy? Let's get you and your pal out.''

He opened the other box, then drew Kayla back. ''We'll just let them get the lay of the land. Once they've catted around some, they'll settle in.'' His eyes skimmed over Laura, lingered, then moved on. ''Whatcha got there, Ali?''

''Kittens.'' Ali's hands and heart were full of them already. ''Mama brought us kittens too.''

''Fuzzy little kitties.'' As he walked to them, he ran his tongue around his teeth. ''Cute.''

''Mama said I could name the gray one myself.''

''Then I get to name the orange one.'' Staking her claim, Kayla took the orange kitten out of Ali's hand and nuzzled it against her cheek. ''Don't I, Mama?''

''Fair enough. We'll have a naming marathon after dinner. We'll just get out of Mr. Fury's way—''

''Can't we show the kittens to Max? Can't we?''

''Sure you can.'' Michael winked at Kayla. ''He's a real softie.'' When the girls raced off, the pup at their heels, Michael shook his head. ''What the hell have you done, Laura?''

''Made my girls very happy.'' She pushed back her hair. ''And saved five lives in the bargain. Do you have a problem with kittens and puppies?''

''Nope.'' The cats had leaped out of their boxes and were slinking around, growling softly. Michael reached over and stroked the nose of his sober gelding. ''You ever do anything halfway?''

''I've been known to.'' She unbent enough to smile. ''I

couldn't stop myself. If you'd seen the girls' faces when I told them that silly little dog was theirs . . . I'll never forget it.''

With the same absent affection he'd shown the gelding, Michael stroked her cheek. He didn't know if he was amused or annoyed when she jerked like a spring. ''You need some training yourself.''

''Excuse me?''

''You shy easy. I appreciate you picking up the cats for me,'' he said before she could think of a response.

''No trouble. The whole lot of them need to go to the vet. Shots. Neutering.''

''Ouch!'' In a knee-jerk male reaction, he winced. ''Yeah, I guess that's the deal.''

''It's the responsible choice—and it's required when you adopt from the shelter. I have all the paperwork. Except I—''

''What?''

''Well, I didn't think to ask about the sex of the kittens. I don't know if they told me. It started to get complicated and confusing, and I think I've heard that it's difficult to tell with young kittens.''

It took an effort, but he kept his eyes solemn. ''I've always heard you shake 'em. If they don't rattle, they're female.''

It took her a moment. Then she broke into easy, appreciative laughter. ''I'll be sure to try it. When the girls aren't around.''

''There you are. I don't suppose I've heard you laugh like that more than a half a dozen times since I've known you. You were always being too dignified when I was around.''

''I'm sure you're mistaken.''

''Sugar, I don't make many mistakes when it comes to women.''

''No, I don't imagine you would.'' To give herself a moment to make her retreat—yes, damn it, a dignified retreat—she turned to the gelding. ''This is a handsome horse.''

"He's smart. Quiet-natured. Jack?"

At his name the horse pricked his ears. Soberly, he turned his head to Michael. "How old are you, Jack?"

In response, the horse stomped a foot four times.

"What do you think of the lady here?"

Jack rolled his eyes toward Laura and let out a quiet and undeniably roguish whinny.

Charmed, Laura laughed again. "How do you get him to do that?"

"Jack? He understands every word you say. Want to take the lady for a ride, Jack?" The response was a decisive nod. "See?" Michael turned his own swift—and undeniably roguish grin—on Laura. "Want a ride, lady?"

"I—" God, she would love one, love to feel a horse beneath her again, let it have its head. Let herself lose hers. "I'd enjoy that, but I don't have the time." She offered Michael a polite, distant smile. "I'll take a rain check."

"Cash it in whenever you like." Too used to Thoroughbreds, he assumed, and shrugged. He'd take Jack over some finicky purebred any day.

"Thank you. I'd better get my motley crew inside. That is, if Annie lets us inside."

"She's a tough nut, Mrs. Sullivan."

"She's family," Laura corrected. "But I should have warned her before I started a small zoo."

"That small zoo is going to keep you up most of the night."

"I'll manage."

She managed, but it wasn't a walk in the park. The puppy whimpered and whined and, despite Kayla's lavish love, was satisfied with nothing less than Laura's bed. She knew it was a mistake, but she couldn't bring herself to banish him when he cuddled so hopefully against her side.

The kittens mewed, fretted, cried, and eventually were comforted by each other, and the hot water bottle that an already doting Annie provided.

As a result, Laura was gritty-eyed and foggy-brained the next morning.

She fumbled at the keyboard in her office at the hotel, cursed herself, then focused on the file for an upcoming writers' convention. Twelve hundred people checking in at approximately the same time, certainly on the same day, were going to present a challenge. Then there were the hospitality suites, banquet and seminar rooms, audio equipment, pitchers of water, requests for coffee services, catering demands.

Cartons of books were already arriving by the truckload. She appreciated the spirit of the planned book signing for literacy, as well as the headaches it was going to cause her and her staff.

Composing a memo one-handed, she picked up her ringing phone. At the sound of the conference coordinator's voice, she struggled not to wince. "Yes, Melissa, it's Laura Templeton. How can I help you today?"

And tomorrow, and for the rest of my natural life, she thought as the woman requested more additions, more changes, just a few more little adjustments.

"Naturally, if the weather's inclement and we're unable to hold your welcoming party at poolside, we'll provide you with an alternate space. The Garden Ballroom is lovely. We often hold wedding receptions there. It's still available for that date."

She listened, rubbed fingers against her temple. "No, I'm not able to do that, Melissa, but if we do book the ballroom, we'll provide another alternate. I realize we're talking more than a thousand people. We'll accommodate you."

She continued to listen, made notes that somehow became mindless doodles. "Yes, I'm looking forward to seeing you again, too. I'll be in touch."

Taking one breath, one moment to clear her mind again, she got back to her memo.

"Laura."

She didn't groan, but she wanted to. "Byron, did we have a meeting?"

"No." He stepped in, seemed to fill her small office with his size. "Aren't you taking lunch?"

"Lunch? It can't be noon."

''No, it can't,'' he said mildly as she looked at her watch. ''It's half past noon.''

''The morning got away from me. I'm due at the shop in an hour. I have to finish this. Is there something urgent?''

Eyeing her, he closed the door at his back. ''Take a break.''

''I really can't. I need—''

''Take a break,'' he repeated. ''That's an order.'' To ensure that she obeyed it, he sat down. ''Now, Ms. Templeton, let's talk about delegating.''

''Byron, I do delegate. It's just that Fitz is running ragged over the Milhouse-Drury wedding reception, and Robyn's swamped. The pharmaceutical convention and a kid with chicken pox. And—''

''And it all comes down to you,'' he finished. ''You look exhausted, honey.''

She pouted. ''Are you speaking as my brother-in-law or as executive director?''

''Both. If you're not going to take care of yourself—''

''I am taking care of myself.'' She smothered a smile. Byron's stand on health and fitness was well known. ''I just didn't get much sleep last night. I went to the pound yesterday.''

He brightened, as she'd known he would. He'd adopted two dogs the year before. ''Yeah? What did you get?''

''A puppy and two kittens. The girls are in ecstasy. And this morning, I caught Annie carrying the pup like he was a newborn baby, and telling him that good dogs mustn't piddle on the Bokhara rug.''

''Start stocking up on newspaper. We'll have to come over and check out your new additions.''

''Come by tonight.''

He raised an eyebrow. ''Before or after the country club dance?''

''The Valentine's Day dance.'' She shut her eyes. ''I forgot.''

''No getting out of it, Laura. You're a Templeton. You're expected.''

''I know, I know.'' There went the long, indulgent bath-

and-early-to-bed night she'd been fantasizing about. "I'll be there. I would have remembered."

"If you hadn't, Kate and Margo would have reminded you. Look, why don't you let your partners handle the shop this afternoon? Go take a nap."

"J. T. is having his checkup this afternoon. I can't leave Kate on her own. We're inundated with the Valentine's Day sale."

"Which reminds me . . ."

Understanding, she smiled. "It's only the tenth, Byron. You still have time to pick up that well-thought-out, loving gift. And no matter what Kate says, don't buy her computer software. Flowers always work for me."

And no one had sent her flowers, she thought, in too long to remember. When her mind drifted to a tiny yellow wildflower, she pulled it back, and called herself an idiot.

"She's not getting that new calculator she's been hinting for, either." He rose. "Do you want a lift to the club tonight?"

So went the life of a single woman, Laura mused. Always tagging along with couples. "No, thanks. I'll see you there."

"I'm not the country club type, Josh." As if someone had already forced him into a suit, Michael rolled his shoulders.

"I'd consider it a favor."

Scowling, Michael measured out grain. "I hate it when you do that."

"And I'd be able to introduce you to a lot of potential horse owners. I happen to know someone who has an impressive stud. You did say you have a mare ready to breed."

"Yeah, she's ready." And he wanted the right sire for her. "So, you'll give me his name, and I'll talk to him. I don't have to go to some lame dance. And I'm the last person your sister wants taking her to some lame dance."

"It's not like a date." So Margo had said when she'd drilled the request into his head. "It's just that Laura's feeling like a third wheel at these things. I didn't realize it myself, but Margo pointed it out.''

And, Josh thought as he watched Michael divvy up grains, had made him feel like a lower form of life. ''Then I realized how often Laura either skips going to events, or cuts out early. It would be nice for her to have an escort, that's all.''

''A woman like your sister ought to have a platoon of likely escorts lined up and waiting.'' And all with the proper pedigree, Michael thought.

''Yeah, well, she doesn't seem interested in swimming with the sharks in the dating pool.'' Was he supposed to do something about that, too? Josh wondered and nearly shuddered. ''She knows you, Mick. She'd be comfortable with you. And it would give you the chance to make some contacts. Everybody's happy.''

''I'm not happy when I have to wear a tie.'' He glanced over his shoulder and grinned. ''Not like you, Harvard, in your fancy Italian suit. Get the hell out of my barn.''

''Come on, Mick. It's just one night out of your fascinating and fun-filled life. We'll hit the game room, play some billiards, tell some lies.''

There was that, Michael considered. And the alternative was a sandwich and an evening hunkered over his drawings for his projected house. ''I can still bury your ass at pool.''

''I'll lend you a tie.''

''Fuck you.'' One of the cats streaked by, pounced in a blur of black. There was a short squeal.

''Christ, that's disgusting.''

''That's life, Harvard.'' Michael moved back to deal with Darling's meal, measuring the additives necessary for her condition.

''You really know what you're doing around here, don't you?''

''Apparently we all have our niche.''

Josh mused over how many niches Michael had already found and rejected. Yet he had a feeling this one was different. They'd known each other too long and too well for Josh to miss the easy contentment in his friend's moves. A contentment, he thought, that had never quite been there before.

"This is the one, isn't it?"

Michael glanced over. He didn't need to explain, not to Josh. He only needed to say one word. "Yeah."

"If I know you, you want to make something big out of it."

He yearned to. "In my own time."

Josh took his, waiting while Michael fed the expectant mother, checked her hay-net, babied her. "Monterey Riding Academy? The owners are friends of the family."

"So?"

"They'll be at the club tonight. Kate was their accountant when she was with Bittle and Associates. They do a lot of buying and selling. So do their students."

Ambition, Michael admitted, was always a trap. "You're a slick son of a bitch, Harvard. You always were."

Josh merely grinned. "We all have our niche."

"Laura might not go for this little arrangement of yours."

"I can handle Laura," Josh said confidently, and checked his watch. "I've got enough time to slip by the shop and do just that before my last meeting today. The dance is at nine. I'll tell her you'll pick her up at eight-thirty—wearing a tie."

"If you don't make this worth my while, pal, I'll have to kick your ass." He brushed grain dust from his hands. "I won't enjoy it, but I'll have to do it."

"Understood." Satisfied with the outcome of his mission, Josh headed for the door. "Ah, you do know the way to the club, don't you?"

Appreciating the sarcasm, Michael tilted his head. "Maybe I will enjoy it after all."

She was furious, livid. And trapped. They'd ganged up on her, Laura fumed as she yanked the pearl gray Miska cocktail dress out of her closet. Josh and Margo and Kate, cornering her at Pretenses and all but presenting her with a fait accompli.

Michael Fury was escorting her to the country club dance. The arrangement would suit everyone. They wouldn't have to worry about her driving there and back alone or about her feeling awkward at an event designed for couples. Michael would gain an entrée and make contacts in the horse world.

Oh, yeah, it suited everyone just fine. Everyone but herself.

It was humiliating, she thought as she jerked the zipper up. A thirty-year-old woman being fixed up by her big brother. Worse, now Michael knew that she was the pathetic divorcée who couldn't get her own date. As if she wanted one in the first place, or the last place, or any place at all, for that matter.

"Which I don't," she told the dog, who had come into her room to watch her every move with adoring eyes. "I don't even want to go to the damn country club tonight. I'm tired."

Sympathetically he wiggled his butt as she stormed over to the closet for shoes and a beaded jacket. She didn't need to hang on to a man's arm to feel complete. She didn't need to hang on to anything, anyone. Why couldn't she just crawl into bed and read a book, she wondered. Eat popcorn and watch an old movie on TV until she fell asleep with the set still on.

Why did she have to dress up, go out in public, and be Laura Templeton?

She stopped, sighed. Because she *was* Laura Templeton. That was something she couldn't forget. Laura Templeton had responsibilities, she had an image to maintain.

So, she told herself as she picked up her lipstick and applied it skillfully, she would maintain it. She would get through the evening, say the right things to the right people. She would be as polite and friendly to Michael as necessary. And when the whole blasted thing was over, she would fall facedown on her bed and forget it. Until the next time.

She checked her hair. God, she needed a trim. And when was she going to fit that in? She turned for her bag and watched in mild horror as the pup wet on her Aubusson.

"Oh, Bongo!"

He grinned up at her and sat in his own pee.

It was only a small rebellion, but Michael didn't wear a tie. He figured that with Laura Templeton at his side they wouldn't boot him out for wearing a black turtleneck under his jacket.

He parked between the island of spring bulbs and the grand front entrance. And if he'd been wearing a tie, he would have tugged at it.

Nerves. They amazed him, disgusted him. But no matter how much he wanted to deny it, he felt like some pimply-faced teenager on a first date.

Ignoring the sky dusted with icy stars, the sheen of silvering moonlight, the scent of sea and flowers, he walked to the door like a man taking his last mile in shackles.

How the hell had he let himself get talked into this?

He'd never used the front door at Templeton House. As a boy, if he came by for Josh, or came along with him, he used the side or rear. The entrance was so damned imposing, grandly tall, recessed, and framed in tile. The knocker was a huge brass affair in the shape of a stylized T. Over his head hung an antique carriage light.

It didn't make him feel welcome.

Nor did Ann Sullivan when she opened the door to his knock. She stood, tight-lipped, in her starched black dress. He noted first that the years sat lightly on her. She was a lovely woman, if you looked past the jaundiced eye. Margo had come by her looks naturally.

"Mr. Fury." The faint hint of Ireland in her voice might have been charming if it hadn't been so damning.

Because for reasons he couldn't name he'd always wanted her approval, she put his back up. His smile was insolent. His voice matched it. "Mrs. Sullivan. It's been a while."

"It has," she returned, clearly telling him it hadn't been nearly long enough. "You're to come in."

He accepted the grudging invitation and stepped into the

soaring foyer. The ivory and peacock-blue tiles were the same, he noted. As was the gorgeously ornate chandelier that sprinkled light. The place was welcoming, even if its doyenne wasn't. It was full of cozy scents, rich color, warming light.

"I'll tell Miss Laura you're here."

But as she turned to do so, Laura came down the wide, curving steps. Though Michael would tell himself later that he was a fool, his heart stopped.

The lights caught the fussy beads of her jacket and shot color. Beneath was a simple dress the color of moondust. There were jewels at her ears, sapphires and diamonds, framing the face that her swept-back hair accented.

She looked so perfect, so lovely, with one ringless hand trailing along the glossy banister. She might have stepped out of a painting.

"I'm sorry to keep you waiting." Her voice was cool, betraying none of her panic at the way those eyes of his bored into her, or her fluster at having to mop up after the dog.

"Just got here," he said, equally cool. Then some of the absurdity struck him. Here he was, Michael Fury, holding out a hand for a princess. "I wasn't supposed to bring, like, a corsage or something, was I?"

She managed a small smile of her own. "It's not the prom."

"Amen to that."

"You be careful, Miss Laura." Ann shot a warning look at Michael. "And you drive responsibly, boy-o. It isn't one of your races."

"Annie, the dog's in with the girls, but—"

"Don't you worry." She gestured toward the door, thinking philosophically that the sooner they were gone, the sooner she'd have her girl back. "I'll take care of him, and them. Try to enjoy yourself."

"And I'll try to bring her back in one piece," Michael added, for the hell of it, as he opened the door.

"See that you do," Ann muttered and began to worry the moment the door closed.

"It's nice of you to drive me to the club." She would put things on the proper footing, Laura determined. And keep them there. "You don't have to feel obliged to entertain me once we're there."

He'd been planning to say pretty much the same thing himself, but he resented her saying it first. He opened her door, leaned on it. "Who are you pissed off at, Laura? Me, or the world in general?"

"I'm not angry with you or anyone." Gracefully, she slipped into the passenger seat of his Porsche. "I'm simply explaining matters so that we get through the evening comfortably."

"And here you said you liked mongrels."

She blinked. "I don't know what you mean."

"Right." He resisted—barely—slamming the door. The evening, he thought as he rounded the hood, was off to a flying start.

Chapter Six

It could have been worse, Michael supposed. He could have been back in some Central American jungle sweating bullets and dodging them. He could have had his skull bashed in, as he had once when a stunt gag went wrong.

Instead he was standing in a room with people he didn't know and didn't care to know.

He'd rather have had his skull bashed in.

He thought the room itself was overly cute, with its glossy red hearts hanging from swatches of paper lace. The flowers were nice, he supposed. He didn't have any objection to flowers. But he thought they carried the obsessive red and white theme too far.

All of the pink-draped tables were centered with a grouping of white tapers ringed by a halo of fluffy red and white carnations. At least he thought they were carnations. And the music. He decided it represented the widest culture clash, with its mild strings and discreet piano, all played by middle-aged men in white suits.

Give him blues or honest rock any day.

But there was a spiffy view of the coastline through a wall of windows. The drama of it, the war of fretful waves against mean-edged rocks, provided an interesting contrast to the quiet, undeniably stuffy group inside the polished, overheated club.

The women had decked themselves out, absolutely dripping bangles and beads and other jewelry, he noted. They wore layers of perfumes and silks and lace. Overdone, in his estimation, like the decor. He preferred Laura's simple and feminine choice. It was class, he supposed, that set her apart. Simple class that came straight through the blood and bone. He might have mentioned it to her, but she had drifted away quickly, making, as he termed it, her Templeton rounds.

Most of the men were in tuxes. A little fact that Josh had conveniently neglected to mention. Not that Michael minded. He wouldn't have worn one anyway. If he'd had one to wear.

Still it gave him another bone to pick with his old friend. If the slippery son of a bitch ever showed up.

On the bright side, he had a cold beer in his hand. The finger food spread out artistically on buffet tables looked delicate, but it tasted fine. He'd already enjoyed a mild flirtation with a woman who mistook him for some Hollywood young gun. Michael hadn't bothered to disabuse her.

He was considering wandering about, maybe taking a turn outside in the fresh air or checking out one of the other rooms. He might find that pool table and a few suckers to fleece. Then Laura moved back to him.

"I'm sorry. There were a few people I needed to speak with." In a gesture that was both absentminded and automatic, she accepted a glass of champagne from a roving waiter, murmured her thanks.

"No problem."

But it was, she thought, her problem. She'd had some time to think about it. "I am sorry, Michael. I was annoyed with Josh for maneuvering me into this evening and I took it out on you." When he didn't respond, she drummed up a smile. "So, what were you and Kitty Bennett talking about?"

"Who? Oh, the ditzy brunette with all the teeth."

Laura choked on her champagne. She'd never heard the chair of the Monterey Arts Council described just that way. Or quite that accurately. "Yes."

"She dug my last flick."

"Did she?"

He decided to be friendly, smiled. "Not *Braveheart,* though I had a couple of nice stunts in it. She thought I was the director of some art house film. Something about foot fetishes."

"Mm-hmm. And you discussed the metaphoric twists on our sex-obsessed society, along with the multiple layers of symbolism representing moral decay."

He started to feel better. "Something like that. She thinks I'm brilliant, and underrated. I think I might be getting a grant."

"Congratulations."

"Of course, she really only wanted my body."

"Well, an artist must make sacrifices. Ah, there's Byron and Kate."

Michael glanced over. His brows rose in surprise as he saw the streamlined brunette in slinky black. The gamine face, all sloe-colored eyes, and the close-cropped dark hair tipped him off, though the girl he remembered had been skinny, coltish—a borderline nerd.

"That's Kate? Kate Powell?"

"She works out now," Laura muttered. "She's gotten obsessive about it, so don't get her started."

"That her trainer?" Michael muttered back, measuring the broad-shouldered, long-limbed man beside her.

"And husband. He's also my boss. Byron." She held out a hand as the couple maneuvered through the crowd toward them. A quick kiss and she turned to Kate. "Margo was right, as usual. The Karan suits you. Byron De Witt, Michael Fury."

"Nice to meet you. Kate's been telling me stories."

"And I didn't even need to exaggerate." Grinning, she

stepped forward and gave Michael a quick, friendly hug.

Her arms might have been lean, Michael noted, but they were tough. Enjoying her, he drew her back. ''Katie Powell. Looking good.''

Because she'd always enjoyed him as well, she wiggled her brows. ''Same goes, Mick.''

''Can I get drinks for anyone?'' Byron asked in a voice that reminded Michael of mint juleps and magnolia.

''I'll have what Laura's having,'' Kate decided.

''Michael?''

''Bass ale.''

''That ought to go down just fine,'' Byron decided. ''I think I'll join you. Excuse me a minute.''

''It's the Southern,'' Kate said, watching him walk toward the bar with a proprietary and satisfied gleam in her eye. ''He's just a gentleman.''

''It doesn't look like it's just the dress that suits you,'' Michael commented.

''It's not.'' Kate turned back, smiled warmly. ''And unlike the dress, which goes back into stock tomorrow, he's all mine. So, how the hell are you, Michael Fury, and when do we get to see your horses?''

It was so easy for Kate, Laura thought as she listened, to make the appropriate comments. She'd fallen right into casual conversation with Michael. Didn't she feel any of those . . . oh, she hated to use the term ''vibes,'' but it was the only word that came to her. Dark, restless, dangerous vibes. It made her jittery to stand next to him, to encounter a brush of his arm against hers, to catch that gleam in his hot blue eyes.

It helped when Josh and Margo arrived. There was more conversation, and laughter. Byron fell into an easy discussion of horses with Michael. Apparently Byron's family owned several. Before the topic switched to cars—another interest the men shared—Byron had arranged to take a look at Michael's stock.

It wasn't difficult to ease away again and draw Margo with her. ''So,'' Margo began, ''are you enjoying yourself? You and Michael are getting some speculative looks.''

Nothing could have been better designed to set Laura off. She could see it now, perfectly, and wondered how she'd missed the master plan.

Her temper hitched, but she controlled it.

''Is that part of your little plot? To give the country club set an eyeful of poor Laura and her escort?''

''When the escort looks like Michael.'' Margo waved an impatient hand. ''Oh, lighten up, Laura. It's only one evening out of your life, and why shouldn't you spend part of it with a good-looking man? God knows, you've been hiding out long enough.''

''Hiding out.'' There was that hitch again. ''Is that what you call it?''

''Don't.'' Regretting her choice of words, Margo put a hand on Laura's arm. ''I just meant that you've been so focused on work and responsibility, you haven't let yourself have much fun. So have some. Ask him to dance, take a walk, whatever, before he and Byron bond like Siamese twins over engine talk.''

''I don't want to dance, or take a walk with Michael,'' Laura said evenly. Now she felt pathetic. The homely younger sister, the neglected wallflower, the pitiable ex-wife. ''And I'm relieved that he's found something to salvage his evening. He's been miserably bored.''

''Then you haven't been doing your job, have you?'' Irritated herself, Margo inclined her head. ''It wouldn't hurt you to be friendly to the man, Laura. In fact, it would be good for you and everyone in close proximity to you if you had a nice hot bout of sex with him and popped your own frustration cork.''

Laura's calm gray eyes turned to steel. ''Oh, really? I hadn't realized that those in close proximity were so affected by my lifestyle.''

''Hey.'' Recognizing the signs of a battle in progress, Kate sidled up. ''Are we fighting?''

''Laura's peeved because we made her come here with Michael tonight.''

''I like Mick.'' Kate chose an olive from her tiny plate and popped it into her mouth. ''What's the problem?''

"I'm peeved," Laura returned, emphasizing the word, "because Margo apparently thinks I should jump into bed with him so that she and my other friends don't have to put up with my sexual frustration."

Kate glanced around to where Michael and Byron and Josh stood. "Couldn't hurt," she said with a shrug. "If I wasn't a happily married woman I'd consider it myself."

"That's nice for you, isn't it? For both of you happily married women. Christ, I hope I wasn't ever so smug." Training overcame temper just enough that she managed to walk away instead of stalking.

"Wrong buttons," Kate muttered. "We definitely pushed the wrong buttons."

"It's past time some of them were pushed." But Margo sighed before sipping her wine. "I don't mind making her angry, but I didn't mean to make her unhappy. I just hoped that she'd enjoy herself, let Michael entertain her. And eventually screw her brains out."

Kate chuckled. "You're a considerate friend, Margo. Hell, are we smug?"

"I'm afraid so."

A few minutes in the ladies' lounge cooled Laura off. She sat on one of the dainty padded stools at the long, mirrored counter and meticulously reapplied her lipstick.

Was she frustrated? Was she becoming difficult to be around? She didn't like to think so. What she was was busy, focused, committed to her family and work.

What was so wrong with that? Then she sighed, propped her elbows on the counter, her head in the vee of her hands. No, it was she who had blown a simple evening out of proportion, she admitted. Because she hadn't had a simple evening in too long.

And because, she could admit privately, she didn't know how to behave with a man, especially one like Michael Fury.

She'd been seventeen when she fell in love with Peter. Eighteen when she married him. Her dating record beforehand had been brief and uncomplicated.

She'd been married for ten years and had indulged in no flirtations, much less affairs. The men she knew were relatives or old family friends. They were casual acquaintances, the husbands of women she knew, or business contacts.

She was thirty years old, she thought miserably, and she didn't know how to date. Even when it wasn't a bona fide date.

When the door to the lounge opened, she straightened quickly and took out her comb.

''Hi, Laura.''

''Judy.'' Her smile warmed. Judy Prentice was a friend and a regular customer at Pretenses. ''It's good to see you. You look wonderful.''

''Holding my own.'' Always ready for a chat or a quick gossip, Judy sat down beside her. ''Did you see Maddie Greene? She had a boob job last month.''

She simply couldn't be overly dignified with Judy. ''It was a little hard to miss her with those twin soldiers.''

''Well, watch yourself. I made the polite comment when she brought it up. I think I said something about them looking very perky.'' She grinned when Laura snorted. ''Next thing I knew, she'd dragged me in here and stripped to the waist to show them off. Up close, my dear, and much too personal.''

''Oh, God, thanks for the warning.''

''I have to admit, they're beauties. Speaking of which.'' Judy set down her jeweled compact. ''I didn't recognize that incredibly gorgeous specimen you're with tonight. Is he from around here?''

''He's an old friend.''

Judy rolled her eyes. ''We should all have such old friends.''

''He's just moved back to the area.'' A little thought leaked through. ''Your daughter takes riding lessons, doesn't she, Judy?''

''She's horse crazy. I went through the same stage, but it seems to be sticking with Mandy.''

''Michael raises horses, trains them. He's working out of

Templeton House for the moment until he can rebuild. His property was destroyed in those mud slides.''

''Oh, God, weren't they horrible? Another friend of mine watched her house slide down a cliff. Just going, going, gone. Heartbreaking.'' Judy dabbed perfume at her wrists. ''Why do we live in California?''

''I hear it's the weather,'' Laura said dryly. ''In any case, you might want to contact Michael if you decide to get Mandy a mount of her own.''

''Actually, we are considering it. Her birthday's coming up, and there's nothing she'd like better than her own horse.'' Lips pursed in thought, Judy replaced her perfume. ''Thanks for the tip. I'll talk to my husband about it. Meanwhile, good luck with your old friend.''

Laura left the lounge in better spirits. The evening was wearing on, she was getting through it. The least she could do was make an effort to enjoy what was left of it.

''Cooled off?''

She jumped a little, muffled an oath. Must the man sneak up behind her? ''I'm sorry.''

''You looked ready to chew steel when you marched off to the ladies' room.'' Michael handed her a fresh glass of champagne.

''Maybe it was indigestion. I ran into a friend in there.''

''You women have little summit meetings in the john, don't you? Isn't that why you usually go inside in packs?''

''Actually, we play poker and smoke cigars, but my point is, this friend of mine has a daughter and she's very keen on riding. They're considering buying her a horse. I gave Judy your name. I hope you don't mind.''

''Hey, anytime you want to toss business my way, feel free. I like your brother-in-law.''

''It showed. I expected the two of you to have a secret handshake by now.''

''Is that a subtle way of telling me I was ignoring you?''

''No.'' She said it too quickly, and then tried to backtrack. ''Not at all. I'm glad you and Byron hit it off.'' She spotted him on the dance floor with Kate. And her eyes warmed. ''They're so happy together. They've only been married a couple of months, but with some people you can just tell that the way they look at each other isn't going to change.''

''Your romantic side's showing.''

She didn't take offense. ''I'm allowed to have one.''

''Then I guess I should ask you to dance.''

She looked up at him. What the hell, she decided. ''Then I guess I should accept.''

Before he could take her hand, he saw her smile fade and freeze, her color drain to white. The hand that had lifted to take his fell to her side.

''What's the problem?''

She only took a quiet, shaky breath. ''Hello, Peter. Candy.''

''Laura.''

Michael shifted, his hand instinctively moving to the small of Laura's back to support her. This must be the ex, he realized, with the perky, cat-eyed redhead clinging to his arm.

He supposed this would be Laura's type. Tall and golden, distinguished, perfectly presented in a tailored tux, diamonds winking discreetly at his cuffs.

''I didn't realize you were in town,'' Laura managed. She knew, though conversations continued, that attention was focusing on the little tableau. ''When I spoke to you about Allison's school supper, you indicated you'd be away.''

''My plans changed a bit, but I'm still not able to attend.'' He said it formally, as if declining an invitation to a polo match.

''It's very important to her, Peter. Just a few hours—''

''And my plans are important to me.'' His gaze flicked to Michael, lingered in speculation. ''I don't believe I know your escort.''

''Michael Fury.'' And Michael didn't offer a hand.

''Of course. I thought I recognized you.'' Candy Litchfield's voice bubbled up. ''Michael is an old friend of Josh Templeton's, darling. You ran away to sea or something, didn't you?''

"Or something," Michael said, sparing her a glance. Her type had always grated on him. Overly bright, overly vicious. "I don't remember you."

The statement had been calculated to deflate and annoy. He usually hit his mark. She bristled a little, then purred. "Well, after all, we didn't run in the same circles, did we? Your mother was a waitress, wasn't she?"

"That's right. At Templeton Resort. And my father ran off with a redhead. I don't think she was related to you."

"I shouldn't think so." After sneering down her nose, she looked back at Laura. "Now don't nag Peter, Laura. We've been so incredibly pressed. We've hardly had time to catch our breath since we got in this morning. We've been in St. Thomas."

"How lovely for you, but the fact is that these pesky domestic details do require some communication. If you'd . . ."

She trailed off as her gaze lighted on the ring Candy was displaying on the hand she deliberately fluttered against Peter's chest. The stone was as big as a hen's egg, sitting atop a platinum Tiffany setting.

Satisfied that she'd finally shifted Laura's attention where she wanted it, Candy giggled. "Oh, dear, you've found us out. Peter and I want to make the announcement quietly, but I'm sure I can trust you to be discreet." And miserable, she hoped. She'd detested Laura for more years than she cared to count, and now she savored her moment of triumph.

Every muscle in her stomach twisted as Laura looked into Peter's eyes. Oh, they were amused. Coolly amused. "Congratulations. I'm sure you'll be very happy together."

"I have no doubt of it." Candace was perfect for him, he thought. Perfect for this new stage of his life, just as Laura had been perfect for another stage. "We're planning a small ceremony in May in Palm Springs."

"Not too small." Candy pouted prettily, but her eyes were gleaming as they stayed locked on Laura's face. "May's such a lovely month for a wedding, don't you think? Something charming and alfresco would be nice. But not too small or informal. After all, a bride needs to show off a bit.''

''And you'd know all about that.'' Laura's hands were threatening to tremble. It couldn't be permitted. ''Are you planning on telling the girls about your marriage, Peter, or is that up to me?''

''I'll leave that to you.''

''I'm sure they'll be delighted,'' Candy purred, as she slid a glass off the tray of a nearby waiter. ''Mine are. Little Charles is very fond of Peter, and Adrianna is thrilled with the prospect of a wedding.''

''How nice for you,'' Laura said stiffly. ''But then, Charles and Adrianna must be used to your weddings by now.''

''Don't be snide, Laura.'' Peter's voice was cool and mild. ''It never suited you. You'll have to excuse us now. We need to mingle.''

''Steady,'' Michael murmured as they slipped away.

''That bitch! How am I going to tolerate that bitch being stepmother to my babies? How am I going to stand it?''

It surprised him that that would be her first thought. Then he realized it shouldn't have. ''They're bright girls, Laura, and she doesn't strike me as the maternal type.''

''I can't stay here.''

Before she could dash, he took a firm hold on her arm. The way he drew her to him made it seem as if they were sharing secrets. ''You run out now, it's going to look like retreat. That's not what you want.''

''I can't stay here.'' There was panic swirling inside her, along with a bubbling brew of fury. ''How could he do this? How could he do this to them?''

Odd, he thought, that she couldn't see that both Peter and Candy had done it to her. Very deliberately, and very well. ''If I'm any judge, everybody in this room is wondering just how Laura Templeton is going to handle this little meeting with her ex and his Kewpie doll. I think we should have that dance.''

He was right, of course. He was exactly, pathetically right. However hurt, however shocked, there was still pride.

She wouldn't allow Candy to snicker over her retreat.

''Okay.''

She walked with him to the dance floor as if she wanted nothing more than a quiet turn. The music was soft, some moody number from the forties. It was designed to be romantic, she thought. Instead it rang in her ears like a battle cry.

''She's not going to get her pinching little fingers on my babies,'' Laura said between her teeth.

''I don't imagine she'd get past you to pinch anyone, if that was her goal. It wouldn't hurt if you looked at me.'' He slipped his arms around her, found they fit well. Discovered her steps matched his smoothly. ''Maybe even smiled.''

''They only came here to slap at me. Neither one of them gave a single thought to the children. She's a mother herself, Michael. How can she not care about the children?''

''Too much in love with herself. Stop worrying about it. She isn't going to make time in her social calendar to play stepmama. Smile,'' he murmured, touching a hand lightly to her cheek. ''You can make everybody believe you're only thinking about me and what we're going to do when we leave here. That'll burn their ass.''

He was right again, and she made her lips curve. ''I'm sorry you got caught in the cross fire.''

''Hell, it's just a flesh wound.'' He was rewarded by a quick, honest laugh.

''You're nicer than I remembered, Michael. And I'm a mess.''

''You look pretty neat and tidy to me. You always did. We've got them wondering now.'' He bent his head so that his cheek brushed hers, his mouth close to her ear. ''Just who is that guy Laura Templeton's wrapped around? How long has this been going on?''

She was beginning to wonder the same thing herself. ''Not everyone's that interested in my business.''

His breath blew warm against her ear. ''Come on, sugar. You fascinate them. Cool, composed Laura.''

''It's been poor Laura for a little too long now.'' Her

voice was tight again. "Poor Laura, whose husband cheated on her with his secretary. Poor Laura, who'll have to hold her head up now that her ex is marrying her former co-chair of the Garden Club."

"Jesus, you played with that irritating little redhead?" He shook his head. "I'm disappointed in you. Tell you what, now that they're wondering, why don't we give them something to talk about over brunch tomorrow?"

His mouth slid around, grazed her cheek. Before she could jolt from the shock of that, it was fixed warmly on hers. The kiss was long and slow. Her head reeled once, and the hand on his shoulder flexed open and dug in.

He eased back, barely an inch so that the only thing she could see was his eyes. "Let's try that again," he said softly. "I think you'll get the hang of it."

She would have protested. She wasn't the kind of woman who indulged in smoldering kisses in public. Or in smoldering kisses in private, for that matter. But his mouth was on hers again, clever, persuasive. Hot. And she was swept along.

The rich male taste, the firm, knowing lips, the confident exploration of tongue and rough scrape of teeth. No one had kissed her like that before, as if her mouth was the source of all pleasure. Something hummed in her throat that might have been shock but was more likely wonder.

As he had wondered. What would she taste like, feel like, be like? What he found was a banquet of contrasts. Heat filtered through cool armor. Shyness fluttering under composure. She was trembling, erotic little shivers that shot need straight to his loins.

And that reminded him that no matter how much he might enjoy the experiment, they weren't alone in a place where they could analyze the results.

"That ought to do it," he murmured. "It sure as hell convinced me."

She could do nothing but stare up at him. Somehow they were still dancing. She knew her feet, however disassociated they seemed from the rest of her, were moving.

"Sugar." Struggling to keep it light when he would have

been happier devouring her in a couple of quick bites, he lifted her hand, nipped at the knuckles. ''You keep looking at me that way, they're going to have more to talk about than a couple of kisses.''

She tore her gaze away, stared determinedly over his shoulder. ''You caught me off guard.''

''That makes two of us. We can leave now, if you want. Nobody's going to think it's a retreat.''

''Yes.'' She kept her back stiff, fighting to ignore the familiar and enticing way his hand continued to stroke it. ''I'd like to go home.''

She didn't speak again until they stood on the wide veranda of the entrance to the clubhouse. One of the eager valets rushed off to fetch Michael's car, and they remained there, sheltered, with the lights and music behind them and the night, moonswept and shadowed, in front.

''Should I thank you?''

''Jesus.'' He rammed his hands into his pockets. She was about as approachable now as polished marble. ''Did it seem like I was making a sacrifice? I've given some thought to kissing you, and if you want to step off that goddamn pedestal again for a minute, you'll admit you knew I'd given some thought to it.''

''I'm not trying to make you angry.''

''Just a happy accident, then. Laura—'' he turned to her, not completely sure of his next move, then swore as the valet zipped his car up to the base of the stairs.

''That's a beauty, sir,'' the boy said, then beamed at the tip Michael all but threw at him. ''Thank you, sir. Drive safely.''

Calmer once he had the car racing away from the club, Michael took a breath. ''Look, sugar, you took a hard knock in there. I'm sorry for it. If you ask me, that jerk you made the mistake of marrying isn't worth a minute of your time.''

She wasn't asking him, was she? Laura thought nastily. ''I'm not concerned about me. It's the girls.''

''Parents get divorced. It's a fact of life. Fathers take off and ignore their kids. Another fact.''

"That's very easy to say when you don't have children to concern you."

A shadow crossed his face. "No, I don't have any children. I've been one who lived through divorce and neglect, though. You get through it."

She shut her eyes. She'd forgotten that his father had left him and his mother. "I'm sorry, but that doesn't make it right. Allison needs his attention, and his disinterest hurts her."

"What about you? Are you still in love with him?"

"No. God, no. Candy's welcome to him. She's just not welcome to my girls."

"I don't see them giving her more than the patented Templeton dismissal. That small, polite smile."

"We don't do that."

"Oh, sugar, yes, you do."

She shifted and aimed a steady glance at him. "Do you know why you call women 'sugar,' Michael? That way, when you roll off one in the middle of the night, you don't have to remember annoying little details like her name."

His mouth twitched into something between a grimace and a smile. "Close enough. I guarantee I'll remember yours . . . Laura. If you're considering letting me roll off of you tonight."

She wasn't sure if she was shocked, outraged, or amused. But she did know that most of the sting from Peter had faded. "That's an incredibly flattering offer, Michael. I don't know when I've had one quite so—"

"Honest," he suggested.

"Crude," she finished. "I'm afraid I'll have to decline."

"Up to you. How about a walk on the cliffs instead?" On impulse, he swung the car to the shoulder.

They speared, magnetic, moon-kissed, and entirely too romantic. Because she could envision herself walking them with him, their hands clasped, she shook her head. "I'm not wearing the right shoes for cliff walking."

"Then we'll just sit here a minute."

"I don't think—"

"I have something to say to you."

Nerves began to hum again. She clasped her hands in her lap. She was parked on a dark road in the moonlight. Something she hadn't done in too many years to count. "All right."

"You're a beautiful, desirable woman." When her head snapped around and he saw her eyes wide and confused, he nearly laughed. "I guess that's something you hear all the time."

It certainly wasn't, which left her at a loss as to how to respond. "I'm flattered you think so."

"I want you."

Now there was panic, fizzing up like champagne in a shaken bottle. "I don't—What do you expect me to say to that? God!" Despite the shoes, she wrenched open the door and stepped out into the night.

"I didn't ask you to say anything. I'm telling you." He came up beside her and turned her to face him. "It's probably a mistake, but I'm telling you anyway. I have memories of you. I didn't realize how many until I saw you again and they just popped out of my head. I used to think about you. Damned inconvenient, and embarrassing to be thinking about you the way I was when you were the kid sister of my best friend. Josh would have kicked my ass for what I was thinking, and I'd have had to let him."

"I'm no good at this." She moved back, retreating quickly. "I'm no good at this sort of thing. You'll have to stop."

"Not till I'm finished. I never stop until I'm finished. Keep backing up that way, sugar—Laura," he corrected himself as he grabbed her arm, "you're going to break an ankle. I don't mind you being afraid of me. I'd be surprised if you weren't." His grin flashed. "Hell, I'd be insulted. Just hold still a minute."

He held both of her hands at her sides and moved in. "I'm not going to hurt you," he murmured as his mouth lowered. "This time."

It didn't hurt. Devastation came too quickly for pain. He simply undid her with one soft, lazy kiss. Then with another, harder, impatient, until that reckless, relentless mouth against hers chipped away at the wall of restraint.

And she knew that marriage hadn't prepared her for this kind of desire—the kind that curled like raw, ragged fists in the gut and twisted in angry frustration.

When she gave, he wanted more. He wanted her there, atop the windy cliff with the moon spotlighting them and the violent thrust of the waves matching the way he imagined thrusting into her. And he knew greed could be his undoing.

"I want you to think about it," he told her. "The horses taught me patience, so I've got a small store where you're concerned. It seems only fair to let you know that I want you. It doesn't have anything to do with saving your face in front of the country club set, or with making your idiot ex-husband steam a little. It has to do with you and me. And it's unlikely when it's done that you'll have to ask whether you should thank me."

"I have children."

Laughter, he discovered, could relieve even a great amount of tension. "Christ Almighty. You've got great children, Laura. But this is between you and me."

"I—let go of me and let me breathe, will you?"

She jerked away, rubbing her hands through hair that the wind had tossed into curling confusion. However shaken she was, she felt the simplest way out was honesty.

"I don't have any experience with affairs." Her voice was composed again, but her hands continued to twist together. "I was married for ten years, and I was faithful."

"You've been divorced how long?"

When she didn't respond, he stared. Then he began to see what she was telling him. There'd only been one man—which made her former husband even more of a fool, in Michael's opinion.

"Is that supposed to make me less attracted to you? You know what it makes me, Laura? It makes me want to toss you over my shoulder and find out if I still know how to pleasure a woman in a parked car."

He saw her glance toward his Porsche, and for a moment

he was sure there was speculation in her eyes. ''Sugar, I'd be willing to give it a shot.''

When he stepped forward, she risked a wrenched ankle and evaded him. ''Don't. Just don't.''

She turned and stared out over the sea where waves slashed white against speared fingers of rocks. It was a long fall, she thought. Reckless jumps were always followed by long falls.

And she had never taken one.

''I don't know how I'm going to react to this. I don't know what I'm going to want to do about it.''

''Think about it,'' he suggested. ''I'm going to be around for quite a while. You want to neck in the car, or do you want me to take you home?''

Now she smiled. How could she help it? ''Another of those intriguing offers of yours. I'll take the ride home, thanks.''

''Your loss, sugar.''

Chapter Seven

''And then Mrs. Hannah said that everyone who'd finished all their assignments could have extra time on the computer. I picked the Art Studio so I got to draw a picture and print it out and everything. Then she put it on the board because she said it was excellent.''

While Kayla chattered about her school day, Michael continued to water brush his mare's mane. Kayla had fallen into the habit of visiting him, and he'd discovered that if a day passed without her poking her head into the stables, he felt deprived.

Her mother, on the other hand, was keeping her distance. He hadn't seen her in three days, since the night of the country club dance.

''Mama's going to get me drawing lessons, and that'll be fun because I like to draw pictures. I can draw you one if you want.''

''I'd like that.'' He sent her a quick smile. ''What would you draw for me?''

''A surprise.'' She beamed at him. Big people didn't

always really listen, Kayla knew. Mr. Fury always listened, even when he was busy. ''Do you have time to teach Bongo a trick?''

''I might.'' Michael tapped the dampened water brush in his palm as he studied the pup, who was currently sprawled on the brick eyeing one of the cats. ''I've got to put this lady through her paces first, though. Got somebody coming by to look at her.''

Kayla's bottom lip poked out as she reached up to smooth the mare's glossy flank. ''To buy her?''

''Maybe.'' Understanding, he crouched down. ''She needs a good home. Like Bongo did.''

''You're a good home.''

He didn't think this called for an explanation of business, the profit-and-loss ledgers that often made him cross-eyed. So he kept it simple. ''I can't keep them all, honey. What I do is take good care of them while they're here and look for people who'll take care of them when they're not. And your mom's the one who found these people. You know Mrs. Prentice?''

''She's nice.'' Kayla gnawed on her lip as she considered. She did like Mrs. Prentice—she had a fun laugh. ''Her daughter rides horses. Mandy's fourteen and has a boyfriend.''

''Does she?'' Amused, Michael tousled Kayla's hair. ''If they like the lady here, and she likes them, she'll be their horse. Do you think Mandy would take good care of her?''

''I guess so.''

''Let's take her out to the paddock, you and me.''

''I'll get her blanket. I'll get it.''

While Kayla raced off, he made a final check of his lady. She was a pretty chestnut hack, her coat gleaming now from his meticulous work with brush and currycomb. Her eyes were clear, intelligent, her heart strong, her hooves healthy and smartly presented, with a coating of oil. At fifteen hands she was a good size, well lined, a cooperative, well-behaved animal who would bring him a good profit on his investment.

He was, he knew as he stroked her neck, going to miss the hell out of her.

Together, he and Kayla saddled the mare, with Kayla watching every move carefully. She hoped that one day Mr. Fury would let her hook the cinches, but she didn't want to ask. Yet.

"Where's Ali today?"

"Oh, she's in her room. She has to clean it and finish all her homework. She can't come outside today because she's being punished."

"What did she do?"

"She had another fight with Mama." With the dog at her heels, Kayla skipped along beside Michael as he led the mare out. "She's mad because our dad's marrying Mrs. Litchfield and he's not going to go to the father-daughter supper at school. She says it's Mama's fault."

"How does she figure that?"

"I don't know." Kayla shrugged her shoulders. "She's silly. Uncle Josh is going to the supper, and he's more fun anyway. Our dad doesn't like us."

The careless tone caused Michael to stop, glance down. "Doesn't he?"

"No, but that's okay because . . ." She trailed off, bit her lip. "It's bad."

"What is, darling?"

She looked behind her toward the house, then back into Michael's eyes. "I don't like him, either. I'm glad he went away and that he's not coming back. But don't tell Mama."

Now there was alarm, and beneath it a silvery rush of defense. "Honey." He crouched down, taking her little shoulders carefully in his hands. "He didn't hurt you, did he? He didn't hit you or your sister?" Even the thought of it churned in his gut like acid. "Or your mom?"

"No." She seemed so baffled by the idea. Michael relaxed again. "But he never listens and he never plays and he made Mama cry, so I don't like him. But don't tell."

"I won't." Michael made an X over his heart, then touched the finger to her lips. How anyone, particularly a father, could not adore this fascinating child was beyond him. "How about a ride?"

Her eyes went huge, hopeful. "Can I? Can I really?"

"Well, let's see." He picked her up, set her on the saddle. "We have to see if the lady likes girls, right?" he said as he adjusted the stirrups. "This here's an English saddle because that's what Mandy uses. Take a rein in each hand. No, like this, sugar," he said and adjusted her grip. "That's the way."

Patiently he explained the proper way to guide the mare while Kayla listened in solemn-eyed concentration. "Now, heels down. Good. Knees in. Back straight." With a hand on the bridle he led the mare into a sedate walk. "How's it feel up there, Miss Ridgeway?"

She giggled, bounced. "I'm riding the horse."

"Now draw back on the left rein, easy now, the way I showed you. See how nice she turns. She's a good girl."

He had work to do, calls to make. And he forgot all of it. For the next twenty minutes he indulged himself, teaching Kayla the basics, hopping up behind her once to take the mare into a quick, circling canter that had the child shrieking with delight.

The day might have been overcast, more rain threatening. But here was sunshine.

When he plucked her off and her arms wound tight around his neck in a hug, he felt, for the first time in his life, like a hero.

"Can I do it again sometime, Mr. Fury?"

"Sure you can."

With easy affection and trust, she wrapped her legs around his waist, grinning at him. "When Mama gets home she'll be so surprised. I rode the horse all by myself and steered her and everything."

"You sure did. And now we know she likes girls."

"She'll like Mandy, so she'll be happy. I'm going to tell Annie right now how I rode the horse. Thanks, Mr. Fury."

She wiggled down and raced off, the pup scrambling after. Michael watched her, stroking the mare's neck. "You've done it now, Fury," he murmured. "Gone and fallen in love with that pretty little blonde.'' He looked into his mare's eyes, kissed her. Sighed. ''Not supposed to fall for what you can't keep.''

Two hours later, he repeated the warning to himself. The Prentices had fallen for the mare at first sight, had barely bothered to dicker over his asking price. Now he had a check in his pocket and the lady was no longer his.

With mixed feelings, he approached Templeton House. He'd made a sale, and that was part of his business. The mare, he had no doubt, was going to be pampered and adored for the rest of her life. And it was a sure bet that the Prentices would spread the word that Michael Fury had good stock for sale.

He had Laura to thank for it, and he intended to do so.

The duty call would give him the opportunity to see her again, to gauge how she reacted to him. Out of habit, and a little fear instilled by the thought of encountering Ann Sullivan, he wiped his feet outside the kitchen door. His knock was answered by a harried call to come in. When he did, fear turned to pleasure.

Mrs. Williamson was exactly as he remembered. Broad back to the room, big, capable hands stirring something wonderful on the huge six-burner stove. The bowl of black hair atop her head wouldn't have stirred in an earthquake.

The room smelled of spices and flowers and the mouth-watering aroma of whatever she had in the oven.

''Got any cookies around this place?''

She turned, wooden spoon in one hand. Her wide face creased into a huge welcoming smile. She'd always had a soft spot for lost boys. And bad ones.

''Well, if it isn't Michael Fury himself. I wondered when you'd come knocking on my door.''

''Ready to marry me now?''

''I might just be.'' She sent him a saucy wink. ''You've grown up handsome enough.''

Because with her he'd always felt at home, he crossed the room, took one of her big hands in his, and brought it to his lips. ''Name the time and place.''

"Oh, you're a one." From anyone else, the sound that bubbled out would have been called a giggle. "Sit down there, boy, and tell me all about your adventures." As she always had, always would, when one of her children came to visit, she took cookies out of the bin, arranged them on a plate. "Selling horses now, are we?"

"Yes, ma'am. Just did." He patted his pocket while she poured his coffee.

"That's fine, then. And you haven't found a woman to suit you in all your travels?"

"I've been holding out for you." He bit into a cookie, rolled his eyes dramatically. "Nobody bakes like you, Mrs. Williamson. Why should I settle for less than the best?"

She laughed again and gave him a vigorous slap on the back that nearly sent him headfirst into his coffee. "Oh, you're a bad one, Michael."

"So they always said. You still do those apple pies? The ones that bring tears of joy to a man's eyes?"

"If you behave yourself I might just send you one over." She went back to her stove and her stirring. "Our little Kayla's been spending a lot of time down at the stables lately."

"I'm going to marry her if you keep turning me down."

"She's an angel, isn't she?" She let loose a windy sigh. "Allison, too. Darling girl, sweet as you please and bright as buttons on a new suit. Miss Laura's done a fine job there. And by herself, too. *He* never paid any mind to them."

When you want information, Michael mused as he took another cookie, go to the source. Mrs. Williamson was a fount of inside information. "*He* isn't very popular around here, I take it."

She sniffed loudly. "And why should he be, I'd like to know? Fussy, stiff-necked, too good to say how do you do? Never gave a minute of his valuable time to those beautiful girls, either. And fooling around with his secretary, and God knows who else, on the side." She pressed a hand to her heart as it swelled with outrage. "I shouldn't speak of it. Not my place."

But he knew she'd speak of it plenty with a little prompting. ''So, Ridgeway wouldn't make father of the year?''

''Hah! He wouldn't make father of the minute. And as for husband, well, he treated our Miss Laura more like an accessory than a wife. Prissy about the staff, too, with his highfalutin ideas.''

Michael ran his tongue around his teeth. ''Laura stayed married to him for a long time.''

''She takes her promises and her duties seriously. That girl was raised right. Near to broke her heart when she filed for divorce, not that it wasn't the proper thing to do or that any of us regretted it for a blink. Good riddance, I say, and I said so straight out to Mrs. Sullivan. Now he's going to be marrying that redheaded cat. Well, they deserve each other, I say.''

To emphasize her sentiments, she rapped her spoon on the edge of the pan, letting the sound ring.

''I bet Ridgeway never got any cookies in your kitchen.''

''Hah! As if he'd have lowered himself to come inside the room. Master of the house, my eye. My hearing may not be what it was, but I hear what I need to hear, so don't think I didn't know he tried to make Miss Laura pension me off so he could hire himself some fancy Frenchman to cook his meals. But she wouldn't do it.''

Her face softened as she turned back. ''Our Miss Laura knows about loyalty, and about what's right. She's a Templeton, and so are her girls, whatever their name might be legal.''

She stopped, narrowed her eyes. ''There you've done it. Got me blabbing and haven't told me a thing. You haven't changed there, Michael Fury.''

''Nothing much to tell.'' She still brewed the best coffee in central California, he thought as he sipped. And the Templeton kitchen, despite its grandeur and shine, was still one of the coziest spots on earth. ''Been there, done that. Now I'm back.''

She could just imagine where he'd been, and what he'd done. Still, she saw in him what she'd always seen: a dark, broody-eyed boy brimming with potential.

"Back where you belong, you ask me. Been out gallivanting long enough."

"Seems like," he agreed and took another cookie.

"Going to make your mark this time around, are you?"

"That's the plan. You come on down to the stables while I'm here, Mrs. Williamson." He grinned wickedly. "I'll give you a ride."

She threw back her head, exploding with laughter just as the door swung open. Ann Sullivan stepped inside. The instant she spotted Michael, lounging at the table with cookies and coffee, her mouth tightened.

"I see you're entertaining, Mrs. Williamson."

"The boy just dropped in to visit." They'd worked together too long for Mrs. Williamson to miss the icy disapproval. Or to pay any heed to it. "Coffee, Mrs. Sullivan?"

"No, thank you. Miss Laura is in the solarium and would like some."

The door burst open behind her, and Kayla rushed in. "Mama said to—Hi!" Instantly distracted, she ran toward Michael, jumped in his lap. "Did you come to see us?"

"I came to talk Mrs. Williamson out of some cookies. And I needed to see your mom for a minute."

"She's in the solarium. You can go see her. I drew your picture. Do you want to see?"

"You bet I do." He kissed the tip of her nose, grinned. "What is it?"

"A surprise." Eager, she scrambled down. "I'm going to go get it. I'm going to tell Ali you came. Don't go away."

Ann stood where she was as Kayla bolted out. If she'd been blind, she would have been able to recognize the easy affection between man and girl. A considering look came into her eye. She was far from ready to soften, but she would consider.

"You can go on to the solarium if you remember the way," she said stiffly. "I'll bring the coffee."

"Fine. Thanks." He rose, equally stiff, until he turned

to Mrs. Williamson. "Thanks for the cookies. And that offer still holds."

"Get on with you."

He got on. He remembered the way to the solarium. The fact was, he realized, he remembered everything about Templeton House. Walking down the polished hallway, glancing into elegant rooms, was like stepping back in time. His time. His youth.

This was a constant, he thought. The soaring ceilings and ornate moldings, the carefully selected and lovingly tended furnishings. The sweep of the stairway in the main hall, the bowl of flowers set just so on a credenza. Candlesticks with their tapers burned down to varying heights.

In the parlor he noticed the quiet fire sizzling. The hearth was lapis, he remembered. Josh had told him that, had explained to him about the deep blue stone. There was a large crystal compote on the piano, a floor-spanning faded rug over the waxed wood.

Flowers everywhere, he observed, fresh and dewy from garden or greenhouse. Not just hothouse roses but simple daisies, sunny tulips. Their scents were subtle, an elemental part of the air.

He knew the Templetons had entertained with lavish parties in this house—he had even been permitted to attend a few. People as glamorous as gods had wandered through the rooms, under the arching doorways, spilled out onto flower-decked terraces.

The house he had grown up in could fit into a single wing of this one with room to spare. But it hadn't been the space that awed him. Or not as much, not nearly as much as the beauty of it. The way it stood looking out over cliffs and hills and banks of flowers. The way the tower speared up into the sky and the windows gleamed with light, day or night. And the rooms inside, streaming into other rooms, with an openness, a welcoming that he'd never been able to analyze.

Of permanence. A statement that he'd always understood said family mattered. At least to the Templetons. Despite its grandeur, Templeton House was a home. And that he had never had.

Shaking himself, he moved through the short breezeway that led to the solarium. There would be lush greenery there, flowers in profusion, padded chairs and lounges, glass tables, colorful mats. The rain that had just started to mist would patter on the glass walls, and you would see the fog rise over the cliffs.

It was exactly as he remembered. The glass walls swirled with fog and rain, lending the room a magical kind of intimacy. A single lamp was lit, casting a soft gold light. Music, something with weeping violins that he didn't recognize, spilled like tears from hidden speakers.

And there was Laura, curled on the pastel cushions of a high-backed wicker lounge. Sleeping.

Perhaps it was the atmosphere, the light, the fog, the music, the flowers, that made him feel as though he were stepping into a spellbound bower. He was rarely a fanciful man, but the sight of her sleeping there made him think of enchanted princesses, castles, and the magic of a kiss.

He bent over her, brushed the hair from her cheek, and laid his lips on hers.

She woke slowly, as an enchanted princess should. Her lashes fluttered, a faint flush rose to her cheeks. The sound that sighed through her lips to his was soft, lovely.

"Doesn't seem like a hundred years," he murmured.

Her eyes stayed on his, heavy, clouded, unfocused. "Michael?"

"Now either we live happily ever after or I turn into a frog. I can never keep the stories straight."

She lifted a hand to his face. Real, she thought. She wasn't dreaming. As reality began to seep in, her color deepened and she hastened to sit up. "I fell asleep."

"I figured that one out." And there were shadows under her eyes. He hated knowing that worry over her daughter gave her restless nights. "Long day?"

"Yes." Concern for Allison had given her some bad moments at three A.M. But so had the man who was studying her now. Then there had been her convention duties at the hotel, a glitch in a shipment at the shop, and a headachy session of sentence diagramming in the homework division. ''I'm sorry—''

The words slid down her throat as his mouth cruised over hers again. ''You made me think of fairy tales when I walked in here. Beauty sleeping.''

''That's Sleeping Beauty.''

''I know.'' His lips curved. ''I didn't have a close acquaintance with fairy tales, but I think I caught the Disney version somewhere. Let's see if I've got it right.''

When he would have kissed her again, she sprang to her feet. ''I'm awake.'' Too awake, she thought as her heart hummed in her throat. Too alive. Too needy.

''I guess that's the best we can do, for the moment. I was in the kitchen charming Mrs. Williamson out of her cookies. I actually came by to see you, but I'm weak.''

''No one can hold fast against her cookies.'' Well aware that she must look rumpled, she tried to smooth her hair.

''Don't. I like it mussed. You never seem to be mussed.''

''You ought to catch me after convincing the girls it really is bedtime now.'' But she made herself stop fussing. ''Kayla said that Judy Prentice was coming by this evening.''

''She did, with her husband and her daughter. Who, by the way, is quite a horsewoman. They bought a good mare. I think they'll work out well together.''

Pleased for him, she said, ''Oh, that's wonderful, Michael. Congratulations.''

He plucked a creamy white hibiscus from the bush beside the lounge and handed it to her. ''I came by to thank you.''

Absurdly touched, violently nervous, she stared at the blossom. ''I didn't do anything but mention your name, but you're welcome. Judy knows a lot of the horse set. I'm sure she'll pass your name along.''

''I'm counting on it. I'd like to take you to dinner.''

She shifted away a full inch. ''What?''

''I'm flush,'' he said, patting his pocket. ''And I owe you.''

''No, you don't. It was just—''

"I'd like to take you to dinner, Laura. I'd like to take you, period, but I think we'll have to do this along more conventional lines. You've been avoiding me."

"No, I haven't. Really." Or hardly at all. "I've been busy."

He imagined her social calendar was full enough. Committees, ladies' luncheons, the jobs she'd taken to fill her time. "I wouldn't imagine a Templeton would scare off so easy."

It was exactly the right switch to pull. "It isn't a matter of scaring off. I have a great deal to do."

"Then take another rain check. You let me know when you can squeeze me in."

When he started to rise, she touched his hand. "I don't mean to sound ungracious."

"You?" He smiled thinly. "Never."

"I wasn't expecting you to . . ."

"Move on you?" he suggested. "Last time I checked, I still had blood in my veins. If you're not interested, just say so. I can probably take a no."

"I don't know what I am, but it's not disinterested." She resisted, barely, tracing the hibiscus along her cheek. "And I don't think I'm prepared to deal with that gleam you just got in your eye. In fact, I know I'm not. I'm going to change the subject."

She drew a deep breath, willing to accept the embarrassment of having him grin at her. "Kayla told me you've been teaching her to ride."

"Is there a problem with that? I guess I should have asked you."

"No." She dragged her hand through her hair again. "No, there's no problem. I'm very grateful that you'd take the time and trouble. I don't want her pestering you, Michael."

"She doesn't pester me. In fact, I'm thinking about giving it ten or fifteen years and asking her to marry me."

Her smile came fast and warm. "She's so easy to fall for. She's so open and loving. She's full of you. Mr. Fury this, and Mr. Fury that. She's certain you're going to turn Bongo into some sort of dog genius."

"I'll have to work on that."

"That's what I wanted to discuss with you. I'd like to compensate you for your time, with Kayla. I—"

"Stop." He said it quietly, the steel of temper a sharp edge beneath. "I'm not a servant."

"I didn't mean that." Horrified that she'd insulted him, she rose again. "I only meant that if you're going to be taking so much of your time to—"

"It's my time, and I'll use it as I please. I don't want your damn money. I'm not for hire as a friend for your kids or as a temporary father substitute or whatever the hell you have in mind."

Now she went pale, very pale. "Of course not. I'm sorry."

"Christ, don't give me that wounded look. You make me feel as though I kicked a puppy." Frustrated, he jammed his hands in his pockets. Compensate him, for Christ's sake. The way you compensate a waiter for good service. He should have expected it. "Just leave it alone."

He spun away to stare out at the swirling fog. Keeping her face blank, Ann stepped inside with the coffee tray. Not by a flicker of the eye did she reveal she'd heard a great deal of that last exchange.

"Your coffee, Miss Laura. The girls are on their way down." If they hadn't been, Ann might have smothered conscience and eavesdropped a bit longer.

"Oh, thank you, Annie." She put a smile on her face, kept it there as her children came in. "I believe Kayla has something for you, Michael."

Kayla held the picture behind her back as she approached. "If you like it, you can hang it on your wall."

"Well, let's see." He took the heavy drawing paper from her, stared. "Damn."

Kayla's face dropped comically. Automatically, Laura put a hand on her shoulder to comfort.

"You don't like it." Kayla's head drooped. "I shouldn't

have drawn it so fast, but I wanted to do it while I remembered everything.''

''No, it's great.'' When he looked up from the drawing, his smile was huge. ''I was surprised, just like you said I'd be. It looks just like the lady, Kayla. Just exactly like her.''

''Really?'' With her tongue caught between her teeth, Kayla peeked over to critique her own work. ''Usually I draw things I see in books, or that are right there. But I thought if you had to sell her, you could have a picture so you'd always remember her.''

''It's beautiful.'' And nothing like the childish drawing he'd expected. She'd captured the mare's springy gait in the movement, the proud head. He supposed a trained eye could find room for improvement, things like perspective and range that he knew nothing of. All he knew was that he was impressed, and touched. ''It's my first original Templeton.''

If anyone noticed he hadn't used her legal name, there was no comment. Kayla merely preened and slipped a hand into his. ''I'll draw you more if you want.''

''I'd like that a lot.'' He scooted her onto his knee and looked at Allison. The older girl stared down at her feet, obviously miserable. ''You finish cleaning your room, Blondie?''

Her head came up, and so did her color. She eyed her sister, and her sister's big mouth with disdain. ''Yes, sir.''

''Good. I figured once you were off the bread-and-water routine, you might want to catch up with Kayla here on the riding lessons.''

Her mouth fell open before she remembered her manners. ''I'd like to learn to ride.'' Though it cost her, she turned to her mother. ''May I?''

''I think that would be a wonderful idea. I may have to brush up myself before the two of you get ahead of me.'' She laid a hand on Ali's shoulder. The stiffness faded reluctantly, but it faded. ''Thank you, Michael. We'll see what we can do to meld our schedules.''

''Mine's flexible.'' After a quick bounce, he set Kayla on her feet and rose. ''But right now I've got to get back.''

"Your coffee," Laura began.

"I'll take a rain check." His smile spread slowly. "You know about redeeming rain checks, don't you, Laura?"

"Yes." How did a mother handle sexual flutters with her two daughters looking on? Laura didn't have a clue. "Thank you for coming by."

"My pleasure."

"I'll see you out," Ali said with great dignity.

To his credit, Michael nodded gravely. "Thank you."

"I'll go, too. Mr. Fury, do you think you can teach Bongo to shake? Uncle Byron's dogs can shake."

Alone, Laura sat again as her daughter's bright voice echoed away. Experimentally, she pressed a hand to her stomach. Yes, it was churning. And to her heart. Yes, it was pounding.

How did a woman with absolutely no point of reference go about redeeming a rain check for an affair?

She had absolutely no clue about that, either.

Chapter Eight

The sun tore away the clouds and fog and the chill of coastal winter. While reports of a Midwest ice storm hit the news, Monterey enjoyed soft blue skies and a breeze that held teasing hints of spring.

On the cliffs, the wind was rougher, whipped in from the sea and tasting, as Laura always thought, of adventure and romance.

The winter grass rustled, and the waves roared, fuming water like froth from a bottle of champagne. Once a young girl had died there, through her own will. An old man had grieved there, through his own memories. And somewhere, gold hidden for more than a century waited to be found.

Laura enjoyed the company and the leisure as much as the search. Nearly every Sunday, she and her friends and her daughters came here with the shadow of Templeton House behind them to look for Seraphina's dowry.

''We could buy a horse when we find it, couldn't we?'' Kayla looked up from her enthusiastic scraping with a garden spade. ''From Mr. Fury. I know how to take care of a horse now. He showed us. You have to feed them and water them, and brush them and clean out their feet—''

''Hooves,'' Ali put in, feeling superior. ''You pick out their hooves. And you have to exercise them, too. And muck out their stalls.''

''Have you been mucking out, Ali?''

Ali shrugged her shoulders, hoping the new earrings in her pierced ears showed off to their best advantage. ''Mr. Fury says it's part of the job. You don't just get on and ride, you have to take care of them.''

''Yes, you do.'' The father-daughter supper was behind them, and Ali had survived it. Laura touched Ali's hair. ''When I was a girl and we had horses, I mucked out my share of stalls. I never minded.''

''Couldn't we have some?'' She'd tried not to ask. Ali wasn't quite willing to forgive her mother for letting her father go away and marry some other woman. ''Mr. Fury's going to build his own stables and house. When he goes away, he'll take the horses.''

''We'll talk about it.''

''You say that when you mean no.'' Ali rose from her crouch.

''I say that,'' Laura returned, praying for patience, ''when I mean we'll talk about it. Right now Mr. Fury's renting the stables and there isn't really time for another horse.''

''He'd sell us one of his if you wanted. If you really wanted.'' Ali turned her back and went over to where Margo and Kate ran the metal detector.

''She's still mad because he's getting married soon,'' Kayla said.

''Hmm?''

''You know, Mama. He's marrying Mrs. Litchfield.''

''I'll talk to her again.'' Though she could think of nothing left to say on the matter. ''Are you mad, baby?''

''No, I don't care if he marries her. I don't know why he wants to when she has that mean smile. And when she laughs it hurts my ears.''

With an effort, Laura muffled a laugh of her own. Leave

it to Kayla, she thought, to sum up Candy in such accurate terms. "People get married because they love each other." Or so she'd once believed, Laura mused as she looked out to sea. So she'd once dreamed.

"Are you going to be in love with someone and get married?"

"I don't know." Dreams change, Laura reminded herself. "You can't plan these things."

"I heard Mrs. Williamson tell Annie that Mrs. Litchfield planned to catch Dad in her trap, and how he deserved it."

"Ah." She cleared her throat. "She just meant that they were going to be happy together."

"I guess." Kayla thought no such thing but was wise enough to let it pass. "I'm going to get some lemonade from the thermos. Do you want some?"

"That would be nice." Laura rose as well and wandered over to her friends.

"I'm not skimming, damn it." Blowing hair out of her face, Margo continued to run the detector. "I'm doing it the way I always do."

"Half-assed." Kate rolled her eyes as Ali giggled. "Sorry."

"She's been hanging around the gym too much," Margo told Ali. "Picking up bad language along with locker room sweat."

"You've got too much jewelry on," Kate complained. "You're going to send the thing into convulsions."

"Bitch and moan." Margo winced herself. "Sorry, Ali. Here, why don't you wear my bracelet a while?"

"Can I?" Thrilled, Ali watched her glamorous aunt transfer the heavy gold links, then held up her arm, watching the sun bounce off them. "It's so beautiful. It glitters."

"What's the point in wearing it if it doesn't glitter?" She winked and flicked a finger at Ali's earlobe. "Those are pretty."

"Mama got them for me. I got an A on my science report." She glanced toward her mother, and her smile bloomed hesitantly. "She said I worked hard and deserved a reward."

"You did—and you did," Laura confirmed. "Would you mind helping Kayla get lemonade? I think we're all dry."

"All right." She took a step, stopped. "Would you like a sandwich?"

It was an apology, Laura realized, and though she wasn't hungry, she smiled. "That would be terrific. Why don't you and Kayla spread out the blanket and we'll take a break for lunch?" Laura murmured as her daughter picked her way around rocks, "She's trying. It's hard for her to accept."

"If I had the prospect of Candy Cane as my stepmother, I'd find it more than hard," Kate muttered.

Margo merely lifted one elegant shoulder. "Candy's too much in love with Candy to give them the time of day. And the girls are smart enough not to give her any more than that back."

"I suppose it would be easier if they liked her—a little." Then Laura sighed and gave in. "And it's probably selfish of me to be glad they don't. But I'm glad they don't."

"Anyone want to take bets on how long the Peter and Candy show runs? My take is—" A little dizzy, Kate sat down abruptly on a rock. "There it goes again."

"Are you all right?" Kate had a history of ulcers, and now Laura leapt to her side. "Is it a flare-up?"

"No." Kate took easy breaths, waiting for the world to settle. Yes, there was the sky, nicely blue and back in its proper place. "You know what? I think I'm pregnant."

"Pregnant?" With a thud, Margo set the detector aside and crouched in front of Kate. "How late are you? Have you taken a test?"

"Late enough." Kate closed her eyes, tried to analyze what she was feeling. "I bought one of those instant things at the drugstore. I haven't used it because I'm afraid it'll say I'm not."

"You're using it first thing tomorrow," Margo ordered, and she cupped Kate's face in her hand to take a long look. "Morning sickness?"

"Not really. A little queasy when I first get up, but it passes." She shifted her eyes. "The two of you stop looking at me with those smug, knowing grins.''

''Not a chance.'' Laura sat beside her. ''What does Byron say?''

''I haven't mentioned it. In case I'm wrong. I don't want to be wrong,'' she said shakily. ''I know we've only been married a few months and we have all the time in the world, but I don't want to be wrong.''

''Another sure sign,'' Laura declared. ''Unstable and heightened emotions.''

Then she heard a voice, slow, deep, and male, and admitted that pregnancy wasn't the only cause of unstable and heightened emotions. Lust was definitely right up there in the running.

With her hand still on Kate's shoulder, she got to her feet.

''Is this club for women only?''

''Depends.'' Margo went to automatic purr. ''On the man. Want to help us look for treasure, Michael?''

''You all would be pretty ticked if I got lucky and found it first shot, after all the time you've put in.''

''He has a point.'' Kate reached up to pat Laura's hand, signaling that she was fine now. ''Anyway, men just don't get Seraphina's dowry. Do they, Mick?''

''Seems to me if she'd had one, she'd have been better off doing something with it instead of burying it somewhere and taking a header off a cliff.''

''See?'' Her point made, Kate rose. ''I'm going to check out lunch. Rumor is Mrs. Williamson made potato salad.''

''I'll give you a hand.'' Enjoying the tension that had leapt into the air, Margo decided to let it hum. She sent Michael a quick wink before following Kate.

''I'd gone upstairs to make some calls,'' Michael began before Laura could retreat. ''Looked out the window and saw five pretty girls scattered over the cliffs. It was hard to think about going back to work without getting a closer look.''

''We try to spend a few hours out here every Sunday. So far we've found two coins. Or rather Margo found one and Kate found one. The girls and I are batting zero.''

"Is it important to you? Finding gold?"

"The hunt's important. And the mood." She shifted her gaze to the sea. "The possibilities. I imagine her there, that young girl standing on the edge of the cliff thinking she had nothing left to live for."

"There's always something to live for."

"Yes, there is." She did retreat, the few bare steps the rocks allowed, when he lifted a hand to her face. "I should help with lunch. You're welcome to have some if you like."

"I wanted to talk to you about the girls, if you have a minute."

"Oh." The wariness in her eyes became concern. "If they're getting in your way—"

"Laura," he said patiently. "Do you really think you're the only one who can appreciate their company?"

"No, of course not." Annoyed with herself, logic hampered by rampaging emotions, she dropped her hands to her sides. "What is it?"

"I've been giving them a few pointers in the saddle. Kayla . . ." He glanced back, grinning as he watched the little blond head bob. "She's a pistol. She'd be doing bareback jumps if I let her."

"Please." Laura shuddered. "My heart."

"Kid wants to gallop full out in the worst way. Wants everything full out. You gotta admire that. But she listens. She learns. I'm crazy about her."

Laura blinked against surprise and sunlight. "She . . . she's full of Mr. Fury and his horses every time she comes back from the stables." Determined to relax, she sat on the rock, and barely jolted when he joined her. "She's starting to lose interest in her dance lessons."

"I don't want to mess with your plans."

"No." Smiling now, Laura shook her head. "She only wanted them because Ali had them. That's Kayla, always determined to keep up."

There were tiny blue flowers fighting out of a crack in the rock toward the sun. In an absentminded move, Michael plucked one and offered it. ''Did you get her that drawing instructor?''

Surprise again flitted into her eyes. How odd that he should remember those little family details. ''As a matter of fact I did find someone.'' She glanced down at the bloom in her hand, wishing she could take those habitual offer of flowers as casually as he did. ''She'll start next week.''

''Kid's got real talent. Me, the only way I can draw is with a ruler. About Ali.''

''She's going through a difficult time. She's not as flexible as Kayla, or as resilient. She's so easily bruised.''

''She'll come around.'' He took her hand, playing with her fingers. ''The riding lessons. I don't know how far you want me to push it.''

With a sigh, Laura studied her older girl, sitting so ladylike on the ground beside Margo. ''If she isn't cooperating, there's no reason for you to push anything.''

''Laura, she's a natural.''

''Excuse me?''

''The kid sits a horse like she's been doing it all her life. She's got this kind of baffling grace. And she listens to me as if what I'm saying is etched in stone. It's scary. If you want to pursue this for her, you might want to look for someone with more experience in teaching than I have.''

Staggered, Laura stared at him. ''She never says anything. Kayla comes back talking a mile a minute, and Ali just shrugs and says it was fine.''

''Kayla's a bullet. Ali's a song. She'll sing when she's ready.''

How could he know her children so well? she wondered. How could he see inside and understand their hearts so well, so quickly?

''She trusts you,'' Laura said slowly. ''Trust isn't easy for Ali these days. If you don't mind, I'd like you to stick with it. She needs something so badly right now, and I don't seem to have whatever it is.''

Annoyed, he cupped a hand under her chin and turned her face to his. ''You're wrong. You have exactly what it is. She's only blaming you because she knows you'll take it. You'll be there.''

He dropped his hand, resisted getting up to pace. He wasn't a damn shrink, but anyone with eyes could see the woman needed something. ''I went through a period when I blamed my mother for a lot of things. But I never said it to her. Because I didn't know if she'd take it. I didn't know if she'd be there.''

Perhaps that was how he saw, she mused. How he understood. ''Maybe it's easier for you to understand her. I never had anyone let me down. My mother and father were—are—as steady as this rock. Never faltered, never wavered. Never failed.''

And she had done all of those, Laura thought. Faltered. Wavered. Failed. It wasn't a simple matter to regain balance after you'd been rocked.

''Then again,'' he said, watching her face, ''maybe she blames you because you blame you. Get a grip, Laura.''

''You've never been married,'' she shot back.

''Yeah, I was. Six months.'' He lifted a brow as he rose. ''And I didn't fuck it up alone. I'll keep working with the kids,'' he continued when she said nothing. ''But I've got a condition.''

He'd been married? Her mind swung there, back, tried to keep up. ''All right. What is it?''

''Stop hiding in the house. Come down and see what they're doing.'' Amused at both of them, he took the flower from her, tucked it in her hair. ''I'm not going to jump you in front of your children.''

''I haven't been hiding, and I never assumed your behavior in front of them would be inappropriate.''

''Christ, it's fascinating to watch you click into that lady-of-the-manor mode. I don't know whether to pull my forelock or jump you after all.''

Cool as snowmelt, she inclined her head. ''I'd prefer you do neither. Now that we've spoken, I certainly will come down and check on the girls' progress. I appreciate your bringing me up to date.''

''Yes, ma'am, Ms. Templeton.''

''Sarcasm suits you, Michael.''

He grabbed her arm before she could stride past him. ''So do you.'' He said it softly, his face close to hers. ''By Christ, so do you. You want to be careful playing princess to peasant with me, Laura. Puts my back up. Makes me want to prove something.''

''You don't have anything to prove to me. Now let go of my arm.''

''When I'm finished.'' He preferred her like this, the challenge of her, encased in ice. The wounded woman made him feel weak and clumsy and eager to soothe.

''Let me remind you who you're dealing with, in case you've forgotten,'' he continued. ''I like to break rules, and if someone puts up a barrier I like to step over it, just for the hell of it. When I'm pushed, I push back. Harder. And meaner.''

She didn't doubt it, any of it. The man who faced her now looked capable of anything—sins, crimes, atrocities. When she had time to think, she would analyze what warped part of her was attracted to just that facet of him. For now, escape would have to substitute for valor.

''I appreciate the reminder. Don't let me keep you from your work.''

''You won't.'' In a rapid shift of mood that left her baffled, he brought her clenched fist to his lips. Watching her, he pried it open, pressed his mouth to the palm. ''Don't forget, sugar, you're still holding that rain check.''

He strolled off, pausing long enough at the picnic blanket to steal a sandwich and make the girls giggle. When there was enough distance, and she was sure the heat had died from her cheeks, she went over to join her family.

''Mr. Fury kissed your hand, Mama,'' Kayla announced. ''Just like in the movies.''

''He was just being funny.'' Laura took a glass of lemonade to ease her dry throat. ''He was telling me how well both of you are doing with the riding lessons.'' Though her stomach was still jumping, she casually chose a slice of apple. ''I think he's enjoying them as much as you are.''

''They're all right.'' Though she pretended disinterest,

Ali studied her mother from under her lashes. The hand kiss hadn't looked at all funny to her. And her mother had a flower in her hair.

"Michael seems to think both of you are doing more than just all right."

"You ought to get back into riding yourself, Laura." Delighted with the progress, Margo nibbled on a cube of cheese. No, that palm buss hadn't looked funny. It had looked perfect.

"I'll think about it." Because she wanted to watch Michael climb the hill back to Templeton House, she looked deliberately west, out to sea.

She couldn't sleep. Being bone-tired didn't seem to make any difference. Laura wanted to believe that it was because the night was so clear, so full of stars, that it would be a shame to waste it. But she knew it was the dreams that kept her from bed.

She had begun to dream of him, and the content, the detail of the content, both shocked and amazed her.

She could, with concentration, control her thoughts during the day. But how could she control what snuck into her dreams?

They were so . . . sexual. "Erotic" was too tame, too formal a word for what went on in her head during sleep.

She should have been able to accept them, laugh at them, even share them with her friends. But she could do none of those things. Quite simply, she mused as she wandered the silent garden, because she had done none of those *things* that her subconscious created.

That rough, sweaty, elemental sex was a far cry from the dreams of her girlhood—except for those few scattered and shocking dreams she'd had about Michael as a girl. Those had been hormonal aberrations, Laura assured herself, not wishes. And they were best forgotten. In any case, most of her dreams had been soft, lovely, when she'd imagined love in all its forms to be tender and sweet. There'd been no ripping of fabric, no bruising hands or frantic cries of release in her innocent fantasies.

And none, she thought with a grimace, in the reality of her marriage.

Peter had never torn her clothes, dragged her to the ground, driven her to screams. He had, long ago, been tender, almost sweet. Then he had been disinterested. She would take the blame for that, for being too inhibited, too naive, too rigid perhaps to inspire in him unthinking lust. It was easier to accept, and perhaps to start to forgive, his faithlessness now that she understood those darker needs.

Now that those darker needs had been awakened in her.

But dreaming of wild sex and acting on such dreams were still two different matters. She slipped her hands into the pockets of her jacket, breathed in the night, and hoped to cool her thoughts before bed.

She would not go to Michael. Whether it was cowardice or wisdom, she would not go to him. He was beyond her scope, she decided as she walked through the arbor and studied the dark stables with the swirl of fog at their base. He was both too dangerous and too unpredictable for a woman with her responsibilities.

And despite the years he had been Josh's friend, she didn't know him. Certainly didn't understand him. Couldn't risk him.

So she would be what she had been raised to be: a strong woman who understood and met her obligations. She would fill her life with what she had been so fortunate to be given. Children, home, family, friends, work.

She needed nothing else. Not even in dreams.

She saw the lights flash on in the apartment above the stables. Like a voyeur caught spying, she slipped back into the shadows. Did he dream too? she wondered. Of her? Did those dreams make him restless and achy and confused?

Even as she wondered, she saw him come bursting out of the door, hair flying. His boots echoed hard on the steps as he raced down them and into the stables.

She stood where she was a moment longer, unsure. But something was wrong. A man like Michael Fury didn't run in a panic for nothing. He was a tenant of Templeton House, she reminded herself. And she was a Templeton.

Self-preservation could never hold out against duty. Laura ran across the lawn with the moonlight chasing her.

There were lights on inside the stable now. Laura shielded her eyes against the glare, but she didn't see him. She hesitated again, wondering if she should leave. Then she heard his voice, the words low and unintelligible. But the concern in them was clear. She walked down the wide brick aisle and looked into the open foaling stall.

He was kneeling beside a horse, his hair falling forward like a black wing to curtain his face. His dark T-shirt was rumpled and revealed arms toughly muscled and the faint shine of a thin scar above his left elbow. She saw his hands, wide, tanned, gently stroking the bulge of the mare's heaving sides.

She had a moment to think that no woman on the brink of childbirth could ever want for more loving comfort, then she was inside, kneeling with him.

"She's going to foal. There, sweetheart." Instinctively, she went to the mare's head. "It's all right."

"Always in the middle of the night." Michael blew his hair out of his eyes. "I heard her upstairs. Guess I've been listening for her."

"Have you called the vet?"

"Shouldn't need him. Last time he checked her out, he said it should go smooth." In an impatient move, he tugged a bandanna out of his back pocket. "What are you doing here?"

"I was in the garden. It's all right, baby," she murmured, shifting the mare's head onto her lap. "I saw your lights go on, and then you ran down here. I was afraid something was wrong."

"She'll be fine." But it was Darling's first, and he was as nervous as an expectant daddy pacing a waiting room. "Go on to bed. This sort of thing isn't usually complicated, but it's plenty messy."

She lifted both brows, and the amusement in the eyes under them was clear and bright. "Really? I wouldn't know anything about that, as I've only been through childbirth twice myself. And when the stork arrived, he was very neat and polite.''

Her attention shot back to the mare as a new contraction began. ''All right now, all right. We'll get through this, honey. He doesn't know anything, does he?'' she murmured, as the mare rolled pain-filled eyes toward Laura's. ''He's just a man. Let him try it, yeah, let him try it once, then we'll see what he has to say.''

''Guess I've been told.'' Torn between worry and laughter, Michael rubbed his chin. ''Should I go outside and pace? Boil water, buy cigars?''

''You could go make some coffee. This could take a while.''

''I can handle this, Laura. I've done it before. You don't have to stay.''

''I'm staying,'' she said simply. ''And I'd like some coffee.''

''Okay.''

When he rose, she noted that he'd taken the time to zip his jeans, but not to button them. With twelve hundred pounds of horse in labor between them, it was no time to have her mouth watering. She looked back, a little blindly, at the mare.

''I take mine black. Please.''

''I'll be right back.'' He paused at the stall door. ''Thanks. I can use the help, and the company. She's . . . special.''

''I know.'' Her lips softened into a smile as she looked up at him. ''I can see that. Don't worry, papa, you'll be handing out cigars by morning. Oh, Michael, what's her name?''

''Darling.'' Embarrassment didn't suit him, but he shrugged. ''She's Darling.''

''Yes, she is.'' Laura continued to smile as his boot heels clicked on the bricks. ''And so,'' she murmured, ''much to my surprise, are you.''

Chapter Nine

It wasn't precisely the way he'd imagined spending the night with her. When he allowed himself to think of it, and he allowed himself often, the circumstances were quite different.

Yet here they were, sweaty, exhausted, and united.

She had more stamina than he'd given her credit for. They'd been at it nearly four hours, the mare rising to pace, lying down again, sweating as she moved from the first to the second stage of her labor.

Laura hadn't wilted. And while the coffee was beginning to jangle his nerves, Laura was calm as a lake.

"Why don't you take a walk?" she suggested. She sat comfortably on the hay, her arms circling her knees, her gaze on the mother-to-be.

"I'm fine." His brow creased as he wiped down the mare. Since he'd tied his hair back, Laura could see his eyes perfectly.

"You're a wreck, Fury."

Okay, okay, he knew it. He didn't care to have it pointed

out to him though. His eyes darkened moodily when they shifted to Laura. ''I've done this dozens of times.''

''Not with her you haven't. She's holding up better than you are.''

Hell with it, he decided, and eased back a moment to stretch his back. ''I'll never understand why something this basic takes so damn long. How do you stand it?''

''A woman in this position doesn't have much choice,'' Laura said dryly. ''And you just focus everything on what's happening to your body. Inside your body. Nothing else exists. Wars, famines, earthquakes. Hell, they're nothing compared to this.''

''Guess not.'' He struggled to relax, to remind himself that Nature generally knew what she was doing. ''First time I went through a foaling, I thought of my mother. Figured I should have cut her more slack. I'd rather have my tongue pulled out than go through this.''

''Actually, it's more like having your bottom lip pulled out and over your head until it reaches the nape of your neck.'' She laughed as he went white.

''Thanks for the visual.''

It would do him good to talk, she decided. And until the mare's water broke, they had time. ''Your mother moved to Florida, didn't she?''

''Yeah, her and Frank. That's the guy she married about ten years ago.''

''You like him?''

''It's hard not to like Frank. He just goes with the flow and manages to turn the current in his direction without making waves. They're good for each other. Up to him her taste in men sucked.''

''The divorce was hard on you?''

''No, it was hard on her.'' Idly, he picked up a shaft of hay, spun it through his fingers. Then, to Laura's amusement, he handed it to her as he had the flowers.

''I don't suppose it's ever easy. Divorce.''

''I don't see why. Something doesn't work, it doesn't work. My father cheated on her from the get-go, never troubled to hide it. She just wouldn't let go. Never could figure that either."

"There's nothing mysterious about wanting to hold a marriage together."

"There is when it's a sham. He wouldn't come home a couple nights running, then he'd show up. She'd rant and throw things, and he'd just shrug and plop down in front of the TV. Then one day he didn't come back at all."

"Ever?"

"We never saw him again."

"Michael, I'm sorry. I didn't realize." Though her hands continued to soothe the mare, her attention was on him.

"Didn't matter to me. Or not much." He shrugged. "But she was miserable, and pissed, and that made it hard to be around her. I didn't spend much time at home for a couple of years. Hung out with Josh, drove Mrs. Sullivan crazy thinking I was going to corrupt him."

She remembered him. Remembered well, now that she allowed herself to, those brooding, dangerous eyes. And her reaction to them. "My parents always liked you."

"They were cool. It was an eye-opener, watching them, you, what went on in Templeton House. Whole different world for a cliff rat like me."

And the world he was describing was different for her. "Your mother married again."

"She hooked up with Lado when I was about sixteen. I hated the son of a bitch. I always figured she picked him because he was the opposite of the old man. He was sloppy and mean and jealous. Gave her lots of attention," Michael muttered, and his eyes were dark with memory. "Lots of it. He used to knock her around."

"God! He hit her?"

"She always denied it. I'd come home and she'd have a black eye or a split lip and make up some lame excuse about tripping or walking into a door. I let it go."

"You were just a child."

"No, I wasn't." His eyes, stormy now, latched onto hers. "I was never a child. By the time I was sixteen, I'd already seen and done more than you will in your lifetime, sugar. It suited me fine.''

''Did it?'' She kept her eyes level. ''Or did it keep you from feeling helpless?''

He nodded. ''Maybe both. But the fact is, Mrs. Sullivan always had the right idea. I was a bad companion, and if Josh hadn't been who and what he was, we both would have ended up in juvie. Or worse. Fact is, he's the reason I didn't.''

''I'm sure he'd appreciate the testimony, but I'd think you had something to do with that yourself.''

For the first time in months he had a strong, nagging urge for tobacco, even patted his pocket before remembering that that part of his life was over. ''You know why I took the hitch with the merchant marine?''

''No.''

''Well, I'll tell you. One night I came home. Been drinking a little, me and Josh and a couple of others down at the cliffs. We were eighteen and stupid, and I'd copped a six-pack from Lado. So I walked into the house, feeling a nice comfy buzz, and there he was, that big fat bastard, using his fists on my mother because she hadn't kept his supper warm or some such shit. I wasn't going to let him get away with it, figured it was my job to look out for her. So I took him on.''

Absently, he brushed a finger over the scar above his eye. Laura's glance flickered at the movement, then held steady.

''He outweighed me, but I was young and fast, and I'd already had my share of dirty fights. I beat the hell out of him. And I kept beating the hell out of him even when he was down and bleeding and unconscious and I couldn't feel my own hands pounding into his face. I'd have killed him, Laura, that's a fact. I'd have beat him until he was dead and I wouldn't have looked back.''

She couldn't envision it, wasn't equipped to. But she thought she could understand it. ''You were protecting your mother.''

''Started out that way, but then I just wanted him dead.

I wanted to make him dead. That was inside me. I would have finished him if she hadn't stopped me. And while I was kneeling over him, while she was holding a hand to her face where it was bleeding and bruised, she told me to get out.''

''Michael.''

''She told me I had no right to interfere. She said a lot of things along those lines, so I got out and left her with him.''

''She didn't mean it.'' How could a mother, any mother, turn on her own child? It was impossible to absorb. ''She was upset and afraid and hurt.''

''She did mean it, Laura. At that moment she meant every word. Later, she changed her mind. She got rid of him and pulled herself together. She got together with Frank. But by then, I was gone, and I've never really been back. Do you know where I went that night I left home?''

''No.''

''I went to Templeton House. I don't know why. It was just there. Mrs. Williamson was in the kitchen. She fussed over me, cleaned me up. She talked to me, and she listened to me. She fed me cookies.'' On a long breath he rubbed his hands over his face. He hadn't realized so much of that night was still inside him. ''She probably saved my life. I don't know what I would have done if she hadn't been there. She told me I had to make something out of myself. Not that I had a choice, or that here were my options, just 'Boy, you've got to make something out of yourself.' ''

''She's always had a soft spot for you, Michael.'' And he deserved one, she thought now. He deserved comfort and care and understanding. Poor, lost boy.

''She was the first woman I ever loved.'' He plucked up another shaft of hay, and to kill the urge for a cigarette, chewed the tip. If he'd had a glimmer of Laura's description of him, he wouldn't have been amused. He'd have been appalled.

''Maybe the last woman,'' he added. ''She told me to go over to the stables, and she went up and got Josh. He and I sat in this place and talked all night. All fucking night.

Every time I talked about doing something crazy, he'd steer me back with that cool lawyer logic of his. The next day I signed up. I stayed here in the stables until I shipped out.''

''Here? You stayed here? Josh never said anything about it.''

''Maybe he understood client confidentiality even then. He always understood friendship. Mrs. Williamson brought me food. She and Josh were the only ones I ever wrote to while I was gone. She was the one who sent me word that my mother had kicked Lado out. I guess Mrs. Williamson went to see her. I never asked.''

He shook it off, grinned. ''You know, her cookies were my claim to fame on ship. Once a month this box would come, full of them. Once I was losing my shirt in a poker game and anted up her—what do you call them—snicker-doodles. I walked away flush.''

''She'd like hearing that.'' Taking the chance, she reached over the mare's neck and touched his hand. ''Any-one Mrs. Williamson takes under her wing deserves it. She recognizes fools, and she doesn't suffer them. You're a good man, Michael.''

He studied her, saw his advantage in her eyes. ''I could let you think that and get you into bed quicker.'' Then he smiled. ''I'm not a good man, Laura, but I'm an honest one. I told you what I've only told two other people in my life because I figure you ought to know what you're getting into.''

''I've already decided, for a variety of reasons, that I'm not getting into anything.''

''You'll change your mind.'' He shifted, winked cockily. ''They all do.''

And the horse's water broke in a gush that soaked the bedding. ''Zero hour,'' he snapped, nerves jangled. ''Keep to her head.''

Laura jolted back. The fatigue, the almost dreamlike state she'd drifted into while he was talking now burst into an adrenaline rush.

The first flood of fluid didn't alarm her. It was a natural process, just as the mare's plaintive whinnies were part of the whole. A process she had shared in, and one, though the mare's eyes rolled in fear and pain, that Laura knew she longed to experience again.

Laura buckled down to the task at hand, following Michael's terse orders without question and issuing some of her own.

"Here it comes. Hold steady, Darling. Almost over." He knelt in blood and birth fluid, laboring as hard as his mare, and those long, thin forelegs appeared. "I've got to give her a hand here, turn it some." Where was the damn head? "You got her?"

"Yes, I've got her." Sweat dripped into her eyes. "Do it. She's exhausted."

"It's coming." He got a grip on the slippery, gleaming limbs and reached inside the birth canal to rotate and ease. There, lying along the forelegs, was the head. "Come on, Darling, just a little more. Just a little more."

"Oh, God." Now there were tears mixed with the sweat on Laura's face as the foal slid out. "There he is."

Once the foal's shoulders were clear, Michael cleaned the membrane away from the nose. The foal was wet, still attached by the umbilical cord. Though Michael wanted to pull it clear, see for himself, he waited with Laura as the foal struggled free of the birth sac, and the cord broke as nature intended.

For a while, there was no sound in the stall but the mare's steadying breathing and her first soft, delighted whinny as she understood she had a child.

"He's beautiful," Laura murmured. "Just beautiful."

"She." Grinning, Michael swiped at the sweat on his face. "We got ourselves a girl here, Laura. A beautiful girl. God bless you, Darling, look what you did."

She looked, and with a mother's instinct climbed to her feet and began to clean her baby.

"It's lovely every time," Laura murmured, easing back so as not to interfere with the bonding. "You're not disappointed?" she asked Michael. "No stud?"

"She's got four legs and a tail, doesn't she? And her mother's coloring."

''Apparently you're not.'' She laughed, delighted with the look of stunned joy on his face, and held out a formal hand. ''Congratulations, papa.''

''The hell with that.'' Riding high, he yanked her into his lap and crushed his mouth to hers.

Instantly breathless. And dizzy. And weak. They were covered with sweat and blood, punchy from a night without sleep. The hay beneath them was filthy, the air thick and ripe.

And they were locked together like hope and glory.

He'd meant it only to share with her that heady exuberance, to thank her, in his way, for being a part of the moment. But he sank into her, into the need, into the heat, into those silky limbs that clung as though she were suspended over a cliff and he was her only salvation.

He was murmuring something, a jumble of the wild and reckless thoughts that jammed into his head. His hand streaked up her hip, closed possessively over her breast. She bucked, arched, moaned.

''Steady.'' He used the same patient, soothing tone he had with the laboring mare. But his teeth nipped at her jaw, scraped over the rampaging pulse in her throat and made the quiet order impossible.

''I can't.'' Can't breathe. Can't think. Can't let go. ''Michael.'' Dazed, she pressed her face against his throat. ''I can't.''

He could, he thought as the ache spread viciously. He could, and more. But he'd chosen his time and place poorly. She'd stood by him through the night, he reminded himself. Taking advantage of her now, as he was, only proved that even an honest man could lack integrity.

''I wasn't angling for a roll in the hay.'' He kept it light, whatever it cost him. ''Relax.'' Careful to keep his hands gentle, he shifted her. ''Look, our little girl's growing up already.''

The hands Laura clenched in her lap slowly loosened as she watched the foal struggle to her feet. After a few comical spills, she gained them.

''Have you . . .'' Laura wiped her palms hard on the

knees of her slacks to ease the tingling. ''Have you chosen a name for her?''

''No.'' He tortured himself a little by sniffing her hair. ''Why don't you?''

''She's yours, Michael.''

''The three of us brought her into the world together. What do you want to call her?''

She leaned back against him and smiled. The foal had already learned how to suckle. ''I had a mare when I was a girl. Her name was Lulu.''

''Lulu?'' He chuckled and buried his face in her hair.

Her eyes closed as he nuzzled, and her heart tilted. ''I rode her over the hills and into dreams.''

''Lulu it is.'' He got to his feet, pulled Laura to hers. ''You're pale.'' He brushed a thumb over her cheek, almost expecting it to pass through like a mist. ''The closer it got toward morning, the more fragile you looked. And the more I wanted to touch you.''

''I'm not going to be able to give you what you want.''

''You haven't got a clue what I want. If you did, you wouldn't have let me within a mile of Templeton House. But since both of us are too tired for me to explain it now, you'd better go get some sleep.''

''I'll help you clean up.''

''No, I can handle it. I'm not that tired, Laura, and you're too damn tempting. Go away.''

''All right, then.'' She stepped out of the stall and looked back. He stretched, a long, lean male wearing black with snug jeans unbuttoned at the waist. Everything that was female in her stirred. And yearned. ''Michael?''

''Yeah?''

His eyes were heavy, she noted. Exhausted. But they still focused on her in a way that made her blood tingle. ''No one's ever wanted me the way you seem to. I don't know how I feel or what to do about that.''

Those exhausted eyes went hot. ''That's not the kind of statement designed to make me want you less.'' Quick as a snake, and deadly, he reached out and snagged her by the shirt front. His free hand circled her throat, squeezed lightly as his mouth came down hard on hers. When he let her go, she stumbled back, her eyes clouded with arousal and panic.

"Go away, Laura," he repeated. "You're not safe here."

She walked blindly out of the stables, into the white flash of morning. Her bones felt bruised, her mind battered. Lifting an unsteady hand, she brushed her fingertips over her swollen mouth. Felt him there. Tasted him there.

Even as she walked toward Templeton House, she looked back over her shoulder and wondered if she wanted to be safe after all. She always had been, hadn't she, and her life hadn't been a rousing success so far. Then again, she had the unsettling feeling that she was thinking with her glands, not with her head. God knew that's what she felt like now, one enormous pulsating gland.

That was a new experience, and she wasn't sure if she wanted to explore it further.

Before she could decide she stepped into the kitchen and all hell broke loose.

"Miss Laura. My God!" Ann leapt at her. While Laura goggled in shock, she was embraced fiercely, yanked back, patted down, and shoved into a chair at the kitchen table. "What did he do to you? That monster, that spawn of the devil. Where are you hurt, my baby?" Eyes wild, Ann smoothed Laura's tousled hair, patted her pale cheeks. "I knew there'd be trouble with the likes of him around, but never did I imagine . . . I'll kill him, kill him with my bare hands. See if I don't."

"What? Who?"

"She's in shock, Mrs. Williamson. The poor lamb. Fetch the brandy."

"Now, Mrs. Sullivan, calm yourself."

"Calm myself? Calm myself? Would you look at what he's done to our Miss Laura?"

After wiping her hands on her apron, the cook bustled over from the stove. "What happened, darling?"

"I was just—"

"I'll tell you what happened," Ann interrupted, the light of vengeance sword-bright in her eyes. "That man happened, that's what. Anyone can see she tried to fight him off. Oh, he'll pay, he will. When I get through with Michael Fury there won't be anything left to scrape off the bottom of a shoe."

"Michael?" Maybe it was fatigue, Laura thought hazily. Hadn't she just left Michael? "What did he do?"

Her lips in a thin, grim line, Ann sat, took Laura's hands in hers. "Now don't be ashamed, and don't worry. None of it was your fault."

"All right," Laura said slowly. "What wasn't my fault?"

"Sweetheart." Obviously the poor girl was trying to block out the horror of it, Ann thought. "Let's get your clothes off and see how bad things are. I'm praying that's his blood on your clothes."

"Blood?" Laura glanced down, looked at the mess of her cotton shirt and slacks. "Oh, Lord." And it began to come clear. "Oh, Lord," she said again and let out a long, wild laugh.

"The brandy, Mrs. Williamson. Fetch the brandy."

"No, no, no." Fighting for control, Laura grabbed Ann before the housekeeper could spring up to exact revenge. "It's not my blood, Annie, or Michael's either. The foal." She hiccupped, managed to get a grip on herself. "I helped Michael birth a foal last night."

"Well, then." Satisfied, Mrs. Williamson went back to her cooking.

"A foal?" Suspicion still gleamed in Ann's eyes. "You were down at the stables birthing a foal?"

"Yes, a filly. A beauty." She sighed and was tempted to lay her head on the table and drift off. Every drop of adrenaline had drained, leaving only floaty exhaustion. "It's a messy job, Annie. I suppose Michael and I both look like we've been in some sort of bar fight."

"Oh." Shaken, and mortified, Ann rose. "I'll get you some coffee, then."

"I've had about all the coffee my system can take for the next couple of years." She sobered then, took Ann's hands again. ''Annie, I'm surprised at you. Michael wouldn't hurt me.''

''I've told her the boy's got gold in him,'' Mrs. Williamson put in. ''But will she listen?''

''I know a rogue when I see one.''

''This rogue,'' Laura said quietly, ''spent the night worrying over a horse. He's taking his own time to teach my children to ride. He's kind to them, and attentive. And from what I've seen of the stables and his stock, he works harder than two men.''

Ann remembered the way little Kayla had run to him, and his easy response. But she set her jaw. She knew what she knew. ''A leopard doesn't change his spots, I say.''

''Maybe not. But a man can remake himself. If he's given the chance. However you feel about him, he is, for the moment, part of Templeton House.'' Dragging herself to her feet, Laura rubbed her hands over her gritty eyes. ''Now I need a shower and a little—'' When she dropped her hands her gaze fell on the clock over the stove. ''Oh, my God, seven-thirty? How can it be seven-thirty? I've got a nine o'clock meeting. The girls, are they up?''

''Don't you worry about the girls,'' Ann told her. ''I'll see that they're dressed and taken to school this morning. You just cancel that meeting, Miss Laura, and go to bed.''

''Can't. It's important. I'll make sure they're getting dressed and grab a quick shower. I can drop them at school on my way to work. See that they have their breakfast, please, Annie.''

''And yours, Missy?''

But Laura was already at a dash. ''Just coffee, thanks. I don't have time.''

''Taken on too much,'' Mrs. Williamson clucked as she whipped up batter for waffles. ''Keeps this up, she's going to drop flat on her face before much longer. You mark my words.''

And she wouldn't mind it if a certain young rogue caught her when she did. She wouldn't mind it one little bit.

''Shouldn't have been up all night worrying over someone else's business.''

"Mrs. Sullivan, you're a fine woman, but you're as stubborn as six mules when it comes to certain matters. And while you mark my words, I'll wager a month's pay you'll be eating your own soon enough."

"We'll see about that, won't we?" Miffed, Ann poured coffee for Laura and prepared to take it upstairs. "That boy is trouble."

"If he is," Mrs. Williamson said placidly, "it's the kind of trouble a smart girl dreams of having. Wish I'd had more of that sort of trouble in my life."

As Ann sailed out, streaming dignity behind her, Mrs. Williamson hummed a bright tune.

It wasn't that she didn't believe there'd been a foal born in the night. It was simply that Ann Sullivan preferred to see with her own eyes. She marched to the stables, grudgingly carrying the basket of muffins Mrs. Williamson had pressed on her. If she had her way, Michael Fury wouldn't be eating from the Templeton House kitchen for long.

She looked up at the apartment first, frowning a bit as she noticed the fresh paint on the trim. Just trying to ingratiate himself, that was all, she thought. Making himself handy and agreeable until he could wreak havoc. Well, he could pull the wool over everyone's eyes but hers.

She strode into the stables, something she had avoided doing since Michael's arrival. Surprise came first. The place was tidy as a drawing room and smelled not at all unpleasant, of hay and horses. She jolted when Max poked his head out and bumped her shoulder in greeting.

"Lord save us, you're big as a house." But his mild eyes made her smile, and checking over her shoulder first to make certain she was unobserved, she stroked his silky nose. "What a pretty boy you are. Are you the one who does all the tricks the girls are forever talking about?"

"He's one of them." When Michael stepped out of the foaling stall down the block, Ann dropped her hand and cursed herself for not looking around more carefully. "Want to try him out?"

"Thank you, no." Stiff as a lance, she moved forward. "Mrs. Williamson sent you some muffins."

"Yeah?" He took the basket, chose one. Steam poured out when he bit in. He could have whimpered in gratitude. "The woman is a goddess," he said with his mouth full. "I don't think you're playing Red Riding Hood, delivering goodies to the wolf, Mrs. Sullivan."

"A lot you know about fairy tales. She was waylaid by the wolf, an innocent girl on her way to her grandmother's."

"I stand corrected." Because she put his back up every bit as much as he put up hers, he went back into the stall to finish medicating the lactating mare and her foal.

"That's a fine-looking horse."

"She is. They are. Had a long night, didn't you, Darling?"

The stall didn't look like the site of a long, messy birth. The straw was clean as a whistle, and both mother and child were well groomed. Since it had been only an hour since Laura had stumbled into the kitchen, it seemed the boy hadn't been wasting his time.

"You've had one as well, Mr. Fury, from what I'm told. I'm surprised you're not snoring in your bed."

"I hope to be as soon as I finish up here. The horses need to be fed and watered first." Because he knew it would annoy her, he grinned over his shoulder. "Want to give me a hand?"

"I have my own duties to see to. You'll keep your own house." And he was apparently keeping it well, she admitted. Tidy habits earned Ann's respect. But . . . "Apparently you had no problem imposing on Miss Laura and keeping her up through the night."

Satisfied that mother and child were settled, he moved out, skirted around Ann's rigid form and began to deal with the feed. "No, I didn't."

"The girl needs her sleep."

"Well, she's getting it now."

"She's on her way to Monterey."

The scoop paused, grain dribbled as he turned back to

her. ''That's ridiculous. She was up all night.''

''She had an appointment this morning.''

''She was exhausted.''

''I know it.'' She was surprised that he did and that he seemed so annoyed.

''Stupid.'' He thrust the scoop back into the grain bin. ''She could get her hair or her nails done later.''

''Get her hair done, her nails?'' Disgusted, Ann slapped her hands on her hips. ''If that's what you think Miss Laura is about, you're stupid. And I've never thought otherwise. She's gone to work, you baboon, at the hotel. And this afternoon she's going to work at the shop. Then, if she's able to stand after you kept her up all night with your horse, she'll tend her children, then she'll—''

''She owns the damn hotel,'' he shot back. ''And the damn shop. And I imagine both could stand if she took a lousy day off.''

''She takes her obligations seriously. And she's got children to raise, doesn't she? Tuition to pay for, clothes and food to buy, bills to pay.''

''Templetons don't work for paychecks.''

''Laura Templeton does. Do you think she'd live off her family? Do you think that even after that heartless bastard took all her money she'd go crying to her parents?''

''What are you talking about, took all her money?''

''As if you didn't know.'' Now she sneered. ''As if all of Big Sur and Monterey and down to Carmel don't know that that man all but emptied all their bank accounts, and the stocks and bonds and properties before the divorce.''

''Ridgeway.'' His eyes flashed, dark, sharp, swords tilted for battle. ''Why isn't he dead?''

Ann sucked in a breath. On this, at least, she could agree even with a rogue. But she had said more than she'd intended. ''It isn't my place to gossip with a stablehand.''

''I'm not a stablehand, and you've never let your place stop you when it comes to me. Why did they let Ridgeway get away with it? Josh could have stopped it, the Templetons could have crucified him.''

"It's Miss Laura's business, and her choice." Ann folded her hands and closed her lips.

"It doesn't add up." He took the grain to Max, who was waiting patiently. "She's got to have family money to wade in. She's got that house, and servants. Nobody lives like that and worries about pennies."

Ann made a derisive sound. "Miss Laura's financial business is none of yours, Michael Fury. But if you've been thinking to soften her into letting loose of some of her money in your direction, you'll have to look elsewhere."

She recognized black fury in a man when she saw it, and also the rigid control that prevented it from spewing out. She'd expected the first, but never the second.

"So warned," he said and went back to feeding his horses.

She started to speak again. Had that been hurt beneath the boiling temper? No, she refused to believe it of a man like him. Still, she bit her lip, wondering how her words would taste if she was wrong and did indeed have to eat them.

"I'll leave you to your business."

When she left, he continued to measure grain, precisely. Then the scoop flew out of his hands, smashed against the stable wall with enough force to snap its handle off. In the stalls several of the horses stirred nervously. Max stopped eating long enough to look out and study his master.

"Fuck me," Michael murmured and rubbed his hands over his face. "I've got enough to do. Goddamn woman should be in bed." He picked up the scoop, threw it again. Then went to find a new one.

Chapter Ten

By two in the afternoon, Laura had entered a new phase of exhaustion. It was almost pleasant, the way she seemed to float just an inch or so off the ground and the way the air around her seemed rather soft and fluid.

She'd handled her meeting with the conference chair for the writers' convention, had briefed her staff one last time for the influx of guests that would be arriving over the following two days, and had checked and rechecked the details with the banquet manager, maintenance and shipping, catering, room service, and housekeeping.

At one, she'd fueled herself with coffee and a candy bar and headed out to Pretenses. The one bright spot in the day had been Kate's semi-hysterical call just as Laura was racing out of the shower that morning.

"It's pink! It turned pink. I'm pregnant. Byron, put me down. Did you hear, Laura? I'm going to have a baby!"

She'd heard, and they'd laughed together, wept a little. Now Kate was wandering in a dream state around the shop.

"How about Guinevere if it's a girl?" Kate wondered.

''Byron's family has this tradition of choosing names from literature.''

''Guinevere was a weak-moraled round heel,'' Margo commented. ''She boffed her husband's best friend. But if that's the kind of thing you want—''

''I've always liked Ariel,'' Laura put in. ''From *The Tempest*.''

''Ariel De Witt.'' Kate took a notebook out of her pocket and jotted it down. Names were a serious matter, she thought, and had to be considered from all angles. Had to sound right, look right. Feel right. ''Hmmm.'' This one definitely had potential. ''Not bad.'' She pocketed her reading glasses as she looked at Laura. ''Laura's nodding off again.''

''I'm not.'' Caught, she jerked her lolling head up, struggled to focus. What the hell had they been talking about? ''Names,'' she said quickly, as though it was a pop quiz. ''Girl names for the baby out of literature. Hester, Juliet, Delilah.''

''And your prize for the correct answer is a complete home entertainment center.'' Kate arched a brow. ''Would you like to move on to round two and try for the trip to Honolulu?''

''Very funny.'' Laura resisted rubbing at her eyes like a cranky child. ''I rather like Juliet.''

''We'll put it before our distinguished panel of judges. Laura, take five before you fall on your face.''

''And if anyone knows the consequences of overextending herself,'' Margo put in, ''it's our pregnant pal with the dopey look in her eyes. Why don't you go in the back and catch a quick nap?'' As she studied Laura, Margo polished glassware. ''Spending the night with Michael's bound to sap a woman's energy.''

Laura winced and looked around to see if there were any customers within hearing distance. ''I told you we were birthing a foal, not tearing up the sheets.''

''Which only proves you've got your priorities skewed. Kate, I think that customer's ready for a little push.'' Margo nodded toward a man contemplating snuffboxes. ''He's got his eye on you,'' she added when Kate walked away.

''The customer?''

''Michael, Laura. Michael. If you don't have yours right back on him, you need to visit your optometrist.''

''I don't have time for . . . all right, maybe I've looked.''

Margo set down a Waterford water glass and turned away. Progress, she thought, at long last. ''And are you ready for a little push?''

Laura blew out a breath. ''He wants to— He wants me.''

''Surprise, surprise.''

''No, I mean, he said it. Just like that. How do you respond to something like that?''

''There are a variety of ways. Let's see, I believe I've tried them all.'' Margo tapped a finger on her cheek. ''Which of Margo's ploys would you prefer?''

''I'm not looking for a ploy.'' Because her knees kept disappearing on her, Laura sat down on the stool behind the counter. ''Margo, I've slept with one man in my life. I was married to him for ten years. I don't have any ploys, or ways, or answers.''

''No ploys, maybe, and good for you. But every woman has ways, and I think you have answers. Try this question. Are you attracted to him?''

''Yes, but—''

''The answer is yes,'' Margo interrupted, and kept one eye on a pair of customers contemplating the jewelry in the display along the side wall. ''You are a responsible, unattached adult female, who is attracted to an attractive unattached adult male.''

''That works fine if you're a rabbit.''

''It can work fine for people, too. Laura, there aren't any guarantees. You certainly know that. Yes, you could be hurt. You could also be happy. Or you could just get your oil checked.''

Snorting, Laura shook her head. ''Sex has always been easier for you than me.''

''I won't argue that, but I'm not particularly proud of it.''

''I didn't mean—''

"I know you didn't. I've slept with more than one man. Some of them were married to someone else. Sometimes it meant something, sometimes it didn't." She could shrug it off now, without regret or recriminations, because she understood that everything she'd ever done had carried her toward where she was now. "Josh is the only one who really mattered."

"Because you love each other," Laura said quietly. "We're not talking about love between Michael and me. It's just plain lust."

"And what's wrong with that?"

"I can usually figure out what's wrong with it, until he puts his hands on me, or kisses me."

As far as Margo could see, that was an excellent sign. "And then?"

"Then I just want, and I've never wanted like that. Everything's too hot, too fast." She shifted uneasily—even thinking about it stirred something inside her. "It's not comfortable."

"Hallelujah!" With a chuckle, Margo leaned closer. "Surprise yourself, Laura, go down to the stables some night and jump him."

"Right. That's just what I planned. Really, Margo, I could use some sensible advice here."

"Sensible's for retirement plans."

"Miss." One of the customers signaled. "Could I see this pin, please?"

"Of course." Taking up the keys, Margo moved away. "Oh, don't you adore Art Deco? That's a fabulous piece. I found it at an estate sale in Los Angeles. They said it once belonged to Marlene Dietrich."

Laura scanned the shop, stifled a yawn. They were busy, she noted, but not overwhelmed. Maybe she could sneak in a quick catnap. She slid off the stool, wandered toward a customer to ask if she needed help. Prayed the answer would be no. And then the door opened.

"Peter." She stopped in her tracks.

"I called your office at the hotel. They indicated I would find you here."

"Yes, this is one of my regular afternoons at Pretenses."

"Interesting." He hadn't been in before, had purposely stifled his curiosity about his ex-wife's little venture into shopkeeping. Now that he was here, he took a slow, measuring study.

Candy's description of the shop as a jumble of secondhand junk hadn't been quite accurate. Then again, understanding his fiancée's feelings toward Laura and her partners, he hadn't expected it to be.

Still, neither had he expected to find the place charming, peopled with well-to-do clientele as well as the tourist trade. He hadn't expected to be intrigued by the displays and more than a little envious of the merchandise.

"Well?" She recognized the appraisal. "What do you think?"

"It's different, isn't it? Certainly a change of pace for you." He looked at her again. Still cool and lovely, he mused. Odd, he'd never have believed Laura or either of her friends had the brains, the wherewithal or the imagination to create something so appealing, so successful.

"It's not a change of pace any longer." She refused to allow the way he studied her, and hers, to upset her. "It is the pace."

"I suppose you're enjoying the distraction."

"It's a business, Peter, not a distraction." Why should she expect him to understand Pretenses? He'd never understood his wife. Perhaps, she thought, he would deal much more comfortably with the new wife he'd chosen. "I doubt you came in to pick up a gift for Candy. She doesn't care for our stock as a rule."

"No, I came to speak with you."

He looked around again, noted the twisting staircase, the open balcony. Then he spotted Margo, watching him with a cold look of calculated dislike. He certainly didn't have to tolerate silent abuse from the daughter of a servant.

"Do you have an office, a private office we can use?"

"We use most of our space for merchandise." There was an office, of course, but she wasn't willing to speak with him in the shop. It was hers; it was not to be soiled with personal problems. ''Why don't we take a walk outside? Margo, I'll be back shortly.''

''If that's what you want.'' Margo smiled thinly at Peter. ''Be sure to give our best to your fiancée, Peter. Kate and I were just saying how delighted we are you've found your match.''

''I'm sure Candace will find your sentiments . . . entertaining.''

Laura merely shook her head at Margo, to forestall another, pithier comment. ''I won't be long.'' She opened the door herself, waited for Peter to step through onto the veranda.

He didn't care for Cannery Row or what he considered its carnival atmosphere. It was crowded, noisy, inconvenient. ''This is hardly private, Laura.''

She smiled at the people strolling on the sidewalk, the busy families, the snarled traffic.

''Nothing's so private as a crowd.'' Without asking him what he preferred, she moved to the curb to wait for a break in traffic. ''We find the location quite a plus. We lure in a lot of browsers who come to the Wharf, or wander down after a tour of the aquarium.''

Idly brushing her hair back as the breeze teased it, she started across the street, wanting to be closer to the sea. ''And, of course, it's pleasant being able to take a break now and again and come out to watch the water, feed the gulls.''

''You'll hardly keep a business afloat by daydreaming over the sea.''

''We're managing.'' She leaned on an iron rail, skimmed her glance over waves and boats. Gulls fluttered and sent a young girl into excited laughter when they landed one by one on her knee as she sat with a bag of crackers. ''What do you want, Peter?''

''To discuss Allison and Kayla.''

''All right.'' She turned to him, leaned back. ''Allison is doing very well in school. Her grades are exceptional. I'm sure you'd approve. Kayla's having a little trouble with math, but we're working on it.''

"That's hardly what I—"

"Excuse me, I'm not finished." She knew he wasn't interested, but she was revved. "Ali played Clara in the *Nutcracker* production put on by her ballet class last December. She was beautiful, and she cried afterward because her father hadn't come as he'd told her he would."

"I explained that I had a conflict."

"Yes, you did. Kayla played one of the mice, and she didn't care particularly whether you were there or not. I believe Ali will continue the dance lessons, and should be *en pointe* in another year. Kayla's losing interest, but her drawing is improving every day. They're also taking riding lessons now from Michael Fury. He's very impressed with both of them. Kayla had the sniffles a few weeks ago, but they didn't slow her down for long. Oh, and I've gotten them a puppy and two kittens."

He waited a beat. "Are you done?"

"There's quite a bit more, actually. They're active, growing children. But that should cover the high points for now."

"I came here hoping to have a calm and civilized discussion, not to be treated to one of your diatribes, Laura."

"That wasn't even close to a diatribe, Peter, but I can oblige you."

He shifted, irritated when someone bumped his shoulder. "Candy and I are to be married in just over eight weeks in Palm Springs. Allison and Kayla should attend."

"Is this a demand or an invitation?"

"People will expect the children to be there. Candy is making arrangements for her children to attend. Her au pair will bring them down the day before the ceremony. Allison and Kayla can travel with them."

How civilized, she thought. And how cold. "You want them delivered by Candy's au pair, and returned the same way, I suppose."

"It's sensible, and it's convenient."

"And it won't infringe on your time at all." She held up a hand before he could speak. "I'm sorry. I'm tired and apparently short-tempered. I'm sure the girls would appreciate being included. If you'd call tonight—''

''I have plans. I hardly see the necessity of running through the details again.''

She turned away, looked once more out to sea. She could and would bury her own resentments and try, once again, to give her daughter what she needed. ''Peter, Ali is very hurt, very confused, and very afraid. You so rarely come to see them or call. She feels abandoned.''

''We've been over this before, Laura.'' And he considered himself infinitely patient for listening to it all again. ''You wanted the divorce. Now it's done, settled, there's been adequate time for her to adjust. I have my own life to think about.''

''And do you ever think of the children?''

He sighed, checked his Rolex. He could spare ten minutes more, and no longer. ''You always expected more than I found manageable in that area.''

''They're not an area, they're children.''

She whirled around, stopped herself from spewing out all the resentment, the bitterness. And simply looked at his face. So handsome, she thought. So cool, so composed. So perfect.

''You don't love them, do you, Peter? You never did.''

''Simply because I refuse to dote on them, to spoil them as you've chosen to do doesn't mean I don't understand my responsibilities.''

''That's not what I asked.'' Surprised at herself, she laid a hand on his arm. ''Peter, it's just the two of us here. We've neither of us anything to lose at this point, so let's be honest. Let's put this in its place so that we can stop going over the same ground again and again and accomplishing nothing.''

''It's you who insists on going over the same ground,'' he reminded her.

''All right, I keep going over it.'' Arguments were useless and, she admitted, just too tiring. ''I want to understand. I need to. It's no longer a matter of what you did or didn't feel for me, or I for you. They're children. Our children. Help me understand why you don't want them.''

For a moment, he stared down at the hand on his arm. Delicate. He'd always found that delicacy appealing. The fact that there was steel under it had been both disconcerting and disappointing.

And perhaps if they cleared up this matter, she would stop her constant requests that he flex his schedule to meet her expectations.

''I'm not father material, Laura. I don't consider that a flaw, simply a fact.''

''All right.'' Though her heart ached, she nodded. ''I'll accept that. But, Peter, you are a father.''

''Your definition of that term and mine are essentially different. My responsibilities are met,'' he said stiffly. ''You receive the child support payments every month.''

And they were banked, she thought, into the college funds that he had emptied before the divorce. ''Is that it? A financial burden, an obligation. That's all there is for you?''

''I'm not a doting parent, and never have been. I thought once that I would do better with sons. That I wanted them.'' He spread his elegant hands. ''The simple truth is that it doesn't matter now. We didn't have sons, and I don't want more children. Candy's are well tended, polite, and don't require my attention. I don't believe Allison and Kayla require it either. They're being raised well and comfortably in a good home.''

Like poodles, she thought, as pity stirred. ''The answer is, you don't love them.''

''I don't feel the connection you'd like me to.'' He angled his head to look down at her. ''Let's both be honest, Laura. They're more Templeton than Ridgeway. More yours than mine. That's always been true.''

''It didn't have to be,'' she murmured. ''They're so beautiful. Miracles. I'm so sorry you can't take what they would give you.''

''And I would say that all of us are better off the way things stand. I was angry initially when you insisted on divorce. Angry that it cost me the position I had earned at Templeton. But over the past few months I've come to see that it was inevitable. I enjoy the challenge of running my own hotel, and frankly, Candace is more the kind of woman who suits my needs and my nature.''

''Then I hope you're happy. Really.'' She shuddered out a breath. ''Do you really want the girls at the wedding, Peter, or is it for form?''

''If they choose not to attend, it's a simple matter to make the proper excuses.''

''All right. I'll talk to them, leave it up to them.''

''I'll expect to hear from you by the end of the week. If we're done, I have an appointment shortly.'' He glanced back across the street. With the air somewhat cleared between them, he chose to be magnanimous. ''Your shop is very impressive, Laura. I hope it's successful for you.''

''Thank you. Peter,'' she said when he turned to leave her. People milled around them, but they didn't matter. She remembered a magical night, with moonglow drifting through the gazebo and the scent of flowers and the promise of a dream. ''Did you ever love me? I have to know. I also have my life to think about.''

He looked at her, standing with the sea at her back, the sun glinting off her hair, her skin pale and fragile. Until the words were out of his mouth he'd had no plans to tell her the truth.

''No. No, I didn't love you. But I wanted you.''

A heart could break again, she realized as she nodded and turned back to the sea. It could break again, and again, and again.

The minute she walked back into the shop, Kate pounced. ''Upstairs.''

''What?'' Dizzy with fatigue and grief, Laura let herself be hauled up the winding steps.

''Upstairs and into bed.''

''But we're open. The boudoir—''

''Is closed for the rest of the day.'' In the boudoir, Kate pushed her onto the slippery satin quilt on the big bed and knelt to pry off her shoes. ''You get in, turn it off. I don't want you thinking about anything. Anything. Especially whatever that creep said to upset you.''

Odd, Laura mused, her vision was all gray at the edges, like a screen narrowing. ''He never loved them, Kate. He told me. He never loved my babies. He never loved me.''

''Don't think about it.'' In sympathy, Kate's eyes began to swim. ''Don't worry. Go to sleep.''

''I feel so sorry for him. So sorry for all of us. I'm so tired.''

''I know. I know, honey. Lie down.'' Fussy as a mother hen over a sick chick, she smoothed the covers over her friend. ''Sleep.'' She sat on the side of the bed, took Laura's hand.

''I used to dream about the way things would be. So perfect. So lovely.''

''Shh,'' Kate murmured even as Laura's voice trailed off. ''Dream about something else. Find a new dream.''

''Is she out?'' Margo said from the doorway.

''Yeah.'' Kate sniffled and wiped her cheek. And thought of the child inside her. Of the man she'd loved and married, who already cherished it, and her. ''I hate Peter fucking Ridgeway.''

''Stand in line.'' Margo stepped in to lay a hand on Kate's shoulder. ''When she walked back in, she looked so . . . broken. I could kill him for putting that look in her eyes.''

''Stand in line,'' Kate echoed. ''She'll be all right. We'll make sure of it.''

Laura's mind was still fuzzy with fatigue when she returned home. She thought briefly about a long, steaming bath, cool, smooth sheets, and oblivion. But she needed her children, and needed them badly.

She found them, as she'd expected to, at the stables. Bongo greeted her first, racing forward with his tongue lolling out in a grin. He skidded to a halt at her feet, promptly sat his rump down, and lifted a paw.

''What's this?'' Charmed, she crouched down to shake.

''Trick dog. Michael's been playing with you. What else can you do, huh? Can you lie down?''

He flopped down into the prone position instantly, looking up for approval, and the expected biscuit.

''Can you roll over? Play dead?''

''We're still working on that.'' Michael strolled over and to Bongo's relief offered him a biscuit. ''You've always got to pay for the show,'' he said to Laura.

''The girls must be thrilled.''

''They're teaching him the rollover. He's making progress.'' But his eyes were on Laura's, and the shadows under them. ''You just getting back?''

''Um. I came down to see the girls and to get a look at the foal. How's she doing?''

''She's doing great, which is more than I can say for you.'' The frustration and annoyance he'd pent up all day spewed out in rough words. ''Are you crazy, going to work a full day on no sleep? You might have nodded off behind the wheel and killed yourself on Highway 1.''

''I had meetings.''

''That's bullshit, Laura. Just bullshit. What's going on around here? What's this crap about you letting Ridgeway walk with your money and you holding down two jobs to pay the bills?''

''Be quiet.'' She glanced anxiously over his shoulder, relieved that the girls weren't in sight or earshot. ''I don't know who you've been talking to, but it's none of their business or yours. I don't want the girls hearing any of this.''

''It's my business when you lose a night's sleep helping me out, then come out here looking as though I could knock you over with a careless breath.'' He yanked her to her feet. ''I figured you were out playing all day at the shop, diddling at an office, and getting your hair done.''

''Well, you were wrong, weren't you? And it isn't your concern one way or the other. Now, where are the girls?''

He vibrated with impotence, with the rage of not being able to help or hinder. With a shrug, he turned on his heel. ''In the paddock.''

"Alone?" Visions of calamities raced through her head even as she dashed toward the stables. When she saw them in the paddock, fear turned to shock.

Her daughters were happily riding in circles on a pair of patient quarter horses.

"I haven't got them jumping through flaming hoops yet or doing flips," Michael said dryly. The woman, he thought, was an open book. "That's next week."

"Aren't they great?" Annoyance with him vanished as she gripped his arm and watched. "Ali's trotting. She posts so well already."

"I told you she was a natural. Kayla," he called out, "heels down."

Her little boots adjusted immediately and, like the pup, she looked over for approval. "Mama! Look, Mama, I can ride!"

"You sure can!" Thrilled, Laura moved to the fence, hooked one foot on the bottom rung. "You both look fabulous."

Her head high, Ali trotted over and drew her mount to a polite stop. "This is Tess. She's three. Mr. Fury says she's a very good jumper, and that he'll teach me."

"She's beautiful, Ali. You look beautiful on her."

"That's why I want her. I can buy her with my own money. I can take it out of my savings." Her eyes tilted down in challenge. "It's my money."

Had been, Laura thought wearily. Peter had taken it, along with the college fund. And she hadn't nearly begun to replace the loss. "A horse is a very big responsibility, Ali. It's not just the buying, it's the keeping."

"We have the stables." She'd thought about this, dreamed about this for days. "I can feed her, and pay for the hay with my allowance. Please, Mama."

Now a headache brewed nastily in the fog of fatigue. "Ali, I can't think about this right now. Let's wait and—"

"Then I'll ask my father." Ali jerked her chin up even as her lips trembled. "I'll call him and ask him."

"You can certainly call him, but he doesn't have anything to do with this."

''You had a horse when you were a girl. You had anything you wanted, but you always tell me to wait. You never understand when something's important. You never understand.''

''Fine. All right. I'm not going to fight with you now.'' Because she was going to break, could already feel the first fissures forming, Laura turned and walked away.

''Get off the horse, Ali.'' When her stormy eyes came to his, Michael reached over for the bridle. ''Dismount. Now.''

''I haven't finished my lesson.''

''Yeah, you have. Now you're going to get another one.'' The minute she hit the ground, he wrapped the reins around the fence rail, then plucked the girl up and sat her beside them so his gaze was level with hers. ''Do you think you have the right to talk to your mother that way?''

''She doesn't listen—''

''No—you don't listen, and you don't see. But I listened, and you want to know what I heard?'' He jerked her chin up when it drooped. ''I heard a spoiled, ungrateful brat sassing her mother.''

Her teary eyes went wide with shock. ''I'm not a brat.''

''You just gave a damned good imitation. You think you can snap your fingers and get whatever you want or have a tantrum if it doesn't happen, or doesn't happen quick enough to suit you?''

''It's my money,'' Ali said hotly. ''She doesn't have any right to—''

''Wrong. She's got all the rights. Your mother just came home from working her butt off so that you can have a nice home and food on the table. So you can have your lessons and your fancy school.''

''I've always lived here. She doesn't have to work. She just goes away every day.''

''Open your eyes.'' Something, he admitted, he should have done himself. ''You're old enough and smart enough to see what she's going through.''

Tears began to leak now. ''She divorced him. She made him go away.''

"I guess she did that just to make you miserable."

"You don't understand. Nobody understands."

"Bull. I understand just fine, which is why I'm not tanning your hide."

"You can't spank me."

He leaned closer. "Wanna bet?"

The very idea was so shocking, so unbelievable, that she closed her mouth tight. "Good choice," he said and nodded. "This horse isn't for sale to you."

"But, Mr. Fury—"

"And you're not welcome in the stables until you've apologized to your mother. If I ever see you sass her again, you will get your hide tanned." He lifted her off the fence and set her down.

On her feet again, Ali fisted her hands at her sides. "You can't make me do anything. You're just a tenant."

"Who's bigger?" Placidly, he stepped over the fence to tend the waiting horse. "And right now, Ms. Ridgeway, you're standing on my property."

"I hate you." It came out on a choked sob, but was nonetheless passionate. "I hate everyone."

She streaked away while Michael stroked the mare. "Yeah, I know how that feels too."

"You yelled at her."

Wincing, he looked over to see Kayla still astride, her eyes huge and fascinated. He'd forgotten he had an audience.

"Nobody ever yells at her. Mama has a couple of times, but she always says she's sorry after."

"I'm not sorry. She deserved it."

"Would you really spank her?" Gray eyes glittered. "Would you spank me if I was bad?"

There was such a poignant wistfulness to the question that Michael gave up. He plucked her out of the saddle, held her hard. "I'd whale the tar out of you." He gave her bottom a light pat. "You wouldn't sit down for a week."

She squeezed harder. "I love you, Mr. Fury."

Hell, what had he done? "I love you too." Which was, he realized with some amusement, the first time he'd said those words to a female in all of his life. ''I was pretty hard on her,'' he murmured, as the picture of Ali's unhappy face swam into his mind. And guilt seeped into his heart.

''I know where she'll go. She always goes there when she's mad.''

He should leave bad enough alone, he told himself. He should stay out of it. He should . . . shit. ''Let's go see.''

Chapter Eleven

With anger and shame snapping at her heart, Ali raced over the lawn, through the arbor of wisteria. Nobody understood her, nobody cared. Those thoughts drummed a miserable beat in her head as she whipped down the stone path through banks of hibiscus and night-blooming jasmine.

She didn't care either, she didn't care about anything or anyone. Nothing could make her care. She burst through arching yews into a sun-dappled alcove with marble benches and a central fountain shaped like spearing calla lilies.

Her headlong rush halted with a skid of her boots on brick. And with shock.

It was her spot, where she came when she needed to be alone. To think, to plan, to sulk. She hadn't known her mother came here too. The cliffs were her mother's special place. Yet her mother was here, sitting on a marble bench. Weeping.

She'd never seen her mother cry, not like this. Not with

her hands covering her face, her shoulders heaving. Not such violent, helpless, hopeless tears.

Staggered, she stared, watching the woman she had always believed invincible sobbing as though the well of grief would never run dry.

Because of me, Ali thought as her own breath hitched. Because of me.

"Mama."

Laura's head shot up. She sprang off the bench, fought for control. Lost. Breaking, she sank down again, too tired, too bruised, too shattered to fight.

"I don't know what to do anymore. I just don't know what to do. I can't take anymore."

Panic, shame, emotions she didn't understand spurted so high so fast that Ali was across the bricks and wrapped around her mother before she'd thought to move. "I'm sorry, Mama. I'm sorry. I'm sorry."

Under the arch, Kayla gripped Michael's hand. "Mama's crying. Mama's crying so hard."

"I know." It destroyed him to see it, to hear it, to know there was nothing he could do to stop it. "It'll be all right, baby." He lifted Kayla up, let her press her face into his shoulder. "They just need to get it out, that's all. Let's leave them alone."

"I don't want her to cry." Kayla sniffled against him as he carried her away.

"Neither do I, but sometimes it helps."

She leaned back, sure that he would hold her. "Do you ever cry sometimes?"

"I do stupid man things instead. Say bad words, break things."

"Does it make you feel better?"

"Mostly."

"Can we go break something now?"

He grinned at her. Lord, what a character. "Sure. Let's go find something good to break. But I get to say all the bad words."

In the alcove, Laura held her daughter close, rocked her.

Comforting, as always, brought comfort. ''It's all right, Ali. It's all right.''

''Don't hate me.''

''I could never hate you. No matter what.'' She tilted her daughter's tear-streaked face up. Her baby, she thought, swamped with love and guilt and sorrow. Her firstborn. Her treasure. ''I love you. Allison, I love you so much, and nothing could ever change that.''

''You stopped loving Daddy.''

Laura's heart shuddered again. Why did it have to be so hard? ''Yes, I did. But that's different, Ali. I know it's hard to understand, but it's so very different.''

''I know why he went away.'' Ali struggled to steady her jaw. She had made her mother cry, and nothing, she knew, nothing she had ever done could be worse. ''It was my fault.''

''No.'' With firm hands, Laura cupped Ali's face. ''No, it was not your fault.''

''It was. He didn't like me. I tried to be good. I wanted to be. I wanted him to stay and to love us, but he didn't want me, so he went away.''

Why hadn't she seen this? Laura wondered. Why hadn't the family counselor? Why hadn't anyone seen it? ''Ali, that's not true. People get divorced. It's sad and it's sorry, but it happens. Your father and I got divorced because of him and because of me. You know I don't lie to you, Ali.''

''Yes, you do.''

Stunned, Laura jerked back. ''Ali?''

''You don't lie, exactly, but you make excuses, and that's the same.'' She bit her lip, terrified that her mother would cry again. But she had to say it. ''You always made excuses for him. You'd say he wanted to come to the recital, but he had an important meeting. He wanted to go with us to the movies, or the zoo, or anyplace, but he had work. But it wasn't true. He didn't want to go. He didn't want to go with me.''

Oh, dear God, how could protecting your child cause so much damage? ''It wasn't because of you. Not because of you, Ali, or because of Kayla. I promise you that's not true.''

''He doesn't love me.''

How could she answer? What was right? Praying that whatever words she chose would be best, she stroked Ali's tumbled hair. ''It might be hard for you to understand this, but some people aren't cut out to be parents. Maybe they'd like to be, or they want to be, but they just can't. Your father never meant to hurt you or Kayla.''

Ali shook her head slowly. ''He doesn't love me.'' She said it quietly. ''Or Kayla. Or you.''

''If he doesn't love you in the way you wish he did, it isn't your fault. It's nothing you did. Nothing you are or aren't. It's not his fault either, because—''

''You're making excuses again.''

Laura drew back, shut her eyes. ''All right, Allison. No excuses.''

''Are you sorry you had me?''

Laura's eyes flashed open. ''What? Sorry? Oh, Allison.'' This part, at least, was easy as breathing. ''Do you know, when I was a girl, hardly older than you, I used to dream that I would fall in love one day, and get married. I'd have a home, and beautiful children to fill it. I'd watch them grow.''

Her lips curved now as she stroked the hair away from her daughter's damp cheeks. ''Not all of that dream worked out the way I thought it would, but the best part did. The best part of the dream, and the best part of my life, is you, and it's Kayla. Nothing in the world could be truer than that.''

Ali knuckled a tear from her cheek. ''I didn't mean those things I said.''

''I know.''

''I said them because I knew you would never go away. No matter what, you'd never go away.''

''That's right.'' Smiling, Laura flicked a finger down Ali's cheek. ''You're stuck with me.''

''I felt bad, and I wanted it to be your fault.'' She had

to swallow before she could speak again. ''Did he go to bed with another woman?''

Just when you thought it was safe, Laura thought with a jolt. ''Where did you hear a thing like that?''

''At school.'' The flush rose up into Ali's cheeks, but she kept her eyes steady. ''Some of the older girls talked about it.''

''That's nothing you—or the older girls—should be talking about.''

Ali's mouth firmed. ''He did.'' She nodded and, leaving a small, lovely part of her childhood on the bench, rose. ''That was wrong. He hurt you, and you made him go away.''

''There were a lot of reasons I asked for a divorce, Ali.'' Tread carefully, Laura warned herself, even as her heart was breaking to see that too-adult look in her baby's eyes. ''None of them is appropriate for you or your friends to discuss.''

''I'm talking to you, Mama,'' Ali said so simply that Laura had no response. ''It wasn't my fault,'' she continued. ''It wasn't your fault, either. It was his fault.''

''No, it wasn't your fault. But two people make a marriage, Ali. And two people break it.''

No, Ali thought, studying her mother. Not always. ''Did you go to bed with another man?''

''No, of course not—'' Laura stopped herself, appalled that she was discussing her sex life with a ten-year-old. ''Allison, that question is completely inappropriate.''

''Cheating is inappropriate, too.''

Weary again, Laura rubbed her brow. ''You're too young to judge, Ali.''

''Does that mean it's all right to cheat sometimes?''

Trapped. Trapped by the unbending logic and admirable values of a ten-year-old girl. ''All right—no, it's not.''

''He took our money, too, didn't he?''

''Oh, good God.'' Laura rose. ''Gossip isn't attractive, and it's irrelevant.''

She understood now, Ali thought, understood the titters from other girls, the murmured conversations of adults.

And all the pitying glances. ''That's why you had to go to work.''

''Money is not an issue here.'' She refused to let it be. ''I went to work because I wanted to. I opened the shop because I wanted to. Templeton Hotels has always been part of my life. So have Margo and Kate. Working is sometimes hard, and it's sometimes tiring. But it makes me feel good, and I'm good at it.''

She took a breath, struggled for the right angle. ''You know how you're tired after a long rehearsal for a recital? But you love it, and when you've done well, when you know you've done well, you feel strong and happy.''

''That's not an excuse?''

''No.'' Laura's lips curved again. ''It's not an excuse. Fact is, I'm seriously considering asking my boss at the hotel for a raise. I'm damned good.''

''Granddad would give you one.''

''Templetons don't pull rank.''

''Can I come with you to the hotel one day and watch you work? I like going to the shop, but I've never gone to your other office.''

''I'd like that.'' She stepped forward, brushed a hand over Ali's hair. ''It's never too soon to start training the next generation in the Templeton organization.''

Settled again, Ali rested her head on her mother's breast. ''I love you, Mama.''

It had been, Laura thought, much too long since she'd heard those words. There were birds singing in the garden, she realized. And the little fountain was playing musically. The air was soft, and her child was in her arms.

Everything would be all right.

''I love you, Ali.''

''I won't sass you anymore, or be a brat or say things to make you cry.''

Of course you will, Laura thought, settling herself. You're growing up. ''And I'll try not to make excuses.''

Smiling, Ali lifted her head. ''But I'm still not going to like Mrs. Litchfield, and I'm never, ever going to call her mama.''

''Oh, I think I can live with that.'' Eyes gleaming wickedly, Laura bent down. Woman to woman. ''I'll tell you something, just between you and me. I don't like her either.'' She traced her finger over Ali's lips when they bowed up. ''Are we better now?''

''Uh-huh. Mama, everyone said our home was broken, but they were wrong. It's not broken at all.''

Laura tucked her daughter under her arm and looked across the gardens to Templeton House. ''No, it's not. We're not. We're just fine, Ali.''

It wasn't an easy thing for a young girl with a great deal of pride to take the first step. Though it had troubled her, and kept her awake a long time during the night, Ali hadn't told her mother what Michael had said to her. Or how it had made her feel.

She wasn't sure what her mother would have done, or said, but she did know when you'd done something wrong, you were supposed to fix it.

She'd gotten up early and dressed for school, then slipped out the side door to avoid any questions. Old Joe was here this morning, humming to his azaleas. Ali cautiously skirted that section of the garden and made her way toward the stables.

She had her speech all worked out, and she was very proud of it. She thought it was mature, dignified, and clever. She was certain that Mr. Fury would nod wisely, impressed, after she was done.

She stopped for a moment to watch the horses he'd let out into the paddock. He would be cleaning the stalls, then. She tried not to pout as she watched Tess and thought about what it was like to ride her and brush her and feed her apples.

Her mother might have evaded the subject of money, but Ali knew, with her new wisdom, that buying and keeping a horse would strain the budget.

Besides, she didn't intend to ask Mr. Fury for anything.

He had yelled at her, scolded her, threatened to spank her. That was simply not permitted.

Head high, she walked into the stables. All the smells she'd begun to love were there. Hay and grain and horse and leather. She remembered the way he'd shown her to saddlesoap the tack, how to curry a horse. How he had put her in the saddle for the first time. And praised her.

She bit her lip. None of that mattered. He'd insulted her.

She heard the sounds of the shovel, and she walked to the end of the row, where Michael was filling a wheelbarrow with soiled straw and manure.

"Excuse me, Mr. Fury." Her voice had a royal ring that she would have been surprised to know closely echoed her mother's.

He looked behind him, took in the slight young girl in the tidy blue dress and trendy Italian sneakers. "You're out early." Thoughtful, he leaned on his shovel. "No school today?"

"I don't have to leave for a little while." She glanced at her watch, folded her hands. The gestures were so like Laura's he had to fight back a smile.

"Something you want to say?"

"Yes, sir. I want to apologize for being rude, and for causing a family scene in front of you."

Little Miss Dignity, he thought, your chin's trembling. "Apology accepted," he said simply and bent to his work.

He was supposed to apologize now. It was, after all, the proper way to close a misunderstanding. When he didn't, her brows drew together. "I think you were also rude."

"I don't." He dumped the last load, propped up his shovel, then gripped the handles of the wheelbarrow. "Better move aside. You'll get your dress dirty."

"You raised your voice, you called me names."

He cocked his head. "And your point is?"

"You're supposed to say you're sorry."

He released the handles, brushed his hands over his jeans. "I'm not sorry. You deserved it."

"I'm not a brat." All her dignity crumbled, as did her face. "I didn't mean the things I said. I didn't mean to make her cry. She understands. She doesn't hate me."

"I know she understands. She loves you. A kid who has

a mother like that in her corner's got everything. Pushing it away's pretty stupid.''

''I'll never do it again. I know better now. I know lots of things better now.'' She knuckled a tear away. ''You can spank me if you want, and I won't tell. I don't want you to hate me.''

Michael crouched down, gave her a long, steady look. ''Come here.''

Trembling, terrified at her images of humiliation and pain, she stepped forward. When he grabbed her, she muffled a cry of alarm, then was dazzled to find herself being hugged.

''You're a stand-up gal, Blondie.''

He smelled of the horses. ''I am?''

''Swallowing pride's hell. I know. You did a good job.''

Full of wonder, she held on tight. It was like Granddad, or Uncle Josh, or Uncle Byron. But different, just a little different. ''You're not mad at me anymore?''

''No. You mad at me?''

She shook her head, and let the words tumble out. ''I want to ride the horses, please. I want to come back and help you and feed them and brush them. I told Mama I was sorry, and I won't sass her anymore. Don't make me stay away.''

''How am I supposed to get things done around here without you? And Tess has already been missing you.''

She sniffed, eased back. ''Has she? Really?''

''Maybe you've got time to say hi to her before you take off for school. But you want to get rid of these.''

He took out a bandanna. Ali, experiencing the thrill of having her tears dried by a man for the first time, fell headlong in love.

''Will you still give me riding lessons and teach me how to jump?''

''I'm counting on it.'' He held out a hand. ''Friends?''

''Yes, sir.''

''Michael. My friends call me Michael.''

* * *

He'd never been inside Templeton Monterey. Though Michael had grown up just up the coast, it wasn't so odd. He'd never had a need for a hotel in the area, and if he had, Templeton would have been beyond his touch.

He'd been to the resort. After all, his mother had worked there. So he knew what to expect. Then again, he mused as he passed the uniformed doorman, you usually got more than you expected from Templeton.

The lobby was enormous, sprawling, with conversation and waiting areas tucked away behind potted palms and greenery to offer the cozy and the private. The bar, long and wide with generous chairs and gleaming tables, was up a short flight of stairs and separated by a trio of brass rails.

Those who wanted a little lift could enjoy their cocktail and watch the people come and go.

There were plenty of them, Michael noted.

They were six deep at check-in, flooding the long mahogany counter while clerks hustled to assign rooms. Two waitresses worked the waiting crowd and passed out glasses of fizzing water.

The noise was huge.

Wherever they stood, sat, or wandered, they talked. Primarily women, he observed, some of them dressed for business, others drooping from travel. And all, he thought, studying the heaped luggage carts, with enough suitcases for a six-month stay.

As he maneuvered out of the way, two women streaked toward each other over the shining tile and met with squeals and embraces. Several others were eyeing him. Not that he particularly minded being ogled, but being so completely outnumbered, he chose discretion as the better part of valor and contemplated retreat.

Then he saw her, and there might not have been another woman in the room. She carried a clipboard tucked atop a fat file. Her hair was pinned up, smoothed somehow into a neat, professional twist. She wore a simple black suit that even one with a fashion-impaired eye could see was painfully expensive.

For his own pleasure, he let his gaze wander down to

her legs. And gave thanks to whatever sadist had convinced women to wear those skinny high heels.

Though she was deep in conversation with the conference chair and frantically sorting out details in her head, Laura felt a flush of heat, a tingle at her back.

She shifted, struggled to ignore it, and at last glanced over her shoulder.

In the midst of all those women—many of whom where rolling their eyes behind his back—he stood with his thumbs tucked in the front pocket of his jeans. Smiling at her.

"Ms. Templeton? Laura?"

"Hmm? Oh, yes, Melissa, I'm going to check on that right away."

The conference chair was as busy, as harried, as Laura. She was also as human, and she felt a quick tug as she looked across the room. "My, my." Grinning, she blew out a breath. "You sure do grow them fine in Monterey."

"Apparently. If you'll excuse me a minute." Tucking her clipboard under her arm, she hurried toward Michael. "Welcome to bedlam. Did you come by to see Byron?"

"I had no idea corporate executives were so sexy." He lifted a hand, flicked it over a glittering heart pin on her lapel. "Cute."

"All the staff are wearing them. It's a romance writers' convention."

"No kidding?" Intrigued, he surveyed the crowd, met several pairs of equally intrigued female eyes. "These women write those books with all that steam?"

"Romance novels are an enormous industry that accounts for more than forty percent of the paperback market and provides enjoyment and entertainment for millions while focusing on love, commitment, and hope."

She reached around to rub the back of her neck. "Don't get me started. I used to read because I liked a story. Now I've become an advocate. Byron's in the penthouse. The elevators—"

"I didn't come to see Byron, though I might swing by. I came to see you."

''Oh.'' She turned her wrist to glance at her watch. ''I'm awfully pressed just now. Is it important?''

''I went by your shop first. Quite a place.'' It had impressed him, as the hotel impressed him with its style and charm. ''You had a crowd there too.''

''Yes, we're doing well.'' She tried to imagine him taking a turn around Pretenses. Not quite the bull in the china shop, she decided. More like the wolf among the lambs. ''Did anything catch your eye?''

''The dress in the front window had its points.'' His eyes slid down her. ''Would have had more with a woman in it. I don't know much about doodads and glitters. Kate fast-talked me into some blue horse.''

''Ah, the aquamarine mare. It's lovely.''

He jerked a shoulder. ''I don't know what the hell I'm supposed to do with it, or how she managed to con me out of three bills for that little statue.''

Laura laughed. ''She's good. But I'm sorry you had to run around looking for me. And now I've—''

''I like looking at you.'' He eased forward.

''Michael.'' She backed up, bumped into a shamelessly eavesdropping guest. ''I really have to get into my office.''

''Fine. I'll go with you.''

''No, it's this way,'' she began when he took her arm. ''I really don't have time.''

''I do. I'm meeting another breeder in a couple hours.'' He saw the glass door with ''Executive Offices'' printed on it. ''Is it always so noisy around here?''

''No. Check-in for a convention livens things up considerably.''

It wasn't much more sedate behind the desk. Phones were ringing, boxes were stacked, people whizzed by. Laura turned into a small office with a central desk piled with tidy stacks of paper. The fax machine was humming away, spitting out an enormous stream.

''Christ, how do you work in here?'' Feeling immediately hemmed in, he rolled his shoulders. ''How do you breathe in here?''

''It's more than adequate, and the limited space demands

efficiency.'' She tore off the fax and skimmed it as she picked up her phone. ''Sit down if you like. I'm sorry, I have to finish this.''

After punching in numbers, she cradled the phone between her neck and shoulder to keep her hands free. ''Karen, yes, I've got it right here. It looks fine. They need to set up their registration desk an hour earlier. Yes, I know, but they've had to readjust their estimate on walk-ins. Yes, I know Mark's handling that, but he doesn't answer his page. No, I don't think he's gone over the wall.''

Chuckling, she set the fax aside and picked up a memo. ''Uh-huh. That's on my list, don't worry. If you could just . . . My life for you. No, I'll buy the bottle when it's over. Thanks. I want to— Hell! I've got another call coming through. I'll check with you later.''

Michael took his seat, rested his ankle on his knee, and watched her work. Who would have thought it, he mused, the cool, pampered princess, up to her elbows in details. Swinging from phone to computer and back like a veteran soldier flanking the enemy.

Depending on the topic, her voice was warm, chilly, brisk, or persuasive. And she never missed a beat.

Actually, her heart missed quite a few—every time she looked over and saw him sitting there. Black denim and worn boots and dark windblown hair. Eyes that watched everything.

''Michael, you don't—''

Before she could finish, even begin to nudge him along, a skinny man with a quick smile poked his head in the door. ''Sorry. Laura?''

''Mark, I've been paging you for an hour.''

''I know. I was trapped, I swear it. I'm on my way to deal with conference registration setup. But there's a small crisis in the Gold Ballroom. They want you.''

''Of course they do.'' She rose. ''Michael, I need to see what this is about.''

''Let's go.''

''Don't you have something to do?'' He made her nervous, matching her pace as she strode back into the lobby.

"I'm having fun watching you. A guy's entitled to an hour off now and again."

As they climbed a flight of wide carpeted steps, he looked around curiously. "I've never been in here before. Hell of a place."

"I didn't realize. I wish I could show you around, but . . ." She shrugged her shoulders. "You can take a tour on your own, but I wouldn't recommend using the elevators. We've got about eight hundred checking in today and they'll be jammed."

"Jammed into an elevator with women who write romance." He shook his head. "I can think of worse things."

The second-floor meeting-room level was as spacious as the lobby, as elegantly appointed, and nearly as crowded. Enormous chandeliers were brilliantly lit, shooting light onto brass and silver, dripping it on pots of flowering begonias in snowy white and blood red. Along one wall, heavy drapes were open to a spectacular view of the bay.

Laura marched toward a bank of six doors topped with an ornate brass plate identifying the Gold Ballroom.

"You have to admire the Templetons."

"What?"

"They know how to build a hotel."

Because she appreciated the statement, she stopped for a moment. "It is wonderful, isn't it? It's one of my favorites, though I can't think of any that don't have some special aspect. The one in Rome rising above the Spanish steps. There are views from the windows that break your heart. Templeton New York has this lovely courtyard. You never expect to find something that quiet in the middle of Manhattan. You take a step off Madison Avenue, and the world changes. There are fairy lights in the trees, a little fountain. And in London . . ." She trailed off, shook her head. "That's something else you shouldn't get me started on."

"I always figured you'd take it for granted. Misconceptions," he murmured as they walked toward the ballroom again. "There's a lot more I don't know about you than I do."

"Templetons don't take anything for granted." And because she didn't, she stepped inside the ballroom prepared for anything.

It was chaos. Half the tables for the evening's mass literacy signing were set up, half were still stacked and waiting. Mountains of boxes lined the walls. Even the thought of what it would take to unpack them and distribute the books to the right spot made her eyes cross. That, at least, was not her job.

"Laura." It was Melissa again, her wire-framed glasses sliding down her nose as she all but leapt across the carpet and into Laura's arms. "I'm so glad you're here. We still haven't been able to locate shipments for six authors, and an entire shipment from one of the publishers is lost somewhere in the bowels of the hotel."

"I'll put a trace on them. Don't worry."

"Yes, but—"

"And I'll go down to shipping and receiving myself." Her smile was meant to be reassuring and not weary. "If necessary, I'll brave the bowels personally and find the books."

"I can't tell you what that means to me. You have no idea what it's like to have to tell an author she doesn't have any books to sign. It doesn't matter if it was flood, pestilence, or Armageddon, she's going to jump you."

"Then we'll see that they're here, even if we have to send someone out to raid the bookstores."

Melissa blew the hair out of her eyes. "I've worked four nationals and six regional conferences. You're the best I've ever worked with. And I'm not saying that just because my life is in your hands."

Relieved, she shifted her gaze to Michael, smiled winningly. "Hello. I'm Melissa Manning when I'm not insane."

"Michael. Are you a writer?"

"Yes, I am, even—maybe particularly—when I'm insane."

"Got a book I can buy?"

She blinked, her eyes lighting with delight behind the lenses of her glasses. "As a matter of fact, I happen to have one in my briefcase, which you can have. Would you like me to sign it for you?''

''That'd be great.''

''Just give me a minute.''

''That was very sweet,'' Laura murmured when Melissa dashed off for her briefcase.

''I like to read, and I might learn something.'' He shifted, slid a hand down her arm until it linked with his. ''How about dinner tonight, maybe a drive, maybe some wild, unbridled sex?''

''As usual, an interesting offer.'' It was humiliating to have to clear her throat, but she had no choice. ''I'm working here tonight.''

''Now that's insane.'' Amused, Melissa strolled back and handed Michael her book. ''You're a stronger woman than I, Laura, choosing work over hot, unbridled sex.''

Michael grinned. ''I'm going to like your book.''

''I hope you will.''

''Count on it. Excuse me a minute.''

He tugged Laura into his arms, lowered his head and kissed her until every ounce of blood in her head drained to her feet and tingled. He let her go and nipped lightly at her chin.

''You're still holding the rain check, sugar. Nice to meet you, Melissa.''

''Yeah.'' Staring after him, Melissa rubbed a hand over her heart. ''I believe in quality, descriptive, and well-crafted writing,'' she began. ''And all I can think of to say now is, Wow.'' she blew out a breath. ''Wow.''

''Yeah.'' Laura made an effort to find the top of her head. It had to be spinning somewhere close by. ''I, um . . .''

''It's okay. Take a minute.''

''I'm going to book on those checks for you right away.''

Melissa tucked her tongue in her cheek. ''Appreciate it.''

''Excuse me.''

As Laura struggled not to stagger to the door, Melissa indulged in a long sigh. ''God, I love this business.''

Chapter Twelve

It was after ten when Laura turned up the drive to Templeton House. She had the good, solid tired of accomplishing a job well. The kind of tired, she realized as she let herself in the house, that didn't yearn for sleep.

Still, she reminded herself, she had another full day coming up starting in just over nine hours. What she needed was a nice hot bath and bed.

After checking in on her daughters and finding them both deeply asleep, she drew that bath, filled it lavishly with fragrant salts and bubbles, and sank in with a long sigh.

She stretched out, gazed up through the tiny skylight over the tub, and dreamed over the stars. Her life was clicking back into gear, she thought. She had her daughter back. There were bound to be some bumps along the way, and she would negotiate them. But everything had been so blissfully normal that morning on the drive to school.

Her family was in order—her parents busily enjoying their lives and their work, Josh and Margo doting on their new baby, Kate and Byron anticipating theirs.

Her job at the hotel was fulfilling, and made her feel part of the Templeton team again. And the shop . . . she smiled and smoothed frothy bubbles down her leg. The shop was an exciting, unexpected fantasy that brought so much pleasure, so many surprises. As busy as she'd been throughout the day, she'd missed swinging in, ringing up sales, talking to customers. Just being with Kate and Margo.

She would manage a few hours the next afternoon, barring any calamity. Then again, she'd begun to enjoy, even to anticipate, certain kinds of calamity. They offered her the challenge of finding the right answer, the satisfaction of knowing that she could find the solution, inside herself.

Like a book, she mused, a whole new chapter of her life was opening up. She was going to enjoy it.

She let the water drain, stepped out of the deep, oversized tub, toweled off slowly, and creamed her skin dreamily. After removing the pins from her hair and placing them in the little silver box where she kept them, she brushed until the curls bounced and shone.

It wasn't until she was dressing again and caught herself humming that she fully realized she wasn't going to bed. Or not alone.

Shocked, she stared at the reflection in the mirror. The woman there, simply dressed in silk slacks and blouse, stared back. She'd been preparing for a man, she realized. The bath, the lotions, the scents. She'd been preparing for Michael.

But now she was thinking again, and she wasn't sure she could go through with it.

He wanted her, but he didn't know her. He didn't know what she wanted, needed. She wasn't certain herself, so how could he be? She didn't know how to offer herself to a man. Not in reality. In dreams, perhaps, where everything was slow and misty, but in the clear dark where there were movements and consequences, she wasn't sure.

Once she had offered herself to another man, in another life. And it hadn't been enough. To do so again, and fail again, would destroy her.

Coward, she thought, closing her eyes. Was she going to

remain alone and celibate for the rest of her life because she hadn't succeeded as a wife, and therefore as a lover?

If he wanted her, she wanted to be taken. Tonight. She wanted him to give her no choice tonight.

She rushed downstairs quickly before she could change her mind.

And the night was thrilling, windswept, full of sound and scent. She ran through it as women had for centuries. Toward fate, toward a man.

And lost her nerve at the base of the steps.

His lights were on. She had only to climb up that one short flight of wooden stairs and knock on the door. He would know, and would take. She would, she promised herself as she crossed her hands over her speeding heart. As soon as she had composed herself, as soon as the giddiness faded a little.

She went into the stables instead, moving down the line of drowsy horses. She hadn't seen the foal since its birth, she reminded herself. She only wanted to look, to admire. Then she would go up and knock.

At the stall door, she studied the mother and child. The foal lay curled on the hay, the mare standing slack-legged beside her.

"I miss having a baby who needs me," she murmured. "They trust you to take care of them. It's the most incredible feeling, isn't it? Knowing that came from you."

She indulged herself another moment, stroking the mare's head when it was offered. Then she turned, and he was there. All in black, he was like a shadow that became real in a blink. She stepped back.

"I was—I hadn't seen the foal since—I didn't mean to disturb you."

"You've been disturbing me for a long time. Longer than I realized." His gaze holding hers, he stepped forward. "I saw you, running across the lawn. In the starlight. You looked like something out of a dream. But you're not, are you?"

"No." She retreated again, nerves shattered. "I should go, I—" She couldn't take her eyes off his as he came closer, boxed her against the stall door. “I should go.”

“Pretty Laura Templeton,” he murmured. “You always look so polished, so perfect. Nothing out of place.” He skimmed a finger over the soft lapel of her blouse, dipped a finger in the vee and watched her eyes go dark. “Makes a man like me want to muss you up, get right under that polish and find out just who the hell you are.”

He closed his hands over her breasts, calloused hands over thin silk. Felt her shudder. “Who the hell are you, Laura? Why are you here?”

Her heart was pounding against his palm, so violently that she wondered it didn’t simply leap out into his hand. “I came to see the foal.”

“Liar.” He pressed her back against the wood, and when the door gave, she would have stumbled if he hadn’t held her. “I bet he never mussed you up, did he? Always polite, always the gentleman. You won’t get that from me.”

“I—” She was panicked now, thrilled, terrified. Her gaze darted from his as hay crackled under her feet. The stall was empty but for them. She was alone with him. Trapped. “I don’t know how to do this.”

“I do. I can make you stay, or I can make you run. I wonder which it’ll be. But you came to me, so it’ll be my way.”

He fisted his hands on the opening of her blouse, shredded it in one quick, shocking yank. “Stay or run.”

His eyes were dark, demanding, focused on hers. Cool air shivered over her bare skin. “If you stay, you’re mine. My way. Stay or run.” He gripped her hair, yanked her head back, and watched her, waited.

“Stay,” he murmured, then crushed his mouth to hers and ravished.

Speed and desperation. She was pummeled by both as he dragged her down into the hay and branded her lips, her throat, her breasts. She cried out when his teeth closed over her, lancing heat from breast to loins until her body was a bucking, writhing mass of sensation.

The asking was over, she knew. The choice was made. Now he would take, as he had in the dreams that haunted her at night. Rough and fast and mercilessly.

And she wanted that, the painful spin out of control, the hard, tough, impatient hands scraping her skin, the relentless, almost brutal mouth feeding on her.

She found his flesh—hot, smooth. The hay beneath her was prickly, abrading her skin and adding one more reeling sensation. The sound of her clothes tearing under his frantic hands, hands that streaked back to squeeze and probe and possess, was unreasonably erotic.

She could hear herself cry out, hear her own short, harsh panting, each gasp of shock and pleasure. Helpless as a raft on a storm-tossed sea, she rolled, thrashed, and gave herself over to fate.

Every time her hands gripped him, those neat lady's nails biting in, his blood swam. Each time she whimpered, moaned, his pulses whipped. The first time her body convulsed and his name—his name—burst like a sob through her lips, his head reeled.

He could see every fresh shock in her eyes, those clouded gray storms that widened, unfocused, closed on a throaty moan. No one had given her this, of that he could be sure. No one had taken her where he would take her. Of all the things she'd been given, all the places she'd traveled in her privileged life, this was new. Though some part of him, deeply buried, hurt that this was all he could offer, he would make it enough for tonight.

For tonight, and as long as it lasted, he would and could be to her what no one had ever been.

He could feel every dark flash of new pleasure sing through her body and explode inside his own. He could hear her shocked gasps, and swallow them. He could take more, still more, and make her arch violently against him in desperate greed. And that delicate ivory skin, so smooth, so fragrant, dewed with the clean sweat of good sex.

His hands, so strong, so quick, so powerful. They cupped her, bruised, destroyed. Her own were lost in his hair, dragging him down until his mouth found hers again, until she could answer that hard, vicious kiss with one of her own.

His body was so tight, so relentlessly male, muscles

bunching under her hands, ridges of old scars sliding under her questing fingers. His skin was hot, burning, and bloomed damp when she bit desperately at his shoulder.

The air was ripe, thick, and tasted of him on each gulping breath she took. Whatever he did to her, she welcomed; whatever he demanded, she gave.

He lifted her hips, high, and his eyes burned into hers. With one violent thrust, he was inside her, hilt deep. The hands she'd gripped on his arms slid limply to the hay as her body simply erupted.

"Stay with me, Laura." His fingers dug into her flesh, and he began to move. "Stay with me."

What choice did she have? She was locked, trapped, steeped. Her breathing was slow now, shallow, her vision misted at the edges, but she moved with him. Stroke now for stroke.

He shuddered when she came, when she closed around him like a damp fist, and he fought a vicious war with himself not to follow. Not yet. There was more. Even as the blood roared like the sea in his head, he wanted more.

And so he dragged her up until her legs locked around him, until her body flowed back so fluidly it might have been made of water. Worked her until her new frenzy was met, matched, until her head dropped on his shoulder.

Then, and then only, he buried his face in her hair and let himself fall.

His weight pinned her to the floor. It was an odd and drugging feeling, having a man's full weight on her again. And it was a triumphant feeling to know that he was incapable of moving, that he was as dazed, as sated, as she.

She didn't have to doubt it. She'd seen his eyes, felt his hands, heard the gritty groan sound in his throat. He had been caught, trembling, on that stunning moment when he had lost himself and come inside her.

There, in the darkened stables with the sweet smell of hay and horses, her clothes in tatters and her blood singing, she felt like a woman again. Not like a mother, a friend, a responsible member of society. Like a woman.

She didn't want to fumble now, to begin stuttering out

foolish truths. That it had never been this way before, that she hadn't known it could be. Better, she thought, for both of them, to keep it light.

So she smiled, found the strength to lift her hand and stroke his hair. "Looks like I redeemed that rain check."

His chuckle tickled her throat. "What was your name again, sugar?"

Gathering his reserves, he rolled lazily over, pulling her with him until she was sprawled on his chest. Her smile was both smug and sleepy. There was hay in her hair.

"God, you're pretty. Such a pretty little thing. The proper Laura Templeton with the surprising, and flexible, steam engine of a body. Who'd have thought it?"

She certainly hadn't, and she raised a brow. "I can't say that I or it has ever been described quite that way before." Her lips quirked. "I think I like it."

"Since you're in such a good mood, why don't you tell me now why you came here tonight."

"To see the foal." Fastidiously, she picked hay out of his hair, then shifted her gaze back to his. "On the way to you. You knew I'd come."

"I was counting on it. If you hadn't I'd have had to breach the castle walls and drag you out. I don't know how much longer I could have done without you."

"Michael." Moved, she laid her hand on his cheek. "Would you have ravished me?"

"Sugar, I *did* ravish you."

"It's the first time anyone has." She waited a beat, watched her own finger trace down his throat. "I hope it won't be the last."

"I wasn't looking for one quick romp in the hay."

Satisfied with that, she nodded, smoothed his hair again. "Then I'll come back." She lowered her mouth to his, lingered over it. "I should go now."

He merely shifted their positions, pinned her again. "Laura, you don't really think I'm going to turn you loose tonight."

She felt the quick, hitching thrill of being overpowered. "You aren't?"

"No." That rough-palmed hand slid up, closed over her breast, and his mouth became busy at her throat.

She arched under him, shuddered out a sigh. "Good."

Still, she hadn't meant to stay until morning. Hadn't meant to fall into twilight sleep in a pile of hay with her body curled around his. Hadn't realized she would awake fully aroused with his mouth on hers, and his hands . . . his hands.

"Michael." And when her eyes fluttered open, he slid slow and deep inside her. Moved inside her with long, lazy strokes that had dreams misting over reality.

He watched her face, that lovely flush from sleep and sex that warmed her cheeks. The eyes smoky and dazed. The mouth, swollen from his, that trembled on each breath.

They would look at each other now in the light, see as they took each other up with a rhythm soft and silky.

Hay motes fluttered in the fragile light of morning, danced in the quiet air. Night birds gave way to the lark. In the stables, horses began to stir, cats stretched and hunted up sunbeams.

And her hands reached for him, cupped his face, guided his mouth once again to hers as they gently slid over.

"Michael," she said again.

"I can't keep my hands off you."

"I don't want you to."

But he'd seen bruises on that delicate skin as she'd slept. "I was rough with you last night."

"Did I forget to thank you for it?"

He lifted his head, grinned. "I guess screaming my name ten or twelve times was thanks enough."

"Well, then." She pushed his hair back from his face, and her eyes were sober. "I don't ever want to be treated like some fragile piece of glass. Not ever again."

"So if I want to break out the cuffs and whips, you're game?"

Her mouth fell open in speechless shock. "I—I—"

"I'm kidding." Christ, what a package she was, he thought on a roar of laughter. And all his. On a spurt of delight, he got to his feet and picked her up. "At least until we've established trust."

"You don't really—I mean, I don't think I could, or would like . . ." When he laughed so hard he nearly dropped her, she lifted her chin. "I don't care to be the butt of your sick joke."

"It wasn't that sick, and, sugar, you've got a first-class butt." He planted a loud, smacking kiss on her mouth. "But since I doubt you want to stroll back to the house showing it off, let's go get you some clothes."

"I'd appreciate it if you would—what are you doing?" She all but squeaked it as he carried her out of the stall.

"Taking you upstairs to get you something to put on."

"You can't just cart me outside this way. I'm naked. We're naked. Michael, I mean it— Oh, my God." Sunlight and cool morning air slapped her as he stepped through the stable door.

"It's early," he said easily. "No one's around yet."

"We're naked." It was all she could say as he started up the stairs. "We're standing outside naked."

"Looks like it's going to be a hell of a day, too. You got anything on for tonight?"

"I—" Didn't he understand that they were standing on his little porch in the full light of day, buck naked? "Get me inside."

"Chilly? I'm working on it." He shifted her and managed the doorknob.

The insult, she fumed. The insensitivity. The outrageousness of it. "Put me down."

"Sure." He set her obligingly on her feet and waited for the show to begin. She didn't disappoint him.

"Are you out of your mind? What if one of the girls had looked out the window and seen us?"

"It's not even six in the morning. Do they usually stare out the window at dawn, with binoculars?"

Of course not. "That's hardly the point. I won't be hauled around that way because you, in your warped brain, find it amusing. Now get me a shirt."

He ran his tongue around his teeth as he considered her.

Even with hay in her hair, and flushed head to toe with embarrassment and temper, she managed to be dignified. It was . . . fascinating.

"Sugar, you're getting me stirred up again, and I don't think we have time for another round."

"You—"

"Peasant? Barbarian?"

With an effort, she reined in. It was impossible to have a reasonable argument under the circumstances. "I'd like to borrow some clothes, please."

"What the hell. It'll only take a few minutes."

"Michael." She jerked back, stunned, when she saw the intention in his eyes. "Michael, I will not be—"

Dragged to the floor, kissed into mindless submission, driven to bone-splitting climax.

"Oh, God." She fisted her hands on the rug and let herself be ravished.

It took more than a few minutes, so that Laura found herself sneaking like a thief into her own house. If she could just get upstairs, she thought, easing open a side door and creeping into the parlor. Into her room.

Her children would be waking for school any minute. Her children. Wincing, carrying her shoes, she tiptoed into the hall. Was she out of her mind? How could she possibly explain herself if—

"Miss Laura!"

If the worst happened, Laura thought fatalistically and turned to face a shocked Ann Sullivan.

"Annie. I was just, ah, out . . . early. Walking."

Very slowly, Ann continued down the stairs. She had been widowed for more than twenty-five years, but she knew the look of a woman who'd spent the night in a man's arms.

"You're wearing a man's shirt," she said stiffly. "And there's hay in your hair."

"Ah." Clearing her throat, Laura reached up and plucked out a bent shaft. "Yes, that's true. I was . . . out, as I said, and . . ."

"You've never been able to lie your way out of an open door." Ann stopped at the base of the stairs, facing down her quarry very much like a mother about to lecture a reckless child. With a mixture of amusement and apprehension, Laura recognized the signs.

"Annie—"

"You've been down at the stables rolling around in the hay with that sharp-eyed, womanizing Michael Fury."

"Yes, I've been down at the stables," Laura said shrugging on her cloak of dignity. "Yes, I've been with Michael. And I'm a grown woman."

"With the sense of a peanut. What were you thinking of?" Ann continued, poking out a finger. "A woman like you wrestling in a hayloft with the likes of him."

Because where she loved, she had patience, Laura's voice was calm. "I imagine you know very well what I was thinking of. Whatever you think of him, or of my sense, the fact remains that I'm thirty years old, Annie. He wanted me. I wanted him. And in all of my life—all of it—no one has ever, ever made me feel the way he did."

"A moment's pleasure for—"

"A moment's pleasure." Laura nodded. If that was all it amounted to, she swore she would go to her grave grateful. "I was married ten years and never knew what it was like to be pleasured or, I hope, to pleasure a man like that. And I'm sorry you disapprove."

Ann's face pokered up. "It's not my place to disapprove."

"Oh, don't give me that dignified-housekeeper-to-mistress routine, Annie. It's years too late." With a sigh, she laid a hand over the rigid one with which Ann gripped the newel post. "I know how much you care. I know that everything you say you say out of concern and love, but even that can't change the way I feel. Or what I need."

"And you think you need Michael Fury?"

"No. I know I do. I haven't decided what to do about it, or where I want to go from here, but I do know that I fully intend to have a great many moments of pleasure."

"Whatever the cost?"

"Yes. For once in my life, the hell with the cost. I need to shower." She started up the stairs, paused, turned. "I don't want you going down there badgering Michael over this, Annie. That is not your place, or anyone else's."

Ann inclined her head, kept it lowered until she heard Laura close the door to her room. Perhaps it wasn't her place to speak to Michael Fury. But she knew her duty, and she would do it.

Without hesitation, she walked down the hall and into the library. The call to France wouldn't take long. Then they would see, she thought, brooding out the window. They would see.

"I'd like to speak with Mr. or Mrs. Templeton, if you please. It's Ann Sullivan, the housekeeper of Templeton House."

"In the stables. In the hay. All night?" In the second-floor kitchen of Pretenses, Kate swiveled on the stool and gaped. The ten-minute afternoon break was a great deal more interesting than she'd expected. "You?"

"Why is that so shocking?" Ignoring her tea, Laura drummed her fingers on the counter. "I'm human, aren't I? Not some sort of windup doll."

"Pal, it sounds like you were pretty wound up to me. And I'm not shocked, exactly. I mean, I wouldn't have imagined bouncing on the hay was your style, but hey, whatever works." She grinned and sampled one of the cookies Laura had picked up at the bakery. "And I take it that it worked just fine."

Mollified, Laura took a cookie herself. "I," she said smugly, "was an animal."

With a snort, Kate raised one of Laura's arms over their heads. "Way to go, champ. So, now—about the details."

"I can't. Well, maybe. No." The gleam in her eye matched Kate's. "No."

"Come on, just one detail, then. One little detail of Laura's Wild Night."

She laughed, shook her head, nibbled on her lip. God knew, she could tell Kate, or Margo, anything. And it had been so rare lately for her to be able to share something so wonderful and reckless. Fastidiously, she brushed crumbs off the counter.

"He ripped my clothes off."

"Metaphorically or literally?"

"Literally. Just tore them to shreds. Just . . ." She pressed a hand to her stomach. "God."

"God," Kate echoed, fanning a hand in front of her face.

"That's it." Laura scooted off the stool and dumped her cold tea into the sink. "I can't do this. It feels like high school."

"Pal, you've graduated and your cap and gown are in tatters. Congratulations." She cocked her head as Laura rinsed out her cup. She knew the woman who carefully washed out china as well as she knew herself. "Are you in love with him?"

Laura watched the water run and drain. "I don't know. Love, this kind of love, isn't as simple as I once thought it was. I'm afraid I could be, and I don't want to complicate everything."

"You once told me that love just happened, couldn't be planned," Kate pointed out. "I found out you were right."

With care, she set the cup to drain. She'd already given Kate's question a great deal of thought, knowing it would be asked by those who cared the most. "If it does happen, I'll deal with it. There's so much more to him than I ever imagined. And every time I see one of those pieces I didn't know was there fall into place, I'm more involved."

Laura dried her hands and turned back to Kate. "I'm not going to get dreamy-eyed this time around, or want more than someone's capable of giving. I'm just going to enjoy it."

"Is that going to work for you?"

"The way I feel this afternoon, it's working perfectly." Feeling loose, she stretched her arms high. "Absolutely perfectly."

"Glad to see you two are enjoying yourselves." Margo stepped into the doorway and scowled. "One of you was supposed to relieve me, remember? I, unlike my feckless partners, haven't had a break in four hours.''

''Sorry.'' Laura dropped her arms. ''I'll go.''

''No, I'll go.'' Kate hopped off the stool. ''It'll give you a chance to fill Margo in.''

''Fill me in on what?''

''Michael screwed Laura's brains out last night in a horse stall.''

Gracefully, Margo fluffed her hair while Laura flushed. ''Really?''

''Ripped her clothes off,'' Kate added as she headed out the door. ''I'll leave Laura to fill in the details.''

On a long hum, Margo settled herself on one of the padded ice cream chairs, crossed her long, shapely legs. ''Pour me some tea, would you, Laura? I'm whipped.''

Automatically Laura poured a cup, brought it to the table. ''Want a cookie?''

''Don't mind if I do.'' Margo debated them, selected, nibbled. ''Now, sit your butt down and start filling in those details. And don't worry about being too specific.''

Chapter Thirteen

Whistling between his teeth, Michael sent Zip into a raging gallop, bursting out of the woods into the sun like a flaming fire. The little demon could run, Michael thought. He'd be sorry to lose him, but the offer that had come in that morning closed the deal.

In a matter of hours, the speedy little colt would be on his way to Utah.

"Going to have some fun with the fillies up there, kid. And breed some champs."

And the asking price meant that Michael could close the deal he'd been negotiating for a particularly fine-looking Palomino mare and her doe-eyed foal.

The mare was ornery, he mused, had twice tried to kick him and her handler during the inspection. Michael liked her the better for it, and for the fact that she'd bred such a tough little foal. A foal he was already planning to raise for stud.

Couple more years, Michael thought, the new colt would

cover twenty mares, and at four his full complement of sixty.

They'd do fine together, he decided. That snippy Palomino mare and the energetic little buckskin she'd birthed would help him start a new phase of his business.

Within two years, he projected, Fury Ranch was going to mean something—something more than livelihood and survival. It was going to mean quality. And that, Michael thought as Zip tore around the stables, was something he'd lived most of his life without.

It would have been impossible and, worse, embarrassing, for him to explain to anyone that he had always wanted quality. Not just for what he had, or what he built, but for what he was. He'd always wanted to come from something. To be something.

And he had come from nothing. That he'd had to face, couldn't be changed. Nor could he change the fact that it left a sore spot inside him that was never really eased.

He'd gone years telling himself it didn't matter what his parents had been, how he'd grown up, or how he'd lived. But it did matter; now more than ever, he knew it mattered. There was a woman in his life who shouldn't have been there.

Sooner or later, he had no doubt, she'd see that for herself. The insult of it, and the inevitability, made him push the colt for more speed. Not for a minute would he have admitted that he was racing away rather than toward. Nor would he admit, even to himself, that his emotions had been in turmoil from the moment he'd stepped inside the stables last night and found her.

As if she was meant to be there, with him. For him. As if he could take, and hold, maybe even deserve something as lovely and fine and vital as Laura. And be for her what she could be for him.

The hell with that, Michael told himself, squinting into the sunlight as the colt flew over the ground. No way he was going to start fashioning pretty little dreams about a life with Laura. If he was one thing, he was a realist. His time with her was temporary, and he would damn well pack as much into it as he could while it lasted.

He was already into the run, the colt bunched for the leap when Michael spotted the figure loitering at the paddock. They sailed over the fence, spewed up dirt and dust.

''That's a hell of a horse,'' Byron called out as Michael trotted to him.

''He is.'' Bending, Michael slapped Zip's neck, then dismounted. ''Sold him today. Guy in Utah.'' After uncinching the saddle, Michael hung it over the fence. ''Wants to breed for speed.''

''He'll get it.'' Byron leaned over, patted the colt's sleek throat. ''Isn't even winded.''

''Nope. He'll tire his rider out first.''

''I'm surprised you're not using him for stud yourself. He's prime.''

''Yeah, he's prime. But I have more foundation to build before I add a stud.'' Couple more years, he thought, picturing the foal again, and we'll both be ready. ''Right now it's horse trading and building on the investment.''

''You've got a good start. That walker there.'' Byron gestured. ''What are you asking?''

''Max?'' Michael glanced around, watched the horse swish his tail. ''I'd sell my own mother first.'' He held up his hand, and Max walked over. ''Glad to see me, Max?''

Max peeled back his lips so his teeth showed and split the air with a horsey laugh. ''Give us a kiss, then.''

Max nibbled affectionately on Michael's chin, and being nobody's fool, snuffed at his pockets. ''True love is never enough. Want one?''

''A kiss from your horse or a carrot?''

''Whichever.''

''I'll pass on both, thanks.'' But he stroked Max's mane as the horse crunched the carrot. ''You got some fine-looking stock here.''

''You in the market?''

''I told myself I wasn't, especially with the baby coming.'' He looked longingly at the mare nursing her foal. ''Shit, this takes me back.''

Michael picked up a dandy brush and began to groom Zip. ''What are you, about two-ten?''

''Twelve,'' Byron said absently. ''Two-twelve.''

''That bay gelding with the two front socks? He'd carry you.''

Byron studied the bay, noted the lines, the flashy white blaze. ''Handsome bastard, isn't he?''

''Good saddle horse, well mannered but no pussy. Needs a firm hand. The right hand.'' Michael tucked his tongue in his cheek as he continued to work. ''Make you a good deal, seeing as you're related to Josh and married to one of my favorite people.''

''I didn't come by to horse-trade.''

''No?'' Placidly, Michael leaned against Zip, lifted a hoof to pick it out. ''Why, then?''

''I was in the neighborhood, more or less, and thought you might want to come by on Saturday night. Poker.''

''I'm usually up for a game.'' Then he paused, narrowed his eyes. ''This isn't going to be one of those enlightened evenings with women asking if a straight beats a flush.''

''Kate would knock you on your ass for that comment.'' But Byron grinned. ''No, it's purely sexist, men only.''

''Then I'm in, thanks.''

''Maybe I'll win that bay from you.''

''Keep dreaming, De Witt.''

''Good heart room,'' he murmured. ''About sixteen hands, isn't he?''

Michael smothered a grin, continued to clean his mount's hooves. ''About. Just turned four. His sire was a walker, his dam a dark-eyed floozy from Baton Rouge.''

''Shit.'' He was sunk. ''You stable?''

''Yep. Here, for now. Then at my place when it's finished. Should be ready to start construction in a couple weeks.''

''Let's take a closer look.'' In his Saville Row suit and Magli shoes, Byron climbed into the paddock.

''I've heard you Southern boys are cardsharps and horse

thieves,'' Michael commented as they strolled companionably toward the bay.

''You heard right.''

How long was she going to make him wait? Michael paced the floor, contemplated the bottle of wine on the counter. It made him scratch his head. He'd actually gone out and bought wine. Not his usual style, but he'd figured sex in a horse stall wasn't Laura's usual either. The least he could do was offer her a civilized drink. Before he jumped her again.

Which was just what he wanted to do.

If she ever got there.

Of course she was coming. He'd reminded himself of that half a dozen times over the last hour. The way it had been between them the night before, she had to be just as eager for a repeat performance. She'd have thought of him during the day, countless times, the way he'd thought of her.

The way he would have sworn he'd smelled her every time he took a breath. The way he'd caught himself going off into some brainless trance because he could see her face in his head, or hear her voice, or . . .

Want her. Just want her.

When had he ever wanted anything like this? Once he'd wanted escape, and he'd gotten it. He'd wanted danger and risk and reckless adventure. And he'd gotten that, too. And when he'd wanted peace, a life he could look at with some measure of pride, he'd gone out and gotten that as well.

But did he have Laura? Was she going to slip silkily through his fingers before he'd gotten a good grip, or before he'd figured out what the hell to do with her? About her.

She was out of his league, and knowing it pissed him off. Made him determined to drag her to equal ground. Sex was a great equalizer, and he had her there. For now.

Furious with himself for niggling at what shouldn't have been a problem, he poured a glass of the wine. He sniffed it, shrugged, downed it.

''When in Rome, Fury.''

But he set the glass aside and began to pace again, prowling back and forth across the length of the room like a cat prowling the confines of a cage.

He'd caught a glimpse of Ann that afternoon, when he supervised the transfer of the colt. From the bullets she shot out of her eyes, he had the feeling that Laura hadn't managed to get past her that morning.

It made him grin to think of it, the elegant lady of the house sneaking in at dawn in a baggy shirt and jeans, caught by the ever-present, cold-eyed housekeeper.

Maybe Sullivan had locked Laura in. His grin vanished as the idea popped into his head. Maybe she had Laura trapped inside, refusing to let her out. Maybe she was . . .

And maybe he should get a grip on himself, he decided.

The hell with it. He headed for the door. He was going after her.

When he yanked it open, Laura jumped back a full step, pressed a hand to her throat. ''You scared the life out of me.''

''Sorry. I was about to rescue you from the dungeon.''

''Oh?'' She smiled, puzzled. ''Were you?''

''But you seemed to have managed it on your own.''

''I couldn't come any sooner. We've been having a little chaos. My parents have decided to come out for a quick visit. They'll be here in a couple of days, and the girls were so excited, I had a hard time getting them to bed. Then we had to—''

''You don't have to explain to me. Just come here.'' He pulled her close and released a portion of frustrated need in one rough kiss. Pressing her back against the doorjamb, he fisted his hands in her hair and released more.

The same, she thought, wrapping herself around him. The same heat, the same rush, the same wonder. When she could breathe again, she kept her clenched hands on his shirt.

''I thought . . .''

''What?''

But she shook her head. ''Nothing.'' Smiling, she lifted her hands to frame his face. ''Hello, Michael.''

"Hello, Laura." He circled her inside, closed the door with his boot. "I was going to offer you some wine."

"Oh, thank you. That would be nice."

"But it's going to have to wait." He swung her into his arms.

"Oh. That's even nicer."

He did bring her a glass when she was sitting on his rumpled bed wearing his shirt. Not having what he considered her misplaced sense of modesty, he sat across from her naked, knee to knee.

"I'm kind of celebrating," he told her, and tapped the glasses together.

She felt so loose she was certain she could slide right into the sheets. "What are you kind of celebrating?"

"I sold two horses today. One to your brother-in-law."

"Byron?" Surprised, she sipped, recognized the rich tang of a good Templeton Chardonnay. "Funny, Kate never mentioned that they were buying a horse."

"I guess he hadn't told her yet."

"Oh . . . uh-oh."

"Does Kate have a problem with horses?"

"No, but it's quite a commitment. I'm surprised they didn't discuss it first. I'm sure she will be, too."

"I'd say he can handle her."

"It's not a matter of handling, one way or the other. Marriage is a partnership, and decisions require discussion and mutual agreement. And what are you grinning at?"

"You look cute, sitting there all mussed up from sex and lecturing me on relationship ethics."

"I wasn't lecturing." She took a small, cool sip from her glass. "I was simply stating. Don't you believe in relationship ethics?"

"Yep." His hand wandered up her thigh. "But I figure like in any partnership, sometimes one end makes a decision on its own, and ethics get bent a little. I like this little birthmark way up here." His fingers skimmed high on her thigh over a small crescent shape. "Looks like a moon. Sexier than a tattoo."

"You're trying to distract me."

"Doesn't take much effort." But he trailed his finger back down to her knee. "I don't want to see the guy get popped by his wife. He fell for the horse, and maybe I gave him a little push." He moved his shoulders. "If Kate has a problem, we can lose the deal."

Laura tilted her head. "And then, in your opinion, Kate would be a shrew, and Byron a Milquetoast."

"I was thinking wuss actually." Amused, he straightened her leg so that he could lift her knee and kiss it. "Did you always talk everything over, nice and civilized with Ridgeway?"

"No, that was part of the problem. I did what I was told and behaved like a proper, dutiful, and spineless wife."

"Sorry." Annoyed with himself for the need to pry open that door to her life, he gave her knee a quick squeeze. "Bad question."

"No, it wasn't." She shifted a little, leaning back on the pillows propped on the iron headboard. "I learned from it. I learned I won't ever be spineless again, or ineffectual, or quietly desperate."

She tapped her fingers against the glass as she put into words what had been in her heart. "What he did, I let him do, which makes it as much my fault as his. I'm only sorry it took finding him in bed with another woman to force me to fix my life."

"You're happy now?"

"Yes, and grateful." She smiled again. "Grateful to you, too."

His thumb skimmed around to rub the back of her knee. "For?"

"For helping me realize I have a sex drive."

Appreciating her, he leaned up, nipping her lips with his as he set his glass on the table beside the bed. "You had problems with that?"

"I'm not having them now."

"Maybe I should check, just to be sure." But before she could circle him into her arms, he slipped back. "I think I'll start down here," he murmured, and lifted her foot.

''You're not going to . . . Oh.'' Her head fell back as his teeth and tongue went to work. ''They do reflexology in the spa at the resort,'' she murmured as he bombarded all manner of tiny, sensitive nerves. ''It never felt like this.''

''You're not going to start fantasizing that I'm Viktor the massage boy, are you?''

She laughed, moaned, shuddered. ''No. The reality's just—Jesus!'' She dropped her glass, splattering wine over herself and the sheets. ''Oh, I'm sorry. Let me—''

''No, you don't.'' He gave her a gentle shove that sent her weakly back onto the pillows. ''Just stay where you are until I finish.'' He scraped his teeth over her ankle. ''Things were a little rushed before. I think I skimmed over some of the finer points.''

He pressed the heel of his hand lightly against her, had her hips rising. ''I suggest you hang on, sugar. I'm going to take you for a long, hard ride.''

It was like being assaulted on all sides. Inside and out, mind and body. She could do nothing but absorb, react, experience. He worked his way up, as if she were a meal to be savored, course by course.

The lights he left burning blazed too bright, burned her eyes even when she closed them. The air, breezy through the open windows, was suddenly too thick, so that each breath she took was a gasp. Her skin, no longer cool, pulsed with the beat of blood beneath and with the skim of hands and mouth.

The long muscles in her thighs quivered as he cruised over them, and the sheets rustled at the bunch and flex of her hands.

She'd never been tasted this way, touched this way, as if she were everything, and all things.

And his mouth closed over her, suddenly greedy, rough and focused on that core of wet heat until she flew up like an arrow with the sharp edge of her own pleasure stabbing her.

He was mad for her now, wild to see her pinned on the jagged peak of her own ecstasy. Her head was flung back, her eyes blind, her hands wrapped around the iron posts of the bed as if only that desperate grip kept her anchored.

And he was mad to drive her farther.

He used his hands until she bucked against him in frantic, pleading rhythm. Watched her, watched her, until his name sobbed out of her, until her hands lost their grip, until her body went pliant as pooled wax.

She lay still, wrecked, unable to do more than moan when he lifted her enough to slip the shirt away from her shoulders.

''You're beautiful, Ms. Templeton. Gold.'' He touched his hand to her hair. ''Rose.'' And her breast. She trembled under his touch.

''Michael.'' She opened heavy eyes, saw the room spin. ''I can't.''

''Can't you?'' Gently now, he lowered his head, flicked his tongue over her nipple. ''I wonder.''

''I know you didn't—you haven't—'' She reached for him, knowing she would find him hard and ready. ''Let me.''

''Some other time.'' He smiled, though his blood had leaped when her fingers closed around him. ''I'll take a rain check. Let's just see if we can finish this the old-fashioned way.''

This time he closed his mouth over her breast and sent the ache echoing down.

''You do things inside me.'' Her breath began to hitch again. That curl of new need began to spread and ache and throb. ''You have no idea what you do inside me.''

It was building again, impossibly strong. She could have wept. He feasted on her breasts, teeth and tongue hungry for the flavor of her, that fragile and floral taste he'd come to crave. He took her hands, wrapping them around the posts again, keeping his clamped over hers.

The thought ran through her reeling head that they were both trapped, both locked in, both prisoners of this.

Accepting, she lifted her mouth to his, linking there as well, and met his fast, desperate thrust.

Then it was only blind speed, blazing heat, gasps and the animal's song of flesh against flesh. Harder, deeper, until he was buried in her. Until, still linked, hands, mouths, sex, they plunged.

Later, when blood had cooled and the air was quiet again, she shifted. His arm curled around her, held.

''I thought you were asleep,'' she murmured.

''Was.''

''I have to go. I can't sneak in the house at dawn every morning carrying my shoes.''

''Little while more.'' He was still half asleep, and his voice was thick with it. ''I wanna hold you.''

Her heart melted. Gently, she brushed the hair back from his face. Wild, untamed hair, she thought. Devil's hair, dark and seductive. ''Only a little while.''

She rested her head on his shoulder, her hand on his heart. But he was already asleep again. So she lay there, for a little while, feeling his heart beat.

Mrs. Williamson slid a stack of pancakes under Michael's nose. It seemed the least he could do was eat them. She watched him take the first bite, her arms folded over her breasts.

''The best,'' he said. ''When I get my place back together, I'm going to miss sneaking over here and having you feed me. Sure you don't want to marry me and come along?''

''You keep asking, you might get surprised.'' She topped off his coffee. The boy had always had a raging appetite, she reflected. For all manner of things. ''Did you finish up that casserole I sent down?''

''I ate it, bowl and all.'' Absently, he reached down to scratch the kitten that wound hopefully through his legs. ''And the pie, and those cookies.'' He grabbed her hand, nibbling on it while she clucked at him. ''If you were to see your way to making one of those chocolate cakes. The one with the cream and the cherries?''

''Black Forest. Miss Laura's favorite.''

''It is?'' Apparently they shared the same taste out of

bed as well. "She probably wouldn't miss a piece, or two, of it."

"We'll see about it." She skimmed her hand through his hair, tugged on the ponytail. "You need a decent haircut. Man your age wearing your hair like a hippie."

"The last hippie emigrated to Greenland in 1979. There's a small commune there where they still make love beads."

"Oh, you're a smart one, you are. Eat your breakfast. I've got to see that those children are fed before they go off to school. And Miss Laura," she continued, bustling back to the stove. "Eats like a sparrow. Never takes the time to sit down and start the day with a decent meal. 'Just coffee,' she tells me. Well, you can't fuel a body on coffee."

Laura's body seemed fueled fine to him, but he didn't think it wise to mention it. Mrs. Williamson might be fond of him, but he didn't imagine she'd approve of him luring the mistress into hot, sweaty bouts of sex.

"She's going to make herself sick, like Miss Katie did last year."

Michael stopped brooding, looked up. "Kate was sick?"

"An ulcer." Even the idea of it insulted her. Mrs. Williamson stopped flipping pancakes to turn around to him. "Can you imagine that? Overdoing, undereating, overworrying until she was flat on her back. Well, we took care of that right enough."

"She's okay now? She looks great."

"Fit and fine. And expecting, too."

"Kate's pregnant?" The grin split Michael's face. "No shit?" He winced when she sent him a narrowed look. He remembered she didn't care for such language in her kitchen. "Sorry."

"We'll overlook it, this time. She's got herself healthy and happy, our Kate. That man she married won't let her get away with that kind of nonsense. There's a sensible man, one who knows how to take care of a woman."

"They look good together." Classy, Michael thought, frowning down at his plate. But then, Byron had grown up in Southern comfort, and Kate was, in every way that mattered, a Templeton. "They fit," he added.

"That they do. It's a good feeling to see Miss Kate happy, and Miss Margo so nice and settled. And what's Miss Laura got but those two angels to raise on her own?" She gestured with her spatula, stopped for a breath. "It's a good thing her parents are coming back for a time. There's no one in the world straightens out a tangle like Mr. and Mrs. T."

When the door opened, she closed her mouth, not wanting to be taken for gossiping.

"Mrs. Williamson, I—oh, hello, Michael."

Laura looked as fresh as a rosebud in her neat pale yellow suit. Not at all like the woman who had sobbed out his name the night before. Unless you looked at the eyes.

"Hello, Laura. Mrs. Williamson took pity on a starving man."

"Blueberry pancakes. The girls will be in heaven."

"Sit down, Miss Laura, and have a plate now."

"No, I can't. Just coffee, please. I was looking for Annie." She accepted the cup Mrs. Williamson handed her. "I've got to go in early. There's a problem at the office." She looked at her watch. "I should be in the car already. I can't find Annie, and I need to see if she can run the girls to school."

"She's gone. It's her day for the farmers' market."

"Oh." Laura pressed her fingers to her eyes. "I forgot. Then I'll have to—"

"I'll run them in."

Busily rearranging her schedule, Laura blinked at him. "What?"

"I'll run them to school."

"I couldn't impose, but—"

"It's no problem, and I don't think you have time to argue about it. Go on to work. I think I can get two girls to school without permanent damage."

"I didn't mean—" He was right, she admitted with another glance at her watch. She didn't have time to argue.

"I appreciate it. Thanks. It's Hornbecker Academy. If you take 1 South to—"

"I know where it is," he interrupted. "Same place you went."

"Yes." She'd had no idea he'd known where she went to school, much less remembered it. "I really appreciate this, Michael. I'm so late." She set the coffee aside, then stood, flustered, when he took her hand.

"Relax. The hotel's not going to collapse if you're late for a meeting."

"No, but my department might. Ali has to turn in her English composition this morning. She has it; I checked. But you might want to remind her. And Kayla should go over her spelling words on the drive in. She has a test. Ali can help her."

"I said I'll handle it."

"Yes, but, if you'd make sure they take umbrellas. I've set them out. It may rain."

"Now." He rose and, forgetting he had an audience, took her face in his hands and kissed her. "Go away."

"I—" She glanced over to where Mrs. Williamson was by all appearances busy humming over her pancakes. "I'm going. But they need to be reminded to feed the dog. Sometimes—"

"Out." Because she apparently needed a boost, he pulled her to the door. "Go nag somebody else."

When she opened her mouth again, he gave her a friendly slap on the butt to send her along. "How does anyone start a morning like that?" he wondered, then turned and found Mrs. Williamson eyeing him soberly.

He cursed, but was wise enough to do it only mentally. "Is it like that around here every day?"

Ignoring his question, she stepped forward, walked around him. He thought he had a pretty good idea of what she was seeing. A man who came in the back door because he didn't belong at the front one.

She stopped, faced him, pursed her lips. "I wondered if you had your eye on anything else around here besides my cooking."

Because she had a way of making him want to shuffle his feet, he tucked his hands in his pockets. "So?"

"So—good." She gave his cheek a brisk pat, and was amused by the surprise on his face. The boy, she thought, had never had a clue of his own worth. "So—good for both of you, and about time, I say. First time in her life that girl's had a real man."

Humbled speechless, he shook his head. When he found his voice again, he took her hands. "Mrs. Williamson, you slay me."

"I will if you break her heart. But in the meantime, you should be good for each other. Now sit down and finish your breakfast before it's cold. If you're going to handle those girls yourself this morning, you need your fuel."

"I love you. I really do."

Her face creased in a wide smile. "I know that, boy. I love you right back. Now sit down and eat. They'll be down in a minute and chattering like magpies."

Chapter Fourteen

Michael Fury had jumped off buildings, fought in jungles, weathered a typhoon at sea, raced cars at high speed and, at one time or another, broken several major bones in his body.

He'd been in bar fights, spent the night in a cell where the artwork on the walls ran to anatomically exaggerated etchings of female organs. He had killed men and loved women.

And he had, he realized, led a sheltered life.

He had never faced the perils and predicaments of getting two girls out of the house on a school day.

"What do you mean you can't wear those shoes?"

"They don't go with my outfit."

His eyes narrowed as he studied Ali's floral skirt and pink sweater. Hadn't she been wearing some green thing a minute ago? "That's what you said the last time. And it looks fine to me. They're just shoes."

In the way of every female since Eve strapped on a fig

leaf, Ali rolled her eyes. "They're the wrong shoes. I have to change them."

"Well, hurry up. Jesus," he muttered as she dashed back upstairs, leaving Kayla tugging on his hand.

"I forgot how to spell 'bedlam.' "

"A-l-l-i-s-o-n."

She giggled at that. "No, really. Is it l-a-m or l-e-m?"

"A." He was pretty sure. Spelling homework wasn't exactly his strong point. And if they didn't get moving, he was going to be late meeting his contractor. The backup with building permits had already put him behind. Now Allison and her shoes . . . "Allison, I'm walking out the door with or without you in ten seconds."

"Sometimes Mama says that, too," Kayla informed him. "But she never does."

"I will. Come on." He tugged Kayla to the door.

"You can't go without her." Eyes wide, Kayla trotted beside him to his car. "Mama's going to be mad if you do."

"We're going. In the car, come on."

"How will Ali get to school?"

"She can walk," Michael said grimly. "In whatever shoes she's picked out this time."

He'd solved the crisis of Kayla's broken barrette, hadn't he? And her hair looked okay to him tied back with the rubber band he'd pulled out of his own hair. He hadn't panicked when Ali claimed to have misplaced her book bag but had found it himself, under the kitchen table, where she'd dumped it during her breakfast.

He'd remained the calm mediator when the two girls had fallen into a minor catfight over whose turn it was to feed the pets. And he had not faltered when Bongo had expressed his sorrow that his young mistresses were leaving him by peeing in the foyer.

No, he had stood strong through all of that, Michael thought as he gunned the engine. But he knew when he was being dicked around, and he wasn't taking it.

Impatience turned to smugness when he saw Ali flying out of the house. Indignation flashed in her eyes as she pulled open the car door. "You were going without me."

"That's right, Blondie. Get in."

Not wanting him to see, under the circumstances, that the nickname delighted her, she angled her chin. "There's only two seats. Where am I supposed to sit?"

"Beside your sister."

"But—"

"In. Now."

At the snapped order, she moved fast, squeezing beside Kayla. Pouting dramatically when Michael reached over to tug the seat belt around both of them, she announced, "I don't think this is legal."

It was her best lady-of-the-manor voice, Michael realized. Her mother's voice. "Call a cop," he muttered and started down the drive.

For the next fifteen minutes, he was treated to a run of complaints. "She's pushing me." "She's taking all the room." "She's sitting on my skirt."

The muscle behind his eye began to twitch. How did anyone—*anyone*—tolerate this every morning of their life?

"I need to go over my words," Kayla wailed. "I'm having a test. Michael, Ali's pushing her elbow in me again."

"Ali, get a grip." He blew away the hair that, thanks to his gift to Kayla, danced in his eyes.

"There's not enough room," Ali informed him loftily. "She's taking up the whole seat."

"I am not."

"You are too."

"I am—"

At the snarl issuing from the man beside them, both girls lapsed into momentary silence.

Satisfied, Michael took a calming breath. "What are the spelling words?"

"I can't remember. I have them written down in my notebook." The wail inched back into her voice. "If I don't get a hundred, I don't get to play on the computer at free time."

"So get the notebook out."

This, as he should have known, caused more complaints.

"You're stepping all over my shoes. You're getting them dirty. Kayla, I'm going to—"

"I don't want to hear about those shoes, Blondie." The twitch was back, double time. "Not a word about the shoes."

"Here are my words." Triumphant, Kayla waved the notebook, conking him on the head in her enthusiasm.

"Well, study them or something."

"No, Ali reads them, and I spell them. And I have to use each one in a sentence."

"I don't want to read them."

Michael sent Ali a narrow look. "Want to walk?"

"Oh, all right." With little grace, she snatched the notebook. "They're just baby words."

"They are not. You're just mad because Tod likes Marcie better than you."

"He does not. And I don't care anyway. And you didn't learn your words because you were too busy drawing dumb pictures."

"They are not dumb. You're dumb because—"

"Cut it out. Right now. If I have to stop this car . . ." Appalled, he trailed off. Had he just said what he thought he'd said? Dear Christ. He was forced to take several calming breaths. "Allison, just read the words."

"I'm going to." She sniffed, peered down her nose at Kayla's carefully written list. "Committed."

"C-o-m-m-i-t-t-e-d." She parroted the letters, then bit her lip. She fumbled for the sentence, looked hopefully at Michael.

"Michael Fury, innocently volunteering to drive two young girls to school, has now been committed to an institution for the permanently insane."

It made Ali laugh. "He's just being silly."

"Don't bet on it, kid." But he racked his brain to come up with an alternative. "The witness pointed accusingly at the man who had committed the crime. How's that?"

"Okay."

They ran through the rest, with Michael nearly cross-eyed by the time he pulled through the gates of the academy. His ancient Porsche merged with shining Mercedes, sedate Lincolns, and snappy four-wheel-drives.

"Scram," he said, unhooking the seat belt. "I'm late."

"You're supposed to say 'Have a good day,' " Kayla reminded him.

"Yeah? Well, have one, then. Later."

"Michael." She rolled her eyes. "Now kiss us goodbye." She pursed her lips, planted one on him.

Amused, he peered over at Ali. "Ali doesn't want to kiss me. She's still mad at me."

"I am not." She sniffed, then graciously leaned over Kayla and touched her lips to his cheek. "Thank you for driving us to school."

"It was my . . . education," he told her, then watched them scurry up the granite steps with hordes of other children.

"Jesus, Laura." He rested his aching head on the steering wheel. "How do you get through that every day without drinking heavy?"

She could have told him it was all a matter of planning, discipline, and priorities. And prayers for patience. At the end of this particular day, because the first three had crumbled in her hands, she was doing a lot of praying.

Could she have anticipated that two women from rival romance magazines would start a fistfight in the lobby? She didn't think so. Could she have guessed that after their efforts to dispel the hair-pulling, teeth-snapping, name-calling furor, two of her bell people would require stitches? She doubted it.

She could have, after the event, predicted the arrival of the press, the cameras, the questions, and the necessity for her to answer questions. But she didn't have to like it.

Things hadn't gone that much more smoothly when she'd arrived, late, at Pretenses to find Kate in an uproar because Margo had delved into her sacrosanct spreadsheets.

Then there had been the customer who instead of watching the three children she'd herded into the shop with her, loitered in the wardrobe room while they ran rampant.

The result was a broken vase, finger-smudged counters, and frazzled nerves. The woman left in a huff after being asked to watch her children and pay for the damages.

Life was no more simple when she returned home, ready to whimper, and found herself faced with an upcoming science project, the request to volunteer to chaperone a field trip to the aquarium, and that parental terror, long division.

It didn't perk up her mood to discover that Bongo had expressed his adoration for her by burrowing into her closet and chewing three shoes—each from a different pair.

And her parents were arriving the next day.

All right. Laura scrubbed her hands over her face after she'd changed into slacks. She would handle it. Homework was done, Bongo chastised, and it was unlikely that Templeton would be sued because a couple of women went ballistic in the lobby.

Still, she needed some air, which would give her an opportunity to make certain that old Joe had the garden up to speed, that the paths had been swept. And since she'd forgotten to ask Ann to see that the pool was vacuumed and readied for her mother's visit, she would see to that herself.

Rolling up her sleeves as she went, she passed Ali's room. She stopped a moment and smiled. She heard both of her daughters inside, chattering away over some recent movie heartthrob who wasn't yet old enough to shave. They were giggling.

Nothing could be really wrong with the world when her daughters were giggling.

She slipped out the side door, knowing that Ann would lecture her to leave the landscaping and pool to old Joe and his grandson. But Laura knew that young Joe was cramming for his final exams. And it would take her ten—well, twenty—minutes to put things right. Besides, she enjoyed the mindless task of manually vacuuming the pool.

It gave her a chance to dream in the garden, which, she noted with pleasure, was blooming beautifully. Old Joe's bursitis must have been behaving itself. He'd put in new beds of annuals, filling in among the perennials with splashes of color and sweeps of shape.

The paths were swept clean, the mulch damp from watering and raked smooth. ''Looks like we're in business,'' she said to the pup, who trotted along with her. She'd had to forgive him for the shoe incident when he looked so ashamed and contritely licked her face. ''Now you sit and behave yourself.''

Willing to make amends, Bongo plopped on the skirt of the pool, watching her over his shaggy paws out of eyes dazed with love.

Of course, Laura thought, if she'd remembered to pick up a new droid, the pool would be cleaned automatically. All she had to do was remember to write it down when she went back in the house. Otherwise, she was going to have to break down and buy one of those electronic pads like Kate kept in her pocket at all times.

But it wasn't a problem to unwind the hoses from their tidy box in the pool shed, or slip the attachments together. She went about it mechanically, daydreaming. She would settle the kids for the night. It was so good to have Ali smile and mean it at their good-night hug.

Perhaps Ali was disillusioned about her father, but she felt better about herself. That was what mattered most.

Then she would go over the household accounts with Annie, Laura mused. Things were looking up there as well. Her dual incomes and the interest on the investments Kate had made for her were holding them above water. By Laura's calculations, in another six months or so, they might actually be able to swim a few laps.

So, she wouldn't sell any more of her jewelry unless absolutely necessary. She wouldn't have to duck and dodge questions from her parents, or Josh.

And maybe, just maybe, she'd be able to juggle funds to buy that horse for Ali after all. She'd take a close look at her own books later. Or tomorrow, she mused, thinking of Michael.

She wanted to go to him again tonight, to forget everything but being. Feeling. He did that for her, made her feel like the center of the universe when he made love to her.

She'd always dreamed of a man who would think of nothing but her when she was in his arms. Who would lose himself in her as she lost herself in him. Of knowing that he was so focused on her when he touched her that there was room for nothing else in his mind or heart.

Oh, she did wish she knew his heart.

That was her problem, she admitted, running the pole smoothly through the water. She wanted that foolishly romantic love she'd dreamed of as a girl.

Seraphina's love, she thought with a quiet laugh. The kind a woman would die for.

Well, she couldn't afford to be dewy-eyed enough to hurl herself off a cliff for anyone. She had children to raise, a house to run, and a career—a surprisingly interesting career—to maintain.

So she would happily settle for whatever she and Michael had between them, and be grateful for it. More than grateful, she thought, tonight, in bed, when he put his hands on her again. Those impatient, rough-palmed hands that took whatever they wanted and made her wild with need.

The way he murmured her name, softly, deeply, when he slid into her to mate.

''What the hell are you doing?''

The pole nearly slipped out of her hands at the sharp tone. Her head jerked up, and there was her lover, scowling, standing spread-legged, hands in his pockets, with his hair loose and flowing.

Fighting against a reckless urge to leap on him and tear in, she tilted her head. ''Why, I'm mixing a souffle. What does it look like?''

''Why the hell are you doing that yourself?'' He was beside her in two angry strides, pulling the pole away. ''Don't you have servants to do this?''

''Actually, no. I let the pool boy go a couple of years ago when I learned that Candy was using him for her personal maintenance as well as her pool. I found it . . . awkward.''

He wasn't going to smile, or even smirk. Coming across

her like this, seeing her laboring over some ridiculous menial chore after putting in a full day burned him.

"Then hire another one."

"I'm afraid it doesn't fit into the scheme of things just now. In any case, I'm perfectly capable of doing it myself." Taking a closer look, she brushed at his hair. "You seem a little frazzled, Michael. Rough day?"

He'd been in a pisser of a mood since his contractor had estimated it would be six months before the rebuilding was completed. There had been a lot of blah-blah about permits, inspections, zoning, but the upshot was that he was going to be Laura's tenant for a great deal longer than he'd anticipated.

He didn't want to be her tenant, to hand over a rent check every month. It wasn't the money, he thought, fuming. It was the . . . It was awkward.

"I've had better." He nudged her aside and began to run the vacuum himself. "But we're not talking about me. You can't raise two kids, hold down two jobs, and deal with this sort of nonsense too. Why don't you just close the damn pool?"

"Because I enjoy swimming, and there are a lot of women who do a great deal more than I do and manage very well."

"They're not you." Which said it all in his mind.

"No, they don't have a beautiful home that no one would ever take from them, and they don't necessarily have a job that they're in no danger of jeopardizing if they need to flex their schedule."

Insulted, she fought with him over the pole. "I am not the pampered princess you seem to think. I'm a—" she hissed, tugged—"capable, intelligent woman who can run her life very well. I'm sick and tired of people patting me on the head and saying 'poor Laura' behind my back." She yanked, swore. "I am not poor Laura and I can clean my own goddamn pool. Give me back the stupid pole."

"No." It had calmed him considerably to see her temper flare. It wasn't much of one, as far as he could see, but there was potential in those stormy eyes, flushed cheeks, gritted teeth. ''Keep messing with me, sugar, and I'll toss you in. It's a little cool for a dip this evening.''

''Fine. Do it yourself. You're a man, after all, and men are so much more capable of doing mindless chores. But I didn't ask for your help, nor do I need it. Nor do I need your sterling advice or your unsolicited criticism on how I handle my life.''

''That's telling me,'' he said equably. ''My hands are starting to shake.''

Her eyes narrowed into slits. ''You, too, could be taking a dip.''

Interesting, he thought. Did she actually have a physical temper in there? ''Is that so? You want to try to take me down?''

''If I did you'd be treading water in—oh, no! Bongo, no!'' Insults paled when she caught sight of the pup busily digging up the newly planted pansies. ''Stop that! Stop that right now!'' She dashed across the pool skirt, snatched up the pup, and frowned at his dirt- and mulch-smeared nose. ''How could you? Didn't I tell you no? It's bad. You're not to dig in the flowers.''

When she set him down to survey the damage, Bongo cheerfully leaped into the mess and began digging again.

''I said no. Stop it. Why don't you listen to me?''

''Because he knows you're a pushover. Bongo.'' At Michael's voice, the pup lifted his head and grinned sheepishly. Michael could almost hear the sentiment: ''Well, gee, Mick, just having a little fun here.'' Michael snapped his finger, pointed, and Bongo padded out, shook himself, and sat politely.

Torn between disgust and admiration, Laura hissed between her teeth, ''How do you get him to do that?''

''It's a gift.''

''That's just great.'' Disgust won. She dragged her hands through her hair. ''I can't control a five-pound puppy.''

''Just takes practice, and patience.''

''Well, I don't have time to practice now.'' She was down on her knees in a flash, salvaging bedding plants.

''And I'm out of patience. Old Joe is going to kill me for this.''

''Laura.'' Though it seemed obvious to point it out, Michael crouched and pointed it out anyway. ''He works for you.''

''A lot you know,'' she muttered, desperately smoothing upturned mulch with her bare hands. ''If I so much as sniff an undesignated rose in his garden, he—'' she broke off, scowling. ''Don't just sit there. Help me.''

''I thought you didn't need any help.''

''Shut up, Michael.'' She brushed a hand over her cheek, smeared it with garden dirt. ''Just shut up and save these pansies before Bongo and I both end up in the pound.''

''Since you ask so nice.'' He shoved roots back into soil and heard her let out a long, keening moan.

''Not like that. For Lord's sake, you're not planting redwoods. Have a little delicacy.''

''Sorry. It's my first day on the job.'' He shook his head as she shifted and knelt in the dirt in a way that was sure to send her trim pastel slacks into the rag heap. And all, he thought, to save the sensibilities of an ancient gardener.

''You run scared of the rest of your staff, too?''

''Damn right. Most of them have been here longer than I have. This could work.'' Her hands, coated now with black soil, smoothed and patted. ''You'll hardly be able to tell when I'm done here. But who am I fooling? He can tell if you pluck a spray of crabgrass, which is fine, as long as you've asked first.''

''It's looking fine to me.''

''Like you'd know a pansy from a geranium,'' she muttered.

''Now you're getting nasty. You've got something . . .'' Casually, he swiped his hand over her cheek, adding a fresh layer of dirt. ''There. And here, you need a little to even out the look.''

''I suppose you think that's funny.'' Struggling for dignity, she brushed at her face and only succeeded in making it worse.

''No.'' He picked up a handful of damp pine mulch and dropped it onto her hair. ''That's funny.''

''A pity I don't have your raucous sense of humor. But let me try.'' She rubbed both of her filthy hands over his shirt. ''There. I'm dying from laughter now.''

He glanced down at his shirt. He'd just washed the damn thing. ''Now you've done it,'' he said quietly.

The tone warned her not to inch back, not to bother with reason and excuses. But to run. She sprang to her feet, sending the dog into frantically joyful barks. She managed two sprinting yards before he snagged her around the waist and lifted her off her feet.

''You started it,'' she managed between choked laughs.

''Uh-huh. So I'm obliged to finish it.''

''I'll have your shirt cleaned. Whoops.'' She watched the world revolve as he flipped her over into his arms. ''Why, Mr. Fury, you're so . . . masterful, so strong, so—what are you doing?'' Amusement turned to panic as she caught a glimpse of his direction and realized his intention. ''Michael, this isn't funny now.''

''Just my raucous sense of humor again,'' he told her as he strode toward the edge of the pool.

''Don't. Now I mean it, Michael.'' In self-defense, she locked her arms around his neck. ''I'm covered with dirt, and it's chilly, and I've just cleaned the pool.''

''Just look at the way it sparkles, too.'' Controlling her frantic wiggling, he toed off his shoes. ''Looks so pretty in the twilight, doesn't it?''

''I will make you pay,'' she vowed. ''I swear I will make you pay if you dare—''

''Hold your breath,'' he suggested and jumped in.

But she was shrieking when she hit the water, swallowed it, came up choking. ''You fool. You idiot. You—'' She swallowed more when he pushed her head under.

What he hadn't counted on was that Laura Templeton had been captain of her swim team, had won a drawer full of medals, and had more than once successfully defended herself against a big brother's bullying.

While he treaded water and roared with laughter, she

nipped fluidly between his legs, grabbed hold where a man was most vulnerable, and squeezed. She could hear the muffled echo of his yelp, smiled grimly, and yanked downward.

Streaking away, she broke the surface and waited smugly for him to wheeze out breaths and flail toward the side.

"Now that," she said, slicking back her dripping hair, "was funny."

He had his breath back, mostly, and eyed her narrowly. "Want to fight dirty, sugar?"

"This is my element, Michael. You're in over your head."

"Think so?" He'd done more than a few water stunts in his day. He pushed off the side and pursued.

She was faster than he'd given her credit for, and slicker. He knew when he was being taunted—the way she nipped just out of reach in a dive for the bottom. The fluidity with which she changed direction and dodged.

They surfaced again, watching each other over the lapping water. "Wet jeans are constricting."

She cocked her head. "If you need an excuse." She snagged one of her shoes as it floated by, sighed. "Four pair in one day. Has to be a record." Philosophically, she planted her feet and stood.

The water streamed off her, glued the thin material of her blouse to the high, full curve of breast, to the narrow torso and subtle flare of hip. In the shadowed light her dripping hair curled wildly and glowed like wet gold.

"Now you are playing dirty," he murmured.

Pouring the water out of her shoe, she looked over at him. Her hand remained aloft, her eyes on his as he slowly skimmed through the water toward her. As he stood, he slid his hands over her thighs, hips, sides, and left them molded to her breasts.

"Michael." The shoe dropped out of her hand and plopped into the water. "We can't."

"I'm just going to kiss you." His hands slipped wetly to her back, down to cup her bottom as he eased back until they were floating again. "And touch you. And drive us both a little crazy."

"Oh." Her head was already spinning as his teeth caught her lip, tugged. "Well, if that's all."

She wrapped herself around him, let him take her through the cool water. It was her mouth that grew hungrier, more avid, seeking his over and over again, going deeper with tongues tangling, breath clashing.

Need pounded through him with anvil shocks. She was destroying him, her legs gripped hard so that her tight little body molded to his, her hips moving seductively so that sex rubbed sex.

"Laura—"

But she answered with an impatient moan, tunneling her hands through his hair, savaging his throat. His loins began to throb like a wound.

"Hold on a minute."

"I want you." Her voice was thick, the words hot against his skin. "I want you. I want you."

"We can't do this here." Could they? His mind went blank when her mouth fit to his again. He sank with her so that the water surrounded them. Her hair floated out, like the mermaid who watched them from the bottom.

He wanted to keep sinking, sinking, just like this with his mouth hard on hers. Sink into a world where air didn't matter, light didn't matter. Where there was nothing but her and this churning, sweet ache of need.

When they surfaced again, he shook his head, trying to clear it. Then kicked once to keep them afloat. "No." It wasn't a word he'd expected to say to a woman under the circumstances. And it came out weak as he pressed her head onto his shoulder. "You'd better give me a minute."

She floated with him, dizzy with desire, dazed with triumph. "I seduced you."

"Sugar, you damn near killed me."

She threw her head back and laughed. "I seduced you," she repeated, her face glowing. "I didn't know I could. It's . . . liberating."

"You come on over to my place tonight and you can be

as liberated as you want. Right now, keep your hands off me.''

She linked her hands behind his neck, easing back so that she could see his face in the falling light. ''You wanted to tear my clothes off again.''

''I'm still thinking about it, so behave yourself.''

''I wanted to tear yours off, too. I wonder what that would feel like, to just rip away at your clothes, and . . . bite you. Sometimes I just want to sink my teeth into your—''

''Shut up.'' In defense, he cupped her head and pulled it to his shoulder again. ''I think I've created a monster.''

''I don't know about that, but you sure hit the switch. I like it.'' She laughed again and arched back so that she was floating from the waist up. ''Let's come back here tonight when everyone's asleep and go skinny-dipping and make love in the water. Then we'll go for a walk on the cliffs and make love there, just like Seraphina and Felipe.''

She rose up again, water streaming from her. ''Let's do something crazy.''

He was about to do something crazy just then, when he caught the sound of footsteps on the path, and movement. Subtly, he hoped, he changed his grip, hoping he wasn't holding any inappropriate part of the daughter of the house.

''Laura?'' Susan Templeton's brows shot up into her spiky bangs. She didn't consider herself to be a woman who was easily surprised, but it certainly rocked her to see her daughter clinging to a man in the pool with the look of a woman who had recently been thoroughly aroused still on her face.

''Mom?'' Shock came first, then the heat in her cheeks from embarrassment. She wiggled, but Michael held firm. Neither of them knew if it was out of stubbornness or habit. ''You're here.''

''Yes. I am.''

''But you were supposed to be here tomorrow.''

''We finished up our business a little early.'' She spoke smoothly. But then, she was a smooth woman. Small and delicately built like her daughter, she looked young and chic in her Valentino traveling suit, her dark blond hair capped gamine style around a sharp, interested face.

"We thought," she said with a faint edge of amusement, "that we'd surprise you. I think we succeeded."

"Yes. I was just—we were . . . How was the trip?" Laura ended lamely.

"Fine." Manners polished to a high sheen, Susan stepped forward, smiled. "It's Michael, isn't it? Michael Fury?"

"Yeah." With a jerk of his head he tossed his wet hair back. "Nice to see you again, Mrs. Templeton."

Chapter Fifteen

"If I'd known you were coming in this evening, I'd have held dinner, called the rest of the family." Composed now, and dry, Laura sat beside her father in the parlor.

"We ate on the plane." Thomas patted her hand. He was, thanks to his wife's discretion, blissfully unaware of what his daughter had been doing in the pool an hour earlier. "And we'll see everyone tomorrow. I swear, those girls have grown a foot since Christmas."

"It seems like." Laura sipped brandy. Her mother was upstairs putting the girls to bed, at her insistence. It postponed the questions, Laura knew. Didn't eliminate them. "They're so excited that you're here. We didn't think you'd be back until summer."

"Got to see our Katie girl," he told her. Only one of the reasons, he mused. But it would do well enough. "Imagine, our little Kate having a baby."

"She's glowing. I know it's a cliché, but she really is. She and Byron go around beaming all the time. Oh, and wait until you see J. T. Oh, Dad, he's so perfect. He's sitting up now, and he laughs all the time. Those wonderful belly laughs. I could just eat him up.'' She curled her legs up, studied him over the rim of her snifter. ''And how are you?''

''Fit and fine.''

It was no less than true. He was a handsome man, one who didn't take his health for granted and disciplined himself with exercise and interests. He wasn't one who took his business or his success for granted; he watched over things with a shrewd and focused eye. Nor did he take his family for granted—he kept them close in heart and mind.

The result was a firm body, still lanky in his fifties, a face that had lived well and accepted the lines and dents of time with gratitude. His eyes were smoke, like his daughter's, and the silver in his hair glinted richly in the lamplight.

''You don't look fit and fine,'' she said and smiled when his brow knit. ''You look dashing.''

''And you look happy.''

It relieved him, but he worried at the cause. Was it, as Annie had prophesied darkly, a transitory state attributable to Michael Fury? Or was his little girl finally finding her feet again?

''You're taking some time for yourself again?''

''I'm enjoying myself.'' It wasn't quite the answer, but it was truth. ''Ali and I have resolved some things. She's happier, so I'm happier. I love my work. My sisters keep giving me new babies to play with.'' With a sigh, she leaned her head on his shoulder. ''I haven't felt quite so content in a long time.''

''Your mother and I worry about you.''

''I know. And I won't bother to tell you not to, but I will tell you I'm fine. Better than fine.''

''We heard that Peter's to be married again.'' Her teeth went on edge. ''To Candace Litchfield.''

''Word travels,'' Laura murmured.

''People are more than pleased to spread that sort of news. Are you all right with it?''

''I was upset initially,'' she admitted, remembering that

hammer blow to the midsection when they'd made the announcement that night at the club. "A knee-jerk reaction, really. It was mostly the idea of Candy being stepmother to my babies and worry about how the girls would handle it."

"And?" he said quietly, his hand over hers.

"And now that it's all settled in, it just doesn't matter." She turned her hand under his, squeezed. "Really doesn't matter at all. The girls have adjusted. They'll go to the wedding in May because it's the right thing for them to do. They don't particularly care for Candy, but they'll be polite. Then they'll come home," she added, "and we'll get on with our lives."

"They're good girls," Thomas agreed. "Good, sharp girls. I know it's not easy for them, but they have you. So it's you I'm concerned with."

"There's no need. In fact, I've come to the conclusion that Peter and Candy are perfectly suited. I couldn't be more happy for them."

He waited a beat, ran his tongue around his teeth. "That's nasty."

"Yes." She sighed lavishly. "It is. I like it."

"That's my girl."

"Now, let's talk about something much more interesting." She sat back again, grinning. "Let me tell you about the impromptu boxing match in the lobby today."

When Susan came back in, it was to the roar of her husband's laughter and the rich undertone of her daughter's. She stood for a minute, enjoying the scene. She could count every week, every month, that had passed since she had seen her little girl laugh that freely.

Gnawing her lip, she considered. If Michael Fury had anything to do with it, she owed him. Whatever Annie might think. As a woman, she understood and appreciated the need of another woman to have, at least once, at least briefly, a dangerous man in her life.

As a mother . . . well, they would see.

"Tommy, your granddaughters want a kiss good night."

He was up like a shot. "I'll have to give them one, then."

"And no more than one story," Susan murmured to him as he passed. "No matter how much you want to play."

He pinched her cheek, winked, and walked on.

"That should keep him busy for an hour." Susan glided over to the liquor cabinet, poured herself a brandy. "And will give you time to tell me about Michael Fury."

Her mother, Laura thought, rarely circled around a point if she could zero right in. "Josh must have told you about the mud slides, how Michael lost his house."

"Yes, I know the background, Laura." Her daughter, Susan thought, could evade like a champ. "He's raising horses now and renting the stables for a time."

"He's got wonderful horses." Laura leapt on the ploy. "You'll have to see for yourself. Several are trained for stunts. It's fascinating. He's teaching the girls to ride, you know. They're crazy about him."

"And are you? Crazy about him?"

"It's been good for the girls to be around a man who pays attention to them."

Patient, Susan reached down to pet Bongo. Only one of the changes, she mused as the dog vibrated with pleasure under her hand. "I was asking about you, Laura. How you feel about him."

"I'm very fond of him. He's been helpful and kind. Are you sure you don't want me to get you something to eat? Some fruit and cheese?"

"No, I don't want fruit and cheese." Susan reached over to still her daughter's nervous hand. "Are you in love with him?"

"I don't know." Laura leveled her breath and met her mother's gaze. "I'm sleeping with him. I'm sorry if you disapprove."

"It's not for me to disapprove over something that personal at this point in your life." But there was a pang. "You're being careful?"

"Of course."

"He's very attractive."

"Yes, he is."

"And nothing like Peter."

"No," Laura agreed. "Nothing at all like Peter."

"Is that why you're attracted to him? Because he's the antithesis of your ex-husband?"

"I'm not using Peter as a yardstick." Restless, she rose. "Maybe I was, to some extent. It's difficult not to compare when you've only been with two men. I'm not sleeping with Michael to prove anything to anyone, but because it's—he makes me . . . I want him. And he wants me."

"Will that be enough for you, Laura?"

"I don't know. It's enough for now." She turned away, paced to the fire. It was quiet tonight, just a warm glow and a subtle hiss. "I failed before. I wanted it to be perfect. I wanted to be perfect. Maybe I wanted to be you."

"Oh, honey."

"It's not your fault," Laura said quickly when her mother got to her feet. "Please don't think I mean that. It's only that I grew up seeing you, how you were, how you are. So competent and wise and flawless."

"I'm not flawless, Laura. No one is."

"You were to me. You are. You never faltered, never stumbled, never let me down."

"I stumbled." She crossed the room, took her daughter's hands. "Countless times. I had your father to help me get my balance."

"And he had you to help him. That's what I always wanted, dreamed of. The kind of marriage and life and family you made. And I'm not foolish enough to think it didn't take effort and mistakes and sleepless nights to make it. But you did. I didn't."

"You make me angry when you blame yourself."

Laura shook her head. "I don't, completely. But I know I'm not blameless either. I set my sights impossibly high. Every time I had to readjust them, lower them, it was harder. I don't ever want to do that again."

"If you set your sights too low, you can miss a great deal."

''Maybe. But I'm not pushing for more here than what I have. Part of me will always want what you and Dad have. Not only for myself but for my children. But if it's not in the cards, I'm through crying over it. I'm going to give them the best life I can, and make the best one for myself too. Right now, Michael's an important part of it.''

''Does he know how important?''

Laura shrugged her shoulders. ''It's often difficult to tell how much Michael knows. But I know this. Peter didn't love me, not ever.''

''Laura—''

''No, it's true, and I can live with that.'' In fact, she discovered it was easier to live with than she had imagined. ''But I loved him, and I married him, and stayed with him for ten years. Both of us, and certainly the children, would have been better off if I hadn't been so determined to make it work. If I had just accepted the failure and let go.''

''I think you're wrong,'' Susan said quietly. ''By doing everything you could do to hold your marriage and your family together, you can look back and know you did your best.''

''Maybe.'' And perhaps one day she would look back. ''With Michael I don't have to carry the burden of making something work, or of living with the illusion that I have a man who loves me and wants what I want. And I'm happier than I've been in too long to remember.''

''Then I'm happy for you.'' And will keep my own counsel, Susan thought, for now. ''Let's go rescue your father,'' she said, tucking her arm through Laura's. ''Before those girls have him wrapped around their fingers so tight he bounces.''

The year Thomas Templeton married Susan Conroy, he added the tower suite as his innovation for Templeton House. The house had already stood a hundred years, with nearly every generation of his family toying with or expanding the original design.

He had built it out of fancy, and a love for the romantic. He had made love with his wife there countless nights, conceived both of their children within the charming rounded walls, in the big rococo bed. Although Susan often said Josh had been made on the Bokhara rug in front of the fire.

He never disputed her on such matters.

Now with flames simmering in the Adams fireplace, a bottle of Templeton champagne chilled in a silver bucket and moonlight filtering in through the high windows, he curled with his wife of thirty-six years on that same rug.

"I think you're trying to seduce me."

He offered her a glass brimming with frothy wine. "You're such a sharp woman, Susie."

"And smart enough to let you." Smiling, she touched a hand to his face. "Tommy. How could so many years have gone by?"

"You look the same." He pressed his lips to her palm. "Just as lovely, just as fresh."

"Now it takes me hours to maintain the illusion."

"It's no illusion." He nestled her head on his shoulder, watched the fire leap as a log gave way to the heat. "Do you remember the first night we slept here?"

"You carried me up the steps. Up every single one. And when you brought me in here, you had flowers everywhere, gardens of them, roses strewn over the bed. Wine chilling, the candles lighted."

"You cried."

"You overwhelmed me. You often did, and do still." She tilted her face up, brushed her lips over his jaw. "I knew I was the luckiest woman in the world to have you, to be loved the way you loved me. And to be wanted the way you wanted me." She shut her eyes, turned her face against his throat. "Oh, Tommy."

"Tell me what's troubling you. It's Laura, isn't it?"

"I can't bear to see her hurt. I can stand anything but that. Even though I know that children have to go their own way, fight their own battles, it breaks my heart. I can still remember the day she was born, the way she curled into my arms. So small and precious."

''And you think Michael Fury is going to break her heart?''

''I don't know. I wish I did.'' She rose, walked to the window that looked out over the cliffs. Cliffs, she knew, that Laura had haunted since childhood. ''It's knowing she's already had it broken that kills me inside. I spoke with her tonight when you were up with the girls. And I realized as she talked to me, that as hard as she's worked to rebuild her life, part of her is still so vulnerable, so raw. So . . . exposed. She believes she's failed, Tommy.''

''Failed, my ass.'' Incensed, he sprang up. ''Peter Ridgeway failed, in every way possible.''

''And did we fail, by not preventing?''

''Could we have stopped her?'' It was a question he'd asked himself dozens of times over the last few years. ''Could we have?''

''No,'' Susan said after a long moment. ''We might have postponed it, we might have persuaded her to wait. A few months, a year. But she was in love. She wanted what we have. That's what she said to me tonight, Tommy. She wanted what we have.''

When he laid a hand on her shoulder, she reached back, gripped tight. ''I hate that she couldn't have it. That she was denied the security and excitement and beauty of it. Now she doesn't believe she ever will have it.''

''She's a young woman, Susie. A lovely and loving young woman. She'll fall in love again.''

''She already has. She's in love with Michael, Tommy. She hasn't admitted it to herself yet; she protects herself by thinking of it as sex.''

''Please.'' He winced. ''It's not easy to think of my little girl that way.''

It made her laugh and turn to him. ''Your little girl is in the middle of a hot affair with Josh's rebellious young friend.''

''Should I get the gun?''

So she laughed again, embraced him. ''Oh, Tommy, here we are, with no way to stop it again. Nothing to do but wait and hope.''

"I could have a . . . little talk with him."

"You could. I could. But nothing we say is going to change Laura's mind, or her heart. He's gorgeous."

Intrigued, Thomas eased her back, frowned into her eyes. "Is that so?"

"Absolutely devastatingly, dangerously gorgeous. Sexy as sin." Her lips trembled at the corners as his frown deepened. "And he still has that the-hell-with-it look in his eye, the one that makes every woman still breathing think she's the one person on earth who could make him care."

"Is that what you think?"

Flattered, she patted his cheek. "I think I admire her taste and, as a woman, her luck. As a mother—I'm terrified of him."

"Maybe I will have a chat with him. Soon." Then he blew out a breath. "Damn it, Susie, I've always liked the boy."

"So have I. There was always something rawly honest about him. And whatever Annie thinks, he wasn't, and isn't, a hoodlum. What he is, is basic."

"And do we want our daughter involved with a basic man who ran off to sea at eighteen and has done any number of things not discussed in polite company?"

She winced. The same thought had passed through her head. "That sounds so snobbish."

"It sounds like parental concern to me. It doesn't matter if she's three or thirty, it's still our job to worry about her."

"And men like Michael come and go on their own whim," she murmured. "They aren't looking for roots. Laura would wither without them. And from what she said, the girls are attached to him. How will it affect them to have another man walk out of their lives?" She burrowed against him. "There's nothing we can do but be there for them."

"Then that's what we'll do. We watched Margo and Kate find the way through their problems. Laura will get through."

"And they have each other." She shifted so that they could look out toward the cliffs together. "The three of them are always there for each other. That shop of theirs has worked magic for them. Whatever happens, Laura has them, and the pride in what they've built together. But I'm greedy, Tommy."

She took his hand, laid it on her heart. "I want her to have her dream. I want her to have what we have. I want to believe that she'll stand at the window, look toward the sea, with a man's arms around her. A man who loves her and will stand by her. A man who can make her feel the way you make me feel."

She cupped his face in her hands. "So I'm going to believe it. And if she's got any of me inside her, she'll fight for what she wants. The way I fought for you."

"You ignored me," he reminded her. "Wouldn't give me the time of day."

Her smile bloomed slowly. "And it worked, didn't it? Perfectly. Then one day I let you find me, by calculated accident, alone in the rose garden at the club. And I let you kiss me, like this." She lifted her mouth, drew the kiss out, warm and slow. "And Tommy Templeton, never seeing the punch, went down for the count."

"You always were sneaky, Susie." He swung her up into his arms and made her laugh.

"And I got exactly what I wanted. Just," she murmured as he lowered her to the rug, "the way I'm going to get exactly what I want right now."

Laura saw the lights in the tower room as she walked toward the cliffs. And for a moment she stood watching the silhouette of her parents embracing. It was a lovely sight, stirred her heart. And her envy.

They fit so perfectly together, she thought, turning back toward the song of the sea. Their rhythms, their styles, their goals, their needs.

She'd learned, the hard way, that what her parents had, what they worked for and preserved, wasn't a given but a rarity to be celebrated.

Her new perspective only brought her more admiration for them.

She walked the cliffs alone, something she hadn't done for weeks. She wanted Michael. The low hum of desire was constant and thrilling, but she wouldn't go to him tonight. Nor, she believed, did he expect her.

They had parted awkwardly. She, undeniably embarrassed at having been caught frolicking in the pool by her own mother. He, obviously uncomfortable. She thought they both would need time to adjust.

The light was strong, glowing, with the clouds chased away to clear skies by a stiff westerly wind. As familiar with the cliffs as with her own parlor, Laura picked her way down, easily negotiating rocks and a path slippery with pebbles until she came to a favored ledge.

There she sat, letting the wind whip at her face and the sea thunder in her ears. And there, listening for the whisper of ghosts, thinking of lost love, she was content.

From his window, Michael watched her go down the slope, the long, loose jacket she wore streaming out behind her like a cloak. Romantic, mysterious. He pressed his hand to the glass as if he could touch her. Then drew it back, irritated with himself.

She wasn't coming to him. Small wonder, he thought, hooking his thumbs in his pockets as he watched her climb down rocks as gracefully as a fawn. Her parents were back, and with them, he expected, came a reminder of the difference in their positions.

Laura Templeton may have been working for a living, she may have scrubbed a few bathtubs, but she was still Laura Templeton. And he was still Michael Fury, from the wrong side of the hill.

She'd be busy now, he supposed. Entertaining, scheduling dinner parties during her parents' stay. Those fancy, flower-bedecked, exclusive affairs that Templeton House was renowned for.

There would be lunch at the club, quick rounds of tennis, erudite conversations over coffee and brandy.

The ritual was more foreign to him than Greek.

And he had no desire to learn either.

So, if she was going to brush him off, what was the difference? With a shrug, he turned away from the window and stripped off his shirt. He could lure her back into the sack another time or two if he wanted. Sex was nothing more than a weakness. He could exploit hers to satisfy his own.

He heaved the shirt aside, frustrated that it wasn't something hard and breakable. Goddamn it, he wanted her. Now. Here. With him.

Who the hell did she think she was?

Who the hell did he think he was?

Eyes grim, he pulled off his boots and threw them both against the wall, where they at least made a satisfying thud.

He knew exactly who he was, and so, he thought, did she. Laura Templeton was going to find herself hard-pressed to shake him loose until he was damn good and ready. He wasn't finished with her yet, not by a long shot.

She could have tonight, he thought, stripping off his jeans. He'd let her have tonight all quiet and safe. Because her nights weren't going to stay quiet, and they weren't going to stay safe.

He dropped naked to the bed and glared at the ceiling. And he would have her right back where he wanted her. The hell with her parents, her fancy friends, and her perfect pedigree.

She'd taken on a mongrel. Now she'd have to deal with him.

From her perch on the ledge, Laura stretched her arms up. Cool, damp air caressed her skin where the sleeves of her jacket fell down to her elbows. She thought of how Michael caressed that skin. Rough and demanding one moment, then the next with surprising and devastating tenderness.

He had so many moods, she thought, so many needs. He had in such a short time awakened so many moods, so many needs in her. No, she was no Sleeping Beauty, she reflected, but she felt as though she'd been sleeping for decades. Waiting for him to find her.

And he had, she realized. They'd found each other. So why was she sitting here alone, trying to reorganize her schedule for the next day, and the day after that? Tomorrow would come anyway. She could be with him right now. She'd go to him. Laura closed her eyes tight, wished. If his lights were still on when she stood and looked back, she would go to him. And he would be there waiting, wanting.

She stood, holding her breath, and turned. And let it out again as she saw nothing but night and the deeper silhouettes of darkened buildings.

He hadn't waited.

She brushed the chill from her arms, calling it foolish. It wasn't rejection, it only meant he was tired and had gone to bed. And she should do that herself. There were dozens of things that needed to be done the next day that would be done better after a good night's sleep.

And they weren't bound to spend every night together. There'd been no promises between them. None at all, she thought, furious that her eyes stung as she turned back to the sea. No promises, no plans, no soft words.

Was that what she wanted, still? After she should have known better? What weakness was this in her that craved those words, those promises, those plans? Couldn't she be content with what was and not always dream about what could be?

It didn't matter what she'd told herself, she realized, as she sat down again. It didn't matter what she'd told her mother, or Margo or Kate. Or what she'd told Michael. It had all been lies. She, who was famous for being a pathetically poor liar, had pulled this one off beautifully.

She was in love with him. She was so stupidly in love with him, and no one had a clue. Part of her had already seen them together, tomorrow, a year from tomorrow, ten years. Lovers, partners, family. More children, a home, a life.

She'd lied to him, to everyone, including herself. And now, as it was with lies, she would have to continue to spin them, and live them, to make the first of them hold.

It wouldn't be fair to him otherwise. For he hadn't lied.

He had wanted her, and she had no doubt that he cared for her. He cared for her children, was willing to offer a hand to help. He gave her his body, had awakened hers, and had offered her a friendship that she valued.

And still she wasn't satisfied.

Selfish, she wondered, or just foolish? It hardly mattered. She had created the illusion and would continue it. Or lose him.

When it was over, whenever it ended, she wouldn't regret it or curse God. She'd go on, because life was long and precious and deserved the best she could give it. When the time came and she had no choice but to live without him, she'd remember what it had been like to feel again, and to love. And she'd be grateful.

Steadier now, she braced a hand on the ground to push herself up. Her fingers closed over the disk as if they'd known it was there, waiting for her. With her heart drumming, loud as the waves below, she lifted it up, turned it under the stream of the moonlight.

It glinted dully, the single gold coin. Untouched, she thought with a shiver, unseen, for a hundred and fifty years. Since a young girl, desperate, had hidden it away to save for her lover. This, the symbol of the dream, the promise and the loss, lay cool in the center of her palm.

"Seraphina," she murmured. And her breath caught as she closed her fingers over the coin, as she felt the wild need of a reckless young girl.

Laura curled into a ball on the ledge, high over the violent waves. And wept.

Chapter Sixteen

The sorrel colt was bright, pretty, and stubborn as a flea-bitten mule. Michael was working hard to prove that he was even more stubborn.

"By God, you'll do it, you little bastard. You know how."

As if to say that was hardly the point, the colt tossed his head, rolled his eyes in Michael's direction, and stood firm. They'd been dealing with each other for just over six months, and both of them wanted to be in charge.

"You think you've got these fancy digs and three squares to stand around posing?" Michael slapped the bat in his hand, and the colt's ears flickered. "You even think about kicking me again and you'll be eating dirt."

He stepped forward, the colt danced back. Michael's eyes narrowed dangerously. "Hold!"

Vibrating, the colt did so, pawing the ground in challenge as Michael approached.

"You and me," Michael said, gripping the bridle as the

colt began to swing around to get a good shot with his back leg, ''we're going to go a round.''

''Don't you dare strike that animal.''

Both Michael and the colt looked up in annoyance at the sharp order and saw the trim form swinging through the paddock gate.

''You should be ashamed of yourself.'' Fired up, Susan grabbed the colt's bridle and stepped between the horse and the bat. ''I don't care if he belongs to you or not. I won't have an animal mistreated on my property.''

As if realizing that sympathy was on his side, the colt lowered his head and nuzzled Susan's shoulder.

''Suck up,'' Michael muttered. ''Look, Mrs. Templeton, I—''

''Is this the way you treat your horses? Clubbing them when they don't behave as you'd like? You brute.'' Color flashed into her cheeks, reminding Michael of Laura. ''If you dare to raise a hand to one of these animals while I'm around, I'll personally kick your butt off Templeton property and halfway to hell.''

Yes, he could see now where Laura got those licks of temper he'd caught a few glimpses of. And he could have sworn the colt was smirking at him. ''Mrs. Templeton—''

''Then I'll have you arrested,'' she barreled on. ''There are laws against cruelty to animals. Laws created to deal with insensitive brutes like you. And if you ever dare to mistreat this sweet horse—''

''There's not a sweet bone in his body,'' Michael interrupted, resisting the urge to rub the thigh that still sang from its rude encounter with a hoof. ''And I wasn't going to use this to beat sense into his hard head, though it's tempting.''

She'd seen the look in his eye, and the bat in his hand. Threw up her chin. ''I suppose you were going to play baseball with him.''

''No, ma'am.'' It might be funny, years later, when he didn't ache everywhere. ''We're not playing at anything here. And if you want to take a good look, you'll see the only one with bruises on him in this paddock is me.''

She did look, noted that although the coat was gleaming with a healthy layer of sweat, the horse was unharmed. In fact, he was magnificent. And the look in his eye wasn't fear, she realized. It was, if such a thing were possible, humor.

Michael, on the other hand, was filthy, and there was the telltale outline of a hoofprint on the leg of his jeans.

"If you threaten him with a bat, his only recourse is to strike out. I would think you'd—"

"Mrs. Templeton." Patience was wearing thin and going ragged around the edges. "Does this little bastard look threatened to you? Right now all he's doing is gloating."

It appeared that he was, Susan admitted, making another close study of the colt's eyes.

"Then explain why—"

"If you'd just let loose of him before he sees I can be slapped around by a woman half my weight and I completely lose the upper hand here, along with six months' work, I'd appreciate it."

She did loosen her grip on the bridle, but warily. "I'm warning you, Michael. If you dare to hurt him, I'll do more than slap you around."

"I believe it," Michael muttered as she took a single step back. "Would you move back to the fence, please? Bastard still has a problem with control."

"Charming name." With her arms folded, Susan took a few more steps in retreat. And stayed poised, ready to leap.

"You've got me in it now, haven't you?" With a firm hand, Michael took the bridle, pulled the colt's head down until their eyes were level. "Make me look like an idiot, pal, and I might just mistake your face for a Spalding. Got that?"

The colt snorted, then jerked his head clear when Michael released it. Michael shifted his grip on the bat, curling fingers around tip and base, then lifted it. After a humming war of wills, the colt reared up, pawed the air.

"Up." Heedless of striking hooves, Michael stepped under them. "Stay up there, Bastard. Nobody'll feed you if you kill me." Shifting the bat again, he grabbed a handful of mane and swung up onto the nearly vertical back.

At the quick and easy grace of the move, the fluidity with which man and horse merged, Susan sighed in admiration. And again when Michael turned the mount in a half circle.

The pressure of Michael's knees brought the horse down. "Stay back," Michael ordered Susan, without looking at her. "This is the part we're having trouble with."

He brought Bastard into a rear again, rolled off and under the dancing hooves. "Don't you step on me," Michael muttered, as he felt the ground shake. "Don't you step on me, you son of a—shit!"

A hoof caught him in the hip. Just a graze, but it was the principle of the thing. He was on his feet again, staring the horse down. "You did that on purpose. You're going to do it again till you get it right."

Limping only a little, Michael picked up the discarded bat and went through the entire routine again. And again.

When they were both winded and he'd managed to complete the drill without breaking anything, Michael, limping a bit more, went over to the bag he'd slung over the fence and took out an apple.

The colt followed him, pushed his head against Michael's back. "Don't try to make up. I'm only giving you this because I'm not on my way to the hospital."

The colt nudged him again, then tried to eat Michael's hair.

"Cut it out. You are such an ass kisser. Here." The apple he offered was taken eagerly. "And you have revolting manners," he added when bits of apple flew.

"I owe you an apology."

Michael stopped rubbing his bruised butt and looked at Susan. In his concentration, he'd forgotten she was still there. "No problem. Maybe I was thinking about bashing him one."

"No, you weren't." She stepped over, ran a hand over the colt's smooth neck. "You're in love with him."

"I hate the bastard. Don't know why I ever took him on."

''Um-hmm.'' She smiled, absently brushed some of the paddock dirt off the sleeve of Michael's shirt. ''He certainly looks ill-kept, ill-used. Ill-fed too.''

Embarrassed now, Michael shrugged. ''He's an investment. A good stunt horse earns good money.''

''I'm sure.'' She simply couldn't stand it—now she broke into excited questions. ''How in the world did you teach him to do that? How do you keep him from trampling you? Aren't you worried? How long have you been working with him?''

Rolling his aching shoulders, Michael settled on the last question. ''Not long enough. He's smart, but he's got some rough edges.'' Then he grinned. ''You had me quaking, Mrs. Templeton. I figured you were going to grab the bat out of my hands and go to work on me with it.''

''I might have.'' She caressed the colt. ''I can't stand to see something abused.''

''Can't say I care for it myself. There was this wrangler on a set a while back. He had this terrific horse, sweet-natured, generous. But the wrangler was never satisfied, always pushing for more, working that horse to exhaustion and never giving anything back. It was bad enough to see him breaking that horse's heart, and his spirit, but then he started using a whip, and his fists, and whatever else came in handy.''

Michael paused to shovel the hair out of his eyes, squint at the sun. ''He got himself a bad rep. Nobody wanted to hire him or work with him anymore. They all said it was too damn bad, 'cause that horse was a rare one.''

''Why wasn't something done?''

''There's politics, the network—the wrangler'd been in the game a long time. I was pretty new at it then, and I never did care much for politics. I talked him into selling me that horse. Made a pretty decent stake working with him.''

''You talked the wrangler into selling?''

Michael looked back at her. ''More or less.''

''Did you use the whip, or just your fists?''

''I don't care for whips. And Max, the walker I bought,

he can't stand the sight of them.'' He nipped the bag away before the colt could investigate the contents. ''You out for a walk this morning, Mrs. Templeton?''

''I could use that for an excuse. But I imagine we both know I wanted to speak with you.''

''Yeah, I figured you or your husband would come down.'' And he'd prepped himself for it. ''You're going to have to talk while I work. My stock need some exercise.''

''All right.'' She went with him as he walked out of the paddock and into the stables. ''Laura tells me you're giving the girls riding lessons.''

''Just a few basics. I've got some quiet saddle ponies.''

''I was treated to a dissertation on Mr. Fury and his horses over breakfast this morning. You've made quite an impression on my granddaughters. Let me help you,'' she said, taking the bridle of one of the horses he'd begun to lead out. ''And you've made an impression on my daughter as well.''

''She's a beautiful woman.''

''Yes, she is. And she's been through hell. In many ways it's made her stronger. But she's vulnerable, Michael, and more easily bruised than either you or she might realize.''

''You want me to promise not to hurt her.'' He stepped back as the horses trotted into the paddock. ''I can't do that.''

''No, you wouldn't do that. As I recall, even as a boy you were careful not to make promises.''

''You don't make, you don't break,'' he said simply and went back to the stables.

''You had a difficult childhood,'' she began, then broke off, raising her eyebrows, when his head whipped around.

''I don't believe in blaming what is on what was. I imagine you had a dandy childhood. Is that responsible for everything you are?''

She nodded slowly as he led out the next horses. ''Well put,'' she murmured. ''No, I wouldn't like to think so, but it did give me a solid foundation to build on.''

''And mine's shaky.'' Though he'd told himself he wouldn't allow it, the bitterness came through. ''You don't have to tell me where I come from, Mrs. Templeton. I know.''

She stopped him by reaching up, closing her hand over his. ''That wasn't a criticism. I'm not blind, Michael, and I don't like to think I'm narrow-minded either. I can see you're building something here. And I know why you left your childhood behind before anyone should have to.''

When he said nothing, she smiled and let him go. ''I know what goes on in my own house, Michael, and I know what goes on in the lives of my children's friends. If your back needs to go up because I felt sorry for that boy, then so be it. My heart broke for you.''

''You wasted your sympathy.''

''I don't think so, but as you said, that's what was. Now is what is. You never cross the wire in the marathon of parenthood, Michael. You never finish the race and take a victory lap. Laura is a grown woman, free to make her own choices and live her own life, but that doesn't stop me from worrying or wondering or hoping she chooses well.''

He knew what she was telling him, had expected it. ''And you've got to wonder, considering things, if she's choosing well this time.''

She nodded slowly. ''Yes. I won't say that sex doesn't last. It can and does if you're lucky. But it isn't enough by itself.''

He'd expected to be warned away, but he wasn't ready to be pushed. ''If you've come down here to ask me to stay away from her, you're wasting your time. I won't do it.''

She measured him. ''I'd be disappointed in you if you would. What I'm asking you to do is be kind.'' She looked away to where the horses pranced. ''Just be kind.''

''You want a promise, I'll give you one. I'll never treat her the way Ridgeway did. I won't cheat or lie or take anything from her she doesn't want to give me. And I won't leave her feeling like a failure.''

Susan's gaze came back and sharpened. It was the words, yes, but more the edgy anger behind them that had her reevaluating. ''You understand better than I gave you credit for.''

''I understand failure just fine.'' And he knew that compared to a woman like Susan Templeton, he might not be a failure, but he could hardly be considered a success. ''If that's all, I've got work to do.''

''Michael.'' Remembering that he'd always been easily roused and prone to impatience, she kept her hand firm and her eyes level with the storm in his. ''It's nice to have you at Templeton House again. Now will you show me the horse you told me about? Is it that walker over there watching you as if he'd die if you asked him to?''

Michael blew out a breath and wondered how a man was supposed to understand any of the Templeton females. ''Yeah, that's Max. He's just hoping for a handout.''

''Why don't you introduce me?''

''I actually told her I was sleeping with him.'' Laura kept her voice low as she slipped clothes back onto hangers in the wardrobe room. ''I can't believe I stood there and told my own mother I was having sex with Michael.''

''Odds are, she'd figured it out for herself.'' Margo slipped discarded shoes back into their slots. ''And probably wasn't all that shocked, as it's likely she knew you'd had sex before. Seeing as you have two children.''

''You know what I'm talking about,'' Laura mumbled. ''It's weird.''

''How'd she take it?''

''Well enough. Poor Dad is tiptoeing around the subject as though if he wakes it up it would start an orgy.''

''Well, you could hardly pretend nothing was going on when Mrs. T caught you and Michael playing lifeguard in the pool.'' She chuckled, checked her hair in the mirror. ''God, I wish I'd seen that one.''

''I'm sure it was illuminating for all parties. It felt like that time Annie caught us necking with Biff and Mark on the cliffs. The cliffs!'' she exclaimed before Margo could comment. ''Lord, my mind is a sieve today! Wait.''

She dashed out, nearly bumping into a customer and

causing Kate to eye her curiously. In the back office, Laura dug her purse out of a drawer and the coin out of the small zippered compartment.

"What's the problem?" Kate demanded, slipping in. "Did Margo forget to order boxes again? We'll be out by Monday if she hasn't—what have you got there?"

"The cliffs." Laura pressed a hand to her heart. "Last night. I forgot."

"You found one!" In a leap, Kate snatched it from Laura's hand. Excitement and triumph spurted straight up into her heart. "You found another one! Seraphina's dowry. And you forgot to tell us?"

"This morning was such a zoo. I didn't know I would be in until Dad insisted he'd cover for me at the hotel, and then Kayla and Ali were begging to stay home from school to spend time with Mom, and—oh, never mind," she finished with a wave of her hand. "Yes, I forgot."

Margo opened the door behind them. "Would the two of you mind terribly if we attempted to run the business today? We have customers who—what have you got?"

"Laura found it. And forgot."

"When?" Letting the door close smartly at her back, Margo took the coin from Kate. "Where?"

"Last night. On the cliffs. On that ledge where I like to sit sometimes. I was just sitting there, thinking, and when I started to go back, I saw it. Well, felt it," Laura corrected. "I put my hand down right on it. I'd been sitting right beside it."

"Just like the other times," Margo murmured. "When one was just there for me and one was just there for Kate. It's a sign."

"There she goes." Kate rolled her eyes and eased a hip onto the desk.

"Well, what would you call it?" Margo snapped back. "We search like maniacs, have been on and off since we were kids. Nothing. We've all but groomed those cliffs with tweezers. Nothing," she said again, gesturing wildly. "Then each one of us goes there, at some turning point in her life, and there it is. A coin. One for each. Which means . . .''

She stopped, looked up from the gold glinting in her hand, and stared at Laura. ''Which means,'' she said slowly, ''you're in love with Michael Fury.''

''What in the world does one have to do with the other?'' To buy time, Laura took the coin back, set it in the middle of the desk blotter.

''The day I went there and found mine, I was thinking about Josh and what I was going to do about being in love with him. And Kate—'' She looked over at her friend, who was frowning in thought. ''She went, thinking about Byron. You were in love with him, weren't you?''

''Yeah, but . . .'' Kate trailed off. ''Look, this is a little too *Twilight Zone* for me.''

''Open that accountant's mind for a minute.'' Impatient, Margo turned back to Laura and took her by the shoulders. ''Are you in love with Michael?''

''That isn't—''

''I asked a direct question, Laura, and I'll know if you lie.''

''All right, yes, but it doesn't—''

''Love matters,'' Margo said quietly. ''We matter. Maybe that's the whole point.'' She released Laura and reached into her pocket, where she habitually carried her coin. ''This matters.'' She placed it beside Laura's and looked at Kate, who rose and took her own out of her purse.

''It matters,'' Kate agreed when the three coins sat side by side. ''We're still in it together. Have you told Mick, Laura?''

''No. And no, I don't know if I'm going to, or how I'll handle it. I can't plan things out like you, Kate, or run on instinct the way you do, Margo. I have to do it my way. Which means, I suppose, maintaining illusions and waiting to see what comes. And my emotions are my responsibility.''

Then she smiled, traced a fingertip over all three coins. ''A sign from Seraphina. Well, maybe it is. Maybe she's telling me not to put all my dreams into one man's hands this time.''

''Or she might be telling you that you can find that dream if you know where to look.'' Margo draped an arm over Laura's shoulders. ''Either way, you can't stop looking. It's the same as jumping off a cliff.''

''I haven't stopped looking.'' She patted Margo's hand before reaching for her coin. ''And I think this calls for a celebration. Why don't we get together tonight and open some champagne?''

''Talked me into it.'' Kate pocketed her own coin. ''I was coming over anyway. Poker night at the De Witts'.''

''That's right.'' Laura grinned. ''Dad's already rubbing his palms together. So, Margo, are you up for it?''

''I'll be there.'' Margo picked up her coin but held it. She hoped Laura wouldn't put hers—or her dreams—away too quickly. ''Maybe we can get Mum and Mrs. T a little drunk and play some poker ourselves.''

''I'm game. Why don't we—'' Kate broke off at the brisk knock on the office door. The customer who poked her head in seemed annoyed and impatient.

''Excuse me, but is anyone working here?''

''I'm so sorry.'' All conciliatory smiles, Laura stepped over. ''We had a small problem. What can I help you with?''

Michael had never been driven to a poker game in a limo, and he wasn't sure how he felt about it. Not that he hadn't ever ridden in one before. After all, he'd worked in Hollywood for five years.

But to a poker game? It felt, well, pretentious.

Then again, as Josh had said when he came to the stables to fetch him, no one would have to worry about how many beers they knocked back.

Obviously at home in the plush surroundings, Thomas leaned back and tapped his finger on his knee in time with the aria playing on the stereo.

All Michael could think was that big limos, opera, and

poker didn't mix. And he began to worry just what the hell he'd gotten himself into.

"I'm feeling lucky." Thomas wiggled his eyebrows. "I hope you two boys brought plenty of money."

Which made Michael realize that his idea of plenty of money and Thomas Templeton of Templeton Hotels' idea of plenty of money were unlikely to be in the same ballpark.

Jesus, he could lose his shirt, and his ego, in one fun-filled evening.

"My wife fell in love with a Tennessee walker you have down at the stables, Michael." Thomas crossed his legs at the ankles and decided to see how much of a rise he could get out of young Michael Fury. "Maybe I'll win him from you before we're done tonight."

"I don't bet my horses," Michael said easily, "or my friends. Nice watch, Mr. Templeton." He flicked a glance over Thomas's slim gold Rolex. "I could use a new watch."

Thomas let out a bark of laughter and slapped Michael on the knee. "A boy needs his dreams. I ever tell you about the time I played seven-card stud for thirty-six hours? That was in Chicago in '55. Now we—"

"Not the 'thirty-six hours in Chicago' story," Josh moaned. "I'm begging you."

"Shut up, Harvard." Almost comfortable, Michael stretched out his legs. "Some of us haven't heard it."

Pleased, Thomas grinned at Michael. "Then I'll tell you, and you can be afraid."

It wasn't such a bad ride after all. And things looked up when they pulled into the driveway of the multi-decked house on Seventeen Mile and the uniformed driver unloaded two cases of Blue Moose beer—a Templeton product—from the limo's trunk.

"Now that's a hell of a beer," Michael said, then hooked his thumbs in his pockets and studied the wood and glass, the decks and gardens of the De Witt homestead. "And that's a hell of a house."

"Easy access to the beach, too," Josh added. "Kate recommended the property to Byron before they got together."

"Good call. It looks like her," Michael decided. "Streamlined, classy, unique. Man, oh, man! '65 Mustang. And it's cherry too." He walked over to the car, ran a loving hand over the fender. "What a beaut. And that 'Vette. First-round Sting Ray. Mmm, sweetheart, let me pop your hood."

"We going to play poker or are you going to make love to inanimate objects all night?"

He shot a look at Josh. "Inanimate, my ass. Honeys like this have more personality and sex appeal than half the women you dated."

"Shows that you haven't met the women I've dated."

"I dated some of them myself." Michael strolled toward the front door, glancing over his shoulder at the cars, then at Josh. "Including your wife."

Josh's grin faltered and so did his feet. "You never dated Margo."

"Didn't I?" Enjoying himself, Michael climbed the short flight of wooden steps. "I seem to recall a couple of interesting evenings in France."

"You're just trying to psych me out."

And it was working. "Ask her," Michael said mildly.

Damned if he wouldn't. His head reeling with visions he didn't want, Josh reached around and opened the door. Two big yellow dogs raced forward and flung themselves at the newcomers.

"Nip, Tuck, sit." Byron called out the order as he stepped into the wide living area. The dogs sat, butt to butt, and continued to vibrate. "You can put the beer in the kitchen. Thanks." He motioned the driver toward the kitchen. "Think you brought enough?"

"We run out," Josh said, "we send for more. Got food?"

"I whipped up a few things."

Unable to resist two lolling tongues and two pairs of adoring eyes, Michael crouched and made friends with the dogs. "You cook?"

"How do you think he got me to marry him?" Kate stepped out, smiled thinly.

"You still here?" Josh moved over to tug her hair. "Go play with your own kind."

She elbowed him away. "I was just leaving. But I want to say that the concept of the all-male poker game is a Neanderthal practice that I find insulting, particularly when it's taking place in my own house."

Being a wise man, Byron limited himself to rolling his eyes behind her back. But Michael didn't have to live with her. He straightened, grinned.

"Yeah, yeah, tell it to Gloria Steinem and get lost."

"I have no desire to stay and listen to a bunch of fools belch, snort, and tell lies about the women they've had." Chin lifted, she snatched her purse from a chair.

"And I was going to tell Byron all about that night I picked you up on Fisherman's Wharf and we—"

"Shut up, Mick." Her brows drew together, her color rose. "I'm leaving."

"Wait a minute." Her husband made a grab, missed. "What night?"

"It was nothing." She seared Michael with a look. "It was *nothing*."

"Aw, sugar," Michael murmured. "Now you've hurt my feelings."

"Men are pigs," she tossed back as she slammed the door behind her.

"Well, that got rid of her," Michael decided. "Where are the cards?"

"Margo *and* Kate?" Josh eyed him narrowly.

"Can't fault my taste, can you?" Michael tucked his hands in his pockets. "Like I said, where are the cards?"

"Men deserve their little rituals." Susan stretched out on the long arm of the conversation pit in the family room. "Just as we deserve ours."

"I don't mind." Snuggled back against a mountain of pillows, Margo nibbled from a bowl of popcorn. "Kate gets huffy."

"Where is Kate?" Wandering to the window, Laura looked out. "She should be here by now."

"Oh, she'd have waited to yank their chains before she left." Margo shrugged and reached for the champagne. "She'll be along. God knows this is better than poker and beer and a bunch of cigar smoke, but she's got to make her point. Ready for a glass, Mum?"

Ann paused in her perusal of the videotapes chosen for the marathon viewing. "Well . . . maybe just a little one."

They had champagne, popcorn, a platter of crudités, fresh fruit, three choices of dip, including white chocolate, and a stack of movies. The baby was sleeping in the nursery and her favorite women were here. Margo judged it the perfect girls' night out.

"I'm going to do your nails."

"I don't want the fussing."

Margo smiled at her mother. "It's fun, Mum. I've got the perfect shade for you. Red Hot Lover."

Ann snorted into her wine. "I won't wear any such thing. As if I'd be painting my fingernails anyway."

"Men go for it." To tease, Margo leaned closer. "And Bob the butcher's had his eye on you for years."

"He certainly has not." Her face flaming, Ann fumbled with the stack of tapes. "That's nonsense. We have a good customer relationship. Nothing more."

"He saves the leanest cuts for Miss Annie." Margo fluttered her lashes, then laughed. "You should give him a break one of these days. Oh, Laura, stop worrying about Kate. She'll be here."

"I'm not worrying, just watching." And thinking of Michael, she admitted. What was he doing? Why was it their paths hadn't crossed once since the night before? But she made herself come away from the window and pour a glass of champagne. "What are we going to watch first? I vote for *To Have and Have Not*."

" 'You know how to whistle, don't you, Steve?' " Susan sighed, dipped a moist red strawberry into creamy white chocolate. "The world's champion come-on."

"World's best brush-off," Margo said, continuing the

theme. ''Bette Davis. 'I'd love to kiss you, but I just washed my hair.' ''

''Best wrenching good-bye.'' Laura said, getting into the swing. ''Bogart to Bergman. 'We'll always have Paris.' ''

When Kate came in ten minutes later, they were in a heated debate over the ten most dangerous men in cinema history.

''Newman,'' Margo insisted. ''It's the eyes. Cold or hot and incredibly blue. You watch *The Long, Hot Summer*, *Hud*, or—''

''Grant.'' Susan sat up to make her point. ''Dangerous because it's unexpected. The charm undermines a woman's defenses, and he has her.''

''Bogart,'' Laura disagreed. ''In anything. Raw, dangerous, elemental, a hero despite his instincts.''

''I can't believe you're discussing men.'' Disgusted, Kate plopped down. ''I just left those four baboons. Is that white chocolate?'' She reared up again and used her finger to dip in. ''And,'' she continued, licking it, ''they were already smug, superior, and sarcastic. Mick's the worst. I can't believe he brought up that time I ran into him on the wharf and we . . .''

''We?'' Laura came to attention. ''We what?''

''Nothing.'' She should have filled her mouth, Kate decided, and began to do so. ''It was nothing. He was home on leave and he looked sort of . . . interesting. We went for a drive, that's all.''

''You went for a drive?'' Laura repeated. ''With Michael? That's all?''

''Well, yeah, mostly.'' Done it now, Kate thought, as every eye in the room focused on her. ''Well, okay, so maybe I experimented a little, for a minute. Who's in charge of the VCR?''

Before she could pop up to take charge herself, Laura clamped a hand on her shoulder. ''Define 'experimented.' ''

''I let him kiss me . . . a couple of times. That's it. Just that. Do we have *Bringing Up Baby*? I could use a laugh.''

''You and Michael necked in his car?''

''Not necked, exactly. I wouldn't call it necking.

Margo—'' She appealed to her friend for help.

''No, a couple of kisses does not constitute necking. I necked with him, so I know this to be true.''

''You—'' Laura choked, grabbed the champagne bottle. ''You—''

''I give him a ten on both technique and style. And since that was a number of years ago, I can only assume he's improved even that.'' She laughed, got up to pop a movie in. ''Now Mrs. T is trying to figure out if she should make a comment or a statement of any kind, and Mum is sitting there steaming over the idea that the disreputable Michael Fury has had his very tasty lips clamped on all three of her girls.''

''That's just the kind of talk I expect from you,'' Ann said with a sniff.

''And I'd hate to disappoint you. He's one of the dangerous men, all right.'' She leaned back and patted her mother's knee affectionately. ''Thank God for them.''

Chapter Seventeen

He wasn't feeling particularly dangerous with the trash Byron had dealt him. He'd held fairly steady in the first hour of the game, keeping his bets conservative, even predictable, while he studied each of his opponents for their tells.

They were good, he admitted, all three of them. This wasn't any sucker's game. They may have been the classy high rollers who normally gambled in palaces, but he had learned his skills aboard ship, where boredom could tempt a man to toss a month's pay into the pot just to break the monotony.

At a card table, any card table, Michael knew a wise man studied his quarries, and his foes.

Josh flicked a thumb over his jaw when he had a solid hand, and his eyes went blank and cool when he was bluffing. De Witt tended to reach for his beer when he had a winner. And Templeton, well, Templeton was a cagey dog, but as the second hour got under way, Michael noted that the man puffed harder on his cigar when he prepared to rake in the chips.

Calculating, Michael discarded, drew into a pitiful pair of treys. He had a choice, considered the practicalities, and decided it was time to shake things up.

"There's your ten," he told Josh, flipping in his chips. "Raise it ten."

"Twenty to me." Absently Byron reached down to scratch one of his dogs. A sign, Michael thought smugly, that he had nothing. "I'm in."

"Twenty." Tommy knocked into the pot. "And ten more."

"Out." Josh tossed his cards down and rose to help himself to one of the fat sandwiches on the counter.

"I'll see your raise and bump it twenty."

"And you two can fight this hand out." Byron pushed back, gulped his beer.

The boy had been bumping the pot since the deal, Thomas mused, and studied the pretty trio of ladies in his hand. Well, they would have to see what he was made of. "Your twenty, and fifty more."

Michael's eyes met Thomas's over the cards, held steady as he pushed chips into the pot. "Fifty. And fifty back. Call or fold."

Thomas studied his opponent, then wheezed out a breath between his teeth. "I'll give you this one," he decided and tossed his cards down. Well?" he demanded when Michael scooped back the chips. "What did you have?"

When Michael merely smiled and began to stack his chips, Thomas hissed out another breath. "You bluffed me. I can see it. You didn't have shit."

"A man has to pay to see, Mr. Templeton."

Eyes narrowed, Thomas leaned back. "Tommy," he said. "When a man bluffs me cold, he ought to call me by name."

"My deal." Michael gathered the cards, shuffled. "Stud. Seven-card." He grinned. "You in, Tommy?"

"I'm in, and I'll still be in when you're writhing on the floor and begging for mercy."

Michael flipped in his ante. "A boy needs his dreams."

Thomas let loose a laugh, then reached into his pocket.

"Damned if I don't like you, Fury. Have a cigar. A real one, not one of those girl smokes Byron puffs on."

"Thanks, but I quit." Still, he sniffed longingly at the clouds of smoke. "Anyway, those Cubans look too much like a dick."

Josh choked on smoke, pulled his cigar out of his mouth. "Thanks, Mick. I'm really going to enjoy this now."

Howling with laughter, Thomas slapped his hand on the table. "Deal the cards—and prepare to lose your shirt."

During hour three, Michael took a pass and walked outside. He peed companionably with the dogs and watched the night-drenched sea.

"Hell of a spot, isn't it?"

Michael looked back over his shoulder as Byron approached. "You sure picked one."

"I was thinking I could put up a small stable there, at the edge of the cypress grove. Simple. Two stalls."

"Two?"

"I figure solo's lonely, even for a horse. I liked the look of that pinto mare."

"She's a sweetheart." He tucked his tongue in his cheek. "You clear it with your wife?"

Byron's eyes were mild and amused. "I know all kinds of ways around my wife. More, I assume than you do even after picking her up on Fisherman's Wharf."

"I was just rattling her cage. And yours." He lifted his hands, palms out. "Never laid my hands on her. Hardly."

Byron chuckled, shook his head. "I think we'll just leave that particular door closed, but if you want to ride Josh about Margo, I'd find it entertaining."

"I don't want to have to fight him. He's tougher than he looks. Loosened three of my teeth when we were twelve." Michael checked them with his tongue. "And his old man's liable to take bets on the outcome."

"That's the Templetons. They'll bet on anything. Look at the way Kate, Margo, and Laura bet on the shop."

"I keep meaning to go by there again. I'm not much on

fancy-lady shops, but I'm wondering how Laura handles clerking.''

''I think you'll be surprised, and impressed. I have been. It's given them something solid and special.''

''Gives them a living.''

''It gives them more than that. It gives them unity, and a goal and love.'' Either the beer or the women were making him sentimental, but Byron went with it. ''I wasn't around when they conceived it, put it together, took the chance. Margo selling off almost everything she owned, my conservative accountant pooling her investments to make her share. And Laura selling her wedding ring.''

''She sold her wedding ring to build that shop?''

''Yeah. It was right after they found out Ridgeway had pretty much cleaned out their joint accounts. She wouldn't take Templeton money for the shop, so she hocked her wedding and engagement rings to make the down payment on the building. What women they are!''

''Yeah.'' Michael frowned out to sea. ''The socialite, the model, and the accountant.''

''They sweated over it. They cleaned and sanded and painted. And figured out how to make it work. It knocks me out to walk in there and see how they are together, how they are together anywhere. You see them out on the cliffs, rooting around in the rocks and dirt for Seraphina's dowry. All these years they're still together, still looking. Kate was wild tonight when she told me Laura had found another coin.''

He was trying to see it all, to settle all these facets into an image in his head. He blinked. ''Laura? She found a coin? When?''

''Last night. Took a walk down on the cliffs. Kate says she does that from time to time when she needs to clear her head or just be alone. She found one, a gold doubloon just like Margo did, and Kate did. Oddest fucking thing. Each one of them finding a coin, months apart, by accident rather than design. Their treasure hunts turn up nothing, then boom, one of them just picks up a gold piece off the ground as if it had been there all along. Makes you wonder.''

The back door slammed open and Thomas's voice boomed out. ''Is this a poker game or a damn church social? Cards are getting cold.''

''Then deal 'em,'' Byron called back. ''Coming?'' he asked Michael.

''Yeah. Laura walks on the cliffs at night?''

''Now and again.'' Byron waded through the dogs, who ran circles around him.

''And last night she just reached down and picked up a gold coin?''

''Spanish, 1844.''

''Son of a bitch. That's weird.''

''I'll tell you what's weirder. I'm beginning to believe they're going to find the whole thing. That they're the only ones who will.''

''Never believed it existed.''

''Ask Laura to show you her coin,'' Byron suggested. ''You might change your mind.''

''I might do that,'' Michael murmured, then walked back into the comforting arena of cigar smoke and beer.

When he dragged himself up the stairs at three A.M., he still had his shirt, his horses, and his ego. He would have counted himself lucky for that. The fact that he was also eight hundred dollars richer was just icing.

He thought he might put it toward buying a pretty yearling Quarter Horse he'd had his eye on.

He stepped through his front door and stumbled over the warm bundle stretched out there.

''Jesus Christ!'' As he hit the floor, the dog yelped, shuddered, then licked humbly at Michael's face. ''Bongo, what the hell are you—Jesus, get your tongue out of my mouth!'' Michael swiped a hand over his face, shifted and ended up with wriggling puppy on his lap. ''Yeah, yeah, you're sorry. How the hell'd you get in here? Learn how to pick locks now?''

''He came with me.'' Laura stepped out of the bedroom.

''He loves me. He didn't want to sleep in my bed all alone. Me either.''

Maybe it was the beer, or his abrupt meeting with the floor, but his voice seemed to have been lost somewhere along the way.

She was standing in the lamplight, smiling. And wearing nothing but one of his shirts. Her hair was tousled, her skin flushed. And when he managed to clear his vision, he noted that her eyes were bright, if a bit unfocused.

She was in simple words, beautiful, sexy, and drunk.

''Did you come for the rent?''

Her laugh was low and frothy. ''It's after business hours. I came for you. Thought you'd never get here. How was the poker game?''

''Profitable. How was the movie marathon?''

''Illuminating. Did you ever watch, really watch, the way people kiss in black and white? It's . . .'' She sighed, ran a hand down her breasts until he had to roll his tongue back into his mouth. ''Wonderful,'' she decided. ''Just wonderful. Come and kiss me, Michael. In black and white.''

''Sugar . . .'' He had very few rules and was struggling to remember this one as he set the dog aside and rose. ''You're plowed.''

''I am, indeed.'' She shook back her hair, leaned against the doorway for balance. ''D'you know, Michael, I have never been drunk in my life. A little tipsy, I will admit to having been, on occasion a little tipsy. But drunk, never. Not done, not acceptable for a woman of my standing in the community.''

''Your secret's safe with me. Bongo and I will walk you home.''

''I'm not going home.'' She straightened, steadied herself, enjoying the liberating way the room tilted as she stepped toward him. ''Until I've had you. Then you can tell me if I kiss as good as Kate and Margo.''

''Shit,'' he muttered under his breath. ''Word travels fast around here.''

''You can even rip my clothes off again.'' She linked her arms around his neck. ''It's your shirt anyway. I like wearing your clothes. It's almost like having your hands on me. Are you going to put your hands on me, Michael?''

''I'm debating.''

''I'll tell you a secret.'' She pressed against him, put her mouth on his ear. ''Wanna know my secret?''

She was going to be sorry come sunrise, but—he skimmed his hands under the shirt—what the hell. ''Yeah, tell me a secret.''

''I have dreams about you. I used to have them before, too. Long time ago, when you would come around with Josh, I had dreams about you. But I never told anybody, because—''

''It wouldn't be appropriate for a woman of your standing.''

She chuckled, nipped his earlobe and sent his blood pressure through the roof. '' 'Xactly. You know what I'd dream about you? I'll tell you. You'd find me. I'd be on the cliffs or in my room or in the forest, and you'd find me. And my heart would start to pound, so hard, so fast.''

She took his hand, pressed it against her heart. To show him. ''I couldn't move or breathe, or even think,'' she continued, and her hand laid over his on her breast. ''You'd come toward me, not saying anything, just looking at me, looking until my knees were weak, until the blood was rushing in my head. You'd kiss me, so rough, so hot. The way no one else ever would. No one else would dare to touch me the way you touched me.''

''No.'' It was like drowning, he thought. Staring into those deep gray eyes was like drowning. ''No one would.''

''You'd rip my clothes, rip them off, and take me right there, wherever we were. Just the way you did that night, just like in my dreams. I must have always known you would one day.''

She circled away, arms lifted like a dancer on point while he stood where he was, aching. Viciously aching.

''That's my secret. I dreamed of you. Oh, my head's spinning.'' She laughed, pressed a hand to it. ''Being drunk feels just like it feels having you on top of me, inside me, pounding in me. God, God, I love it.''

She combed her hair back from her face, grinned at him. "Look at you, standing there, watching me. Never expected to hear such talk from Laura Templeton, did you?"

He knew, standing there, watching her, that if he'd been dying of thirst he would have begged for her rather than a single sip of water. "No. And if you don't remember this in the morning, I'm going to be damn sorry."

"I'm just full of surprises tonight." She lifted her arms, hooked them behind her head and stretched. "I watched all those movies, drank all that wine. Ate chocolate and laughed. And cried, and sighed. All those things women do."

Laura lowered her hands again and turned a slow, fluid pirouette that made his shirt flow up, out.

"I watched Margo talk Annie into having her nails painted, and Kate dozing off with her head on my mother's lap. Margo nursing the baby when he woke. I loved it all so much, loved being with them. My life is them and my babies, but through it all, you were in the back of my mind. Where is Michael? Does he still want me? And I thought, we'll see. I'll be there when he comes home, and we'll see if he does. If I can make him want me. Do you?"

He didn't speak, couldn't have. Simply crossed to her, dragged her against him and plundered. Joy and need and pleasure burst through her in one sizzling ball of heat. Her laugh was smoke, like her eyes as he pulled her to the floor.

"No, no." Giddy now, and brave enough, she rolled on top of him. "Let me. This time. I want to see if I can."

He was ripe to explode and pulled her down again. "Laura, for Christ's sake—"

"Me." She jerked back, shook her reeling head. "I want to do things to you, things that might be considered inappropriate for a woman of my station."

He struggled to clamp down on hurry when she straddled him. "Want to use me, do you?"

Her lips quirked at the gleam in his eyes. "That's right. Look, we scared Bongo. He's curled up in the corner."

"He'll get over it. What do you want to do to me?"

"I have to figure it out." She blew out a breath, toyed

with the buttons of his shirt. "I've got another secret."

"If it's anything like the last one, it'll probably kill me."

"It's not a good one." Now her lips pouted. "Well, maybe since it turned out this way it is. Peter never ripped my clothes off."

"Christ. Forget it, and him."

But when he reached up, she evaded him. "I want to tell you so you'll know. It's kind of funny, really. We always had very appropriate sex. Not like with you." She traced the vee above the button with a fingertip. "Always proper sex, except when we didn't have sex at all which was most of the time and all through the last year we were married. And you know what?" She placed her hands on either side of his head and leaned down, a heavy-eyed, more-than-tipsy woman.

"What?"

She hummed in her throat as he stroked her breasts. "You can do that," she murmured. "I don't mind at all. But I was saying. We had a system. No, he had a system, I was just there. He would put on classical music. Chopin, always the same sonata. I sometimes still get a tick in my eye when I hear it. He would close the door, lock it, lest a wandering servant be shocked by the goings-on, though the staff would hardly have business in there at ten forty-five in the evening. It was mostly always at ten forty-five."

"So he was a creature of habit." Michael flipped open buttons and found her flesh.

"Umm. No, you don't." She sat up again. "You're trying to distract me. He would turn off the lights, get into bed. He would kiss me three times. Not two, not four, but three times. Then he would—"

"I don't think I want a play-by-play here of Ridgeway's style in the sack."

"In the marital bed, please. Well, we'll just skip right along, then, since it isn't very interesting anyway. At eleven-oh-five, he would wish me a pleasant night and go to sleep."

"The twenty-minute special, huh?"

"You could set your clock by it. Oh, Michael." She

stretched her arms up, giving him tempting glimpses of soft white swells. ''I thought it was me. I thought that was just the way it was, had to be. But it isn't, it wasn't, it doesn't.''

She cupped her breasts in her hands, let her eyes close. ''It's never predictable with you. I never know what you'll do, where you'll touch me next, or how. And it's never proper. It's so wonderfully improper. The things you do with your hands, with your mouth on me.'' She dropped her hands to his chest. ''Do you have any idea what it's like to discover, at thirty, that you have a sex drive?''

''No.'' He couldn't help but smile at her. She was so beautifully drunk. ''I found mine at sixteen and never lost sight of it.''

She laughed, flinging her head back and making his teeth ache with the need to bite into that slim white throat. ''Oh, but this is better. Has to be. It's like finding Seraphina's dowry. Somehow you know it's there, somewhere, or hope it is. And then when you find it, after all that time, all that wondering, it's so sweet.''

''Since you found that elusive sex drive''—his hands slid up her torso—''why don't we put it to use?''

''I'm going to make you sweat.'' She eased down again, scraped her teeth over his jaw. ''You might even beg.''

''Now you're getting cocky.''

''I take that as a challenge.'' To demonstrate, she shoved up her sleeves, which fell right back down again. ''Are you man enough to agree not to touch me until I say you can?''

He lifted a brow, wondering just what the lady had in mind. ''Your loss, sugar.''

''I don't think so, ultimately. No hands,'' she murmured and pressed his to his sides. ''Except mine.''

She lowered her lips to his, brushed, teased, nibbled. ''Margo said you had a very tasty mouth.'' She smiled when he winced. ''She was right. I think I'll stay right here a while.''

She lingered on his mouth, changing the angle, the depth, the tone of the kiss. Light one moment, intense and urgent the next, then sultry, smoky.

His fingers, aching, curled into the carpet. ''Not bad for

a beginner,'' he managed in a voice rusty with need.

''And I learn fast. Your heart's pounding, Michael.'' She nipped at the pulse in his throat, cruised over dampening flesh. Then she gripped his shirt at the shoulder, pulled. When the seam stayed fast, he chuckled from both humor and frustration.

''Want me to do that for you?''

''I can handle it.'' She eased back, kept her eyes on his as she yanked hard. The seam ripped, exposing muscle and skin. She pounced on it like a starving cat. ''Oh, your body,'' she whispered, then crossed her hands, taking hold of his shirt and sending cloth and buttons flying. ''You have such a body. Tough and scarred and tight. I want it.''

Her mouth streaked down his shoulder, over his chest. Quick, greedy bites and sucks, feathering openmouthed kisses and flicks of tongue. But when his hands came up to grip her hips, she shoved them away with a single word.

''Mine.''

Rising up, she shrugged off the shirt, then once more bent to her task.

She was destroying him in a way he hadn't known he could be destroyed. Slowly, inevitably. She was taking him in a way he hadn't known he could be taken. Greedily, intently. His breath thickened, caught, released on a groan when she laved her tongue low on his belly. Every muscle quivered, taut wires close to snapping.

Thoughts filled and emptied from his mind so rapidly that he couldn't gain hold. Sensation rammed violently into sensation like two clenched fists. The scent of her, elegant as royalty, the sheen of her skin, glossy as a damp rose, and the stroke of her hands, restless as lust.

Giddy on her own power, she tugged open the button of his jeans, felt his body tense like a runner on the mark. She lowered her mouth, tasting there, just there where denim and flesh met. And heard him choke out her name.

She could do this to him, she thought as she dipped her tongue under the denim to tease. She could create this desperation, and weakness, this violent need in a strong, vital man. She could make him want her to the point of madness, and she could take whatever she wanted from him.

She nudged the material down, closed her teeth over his hip. And heard the breath explode out of his lungs. He was helpless, she knew, lost in her. And she could make him ache.

She took him into her mouth, clamped him in a wet velvet vice and shot his system into chaos.

His hands fisted in her hair as his body bucked under her. When her mouth cruised up to his belly again, over quaking muscle, he was ready to kill to have her.

Still gripping her hair, he yanked her head back, reared up. She felt one shocking jolt at the dark burn of his eyes, then his mouth was clamped on hers.

"I didn't say you could touch me." She panted it out as his lips branded her throat, her shoulders, her breasts. "You didn't beg."

"I need you." He found her with his hand, shoved her over the peak he was still clinging to. "Now. Goddamn it, take me in."

Triumphant, she threw her head back, and her laugh was rich and wild. Locking her legs around his waist, she arched back, "Yes." Bowed like a bridge when he drove himself into her.

She cried out, no longer surprised but shuddering nonetheless over the speed and violence of the orgasm. She arrowed up again, her body locked to his, her hips pumping.

"More," she demanded, tearing nails down his back. "Michael. More."

Blind with greed, she shoved him back, dug her hands into his waist, and took more.

The storm raged through him, whipping toward peak, but he could see her. Rising and falling over him, her eyes closed to heated slits, her head back in abandon. The animal inside him mated with hers until she'd ridden both to exhaustion.

Through hazy vision he saw her melt down on him. And felt the quakes of the aftershocks rush through her. His own body felt bruised, numbed, weightless so that he wasn't even aware that his arms were locked tight around her, like a man holding everything that mattered.

"Told you I could do it," she murmured, turning her lips to his throat.

"Yeah, you sure showed me." He pressed his lips to her hair, wallowed there. "Laura." He said her name quietly, almost to himself. Then closed his eyes and tried, for both their sakes, not to hear the rest of it. *I love you. Love you.*

"You wanted me."

"Yes. I wanted you." Her hair smelled like sunlight, weakened him all over again.

"Will you do something for me, Michael?"

"Yeah." Anything. Terrifying thought. Anything.

"Will you carry me to bed? I'm still drunk."

"Sure, baby. Just hold on." He rose with her, a feat that even in her impaired state made her heart flutter.

"And one more thing." Her head dropped limply against his shoulder, and when she moaned he had panicked visions of finding a basin to shove under her face before she was sick.

"Okay, don't worry. I'll take care of you. It'll be fine."

"All right." Warm and soft and trusting, she curled into him, then blinked against sudden hard light. "What? What?" Her head cocked curiously. "Why are we in the bathroom?"

"It's the handiest place to be sick. Go ahead and toss up that wine, sugar, you'll feel better."

"I'm not going to toss up perfectly good champagne." She wrapped her arms tighter when he tried to set her down. "I'm not going to be sick." Then she flopped back, dead weight, like a woman in a faint and laughed until it echoed off the walls. "Oh, that's so sweet. You were going to hold my head while I vomited. God, Michael." She raised up again, kissed him sloppily. "You're the cutest thing. Just so cute and sweet I could eat you right up. My hero."

Embarrassed, he narrowed his eyes. "Maybe I'll just stick your head in the toilet anyway. If you're not going to lose the champagne and chocolate, what do you want?"

"I told you to carry me to bed. I would think it would be obvious." Smiling, she traced a finger down his chest. "I want you to want me again. If it wouldn't be an imposition."

He glanced down at her, warm, rosy, naked female. His female. "I guess I could manage that."

"Good, and do you think you could, well . . ." She leaned over and whispered something in his ear that made his blood take a quick trip to his loins.

"That's pretty inappropriate behavior, but . . ." He made a beeline for the bed. "Under the circumstances . . ."

Chapter Eighteen

Experiencing a first hangover, Laura discovered, wasn't nearly as much fun as experiencing a first drunk. Instead of having a head filled with light and color and gloriously rambling ideas, she had one crammed with noise—along the lines of a poorly directed high school band, with the percussion section banging away gleefully at her left temple.

Her system didn't feel free and floaty, but clogged, the way her mouth seemed clogged with enough dirt to make half a dozen mud pies.

She was grateful that Michael had left her alone rather than witness the humiliation.

She wouldn't think about the fact that she'd spent the night in his bed and now would have to stagger into the house, where her family and the staff would shoot her questioning looks.

She tried to drown those unmerciful drummers under the shower, then bit down on her lip when she realized the new sound she heard was her own whimpering.

Under normal circumstances she would never have gone through any of Michael's things, but she finished up a fumbling search through the mirrored medicine cabinet and bathroom drawers and nearly wept when she found a bottle of aspirin.

She took four, another break in tradition; then, deciding she couldn't be much more intrusive, used his toothbrush.

She didn't look in the mirror until she'd dressed, and even then it was a mistake. Her face was deathly pale, her eyes smudged and swollen. And as she didn't have so much as a tube of lipstick with her, there was nothing she could do about it.

Knowing she had to get it over with, she stepped outside and moaned quietly as the sunlight sent hot little spears into her eyes. Her head didn't feel like the practice field for a marching band now; now it felt like glass. Very thin, very fragile glass. And it was balanced precariously on her neck.

"How's it going, sugar?"

She winced, jerked. Her head fell off, smashed on the steps at her feet. Thank God she had another one. She turned it, struggled to smile as Michael dusted his hands on his hips and walked toward her.

"Good morning. I'm sorry I didn't hear you get up."

"The way you were sawing them off, I figured you'd sleep till noon."

The insult of the headache faded. Snore? She certainly did not snore. She wouldn't dignify such a lie with a comment. "I have to be at the shop in a couple of hours."

"You're working today?" She didn't look to be in any shape for it to him. "Give yourself a break, Laura, and go crawl back into bed."

"Saturdays are our busiest day."

He shrugged his shoulders. Her choice. "How's the head?"

"Which one?" Now she did smile, a little. Certainly a man like Michael would understand hangovers. "It's bad, but no longer unbearable."

"Next time you go on a bender, chug plenty of water

and pop a couple aspirin before you pass out. It usually helps take the edge off the morning after."

"I don't intend to have a next time, but thanks."

"Now that might be a shame." He trailed a finger over the back of her hand. "You make a very inventive drunk. How's the memory?"

Her blood must have been moving still, for she felt it rise up to sting her cheeks. "It's good. A little too good. I certainly wouldn't have—I can't believe that I—" She shut up, closed her eyes. "You can stop me anytime from making a total fool of myself."

"I kinda like it. Come here." He drew her against him, cradling her aching head on his shoulder. "Ice water," he murmured. "Stick your face right into a bowl of ice water, try to get some food in your system, then you just have to tough out the rest of it."

"Okay." She'd have preferred just staying there for the rest of her life. "I have to go. I shouldn't have slept here last night." With her face pressed against him she didn't see the disappointment and the hurt shadow his. "I can't imagine what everyone will think."

"Right." His eyes were impassive again when he drew her away. "You go on and shore up the damage to the Templeton name."

"I didn't mean—"

"Forget it." He wasn't going to let it touch him. "Forget it," he repeated. "Why don't you go riding with me tomorrow?"

"Tomorrow?" She pressed her fingers to her eyes. If she didn't get them out of the sun soon they were going to implode. "We have the treasure hunt."

"We'll go in the morning. You'll be back for Seraphina."

Riding. It had been years since she'd ridden in the hills, through the forest. "All right. I'd love it. Can we go about eight? That way I can—"

"Sure, eight." He gave her a quick pat on the cheek before walking away. "Don't forget the ice water."

"No, I—" But he had already disappeared around the

side of the building. Baffled by his rapid shift of mood, she considered following him. Then she looked at her watch and accepted the reality that her obligations for the day didn't allow time to puzzle out the enigma of Michael Fury.

No one asked questions, demanded answers, or voiced disapproval. When Laura tucked her children into bed that night, she realized she had gotten through the entire day without having anyone question her absence from her own bed.

Oh, there'd been vibes in the air. Worry, curiosity, but she'd dodged even those. She'd survived a hangover as well, and the world had not come to an end.

Maybe, just maybe, Laura Templeton did not have to be perfect after all.

She left her daughters and crossed the hall to her own room. There she freshened her lipstick, brushed her hair. She needed to go and join her parents and the old friends who had come for dinner. She needed to make certain everyone was comfortable and entertained.

And, oh, she needed to stretch out for five minutes. Just five, she promised herself as she lay down crosswise on the bed. A quick catnap would set her up, help her get through the rest of the evening.

The minute she closed her eyes, she was dead to the world.

''Something has to be done, Mrs. T.'' Hands gripped tight at her waist, Ann stood in Susan's quiet sitting room in the tower suite. ''It has to be.''

''All right, Annie, sit down.'' It had been a long evening, and though she'd been pleased to see old friends, Susan had hoped for a few moments of solitude before bed. The look on Ann's face warned her she wouldn't get it. ''Now what's the trouble?''

''You know what the trouble is, Mrs. T.'' Too fretful to sit, Ann wandered the room, fussing with curtains, realigning candlesticks, fluffing pillows. ''You saw how pale and tired Miss Laura was today. You had to see for yourself.''

''Yes, I did see. And I've been pale and tired myself the day after I've overindulged in champagne.''

''Oh, as if that was all of it. And that's something she's never done before him, either.''

Perhaps she should have, Susan thought. She sighed. ''Annie, stop tidying the room and sit down.''

''She spent the night with him. The whole of it. Over there with him above the horses.''

Because her lips wanted to twitch, Susan glanced down at her own hands as Ann sat across from her. ''Yes, Annie. I'm aware of that.''

''Well, it can't go on.'' And that, Ann felt, was that.

''Just how do you expect to prevent a grown woman from doing as she chooses? The fact is, Laura is very attracted to Michael, perhaps more than attracted. She's been lonely and unhappy, and now she isn't.''

''He's taking advantage of that. He's a bad influence. Why, she didn't even come down and say good night to her guests. She's never shirked her duties that way.''

''She was tired, Annie, and the Greenbelts are my and Tommy's friends. Which isn't the point at all, really. You can't worry yourself so about all of this.''

''You're her mother, but you know I love her, just as you love my girl. When Margo had troubles, you worried yourself for her.''

''Yes.'' Understanding, Susan laid a hand over Ann's. ''They're our children, and that's as it's always been. But children grow and go their own way no matter how we worry. That's how it's always been, too.''

''She'd listen to you, Mrs. T. I've been thinking on it.'' The words came out fast now and seemed so logical to her. ''Miss Laura, she hasn't gone away with the girls for such a long time. She's been working hard and hasn't had a holiday. The spring vacation's coming up for Ali and Kayla. They could go away for a while. You know how the girls love to go to Disneyland. If you put the notion in Miss Laura's head, she'd take them. And it would give her time, and distance. She'd have a clearer eye about what she's doing.''

''I think Laura and the girls deserve a break, but a week in Disneyland isn't going to change her feelings for Michael, Annie.''

''She's just caught up right now. If she had some time without him clouding her mind, she'd see that man for just what he is.''

At a loss, Susan threw up her hands, let them slap down on the arms on her chair in a show of impatience. ''For God's sake, Annie, what is he? Why do you dislike him so intensely?''

''He's a brute is what he is. A brute and a user and probably a fortune hunter as well. He'll hurt her in more ways than one, and I'm not having it.'' She pressed her lips tight together. ''I'm not.''

To clear her own temper, Susan took a long breath. ''I want you to explain to me what he's done.''

''You know very well that when he was no more than twelve he was sneaking around this house.''

''He was Josh's friend.''

''And giving Mister Josh stolen cigarettes, daring him into all manner of foolishness.''

''Boys do foolish things at twelve. Christ, Annie, I taught my best friend how to smoke when we were fourteen. It's stupid, but it's children.''

''And was it a child's foolishness that sent him to jail?''

''What's this?'' Susan's face paled a bit. ''Michael was in jail? How do you know?''

''I hear things. He was locked up for fighting. In a bar. Oh, they didn't keep him but overnight, but they locked him up right enough. The man likes to use his fists.''

''Oh, for heaven's sakes, I thought he'd robbed a bank or killed someone. I may not approve, but I can't condemn a man for sleeping in a cell overnight because he punched someone in a bar. You don't even know who started it, or why, or—''

''How can you make excuses?'' Suddenly furious, Ann sprang up. ''How can you? The man is with your daughter night after night. He'll use them on her eventually. She'll do or say something and he'll use his fists on her the way he did on his own mother.''

''What are you saying?'' A jiggle of fear settled low in her stomach.

''A man who will strike his own mother, bloody her mouth and blacken her eye, won't think twice about doing the same to another woman. She's so small and delicate, Mrs. T. I can't bear the thought of what he could do to her.''

''You believe Michael Fury beat his own mother?'' Susan said slowly.

''She told me so herself. Came looking for him here with her poor face all black and blue. I took her into my room and did what I could for her, and she told me Michael had come home the night before, drunk, and had hurt her, had driven her husband off, then left her there alone. I wanted to go to the police, but she wouldn't have it.''

She whirled away, emotions choking her. ''Ah, he belonged in a cell. He belonged in a cage. If you had only seen her face. If that man raises a finger to Miss Laura, I—''

''Annie, I did see Michael's mother.'' Susan rose. ''I did speak with her.''

''Then you know. He ran off to sea just after that rather than face what he'd done. Mrs. T, we have to make him go away from here. We can't have a man who's capable of what he is near Miss Laura and her babies.''

''I'll tell you what she told me, Annie, after she came to shout at me for keeping Michael here after that night.''

''Here?'' Ann had to press a hand to her outraged heart to keep it in place. ''That man was here? You let him stay here in this house after—''

''He slept in the stables until he shipped out. He never laid a hand on that woman.''

''You saw her. She told me—''

''She blamed him. She couldn't blame herself, not then. But I had the truth out of her. It was her husband who beat her, and who had done so before. She had come to work with black eyes before, and Michael didn't put them there.''

''But she said—''

''I don't care what she said,'' Susan shouted. The memory of it still made her blood burn. A mother blaming a child for her own failings. ''That boy came home and saw his stepfather beating his mother. And he protected her. The thanks he got for giving that beast what he deserved was having his own mother kick him out of the house, tell him he had no right to interfere, that he was to blame.''

She stopped for a moment, struggled to calm herself. ''And when Michael was gone, when she knew she'd lost him, she sat right here in this room and broke down. She told me everything.''

''But she told me . . . I believed . . .'' Ann sank down in a chair. ''Oh, sweet God.''

''She begged me to help her find him, to persuade him to come back. She was alone, you see, and Michael's mother was a woman who didn't know how to be alone. I want to believe that somewhere inside, she regretted what she'd done, what she'd said to him, and she loved him. But all I saw was a miserable, selfish woman who was afraid to be without a man, even if the man was the son she'd driven away.''

''Oh, Mrs. T.'' Ann pressed her hand against her mouth. The tears that swam in her eyes were tears of guilt and pity. ''You're sure of this?''

''Annie, forget what she told you, even what I've just said, and tell me, honestly, what you see when you look at him. As if you knew nothing more about him than what you've seen since he came here.''

''He works hard.'' She sniffled and tugged a tissue from her pocket. ''He's good with children and his animals. He's kind to them. He's got the devil in his eye, and something hard comes into it. He doesn't watch his language as he should around the children, and I don't think . . .'' She trailed off, wiped her eyes. ''He's good to them. And he's been good for them. I can't deny it. And I'm ashamed.''

''There's no shame in worrying over the ones you love. I'm sorry you were living with the fear that Laura had gotten herself involved with the kind of man you thought he was.''

''I've hardly slept since he's been here. I kept waiting for him to— Oh, the poor boy. What a terrible thing to go through. And him barely old enough to shave regular.''

''You'll sleep better now,'' Susan murmured.

''But I'm still keeping my eye on him.'' She managed a weak smile. ''Men who look that way, they're not to be trusted around a woman.''

''We'll both worry.'' Susan squeezed Annie's hand. ''We know our Laura, don't we? She needs home, family, love. When everything else is brushed aside, that's what she is. I don't know if she'll find that with Michael, or what it will do to her if she doesn't.''

She'd found something else. The thrill of streaking over the hills, of racing through low-lying fog that hugged the ground like a river. Of hearing the thunder of hooves and feeling the strong, sleek mount beneath her gather itself to jump.

She sailed over a fallen log and burst into a clearing where the sun flashed white.

''Oh, God, it's wonderful!'' After reining in, she leaned low over the horse's neck. ''I'll never be able to do without this again. You're a clever man, Michael Fury.'' She straightened and turned to study him as he sat easily on Max. ''How could I buy a horse for myself and not buy that mare for Ali?''

''I'll give you a hell of a deal on three. The little bay gelding fits Kayla like a glove. You ride like a demon, Laura.'' He reached down to pat the neck of the mare Laura rode. ''And Fancy here suits you. I figured she would.''

''Apparently you know your horses, and your women.''

His eyes flicked up to hers. His woman. For the moment. ''Apparently. You look . . .'' Stunning, vital. ''Rested.''

''I slept like the dead last night. Nearly ten hours.'' Trying her hand at flirting, she sent him a sidelong look under her lashes. ''Did you miss me?''

He'd reached for her half a dozen times during the night.

''Nah.'' When her face fell, he laughed. Grabbing her by the shirt, he tugged her sideways just enough to meet her lips. ''What do you think?'' He dismounted. ''Let's give them a rest. We've been riding them hard.''

He tossed the reins over a branch as she slid agilely to the ground. ''Did you find any more coins yesterday?''

''Nothing. Not even a bottle cap. I can't— Oh, I didn't tell you, did I? The other night—''

''I heard.'' For reasons he couldn't pin down, it had annoyed him that she hadn't come running to him with her coin. ''Good for you.''

''It was the oddest thing.'' She stretched muscles unused to riding. ''I put my hand right on it. Just the way you would if you'd dropped a quarter and reached down to . . .''

She blinked, lost her train of thought. He was standing there, just standing there with the sun at his back and his eyes focused on her face. ''What is it?''

''You said you'd dreamed of me. Now, and years ago. On the cliffs, in your room, in the forest. You'd turn and I'd be there.''

''Yes.'' Wasn't it foolish to have her heart lodged in her throat? To feel both fear and anticipation prickle hot on her skin. ''Michael.''

''And I'd touch you.'' He floated a palm over the curve of her breast, felt the quiver. There were parts of her life that were barred to him, parts of his that he would keep barred from her. But here . . . here was equal ground. ''And taste you.'' Laid his mouth over hers, felt the heat. ''And take you.'' Swept her into his arms, felt the ache. ''And I will.''

She lay beside him, naked in the sunlight, with birds singing in the trees. He hadn't torn her clothes. It amazed her that she wouldn't have stopped him from doing so even if she'd had to ride back to Templeton House bare as Lady Godiva.

Instead, he had been so gentle, so tender that even now she could have wept.

''I've never made love outside,'' she murmured. ''I

didn't know it could be so lovely.'' She sat up, stretched. ''So many firsts. I don't suppose there are many firsts I can give you.'' She smiled down at him. ''Bad Michael Fury's already done them all.''

''And then some,'' he said with his eyes closed.

''There's so much you don't talk about.'' Knowing it was all too typical to pry into a man's past when you were in love didn't stop her. She traced a finger down his chest. ''So many secrets inside.''

''You told me a couple of yours last night. Quid pro quo?''

''No, of course not.''

He opened his eyes. ''You want to know something about me, ask.''

She shook her head and started to shift, but he reached up and held her still. ''Afraid of the answer?''

''No,'' she said steadily, ''I'm not. And I'm surprised you'd think I would be.''

''Fine. Ask.''

''I—'' she hesitated still, then gave in. ''All right. You said you were married before, but you never mentioned her or what happened.''

''Her name was Yvonne. We got divorced.''

''All right.'' Miffed by the terse response, she reached for her shirt. ''We should be getting back.''

''Shit.'' He rubbed his hands over his face and sat up as she shrugged into the soft—and now wrinkled—broadcloth. ''Okay, you want to know. I met her when I was racing. She liked to party with drivers.''

''And you fell in love with her?''

''Christ, you're a child in so many ways.'' He stood and dragged on his jeans. ''I fell into bed with her. We liked each other, we had good sex. So we kept falling into bed, and we kept having good sex. Then she got pregnant.''

''Oh.'' She rose slowly and kept her eyes on her trousers as she slipped them on. ''You said you didn't have children. I assumed—''

''Do you want to hear this or not?''

She looked up, surprised by the bitterness in his voice. ''Not if you don't want to tell me.''

''If I'd wanted to talk about it, I probably would have.'' He swore again, then took her arm as she bent to retrieve her boots. ''Sit down. Just sit, goddamn it. Nobody uses that wounded look the way you do.''

He pressed his fingers to his eyes and struggled for control. Once he'd opened up this part of his life, he would have to open others. She would ask more questions, he would give her the answers.

He accepted it there, in the sun-washed woods, with his body still warm from hers, that this was the beginning of the end.

''Okay, she got pregnant. So we talked about it. The best thing for everybody was to go for the abortion. Simple, quick, done. So we made the arrangements.''

''I'm sorry. That's a difficult decision. You—you never questioned that you'd been the one who—''

''That I'd gotten her pregnant? Yvonne wasn't a liar or a cheat. She said the kid was mine, it was mine. We were friends, Laura.''

''I'm sorry. It was hard for both of you.''

''We figured we were doing the smart thing. I was trying to make a name for myself on the circuit, she had just started a new job. A baby didn't fit. Hell, neither of us knew anything about kids, about parenthood. We were what we were.'' He looked her in the eye. ''Scrabblers, looking for a good time.''

She kept her gaze level. ''Are you telling me it was easy? A casual shrug. An oops?''

''No.'' His eyes shifted, stared off into the trees, into the shadows. ''No, it wasn't easy. It just made sense. We agreed it was the best solution. But the night before we were to go in for it, we figured out something else. We both wanted it. We both wanted the baby. It didn't make any sense, we didn't know what we were doing, but we both wanted the baby.''

''She didn't have the abortion.''

''No. We got married. We figured what the hell, let's do

it, let's have a baby. She tried to knit things.'' A smile ghosted around his mouth. ''She didn't have a clue. We read books. Went in for one of those sonogram things. Jesus Christ, it was just . . . beautiful. We argued about names and did all the things I guess everybody does.''

The smile went away and, she thought as she watched his eyes, so did he.

''Middle of the night, she was about four months along, she started bleeding, bad. She was in pain and scared. We were both so scared. I got her to the hospital, but it was already pretty much over by then. We lost the baby.''

''I'm sorry.'' She rose again, but didn't touch him. ''I'm so sorry, Michael. There's nothing more painful than losing a child.''

''No, there's nothing. The doctors said she was young and healthy and we could try again in a little while. We pretended we would. Tried to keep it together. But we started fighting, sniping at each other. I'd slam out, leave her alone. She'd slam out, leave me alone. One night I came home and she was waiting for me. She'd figured it out before I had. She was a smart woman. We'd stopped being friends. All we'd had to keep us married was the baby, and the baby was gone. Now we were stuck, and we didn't have to be stuck. She was right. So we decided to start being friends again and stop being married. End of story.''

She touched him now, took his face in her hands, felt the tension. ''There's nothing I can say to ease that kind of grief, the kind you carry with you forever, no matter what.''

He shut his eyes, let his brow rest on hers. ''I wanted the baby.''

''I know.'' She eased her arms around him. ''You loved it already. I understand. I'm sorry, Michael.'' Gently, she stroked his back. ''I'm sorry I made you tell me.''

''It was almost ten years ago. It's done.'' He drew back, then swore at the tears on her cheek. ''Don't do that. Hell, you should have asked me something else.'' Uneasy, he brushed the tears away. ''Like about how I used to stunt double for Mel Gibson.''

She sniffled, struggled to give him the smile he wanted. "Did you? Really?"

"You women always go for Mel. Maybe you should come down to Hollywood with me. I could introduce you." He twined a blond curl around his finger. "Me and Max, we have to go down tomorrow."

"Tomorrow?" She shook her head. "You're going to L.A.? You didn't mention it."

"Just got a call Saturday." With a shrug, he sat down to tug on his boots. "Action western with your pal Mel. He wants me and Max. So we got to do some meetings, some test shots. See if we can give them what they're looking for."

"That's wonderful. I'd think you'd be more excited."

"It's a job. I don't suppose you're interested in tagging along."

"I'd love to, but I can't leave the girls, and work. How—" How long will you be gone? She bit the question back. "They'll be so impressed when I tell them."

"I've got a guy coming in for a few days to see to the stock while I'm gone. I should be back by Friday."

"Oh." Only a few days. She smiled again. "If you are, I have this opening I have to go to on Friday night. Would you like to go?"

"An opening of what?"

"It's an exhibit at the art gallery. Expressionists."

To his credit, he didn't snort. "You want me to go look at paintings and make all sorts of idiotic comments on brushstrokes and underlying meanings." His cocked his head. "Do I look like a guy who's going to stand around sipping espresso and talking about the use of color on canvas?"

"No." He was sitting on a stump, bare to the waist, with faint purpling bruises on his ribs. His hair was wild and tousled. "No, you don't."

No more, he thought, than she looked like a woman who would toss aside responsibility and run off to L.A. with her lover for a week.

What the hell is she doing with me? he wondered as he

rose. And to me? If this goes on much longer, what will we do to each other?

"We'd better get back." He shrugged into his shirt. "You don't want to keep Seraphina waiting."

"Michael." She laid a hand on his chest. "I'll miss you."

"Good." He lifted her into the saddle.

Chapter Nineteen

He wasn't gone a few days, but nearly two weeks. Laura reminded herself every night that he was under no obligation to call her, to tell her what was delaying him. Or just so that she could hear his voice.

She reminded herself that they had an adult relationship in which each party was free to come and go as he or she pleased. It was because she'd never had a relationship like it before, she told herself, that she was fretting. Worrying. Feeling hurt.

She certainly had plenty to keep her busy. And she had learned the hard way never to allow a man to be responsible for providing her with a fulfilling life. That was her job, one she intended never to neglect again.

With her work, her children, her family and friends, she had a full, contented life. Perhaps she wanted to share it with Michael and to be a part of his life, but she wasn't a lovestruck teenager who sat by the phone hour by hour waiting for it to ring.

Though she did try to will it to ring a time or two.

At the moment, though, she wasn't worried about the phone. She had other problems on her hands. Ali's spring dance recital would begin in less than two hours. Not only was no one ready but one of the kittens had coughed up a hairball in the middle of Kayla's bed, causing much dismay and more female disgust—and one of the barn cats had gone exploring, seducing Bongo into giving mad chase through the herb garden, which resulted in bad news for the chamomile and tansy and earned Bongo a bloody nose.

Nothing Laura did could lure the insulted, hissing cat down from the cypress tree where he had taken shelter. And Bongo continued to whimper pitifully under her bed.

Despite all of that, her biggest problem was Ali herself. The girl was moody, uncooperative, and whiny. Her hair was terrible, she claimed. Her stomach was upset. She didn't want to go to the recital. She hated recitals. She hated everything.

Her patience strained, Laura tried one more time to style Ali's hair to the child's specifications.

"Honey, if you're nervous about tonight, it's all right. You'll be wonderful. You always are."

"I'm not nervous." Ali pouted into the mirror. "I never get nervous before I dance. I just don't want to go."

"People are depending on you—your instructors, the other girls in your troupe. The family. You know how excited Grandma and Granddad were when they left for Uncle Josh's. Everyone's looking forward to tonight."

"I can't depend on anybody, can I? I have to do what I say I'll do, but nobody else does."

Around the circuit again, Laura thought. "I'm sorry you're disappointed your father won't be there. He's—"

"I don't care about him." In a bad-tempered move, Ali shrugged and scooted out from under her mother's hands. "He never comes anyway. It doesn't matter."

"Then what's the problem?"

"Nothing. I'll go. I'll do it because I keep my promises. My hair looks much better now," she said with dignity. "Thank you."

"Honey, if you'd—"

"I have to finish getting dressed." She pressed her lips together, a small girl, pretty in her tights and ballet skirt. "It's not your fault, Mama. I didn't mean it to sound that way. I'm not angry with you."

"Then what—"

"Mama!" Kaya's wail bounced down the hallway. "I can't find my red shoes. I want to wear my red ones."

"You can go help her," Ali said and tried to smile. "I'll be downstairs in a minute. Thanks for doing my hair over."

"It's all right." Because she could see the sorrow haunting Ali's eyes, she leaned down and kissed her on both cheeks. "I love playing with your hair. And I suppose if you wanted to put just a little of that lip gloss on, it would be all right."

"You mean before we go, not just for onstage?"

"Just for tonight." Laura tapped her fingers against Ali's lips. "You're not growing up on me any faster than I can help it."

"Maaamaaa, my shoes."

"And neither is she," Laura murmured. "I'm coming. Downstairs, Ali, ten minutes tops."

She found the shoes. Who would have expected to find them right there on the shoe shelf in the closet? After pulling a brush through her own hair, Laura herded her girls toward the door.

"Come on, troops, get a move on. This train leaves in five minutes. I'll get it, Annie," she called out when the doorbell rang. "Could you check on Bongo before you leave? He's under my bed and—"

She broke off as she pulled the door open and found Michael standing on the other side.

"Michael! You're home."

"It looks that way."

If she had leapt into his arms, right there in her own home, there in front of her children, he doubted he could have stuck with the decision he'd made. But she didn't. She only smiled at him, held out a hand.

It was Kayla who leapt. "Did you bring Max back?" With the simplicity of childhood, she hugged his waist and lifted her mouth for a kiss. ''Did he come home too?''

''Sure. Max and I travel together. Where'd you get the red shoes, kid? Pretty snappy.''

''Mama bought them. They're my favorites.''

''You came.''

Michael halted his admiring study of Kayla's red shoes and lifted his gaze to Ali's face. She looked, he thought, so much like her mother just then, with that stunned wonder on her face and the emotion swimming in her eyes.

''I told you I would.''

''I thought you'd forgotten. I thought you were too busy.''

''Forget an invitation from a beautiful ballerina to watch her dance?'' He shook his head as he straightened. ''Boy, that wouldn't say much about my memory.'' Head cocked, he held out the bouquet of pink baby roses. ''We do have a date, right? You didn't go call some other guy to take my place?''

''No. Are these for me?'' Mouth open in a litle O of confused delight, she stared at the roses. ''For me?''

''Who else?''

''For me.'' She breathed it, taking the flowers in her hands. ''Thank you. Mama, Michael brought me flowers.''

''I see.'' And her eyes stung a bit. ''They're lovely.''

''We'll use the Waterford.'' Annie stood a few steps back in the hall, her hands folded, her eyes on Michael's face. ''When a girl receives her first flowers from a man, they should be treated as something very special.''

''I want to put them in the vase myself.''

''And so you should. It will only take a moment, Miss Laura.''

''Yes, all right. Thank you, Annie.''

''I'll help.'' Kayla raced down the hall. ''Let me smell them, Ali.''

''Her first flowers,'' Laura murmured.

''Man, why do females always get wet-eyed over a bunch of posies?''

Which reminded him that he'd never given Laura flowers. Never real ones, just something plucked carelessly out of the ground. He'd never thought of it. Had never, he realized, given her anything but good, hot sex.

"Flowers are symbolic." And she remembered the pretty little wildflowers he'd given her. So sweet, so simple. So right.

"Everything is to women."

"You could be right." She turned back, beaming at him. "It was so thoughtful of you to bring them. And to come. I didn't realize she'd asked you. Had no idea she was counting on it."

"She asked me a couple of weeks ago." He dipped his hands in his pockets. Laura hadn't asked him, he remembered. Hadn't mentioned it. "I've managed to avoid ballet for thirty-four years. This ought to be an experience."

"I think you'll find it painless." She started toward him now, and he took his hand out of his pocket to take hers before she could touch him.

"So how are you?" he asked.

"Fine." Was he just tired, she wondered, or was this distance she felt? "Did things go well in L.A.?"

"Yeah, it went. They'll start shooting in about three weeks. We'll get a couple months' work out of it. Maybe more."

"You'll stay in L.A. during the filming," she said slowly as a weight sank in her stomach.

He shrugged. It wasn't the time to get into all of this, and he was spared when Ali marched back down the hall, bearing her vase of baby roses like a trophy.

"Don't they look beautiful, Mama? Annie's going to put them in my room."

"They're perfect. We really need to go. Performers have to be there thirty minutes before curtain."

"I'll take those now, sweetheart." Annie slipped the vase from Ali's hand. "And I'll be there to see you dance." She inclined her head toward Michael in what, from anyone else, he would have taken as a friendly smile. "We all will."

* * *

It wasn't impossible to put everything out of his mind for a couple of hours. The kid was so cute. All of them were. But it was hard to sit beside Laura, in the middle of all those people—the families, the partners, the couples—and not be miserable.

But he'd had time, and he'd had the distance to allow himself to take a good hard look at what was going on. And what was happening to him. He'd fallen for her, all the way.

It would never work.

He'd seen himself in the dingy little bar in south L.A., drinking beer and swapping stories with wranglers. Going back to his hotel room after a long day, sweaty, dirty, smelling of horse. And he'd seen himself growing up in a house that had breathed neglect and violence and tension.

He'd seen himself for what he was. A man who had chased all the wrong things most of his life and had found plenty of them. A cliff rat, son of a waitress and a wastrel, who would in time and with effort be able to make a decent living.

And he'd seen Laura, the Templeton heiress, sitting in her plush country club drinking tea, dressed in her tidy suit, running a fancy boutique, strolling through a grand hotel that she owned.

He didn't doubt that he'd given her something. Or that under different circumstances, they could give each other more. But it would be only a matter of time before the haze of lust cleared from her eyes and she saw what she was doing. Having an affair with a horse trainer.

They were both better off that he'd seen it first. Knowing her, he doubted she would be able to break it off clean. She was too soft, too kind, to walk without guilt. Worse, she might continue the relationship long after she'd realized her mistake because of that sterling sense of obligation.

He was no good for her. He knew it. The people who knew both of them understood it. Eventually she would know it. And it would kill him.

Maybe if he hadn't run into that old buddy of his in L.A., the old merchant marine stevedore he'd shipped with, drunk with, raised hell with. One of the men who had gone to war with him for profit after the sea lost its lure.

But they had run into each other. And the stories were rehashed, the memories swam back. And for one harsh, illuminating moment, he had looked into the surly, bitter, used-up face of the man across from him. And had seen himself.

Michael Fury was a man he never wanted to touch Laura, a man he never wanted her to know. If such a man tried to touch her, to know her, she would cringe in shock.

Before either of them had to cope with that, he would do her a favor and slip out of her life.

As Ali twirled on stage, Laura laid a hand over his and squeezed. And broke his heart.

''Don't they look wonderful?'' Margo murmured.

Beside her, Josh tapped his foot absently to the music and continued to watch his niece. ''They're all great, but Ali's the best.''

''Naturally.'' She chuckled a little, leaned closer to his ear. ''But I was talking about Laura and Michael.''

''Hmm?'' Distracted, he shifted and glanced at the couple one row in front of them. ''Laura and Michael what?''

''They're wonderful together.''

''Yeah, I guess . . .'' He trailed off, stunned as the meaning seeped in. ''What do you mean 'together'?''

''Ssh.'' She shushed him, fighting back another laugh. ''Together, together. What, are you blind?''

His throat went dry and tight. ''They're not seeing each other. They're not dating.''

''Dating.'' She had to clamp a hand over her mouth. ''For God's sake, Josh, they've been sleeping together for weeks. How could you not know?''

''Sleeping—'' Shock, rage, disbelief all slammed together against the words. ''How the hell do you know that?''

''Because Laura told me,'' she hissed into his ear. ''And because, if she hadn't, I have eyes in my head. Ssh,'' she ordered when he opened his mouth. "You're annoying people. And here's Ali's solo."

He shut his mouth, but not his mind. He had a great deal to think about. And as far as he was concerned, his old pal Michael Fury had a great deal to answer for.

There'd been nothing he could do about it that night but go home and grill his wife. Then argue with her over the situation. Josh put her attitude down to female hormones. Women found Michael romantic—which had always been his good luck and was the crux of the current problem.

Josh found him in the paddock, working a yearling on the lounge line. "I need to talk to you, Fury."

Michael recognized the tone. Something was stuck in Josh's craw. He wasn't in the mood for it, not when he was still thinking about the baffled hurt on Laura's face the night before when he'd given her a quick pat on the head and told her he was beat.

In other words, I'm going to bed, sugar, and you're not invited.

Still, he released the yearling and walked to the fence where Josh waited. "So talk."

"Are you sleeping with my sister?"

Ah, well, the time had come. "We don't sleep much," Michael said easily and braced when Josh's hand whipped out and gripped his shirt. "Watch it, Harvard."

"What the fuck do you think you're doing? Who the hell do you think you are? I asked her to rent this place to you. Do you a favor, and you just jump right in."

"I didn't jump alone." Damned if he'd take the rap for that. "She's a big girl, Josh. I didn't lure her into the stables promising her candy. I didn't force her."

The idea of it curdled his blood, then shamed him. "You wouldn't have to," he shot back. "You forget who you're talking to. I know you, Mick. I know your style. Christ, we cruised together often enough."

"Yeah, we did." Eyes level, Michael pried Josh's fingers off his shirt. "But that was all right, the two of us going out sniffing out babes."

"This is my sister."

"I know who she is."

"If you knew, if you had any idea what she's been through the past few years, how easily bruised she is, you'd stay the hell away from her. The women you played with always knew the rules, went in for the game. That's not Laura."

"And because she's your sister, because she's a Templeton, she's not entitled to play." Bitterness rose like bile. "Certainly not with me."

"I trusted you," Josh said quietly. "I always trusted you. It's one thing for you to hit on Kate, and on Margo, but I'm damned if I'm going to stand back and watch you make it three for three."

His eyes went very cold, very hard. At his side his fist clenched, and in his mind he saw it strike out, fast. It took all of his will and a lifetime of friendship not to follow through.

"Get the fuck away from me. Now."

"You want to take a swing, you take one. We've gone around before."

Not like this, Michael thought as his system revved toward violence. Now they were men, and the stakes were higher. And if he had any family, any that really mattered, this was it, standing here right now, prepared to break his neck.

"Why don't we try this instead—I'll be out by the end of the week. I've already started making the arrangements."

Torn now between friendship and family, Josh narrowed his eyes. "What arrangements? You barely have your foundation up on the new construction."

"I'll probably sell it as is once I've relocated to L.A. Is that far enough away from your sister, Harvard? Or do I have to go to hell?"

"When did this come up?"

"Do I have to check that with you too? Go away, Josh. I'm busy here and you've made your point."

"I'm not sure I have." And as he watched his oldest

friend walk away, Josh was no longer sure what the point was.

He knew she would come. There was no way to avoid or prevent it. They hadn't been together in two weeks, and she would expect him to want her. Of course he did, pitifully.

But he wouldn't touch her. It was only worse now. He'd nearly talked himself out of his earlier decision, had told himself he could find a way to make it work between then. The visit from Josh had snapped things back into reality.

He would make it clean, he would make it quick.

She would be hurt, a little. There was no way to avoid or prevent that either. But she would get over it.

Still, though he'd known she would come, he hadn't expected her so soon, hadn't expected himself to be so unprepared when he saw her standing in his doorway with the sun in her hair and her eyes so pure, so gray, so warm.

"I took off from the shop a little early," she began. She knew she was talking quickly, bubbling over with nerves. Something was wrong. She could have been deaf and blind and still have sensed it. "I thought since my parents were taking the girls into Carmel for dinner, I'd see if you'd like me to fix yours."

"Women like you don't cook, sugar. They have cooks."

"You'd be surprised." She came in, not waiting for the invitation, and swung past him into the kitchen. "Mrs. Williamson taught us all, including Josh, at least the basics. I make an exceptional fettuccine Alfredo. I thought I'd see what you had before I brought over ingredients."

Seeing her poking around the kitchen as if she belonged there, as if he could come home after a hard day and find her cheerfully waiting for him, tore him apart. So his voice was cool and careless.

"I'm not much on fancy sauces, sugar."

"Well, we'll try something else." Why wouldn't he say her name? she wondered, fighting panic. He hadn't once said her name since he'd come home. She turned to him and couldn't prevent herself from leading with her heart. "Oh, I missed you, Michael. So much."

She was halfway across the room, reaching for him. He could all but feel the way her soft, delicate arms would wrap around his neck. He stepped back, lifted both hands to ward her off.

"I'm filthy. I haven't had a chance to jump in the shower. You wouldn't want to mess up a nice silk blouse."

Why should it matter? He'd once torn one off her. He hadn't held her in days. Yet he stood there now with—was it boredom in his eyes?

"What is it, Michael?" Her stomach jittered, echoed in her voice. "Are you angry with me?"

Deliberately he tilted his head. "Why do you do that? Why do you always assume that whatever's going on around you is your fault or your responsibility? That's a real problem you've got there," he added as he walked past her to get a beer out of the refrigerator.

He twisted off the top, drank deep. "Do I look mad to you?"

"No." She folded her hands, gathered her composure. "No, you don't. You look vaguely annoyed that I'm in your way. I assumed you'd want me to come, that you'd want to be with me tonight."

"It's a nice thought, but don't you think this has run its course?"

"This?"

"You and me, sugar. We've taken this about as far as it's going to go." He tipped the beer back again, wiped his mouth with the back of his hand. "Listen, you're a hell of a woman. I like you. I like your style, in bed and out. But we both know we've got to move on eventually."

She would breathe, she told herself. However tight the fist was around her heart, she would breathe, slow and easy. "I take that to mean you've decided to move on now."

"Some things came up when I was in L.A. Changed my plans. I like to be fair with a woman I've slept with, so I figured I should let you know I'm moving down there next week."

"You're moving to L.A.? But your house—"

"Never meant a damn to me." He jerked his shoulder. "Just a place. One's the same as the other."

One's the same as the other, she thought dully. One house. One woman. "Why did you come back at all?"

"I left my horses." He forced his lips into a grin.

"You went to Ali's recital. You brought her flowers."

"I told the kid I'd go. I don't make many promises, so I don't break the ones I do make." In this at least, he didn't have to improvise. "You've got terrific kids, Laura. I've liked getting to know them. And I wouldn't have let her down last night."

"If you go, they'll be devastated. They'll—"

"Get over it," he said, his voice roughening. "I'm just a guy who passed through."

"You can't believe that." She stepped toward him. "You can't believe you mean so little to them. They love you, Michael. I—"

"I'm not their father. Don't lay that guilt trip on me. I've got my own life to worry about."

"And that's it." She drew in another breath, but it wasn't slow, it wasn't easy. " 'See you around, it's been fun?' We meant nothing to you."

"Sure you did. Look, sugar, life's long. A lot of people walk through it. Both of us gave each other what we were looking for at the time."

"Just sex."

"Great sex." He smiled again. Then, because his reflexes were good, dodged by inches the bottle she picked up and heaved at him. Before he could recover from the shock of that, she was using her hands. Both of them shoved hard enough against his chest to knock him back two full steps. "Hey."

"How dare you! How dare you lower what we have, what I felt, to some animal urge? You son of a bitch, you think you can brush me off like an inconvenient speck of lint, then walk away?"

A lamp went next, and he could only watch, speechless,

and duck, fast, when she threw whatever came to her hand at his head.

"You didn't think I'd cause a scene, did you?" She picked up an end table, toppled it. "Wrong. Finished with me, are you? Just like that." She snapped her fingers under his nose. "And I'm supposed to meekly walk away, sob into my pillow and say nothing?"

He backed up. "Something like that." So it wasn't going to be quick and clean, he decided, but messy. Nonetheless, it had to be done. "Break the place up if it makes you feel better. It's your stuff. I expect even royalty has to have its tantrums."

"Don't you speak to me that way, as if I were some interesting toy that's suddenly run amok. You came into my life, you exploded into my life and changed everything. Now you're just finished?"

"We've got nothing here and we both know it. It's just one of those times I saw it first."

She snatched up a bowl and sent it crashing through his kitchen window. Another time he might have been impressed with the force and velocity. And her aim. But at the moment he could only suffer.

"I ain't paying for the damages, sugar. And I never made you any promises, told you any lies. You knew yourself what you were getting when you came looking for me. You wanted me to take the choice out of your hands. You wanted me to take you so you wouldn't have to say it. That's fact."

"I didn't know how to say it," she shot at him.

"Well, I did, and that was fine with both of us. You haven't got a choice here either. It's just done."

Her breath was heaving, shuddering as she tried to calm it. Temper—her temper—she knew, was horrible when unlocked. And when the key was turned with pain, so much the worse. "That's cruel, and it's cold."

Where the temper had missed its mark, the quiet words arrowed straight into his heart. "That's life."

"Just done." She let the tears come, they hardly mattered. "So that's how this sort of thing is accomplished.

You say it's just done, and it is. So much less complicated than divorce, which is the only way I've ended a relationship.''

''I didn't cheat on you.'' He couldn't bear having her think that of him, or herself. ''I never thought of another woman when I was with you. This has nothing to do with you. I've just got places to go.''

''Nothing to do with me.'' She closed her eyes. The temper was gone now, quickly as always. Drained to exhaustion. ''I never would have said you were a stupid man, Michael, or a shallow one. But if you can say that, you're both.''

She lifted her hands, rubbed away the tears. She wanted to see him clearly, since it would be the last time. He was rough, wild, moody. He was, she thought, everything.

''I wonder that you don't even know what you're throwing away, what I would have given you. What you could have had with me, and Ali and Kayla.''

''They're your kids.'' This was another hurt, just as deep, just as bloody. ''Templetons. You wouldn't have given them to me.''

''You're wrong, pathetically wrong. I already had.'' She walked to the door, opened it. ''You do what you have to do and go where you have to go. But don't ever think it was just sex for me. I loved you. And the only thing more pitiful than that is that even as you turn me away like this, so carelessly, I still do.''

Chapter Twenty

Michael took a step forward, then stopped himself. She didn't know what she was saying. Couldn't know.

He forced himself to step back from the door, then turned and watched her walk away across the lawn. Continued to watch when she changed directions, broke into a run.

She'd go to the cliffs, he realized. She was angry and hurt, so she would go to the cliffs to finish crying. When she was finished she would think. She would stay angry and hurt for a while, and hate him longer than that, but he knew that eventually she would see it was for the best.

She wasn't in love with him. He scrubbed his hands over his face. It already felt raw and battered. Maybe she thought she was, or had talked herself into it, he decided. It was a knee-jerk female reaction, that was all. It fit a woman like Laura—sex and love, need and emotion. She wasn't seeing the big picture.

But he could.

Men who had lived as he had lived didn't end up happy ever after with women of her class, her breeding. Sooner or later she'd have come to the same conclusion, found herself drawn back to the country club style. Maybe she would never forgive him for seeing it first, but that couldn't be helped.

It would kill him to be with her and wait. To know that when the passion had dimmed she would still stay with him. She'd be kind. She couldn't be otherwise. But he would know when he had become just another obligation.

He was doing them both a favor by getting out of her life.

Josh was right. And no one knew him better.

But he continued to stand, staring out at the cliffs and the lone figure who stood there twisting the knife in his own heart. Finally he turned away and left the room that was as disrupted as his life to go down to his horses.

She hadn't known how completely a heart could shatter. She'd thought she knew. When her marriage had ended, Laura had been certain she would never grieve in quite the same way again.

She'd been right, she thought now and pressed both hands to the ache in her heart. This was different. This was worse.

Her feelings for Peter had eroded so slowly over the years that there had barely been any left by the time it was over. But this . . . she squeezed her eyes tight, and though the air was still and warm, she shuddered.

She'd never loved anyone the way she loved Michael. Wildly, outrageously. Brutally. And all those feelings were so fresh. So bright and new. She had treasured them. She'd treasured discovering that she could feel again, realizing she could want and be wanted as a woman. She'd admired what he was, what he'd made himself, and she had fallen as much in love with the rough and dangerous man as the kind and gentle one within.

Now he wanted it over, and there was nothing she could do. Crying didn't help, and her tears were already dry. Temper changed nothing, and she was already ashamed of the way she had snapped in front of him. He'd think her pitiful now, but that couldn't be helped either.

She stepped closer to the edge to watch the waves beat against rock. She felt that way, she mused. Battered by forces that were beyond her control, trapped in a violent, endless war with no choice but to stand.

It didn't help, it simply didn't help, to tell herself she wasn't alone. That she had her family, her children, her home, her work. Because she felt alone, completely alone, there on the edge of the world with only the thunder of the sea for company.

Even the birds were gone. No gulls cried today, none wheeled white toward the hard blue sky or dipped toward the spewing waves. She could see nothing but the rolling of the endless sea.

How could she accept it that she would never love this way again? Why was she expected to go on, to do everything that needed to be done, alone, always alone, and know that she would never turn in the night and find someone there who loved her?

Why had she been given this glimpse into what she could have and feel and want if it was only going to be taken away? And why was the one thing she had dreamed of all of her life always, always, just out of her reach?

She imagined that this was what Seraphina had felt as she stood here so many years before grieving the loss of her lover. Laura looked down, pictured that dizzying, somehow liberating plunge into space and the fierce, furious heart that had taken it.

Had she screamed as the rocks rushed up, Laura wondered, or had she strained to meet them?

Trembling, Laura took a step back. Seraphina had found nothing but an end, she thought, a horribly easy end to pain. Her own wouldn't be easy, because she would have to live with it. Live without Michael. And finally accept that she would live without her dream.

She barely noticed the rumble, took it at first for the sea's thrashing. The ground seemed to jitter under her feet. Blank for a moment, she stared down, watched pebbles dance. Then the roar filled her ears, and she knew.

Panicked, she tried to stumble back, away from the edge. The ground rolled, unbalancing her as she grabbed frantically for a rock. The wave of earth lifted her up and pushed her hard over the rim of the world.

The horses sensed it first. Eyes wheeling white, panicked whinnies. Michael reached up to calm the mare he was grooming. Then he felt it. The ground shuddered under him. He swore as the noise grew and horses plunged. Above his head came the sound of crashing glass, straining wood.

The freight train roar deafened him as he fought to keep his balance. Tack leapt off the walls and fell jangling on the shuddering brick.

He yanked stall doors open, focused on getting his horses out. In the wild confusion of the moment, one thought pierced like a lance.

Laura. My God. Laura.

He stumbled forward, fighting free when the earth tried to heave him back. He raced into the brilliant sunlight, ignoring the violent undulations of the tidy green lawn. When he was knocked flat, he clawed his way back up, skidded down the slope. No one would have heard him screaming her name as he ran toward the cliffs. He didn't hear it himself.

It lasted no more than two minutes, that stretch and shift of the earth. All was still, preternaturally still, when he reached the cliffs.

She'd gone home, he told himself. She'd gone back to the house, was safe, secure. A little shaken perhaps, but a native Californian didn't panic at every trembler. He'd go check on things himself as soon as he . . . as soon as he made sure.

When he looked over the edge and saw her, his legs buckled. On a ledge fifteen feet below, inches away from oblivion, she lay white as death. One of her arms was flung out so that her hand dangled over that narrow bed of rock into space.

He wouldn't remember the climb down to her, the sharp

bite of rock into his hands, the small, nasty avalanches of dirt and pebbles where his feet slid, the stinging slices as roots and rock tore viciously at his clothes and flesh.

Blind terror and instinct took him down fast where a single misstep, one incautious grip, would have sent him plunging. Cold sweat dripped into his eyes, skidded along his skin. He thought—was sure—she was dead.

But when he reached her he fought back the panic and fear and placed a trembling finger on the pulse in her throat. And it beat.

"Okay, okay." His hands trembled still as he brushed the hair from her cheeks. "It's all right, you're all right." He wanted to drag her up, hold her, rock her to him until this greasy sickness in his gut passed.

He knew better than to move her, even with thoughts of aftershocks spinning in his head. He knew he had to check the extent of her injuries before he risked shifting her.

Concussion, broken bones, internal injuries. Christ, paralysis. He couldn't get his breath and had to squeeze his eyes shut for a moment and force air in and out until he was calm. He made himself move slowly, carefully. Lifting her eyelids to check the pupils, gently moving his hands over her head, gritting his teeth at the blood that smeared on his fingers.

Her shoulder—she'd dislocated it, he realized as he probed. It would be screamingly painful when she woke. Dear God, he wanted her to open her eyes. His breath came fast and harsh as he continued to check her. No breaks—a lot of bruises and some bad cuts and scrapes, but nothing was broken.

He agonized over her back and neck, knew he had to leave her to call for an ambulance. And the thought of leaving her alone there on that ledge, knowing that if she woke it would be to terror and pain, ripped him.

"It's going to be all right." He took her hand, squeezed gently. "Trust me. I won't be long. I'll be back."

When her fingers flexed in his, relief burned through him in cold fire.

"Laura, can you hear me? Don't move, baby. Open your

eyes if you can hear me, but I don't want you to move.''

Her world was white and thick and cold, so cold. Then there were shadows, shifting, receding, voices whispering under a brilliant roar. Then his face, close to hers, dark eyes so blue they burned.

''Michael?''

''Yeah.'' He had to swallow, couldn't. Fear had dried up every bit of the saliva in his mouth. ''Yeah. You're going to be all right. You just took a little fall. I want you to—''

''Michael,'' she said again, then her white world flashed red. Pain sliced through her, long, ragged blades of it that had her crying out, rearing against his hands.

''Stop. I know it hurts, but I don't know how bad it is. You have to lie still. Lie still.'' But the way she'd already twisted terrified him. ''Look at me. Look at me. Tell me if you can feel this.''

He put a hand on her thigh, pressed. When she nodded, he pressed her other leg. ''Move your feet for me, Laura. Okay, good.'' Part of his throat opened again when he saw her feet move and flex. ''You're a little banged up, that's all.'' And in shock, he noted, studying her pupils. And in pain. ''I'm going to get you up.''

''My shoulder.'' She tried to reach for it, fought off a wave of nausea. Black and boiling nausea. The pain was unspeakable, and even breathing threatened to make her retch. ''Did I break it?''

''No, just knocked it out of joint.'' His hands were clammy when he closed them over hers. Blood oozed from a dozen gashes he didn't even feel. ''Done it myself a couple times. Hurts like hell. I'm going to be right back, okay? Just a couple minutes.''

''No, don't—'' The wrenching pain slammed into her. She tried to move away, escape it. Sweat pearled on her face and her eyes went glassy.

''Okay, hold on.'' He couldn't leave her like this, in shock and pain. Simply couldn't leave her here, suffering. He could fix it—though the thought of what it would take out of both of them churned like acid in his stomach. ''I can pop it back in. I'll hurt you, but it'll give you relief. You're better off with a doctor, though. Just hanging on until I can get—''

''Please.'' She closed her eyes. Agony was an icy white knife digging into muscle and bone. ''I can't think. I can't think over it.''

He shifted, braced himself beside her. He wiped a hand over his mouth, smearing blood. ''Don't think. I want you to scream. Let out one long, loud scream.''

''What?''

''Scream, goddamn it.'' He held her down with one hand, took a firm grip on her arm, hissing when her eyes opened wide and stared into his. ''Now.''

She felt the jerk, the sick roll of it echoing in her stomach. And white again, white-hot. Then nothing.

His hands were slick with sweat and blood, slippery enough that he nearly lost hold. His stomach churned as he watched her eyes roll back, felt her go limp under him. Gritting his teeth, he snapped the joint into place. Then his breath whooshed out and he lowered his brow to hers.

''Oh, baby, I'm sorry. I'm sorry.'' He did lift her now, cradling her in his arms, rocking them both. He lost track—ten seconds, ten minutes, he had no sense of time passing until she stirred again.

''It's all done, don't worry.'' He pressed his lips to her hair, buried his face there until he managed a greasy grip on control. ''It's better now.''

''Yes.'' She was floating. Pain was everywhere, but it was dull now, throbbing almost gently in her limbs. ''It's better. I can't remember—what happened? An earthquake?''

''It knocked you off, onto the ledge.'' Gently, he checked her head. The bleeding had stopped, but he worried over the lump and the broken skin. ''You're going to have some champion bruises.''

''Knocked me off—my God.'' She turned her face into his chest, shivered. Off the cliff, nearly into the sea, she thought. Onto the rocks below. Like Seraphina. ''How bad? The house—the horses? Oh, Michael, the girls.''

"It's fine. Everything's fine. It wasn't a big one. I don't want you to worry." He'd do that for both of them.

Now that he was calmer, he was taking stock. The quake had shifted rock and earth. There was nothing left of the rough path leading back up. He'd have to leave her, climb back up and get ropes.

"Let me look at you." He studied her face. Too pale, he thought, and her pupils were still dilated. "How's your vision? Blurry?"

"No, it's fine. I have to see if the girls are all right."

"They're fine. They're with your parents, remember? In Carmel." She was lucid, he told himself. Her pulse was rapid but strong. "How many fingers?"

"Two," she said and gripped the hand he'd held up. "Annie, the house—"

"I said everything's fine. Trust me."

"All right." She closed her eyes again and let herself float. "I fell off the cliff."

"That's about it." He pressed her hand to his lips, held it there until he could speak again. "Now, listen—I'm going to have to leave you here for a couple minutes. Then I'm coming back and I'll get you up."

"You have to leave me."

"You can't make the climb. I want you to lie right here, stay still. Promise me. Laura, open your eyes and look at me. Promise me you won't move until I come back."

She looked at him. "I won't move until you get back. It's cold."

"Here." He stripped off his denim jacket, laid it over her. "That'll help a little. Just relax now. Relax and wait for me."

"I'll wait for you," she murmured.

The world seemed to revolve in slow motion. She watched him rise, turn. Confused, she saw him scale the cliff, his hands and feet finding purchase, showering down little cascades of dirt. She smiled dreamily, thinking he looked like a hero scaling castle walls.

Was he saving her from the tower? Climbing up, so high, to kiss her awake? No, no, he was leaving her, she remembered. He was leaving her, she thought dully, and watched, too buffered by shock to feel alarm as he slid five full feet down the cliff face. She watched as he swung a hand up, dug in with bare fingers, and fought his way up the rough, unforgiving wall.

He was going away, she thought, but he would come back for her. He'd come back, then he would leave again.

When he reached the top, he stared down at her. His eyes seemed oddly close again, as if she could reach up and touch his face. Then he was gone, and she was alone.

He'd left her. He didn't want to be part of her life any longer. Or to allow her to be part of his. He would come back, she didn't doubt that he would come back and do as he'd promised. But she would still be alone.

And she would survive, Laura thought. Because there really was no other choice. She hadn't leapt from the cliff. She hadn't tossed her life aside. Fate had pushed her, but she would survive that as well. And go on.

Poor Seraphina. Drifting a little, Laura turned her head. She hadn't fought for life, hadn't survived. And had lost all of her dreams.

A tear trickled down her cheek, in sympathy, in sorrow, and as she turned to brush it away, her gaze fell on the small, dark hole in the wall of the cliff.

A cave? she thought hazily. There was no cave on this ledge. The rocks had moved, she realized, and sighed a little. Everything had moved. She inched her way toward the opening. A secret place, she thought. A hiding place. A lovers' place. She was smiling as she pushed herself up, sat, smelled—surely she smelled the faint scent of a young girl's perfume.

"Seraphina," she murmured even as she reached her hand inside the opening and laid it on the polished wood of a chest. "I've found you. Poor Seraphina, lost for so long."

She continued to speak, and if the words were incoherent, there was no one to hear. She knelt, waited for her head to stop spinning, and tried to drag the chest into the light.

''Laura, goddamn it.''

Her smile soft, her eyes vague, she lifted her face and saw him atop the cliff. ''Seraphina. We've found her. Michael, come and see.''

''Stay put. Stay just where you are.''

It was the hit on the head, he thought, and worked rapidly to secure the rope to the horn of Max's saddle. She was disoriented, confused. His heart drummed in his throat at the idea that she might try to stand. She might fall before he could get back to her.

''Hold steady,'' he ordered Max, then played out the rope. He went over the edge with more speed than caution, the rope burning his wounded hands and the cliff striking out to punish him.

His ankles sang when he landed, and his breath came fast. But he had her again, hard against him. Safe.

''You promised not to move.''

''Seraphina. In the cave. I can't get it by myself. It's too heavy. I need Margo and Kate.''

''In a minute. Let's get this on you.'' Working fast, he looped the rope around her. ''You're not going to have to do anything but hold on to me. Max and I will get you up.''

''All right.'' She didn't question it. It was all so simple, after all. ''Could you get it out for me? Just out here in the light. It's been in the dark so long.''

''Sure. Now I'm going to lift you up. You look at me, nothing but me.''

''I will—but the chest.''

''What chest?''

''In the cave.''

''Don't worry about it. I'll—'' But he glanced over at the gesture of her hand. And saw the dull gleam of brass against wood, the shadow of shape. ''Jesus Christ!''

''Seraphina's dowry. Would you pull it out into the light?''

It was small, no more than two feet long, a domed box of cedar fitted with brass hinges. And no more than twenty pounds, he judged as he hefted it out. A simple box, uncarved, yet he could have sworn he felt something as his hands closed over it. Heat where there should have been none, a faint vibration that tickled his fingertips. It lasted only a moment, no more than two heartbeats, then it was just a small chest fashioned out of smooth wood and brass.

"All of her dreams locked away," Laura said softly. "All locked away because the one she wanted most was over."

"The quake shifted the rocks." Frowning, Michael studied the cave, cut so neatly in the wall. "I'd say another one some time ago covered it up."

"She wanted us to find it. She's been leading us here all our lives."

"Now you have it." However intriguing the find, he had priorities. "I want you to put your arms around my neck and hold on. Can you do that? How's the shoulder?"

"It's sore, but I can manage. How are we going to—"

"Let me worry about it." He helped her to her feet, kept himself between her and the edge. "Just keep looking at me," he continued, pulling her arms up until they linked around him. It's a good strong rope. You've got nothing to worry about."

"Did you climb up the cliff? I thought I saw you climbing up."

"Nothing to it," he said, aware that her mind was drifting. "Fell off a few, too, on film." He continued to talk as he tested the rope. "Hold tight now, we're going up. Max! Back. Back." The rope went taut. With one arm firmly around Laura's waist, Michael let his feet leave the ground and put himself in the walker's hands.

Rocks scraped painfully against his back. He used his heels to aid the ascent while sweat ran down his face and the muscles of his arms screamed.

"Almost there," he told her.

"We didn't get Seraphina. We have to get her."

"I'll go back and get her. Just hold on. Look at me."

She snapped back into focus, stared into his eyes. "You came back for me."

"Sure. Hold on." For an instant his heart stopped. They

were inches from the edge, dangling between sky and sea. If any one of them faltered, they would lose. "Reach up. Just one hand now. Reach up, Laura, and grab hold."

She did as he asked, watched her own hand grip the edge of rock and dirt, slip away, grip again.

"That's it! Pull."

Ignoring his tortured muscles, he levered her up, dragging himself behind her as his horse strained to pull them the last foot. Michael bellied up to level ground, then simply lay there, his body sheltering hers, his face buried in her hair.

"Laura. God. Laura."

His mouth sought hers, and for a moment he sank out of terror and into oblivion.

"We'll get you home. We'll get you home now." He drew back. "Pain?"

"My head. It's all right."

"Lie still, let me take care of you." He released the rope, let it dangle and gathered her into his arms.

"Max?"

"He'll come. Don't worry, he'll come." He carried her away from the cliffs and up the long slope to Templeton House, with Max following placidly behind.

His legs didn't begin to shake until Ann burst out of the front door.

"Oh, sweet Lord, I've been looking for her everywhere. What happened? My poor lamb."

"She took a fall." He continued moving through Ann's fluttering hands. "She needs to get inside."

"In the parlor." Sprinting ahead, Ann called desperately up the stairs. "Mrs. Williamson, Jenny! I've found her." Then, to Michael, "How bad is she? Everyone's on the way. I called when I couldn't find her. Lay her down here on the sofa and let me see. Oh, sweetheart, your head."

"What in the world—" Mrs. Williamson stopped, out of breath, in the doorway.

"She's had a fall," Ann snapped out. "We need hot water, bandages."

''I fell off the cliff,'' Laura said as her head settled back into place.

''Oh, my dear God. Where does it hurt? Let me look at you.''

She broke off when she heard the sound of cars speeding up the drive, doors slamming. ''Everyone's here.'' Ann pressed a kiss to Laura's brow. ''Everything's all right now.''

Susan burst through the doorway first, stopped, braced herself as her heart tilted. ''Well,'' she managed calmly enough, ''what's all this?''

''I fell off a cliff,'' Laura told her. ''Michael got me up. I hit my head.''

That was all she got out before the room filled with people and hands that wanted to touch and voices that babbled questions.

''Quiet.'' Thomas took his daughter's hand, shot the order out to the group at large. ''Josh, call the doctor, tell him we're bringing Laura in—''

''No.'' Rousing herself, Laura sat up and patted Kayla's head as her daughter laid it in her mother's lap. ''I don't need the doctor. I've just hit my head.''

''It's a nasty bump,'' Mrs. Williamson tutted as she continued to clean the blood and dirt from Laura's head. ''Wouldn't be surprised if you have a concussion here, little girl. Michael?''

He didn't notice all the eyes that focused on him. All he could do was stare down at Laura. ''I don't know how long she was out. Five, six minutes. But she's been lucid, her vision's not blurred. There's nothing broken.'' He wiped a hand over his mouth. ''She had a dislocated shoulder. She probably fell on her left side. It'll be sore, but she's got good rotation.''

''I don't want to go to the hospital. The ER will be packed with people after a tremor. I don't want to be one of them. I need to be home.''

''Then you should stay home.'' Margo crouched beside her. ''We can take care of you. You gave us a scare.''

''Gave myself one.'' Murmuring, she wrapped her arm

around Ali as the girl burrowed into her side. "I'm fine. Just a few bumps and bruises. It was quite an adventure."

"Try scuba diving the next time you want an adventure." Reaching over the back of the couch, Kate laid a hand on Laura's shoulder. "My heart can't take this."

"We found Seraphina's dowry."

"What?" Kate's fingers gripped. "What?"

"It's there, on the ledge where I fell. There was a cave, and it was there. Wasn't it, Michael? I didn't imagine it, did I?"

"It's there. I'll get it for you."

"You'll be getting nothing," Mrs. Williamson said, lifting her voice over the fresh spurt of questions. "Sit down before you fall down, boy, and let me see to your hands. You've made a fine mess of yourself."

"Oh, good Lord." Focusing on someone other than her daughter for the first time, Susan snagged Michael's wrist. His hands were coated with dirt and blood, the knuckles mangled. "You've cut them to pieces." Her eyes lifted to his, swam, overflowed as she realized what he'd done. "Michael."

"They're fine. I'm fine." He jerked away. Abruptly, he couldn't breathe, wasn't certain how much longer he could stand. "I've got to see to my horses."

When he staggered out, Susan took a step after him. "Mom." Josh put a hand on her arm. "Let me. Please."

"Bring him back here, Josh. He needs tending to."

"He won't come," Josh said to himself as he went after his friend. "Michael." He hurried across the terrace, over the yard, feeling like a fool for chasing a man who walked like a drunk beside a clopping horse. "Goddamn it, Michael, wait." He caught Michael by the shoulder, spun him around, and stepped back involuntarily at the molten fury that spurted out.

"Get away from me. I'm done here."

"I'm not. You listen—"

"Don't fuck with me now." Ignoring the pain in his hands, Michael shoved Josh back. "I'm in the mood to hurt somebody, and it might as well be you."

"Fine. Take a shot. The shape you're in, I could blow on you and knock you down. You idiot, you stupid son of a bitch, why didn't you tell me you were in love with her?"

"What the hell difference does it make?"

"Only all. You stood there and let me dump a pile of shit on you and did nothing. All you had to do was open your mouth and say it. I thought you were using her."

"I did use her, didn't I? I used her, then I tossed her aside just like you said I would. Ask her."

"I know what it's like to be in love with a woman and be scared boneless you won't make it work. And I know what it's like to want it so much you screw it up. Now I know what it's like to be a part of making two people I care about miserable. And I don't like it."

"This isn't about you. I'd figured out it was time to move on before you had your say. I've got other plans. I've got things . . ."

He trailed off, turned to press his face into Max's warm throat. "I thought she was dead." His shoulders shuddered, and he didn't have the will or the energy to shrug off Josh's hand. "I looked down and saw her lying there and thought she was dead. I can't remember anything else until I was down there and put my hand on her throat. Felt her pulse beating."

"She's going to be all right. Both of you are."

"She wouldn't have been down there if I hadn't told her it was done. If I hadn't hurt her." He drew back, rubbed his hands over his face, smearing blood. "She's being taken care of, so that's fine. I've got no place here."

"You're wrong. No one's shutting you out but you. Christ, Mick, you're a mess." He took a good look at the battered hands, the torn and bloody clothes. He didn't want to think, quite yet, of how close his sister and his friend had come to dying. "Come back inside, let Mrs. Williamson fuss over you. You look like you could use a drink, too."

"I'll get one when I'm done."

"Done with what?"

"I told her I'd get the damn chest, didn't I? I'm going to get it."

Josh opened his mouth as Michael started away again. Arguments, he decided, were fruitless. "Hold up. I'll get Byron. We'll do it together."

Chapter Twenty-one

An hour later, dirty and a little sore, Josh and Byron brought the small chest into the parlor. There'd been a couple of dicey moments during an aftershock when the three of them had been caught crouching on the ledge, wondering if they'd lost their minds. Fortunately it had passed, and now the chest, still unopened, sat on the coffee table. Waiting.

"I can't believe it," Margo murmured. She brushed the wood with her fingertips. "It's real. After all this time." She smiled over at Laura. "You found it."

"We found it," she corrected. "We were always meant to." Her head throbbed dully as she reached for Kate's hand. "Where's Michael?"

"He didn't—" Josh bit back an oath. "He needed to check on his horses."

"I'll get him for you," Byron offered.

"No." It was his choice, Laura reminded herself. And her life had to continue. "It's so small, isn't it?" she mused. "So simply made. I suppose all of us had imagined something huge and ornate and extraordinary, but it's just a plain, serviceable chest. The kind that lasts.'' She took a deep breath. ''Ready?''

With Margo and Kate beside her, she put a hand on the latch. It opened easily, soundlessly, the interior releasing a scent of lavender and cedar.

Inside were a young girl's treasures, and dreams. A rosary fashioned from lapis with a heavy silver crucifix. A brooch of garnets, rose petals drying to dust. Gold, yes, there was gold, glinting as it was poured out of a leather pouch.

But there were linens, meticulously embroidered and carefully folded. Handkerchiefs with lacy edges turning yellow. An amber necklace, a ring crafted to fit a small finger and studded with little ruby stones that glistened like new blood. Pretty pieces of jewelry that suited a young woman not yet married and a locket that held a curl of dark hair bound by gold thread.

Tucked in with them was a small book with a red leather cover. Inside was the careful convent-school writing of a well-bred woman: ''We met on the cliffs today, early, when there was still dew on the grass and the sun was rising slowly from the sea. Felipe told me he loved me, and my heart was brighter than the dawn.''

Laura rested her head against Margo's shoulder. ''Her diary,'' she murmured. ''She put her diary in with her treasures, locked away. Poor girl.''

''I always thought I'd feel thrilled when we found it.'' Kate reached into the box, stroked a finger over the amber beads. ''I just feel sad. She hid away everything that was important to her in this little box and left it behind.''

''You shouldn't feel sad.'' Laura laid the open diary on her lap. ''She wanted us to find it and to open it again. I like to think it had to wait until all three of us faced something we thought we couldn't face. But we did. We have.''

She reached out, took each of their hands in hers. ''And we should put these in the shop, in a special case.''

''We couldn't sell any of it,'' Margo murmured. ''We couldn't sell Seraphina's treasures.''

''No, not to sell.'' Laura smiled at the simple box. ''To let other people dream.''

Michael left the rubble of his living room just as it was. He was going to stand in the shower and drown out the aches and pains. After he'd had a drink. In fact, now that he thought of it, getting piss-faced drunk was probably a much happier way to drown out the pain.

He bypassed beer and took out a bottle of Jameson's. As he poured a tumbler half full, he ignored the insistent knocking on his door.

''Go the fuck away,'' he muttered and took one long swallow. It did little to improve his mood when Ann Sullivan pushed open his door.

''Well, I see you're already drowning your sorrows in the middle of this chaos.'' She set down a box on the counter and frowned at the destruction. ''I wouldn't have thought there'd be this much damage. We lost only a few breakables at the main house.''

''Laura did most of it.'' He lifted his glass again as Ann pursed her lips.

''Did she? It's rare for her to let her temper loose, but a wicked one it can be. Well, sit down, we'll tend to you before we clean up the mess.''

''I don't want to clean it up, and I don't want to be tended to. Go away.''

She merely reached into the box and took out a covered plate. ''Mrs. Williamson sent you food. I asked her to let me come instead. She's worried about you.''

''Nothing to worry about.'' He studied his hands. ''I've had worse.''

''I've no doubt, but you'll sit down and let me clean those cuts.'' She set a basin, bottles, bandages on the counter.

''I can take care of myself.'' He lifted the glass, peered at the level of whiskey. ''I've already made a start.''

In her no-nonsense style, Ann came around the counter and shoved him into a chair. ''Sit when you're told.''

''Shit.'' He rubbed his shoulder where she'd pushed. It burned like fire.

''And keep a civil tongue in your head.'' She busied herself filling the basin with hot water. ''Got infection brewing already, I've no doubt. The sense of a bean is what you've got.'' She snatched one of his hands and got to work.

''If you're going to play Nurse Nancy, at least—goddamn, that hurts.''

''I imagine. Don't you swear at me, Michael Fury.'' Her eyes stung when she saw just how badly he'd damaged his hands, but her movements remained brisk and not particularly sympathetic. ''This'll bite some.''

The burn of the antiseptic that she generously poured over open wounds made his eyes cross and filled the air with wild blue curses.

''You've a raw Irish tongue. Reminds me of my Uncle Shamus. What part does your family come from?''

''Galway. Goddamn it, why don't you just use battery acid and be done with it?''

''Big, strong man like you, whining over a little peroxide and alcohol. Take another drink, then, as I haven't a bullet for you to bite on.''

It scored his pride, as she'd meant it to. Michael tipped back the glass and scowled at her. He decided to brood while she wrapped gauze over his hands.

''Done?'' he demanded.

''With those, for the time being. You'll want to keep the bandages dry and they'll need to be changed regular since I assume you'll be as stubborn as Miss Laura about a doctor.''

''Don't need a doctor.'' He jerked his shoulder but regretted it when it throbbed. ''She'll be fine, too. She's got enough people hovering over her.''

''She inspires love and loyalty because she's generous with giving both.'' Rising, Ann emptied the basin, refilled it. ''Take off what's left of your shirt.''

He cocked a brow. ''Well, Annie, I'm a little impaired, but if I'd known you had an urge to— Ow!'' He gaped, shocked speechless as she gave his ear a hard twist.

"I'll twist more than your ear if you behave like a baboon. Take that shirt off, boy."

"Christ!" He sat for another moment, rubbing his stinging ear. "What's your problem?"

"Your hands aren't the only things you've cut to blazes. Now get the shirt off so I can see what you've done to yourself."

"What the hell do you care? I could bleed to damn death and you wouldn't bat an eye. You've always hated me."

"No. I've always been afraid of you, and that was foolish. You're just a pitiful man who hasn't a clue of his own worth. And I made mistakes I'm sorry for, and I hope I'm woman enough to admit it." Because he wasn't cooperating, she tugged off his tattered T-shirt herself. "I thought you had beaten your mother."

"What? My mother— I never—"

"I know that. Be still. Oh, Jesus, boy, you've done a job here. Oh, poor lad." She crooned now as she dabbed gently at the gashes on his back. "You'd have killed yourself for her, wouldn't you?"

Suddenly tired, unbearably tired, he laid his head on the counter, shut his eyes. "Go away. Leave me alone."

"I won't. Nor will anyone else. You'll have to be the one to do it. Hold on now, this is going to hurt."

He hissed between his teeth as the antiseptic bit. "I just wanna get drunk."

"You will if you must," she said easily. "But a man who would brave an earthquake to get to his woman should have enough nerve to face her sober. This bruising could use liniment. Well, we'll see to that after we've seen to the rest. Take off your pants."

"Oh, for Christ's sake, I'm not going to—Christ!" He yelped when she twisted his other ear. "All right, all right, you want me naked, you got it."

He rose, wrenched the button of his torn jeans, tugged them off. "I'd have gone to the hospital if I'd known what the alternative was going to be."

''That cut on your thigh could use stitches, but we'll do what we can.''

He sat bad-temperedly but shoved the tumbler aside. He didn't feel like drinking any longer. ''Is she all right?''

A smile ghosted around Ann's mouth, but she kept her head lowered. ''She's hurting, in more ways than one. She needs you.''

''No, she doesn't. The last thing. You know what I am.''

Now she lifted her head, looked him dead in the eye. ''Yes, I know what you are. But do you, Michael Fury? Do you know what you are?''

He worried over it like a man worrying over an aching tooth. How could he concentrate on what he needed to do when he kept seeing her the way she had been, white and still on that ledge? Or the way she had looked, eyes filled with hurt and temper, as she'd turned at the door and told him she loved him.

Distractions didn't help. He'd dealt with the mess of the apartment—because Ann had ordered him to get up off his butt and take out the trash. He'd calmed his horses, rehung his tack, then taken the tack down again and packed it.

He wasn't staying anyway.

In the end he'd given up and started across the lawn to Templeton House. It was reasonable, wasn't it? he argued with himself, to want to check on her. She probably should be in the hospital. Her family wouldn't push her. It was obvious to him that when Laura Templeton dug her heels in, no one could push her.

He would just check, then he'd make arrangements to stable his horses elsewhere until he could get the hell out of Dodge.

As he walked through the garden, Kayla and Ali popped up from their perch on the terrace where they'd been playing jacks. His first thought was that he hadn't known kids still played jacks. Then they launched themselves at him.

''You saved Mama from the earthquake.'' Kayla, all but climbing up into his arms, made his fresh bruises throb.

''Not exactly,'' he began. ''I just—''

"You did." Solemn-eyed, Ali looked up into his face. "Everyone said so." He started to shrug, uncomfortable in the role of hero, but she took his hand and her eyes were clouded with worry. "They said she was going to be all right. Everyone said she was going to be all right. Is she?"

Why ask him? Damn it, how did he get to be the authority? But he crouched down, unable to resist that trembling lip. "Sure she is. She just got some bumps, that's all."

Ali's lips curved a little. "Okay."

"She fell off the cliff," Kayla continued. "And found Seraphina, and she got hurt, but you and Max came to pull her back up. Mrs. Williamson said Max should have a whole bushel of carrots."

He grinned, tousled her hair. "What do I get?"

"She said you already got your reward. What is it?"

"Search me."

"You got hurt too." Soberly, Kayla lifted his bandaged hands one at a time and kissed them. "Do they hurt? Does that make it better?"

Emotion swarmed through him, a stinging hive of bees that left behind a sweet ache. No one, in all his life, had ever kissed his hurts. "Yeah, much." He pressed his face into her hair for a moment. Wishing. Wanting.

"Is it all right if we go down and see Max?" Instinctively Ali stroked Michael's hair to soothe him. "To thank him."

"Yeah, he'd like that. Ah, your mom . . ."

"She's in the parlor. Everyone's supposed to be quiet so she can rest. But you can go in." Ali beamed at him. "She'd want to see you. And Kayla and I are going to get up every morning early before school and clean the stalls until your hands are better. You don't have to worry."

"I—" Coward, he thought. Tell them you won't be here. Tell them you're leaving. Couldn't. Just couldn't. "Thanks."

As they dashed off, he watched them, two pretty young girls racing away through fanciful gardens. He stepped over the scattered jacks, and after three tries managed to lift his hand and open the terrace door.

She wasn't lying on the couch as he'd expected, but standing at the window, her back to the room, looking out toward the cliffs.

She was so . . . small, he thought. Everything about her telegraphed fragility, and yet she was the strongest woman he'd ever known.

She should have seemed delicate just then, highly breakable, with her hair pulled back, the soft, fluid folds of a white robe wrapped around her. But when she turned, and those last gilded beams of the setting sun danced against the window at her back, she seemed simply indestructible.

"I was hoping you'd come." Her voice was calm, as was she. A close brush with death had shown her that she could indeed survive anything. Even Michael Fury. "I wasn't able to thank you coherently before, or to see how badly you were hurt."

"I'm fine. How's the head?"

She smiled. "It feels as though I smashed it on a rock. Would you like a brandy? I'm not allowed, myself. My many medical advisers tell me I can't have any alcohol for twenty-four hours."

"No, I'll pass." The whiskey he'd downed earlier wasn't sitting very well as it was.

"Please, sit down." Leading with manners, she gestured to a chair. "We've had quite a day, haven't we, Michael?"

"I won't forget it anytime soon. Your shoulder—"

"I've had enough fussing. It's sore." She sat, smoothing down her robe as she did. "I'm sore. My head aches, and occasionally I get this quick twist in my stomach when I let myself think about what might have happened. What would have happened if you hadn't found me."

Her brow lifted as she watched him prowl the room. Other than that first long stare when she'd turned to him, he'd barely looked at her. To keep her own hands still, she linked them in her lap.

"Is something else on your mind, Michael, other than my medical report?"

"I just wanted to see—" He stopped, hooked his thumbs in his pockets, and made himself look at her. "Listen, I don't see any point in leaving this business hanging between us."

"What business?"

"You're not in love with me."

Patiently attentive, she angled her head. "I'm not?"

"No, you've just got it all mixed up with sex, and now probably with gratitude, and that's just stupid."

"So now I'm stupid."

"Don't twist things around."

"I'm trying to untwist them." She leaned forward to touch the box, still open on the coffee table. "You haven't seen Seraphina's dowry. Aren't you curious?"

"It's nothing to do with me." But he looked down, saw the glint of gold, of silver, of glossy beads. "Not a hell of a lot, considering."

"You're wrong, it's quite a bit, considering." Her gaze lifted to his again. "Quite a bit. Why did you go back down for it?"

"I told you I would."

"A man of your word," she murmured. "I was fuzzy at the time, but things are clearer now. I remember lying there watching you climb up that rock wall. Clinging like a lizard. Your hands bleeding, slipping when the wall would give way. You could have been killed."

"I guess I should have just left you there."

"You couldn't have done that. You'd have gone down for anyone. That's who you are. And you went back, for this." She stroked the lid of the box. "Because I asked you."

"You're making it bigger than it was."

"You brought me something I've looked for my entire life." Her eyes, swimming with emotion, stayed on his. "I can't make that bigger than it is. How many times did you climb up, climb down, for me, Michael?" When he said nothing, only turned away to pace again, she sighed. "It makes you uncomfortable—gratitude, admiration, love."

"You're not in love with me."

''Don't tell me what I feel.''

Because her voice had sharpened, he glanced back warily. If she started throwing things again, he doubted he had the energy to dodge.

''Don't you dare to tell me what I feel. You're entitled not to feel the same way, entitled not to want me to love you, but you're not entitled to tell me what I feel.''

''Then you are stupid,'' he exploded. ''You don't even know who I am. I killed for money.''

She waited a beat, then rose and walked over to pour herself a glass of mineral water. ''You're referring to when you were a mercenary.''

''It doesn't matter what title you put on it. I killed, I got paid for it.''

''I don't suppose you believed in the cause you were fighting for.''

He opened his mouth, shut it. Wasn't she hearing him? ''It doesn't matter what I believed or didn't. I killed for profit, I've spent the night in a cell, I've slept with women I didn't know.''

Calmly, she sipped. ''Are you apologizing, Michael, or bragging?''

''Christ Almighty, don't pull that snotty lady-of-the-house routine on me. I've done things you can't even imagine in this rarefied world you live in.''

She drank. ''Rarefied, is it?'' she murmured. ''As compared to the reality you live in. Michael Fury, you're a snob.''

''Jesus Christ.''

''You are. As you see it, I'm above desperation or needs or sins because I come from money and maintain a certain social status. I'm not supposed to understand a man like you, much less care for him. Is that right?''

''Yeah.'' He ached everywhere. ''That about sums it up.''

''Let me tell you what I see, Michael. I see someone who has done what he had to do to survive. And I understand that very well, even living in my pathetic, rarefied world.''

"I didn't mean—"

"Someone who didn't give up, no matter what got in the way," she interrupted, staring him down. "I see someone who decided to take a new direction in his life and is making it work. He has ambition, decency, and courage. And I see a man who can still grieve over a child he never had a chance to know."

She was making him into something he wasn't, and she was scaring the life out of him. "I'm not what you're looking for."

"You're what I found. I have to live with that, and when you go, I will."

"I'm doing you a favor," he muttered. "You can't even see it. You'd have figured it out for yourself sooner or later. You've already got the seed in your head."

"Which means?"

"You know it isn't going anywhere with us. It can't, and you knew it."

"Did I? Why don't you explain how you've come to that conclusion?"

There were dozens of examples, but only one stuck out. "You're damn careful not to touch me when anyone's around."

"Is that so?" She set down her glass with a snap. "Stay right there." Incensed, she marched to the door and out, leaving him scowling after her.

Why the hell was he getting into all this? he asked himself. Why was he arguing with her? Why couldn't he just touch her one more time, just hold her one more time. Then he'd go.

Laura strode back in, dragging Thomas in her wake. "You're supposed to be resting," her father scolded. "Oh, hello, Michael. I was about to go down and—"

"Talk later," Laura ordered, then marched straight to Michael.

"Hey," was all he managed before she grabbed him by the hair, dragged his head down, and fixed her lips hotly on his. He lifted his hands, dropped them again, then gave up and crushed her against him. Her body was drum-tight, all but vibrating with fury, but her mouth was soft, sweet, and the kiss weakened his knees.

''There.'' She pulled away, spun toward a baffled and grinning Thomas. ''Thanks, Dad. If you wouldn't mind leaving us alone again?''

''No, fine. Michael, I believe you and I will have a little talk later.'' Thomas closed the door discreetly behind him.

''Satisfied?'' Laura demanded.

Not nearly. She'd just churned up all the urges he'd nearly managed to quell. Saying nothing, he yanked her against him again. ''What the hell was that supposed to prove? It doesn't change—''

And then he broke, just broke. Shuddering, he buried his face in her hair, fought to find his breath. ''I thought you were dead,'' he managed. ''Oh, God, Laura, I thought you were dead.''

''Oh, Michael.'' Every drop of temper drained out of her as she stroked his back. ''It was horrible for you. I'm sorry, so sorry. We're fine now. You saved me.''

Gently, she cupped his face and studied those dark, stormy eyes. ''You saved my life,'' she murmured and touched her lips to his.

''No.'' He jerked back, shocked at how close she'd come to bringing him to his knees. ''We're not going that route, we're not mixing this up again.''

She stood where she was, watching all those violent emotions flit over his face. And slowly, her aching heart began to swell, and to heal. Her smile bloomed. ''Why, you're afraid of me, aren't you? Afraid of us. I see I have been stupid after all, thinking it was only me. You're in love with me, Michael, and it scares you.''

''Don't put words in my mouth,'' he began, then backed up a full step as she came toward him. ''Don't.''

''What'll happen if I touch you now?'' The sense of power, of right, glowed inside her. ''You might shatter. Tough guy, holding it all in. I could break you, just by doing this.'' And she laid her hand on his cheek.

''You're making a mistake.'' He clamped a hand on her

wrist, and his fingers trembled. ''You don't know what you're doing. I can't be what you need.''

''Why don't you tell me what you think I need, then?''

''You figure I'll polish up and start playing tennis at the club? Go to the gallery openings and buy a tux? It's never going to happen. I'm not going to start drinking brandy and playing billiards or sit in a steam room with a bunch of overweight rich guys and talk about the latest stock reports.''

She began to laugh, and the laughter made her head ache and spin so that she had to sit on the arm of the settee until she caught her breath. ''That's telling me.''

''You think this is a joke? So will all your fancy friends. There goes Laura Templeton with that mongrel she picked up.''

She sobered quickly. ''I could slap you. I could actually slap you for that.'' In fact, she had to grip her hands together to stop herself from doing just that. ''That's insulting, to me and to those I consider my friends. You think I care about any of that? Do you really think so little of me?''

''I think everything of you,'' he said and stopped her tirade before it could begin.

''If that's true, then you should respect what it is I do need. With some alterations it's the same thing I've needed my whole life. I need my family and my work. My home. I need to feel that I put in as much as I take out. I need my children to be happy and safe. And I need someone I love, and who loves me, to share it all, to be there for me. I need someone who'll depend on me and whom I can depend on. I want someone who'll listen and understand, who'll touch me when I need to be touched. Who'll make my heart beat a little faster when he looks at me. The way you look at me, Michael. The way you're looking at me right now.''

''You're not going to let me walk,'' he said quietly.

''Yes, yes, I will.'' She reached into the box, took out the locket. ''If you need to go, to prove something, to escape from something, even if that something is what we feel for each other, I can't stop you.''

She laid the locket down again, gently. ''But I won't stop loving you, or needing you. I'll just live without you. I'll live without the life we could make, without seeing my children light up when you walk into the room, without the other children we could make together.''

She narrowed her eyes when she saw the flicker in his eye. ''Did you think I wouldn't want more children? That I haven't already dreamed what it would be like to hold a baby we made together?''

''No, I didn't think you'd want more children, with me.'' She was breaking him, bit by bit. ''Laura . . .''

She rose, waited, but he only shook his head. ''A family, Michael, that's all I've ever really dreamed of. You changed a great deal inside of me, but never that. You gave me all those firsts, and because I was so dazzled by you, so in love with you, I didn't see that I could give you something back. I'll give you a family, Michael.''

He wondered if he could speak, how any man could when faced with the gift of everything he would ever need. Every treasure imagined and sought and despaired of.

''I'm wrong for you. I've got to be wrong for you, and it was never supposed to come to this between us. I took you because I could, because I wanted you more than I'd ever wanted anything.''

''You're right for me,'' she corrected. ''You have to be right for me. And what was it never supposed to come to between us, Michael?''

''To plans. To futures.'' His gaze was drawn to the open box again, and all those tiny, precious treasures. ''I've barely started to get my business off the ground, hardly made a dent in getting my life into some kind of decent order. I've got nothing for you.''

''Don't you? Don't you have dreams, Michael? And aren't some of them the same as mine?'' She wanted to reach for him then, but this time he would have to reach first.

She would let him walk, he realized. If he turned and stepped back out the door, they would both go on.

She was waiting for him. She was willing to take him

just as he was. And with her, he realized, he might find there was more in him, more for him, than he'd ever allowed himself to dream.

''I'm going to give you one more chance before I say what I have to say. What I wasn't going to say. What I didn't think you'd want to hear.''

How many chances did a man get? he wondered. How many lives? How many offers of everything that mattered? He took a step toward her, stopped.

''Once I say it, the door closes. For both of us. Do you understand that?''

Her lips curved. ''Do you?''

''I understood it the minute I saw you again.'' His eyes went dark, dangerous. ''Stay or run, Laura.''

She lifted her chin. This time she would say it. ''Stay.''

''Then you'll have to live with it. And me.'' He took her hand. Not gently, but possessively, his battered fingers clamping onto hers. ''I've never loved another woman. That's a first you gave me.''

She closed her eyes. ''I feel as though I've waited my whole life to hear you say that.''

''I haven't said it yet.'' He lifted his free hand to her face. ''Look at me when I do. I love you, Laura,'' he said when her eyes opened. ''Maybe I always did. I know I always will. I'll never lie to you or leave you to handle things alone. I'll be a father to your children. All of them. I'll love them, all of them. And they'll never have to wonder if I do.''

''Michael.'' Overcome, she turned her lips into his palm, kissing his hurts much as Kayla had. ''That's everything.''

''No, it's not. So here's the rest.'' He waited until her eyes cleared and met his. ''If you want to take a chance on this, I'll give you whatever I have, whatever I can make and whatever I can be.''

The words were just there, he realized. Just there, waiting to be said. Absently he reached over, plucked a tulip from the vase on the table beside them. Held it out to her. ''Marry me. Be my family.''

Rather than take the flower, she closed her hand over his

around the stem. "Yes." She touched her lips to his cheek, settled her head with a sigh on his shoulder. "Yes," she said again, feeling his heart thud against hers as she looked into the simple box filled with dreams.

"I've found you," she murmured, turning her mouth up to Michael's. "We've found each other. Finally."